He'd warned them she was a murderer, and now she was on the run...

John put the surgical booties on. "Now you can show me. Anyone see anything?"

"No one saw a Barbara Montgomery."

"Who did they see?"

"A doc in a red suit with black shoulder-length hair."

"I'm checking out her room, then the nurse's station. Sergeant, call Carlson and our team to get here."

"On the way."

John reached her room and leaned over the barricade tape without touching it. The boots were lying on the bed with her knitting bag and its contents strewn all over.

Wow. She left these. Must have really thought about this one. "Okay. Again, Phil record. McDonald, you click. I see the paisley lining of the knitting bag pulled inside out. At the top, I see a zipper. I see the lining. It's a paisley zipper to a hidden compartment—I'm guessing hidden." He took the phone from McDonald. "I see a black hair in the zipper. Suspect it's a wig. Montgomery's hair is highlighted-blonde. She must have another ID. I'll speak to the nurses to see what tag she had on."

Paul, didn't you even check this thing? Why is she being so careless? It's almost like she's toying with me. What does she want? Does she want this to be over with? How did she get away with all that she did being so blatant?

The bathroom was at an angle to the door. A knitting needle with the rusted tip on the floor lay wrapped in a rust-ridden towel. "She pried it out with this."

Damn, Barbara, how did you know?

"That stuff on your hand is the rust and some grease she used," Sergeant McDonald said.

"Damn, shea butter body cream."

"Excuse me?"

"Moisturizer. I gave it to her. Brought it from her apartment. Damn!"

His life is exactly the way he wants it to be—until he meets her…

Both psychic and clairvoyant, Dr. John Trenton is a forensic psychiatrist who has a wife he worships and a position as a department head at a hospital for the criminally insane in Manhattan. His patients—young adult men, who are some of the most psychotic and psychopathic criminals in NYC—enable him to live his life on the edge, just the way he likes it. Then he meets a woman who changes everything.

She is two days from accomplishing the revenge she lives for—until she meets him…

Stripper by night, school psychologist by day, Gemini obsessed Barbara Montgomery makes a critical mistake and is committed for seventy-two hours of observation, where she risks it all in an unnerving escape. Furious with Dr. Trenton for interfering in her life, she is now determined to kill his wife and unborn child, along with everyone else who has ever caused her pain—real or imagined.

As the killing spree continues, John is forced to use all his ESP, as well as his knowledge and expertise, to interpret this psychopath's Gemini obsession and unravel her dark and murderous past. But can he track her down and bring her to justice—before she destroys his world completely?

<h1 style="text-align:center">KUDOS for Gemini</h1>

In *Gemini* by Ronnie Allen, Dr. John Trenton is a New York forensic psychiatrist who deals with young adult criminals mentally incapable of standing trial for their crimes. John is a clairvoyant and psychic and uses his paranormal skills in his work. He is well-known and respected in his professional life, but his personal life is going to hell. His wife is leaving him and going back to Florida, his relationship with the New York cops is deteriorating, and his new patient is a serial killer who escapes from his custody. Allen has crafted a chilling tale of murder and revenge, of psychological obsessions, and man's inhumanity to man. Her characters are complex, realistic, and extremely well-developed. Her plot is strong and well-crafted. The book is a page-turner and will keep you on the edge of your seat from beginning to end. ~ *Taylor Jones, Reviewer*

Gemini by Ronnie Allen is a story about duplicity. The zodiac sign of Gemini is the sign of twins, Castor and Pollux, who died tragic deaths. In Allen's story, the protagonist, Dr. John Trenton, a forensic psychiatrist, works at a mental hospital in New York, where he treats criminally insane young adults. A consummate and extremely competent person in his professional life, John's other half, his personal life, shows a very different side. Here he is needy and insecure. His wife, whom he adores and cannot live without, hates New York and goes home to Florida. John has certain paranormal skills, which he uses to his advantage in his work, but they seem to fail him completely in his personal life. The antagonist, Barbara Montgomery, is an identical twin. She's also a stripper, a school psychologist, as well as a serial killer. Barbara makes a critical mistake when she loses her temper and attacks some New York police. The cops restrain her and send her to Dr. Trenton's hospital for observation and diagnosis. John runs tests, talks with her, and diagnoses that she is a murderer. However, the cops think he's nuts and fail to back him up, so John is unable to transfer her to maximum security. Naturally, she escapes and all hell breaks loose. *Gemini* is a well-crafted, chilling, and entirely too realistic story about both sides of the coin of humanity and darkness that lives within us all. The book is too long to read in one sitting, but give yourself plenty of time when you start reading because this isn't a book that is easy to put down. *~ Regan Murphy, Reviewer*

ACKNOWLEDGEMENTS

Miracles. They've been happening to me since I was born. According to medical science, I shouldn't be here. Well, surprise, surprise, I am. More miracles happened in the summer of 2012, when my main supporter—my husband Bob—found an article in the *Citrus Chronicle* about a writer's workshop on plotting. I went. And I was introduced to the most relentlessly giving group of men and women, multi-published authors on the planet, Sunshine State Romance Authors, Chapter 225 of Romance Writers of America. I thank them all with special gratitude to Loretta Rogers and Flossie Benton Rogers to whom no question went unanswered. Then at the Christmas party, I won a raffle of a full manuscript critique from Dylan Newton. She was my first critique partner and spent hours on *Gemini*, and then hours with me, all the while validating *Gemini* was ready to leave the nest and fly into the world of publishing.

I also want to thank my friends, Susan Pellegrino for an awesome critique, and Rhoda Kwartner and Sherry Wilson for spot-on beta reads. These gals made a big difference. Together with their advice and Dylan's, I let my baby go.

I want to remind you that *Gemini* is a work of fiction. Any misinterpretation of police procedure, any stretching of the protocols—medical or police—any fictionalization of locations and associations is on me. Now, thank you, Detective Michael and Captain David M. DeCarlo, Criminal Investigation Division, Citrus County Sheriff's Office. From different parts of the country with different police department procedures, you both helped to make *Gemini* more credible.

In May of 2014, another miracle happened. I met my publisher Black Opal Books. I want to thank my editors, Lauri, Faith, and Joyce for diligently working on my manuscript with me, and Jack in the arts department for the striking cover.

And I want to thank my husband Bob for understanding that I couldn't spend as much time with him as he would have liked because I needed to be inside my characters' heads.

GEMINI

The Sign Behind The Crime
Book 1

Ronnie Allen

A Black Opal Books Publication

GENRE: PSYCHOLOGICAL THRILLER/ROMANTIC & PARANORMAL ELEMENTS/WOMEN'S FICTION/MYSTERY/SUSPENSE

GEMINI ~ The Sign Behind The Crime ~ Book 1
Copyright © 2015 by Ronnie Allen
Cover Design by Ronnie Allen
All cover art copyright © 2015
All Rights Reserved
Print ISBN: 978-1-626942-79-0

First Publication: JUNE 2015

Published by Black Opal Books **http://www.blackopalbooks.com**

DEDICATION

For all the teachers out there who through blood, sweat and tears every day in their classrooms, protect and rescue children from the horrors of abuse they endure in their lives.

CHAPTER 1

Present Day:

*O**kay, girlfriend. Let's get serious here. Tonight's gotta be the night. Time's runnin' away from me.*

She jammed her eyes shut, swallowed hard, and blew out a prolonged breath. Tonight could be rough. Or impossible. Her heart thumped in expectation of finding the right person to accompany her in the train wreck of her life.

She had no choice, but to make it work.

Her life depended upon it.

Before she could overthink it, she grabbed the pink paisley duffle bag, which held her outfit for the job, off the Queen Victoria chair that graced the corner of the hallway. The entire getup could fit in her jeans pocket but she had to go fancy. She zipped up the black patent leather stiletto heeled boots, hesitating for a moment, contemplating if she was getting too old to wear them. After a last minute once-over in the full length mirror on the adjacent wall, she reconsidered. Nah, not with her knockout bod. Women half her age didn't look so good. Not even any laugh lines around her eyes to give it away. She winked in the mirror and her emerald contact lenses twinkled back.

She eased the door closed to her ritzy Manhattan apartment at one a.m. with her right hand on the knob and her left palm on the door, guiding it to the latch so that her ears alone heard the soft clicks of the bolt.

Can't wake those old geezers next door. Otherwise, I'll just have to do what I do best.

Chills of anticipation snaked through her as she traversed the darkened hallway to the elevator all the while listening for footsteps in her neighbor's apartment. The elevator door opened. She slipped in.

All was good.

They got to live another night.

ↄ⊃ↄ⊃

Undulating her body on stage, she made the most of the techno and house music in Zodiac, the dark and dingy strip club on the lower west side of Manhattan. She encircled her legs around the glistening pole as if she was the giftwrap for a valuable prize for the men watching her. Very expensive giftwrap. The embroidered red dragon on the outer side of her right boot reflected in the glaring lights as she raised her leg and arched her firm midriff. She held onto the pole with her left arm as she extended the right. Her impressive breasts popped out of her skimpy top. Standing upright and feigning embarrassment, she put her hand over her mouth. After a few moments to entice the enthralled men, she cupped her breasts in the palms of her hands sliding her thumbs over her nipples and they slithered back into the cups. She bent over and gave a flirty wiggle to make sure the girls were back in place. Wearing a Lucille Ball flame-red wig, and so much makeup, with bright emerald contact lenses, she camouflaged her true self. She wouldn't want anyone to see her true self. She didn't want to see her true self.

While she danced to the hard and fast music, keeping the rhythm and gyrated her hips, her gaze wandered around the room, focusing on some shirtless men whose bodies weren't worth a second look, and then down the stairs. Then she saw him.

The bum who was older than the rest.

The bum pushed people aside on the dance floor to get through the crowd on his way to the stairwell. His ratted knapsack swiped against two twenty-something guys in the middle of an E exchange who were too engrossed in what they were doing to notice him. But she could read him. She could tell he was the type who would go unnoticed. Medium height, medium build. She'd wait to make her decision when he got closer.

Ignoring everyone, the bum walked steadily up the stairs to the second floor. The black light illuminated the astrological signs painted in neon on the wall behind him. Those going up and down the stairs needed to squint from the glare. Blindness and burning eyes from the artificial smoke overwhelmed them. The bum clung to the banister, banging his knee on the top step, the steepest one.

Good. He's getting too old for this. Perfect.

The bum settled on a bar stool in front of the rack. The stripper preferred to acknowledge it as Pervert's Row. Her stare was glued to him as he took unhidden slugs from the bottle of whisky he pulled from his knapsack. She saw him as a ruined man, haggard and wrinkled beyond his forty-five or so years. His nicotine-yellowed fingernails helped to give him away. Smoking must have been the culprit, adding wrinkles of a much older man. He probably survived by ignoring his tattered clothes and receding hairline, though he'd let his blond hair grow long around his ears and longer in the back. Gray roots over dark brown had emerged. He needed another bleach job.

Dancing in front of him, she enticed him with her narrow waist, slightly wider hips, and strong defined legs to match her moves.

"Hey, baby, how about giving me some of that?"

The stripper gave him the up and down. "You're not green enough, pal."

"I can share this with you," he said, holding up the bottle. The haze of despair in his eyes reflected in the bottle of whiskey. She often had that same look.

"Don't drink on the job, baby." She was there to make money and she'd found her mark. Her attention followed the men tempting her with the largest bill. She was determined to make, at the minimum, the two hundred bucks she had to pay the club owner for tonight, plus an additional ten percent for the server who catered to her customers. Otherwise, all her bumping and grinding would leave her in the red. On a good night, she pulled in over a grand. However, from the looks of the crowd she surveyed tonight, she would have to work hard for anything close to that.

If she had only gone to one of the high-end clubs in Chelsea that she had worked in, she'd make five times that amount. But that wasn't in her agenda for the immediate future. She had more dough than she'd ever need in off-shore accounts through other means, and ugh, her legal day job, a real farce of a day job, but she wanted more than money, now.

Now she wanted revenge.

For the past twenty-two years, more than half her life, she craved this revenge. It encompassed her mind, body, soul, and every cell within her. Her body shivered at the thought. She lifted high toward the heavens. It was her spirit lifting. She could taste it. She could smell it. The scent of sweet mango teased her nose. Her universe gave her that scent as a signal. She was on her way to getting what she craved.

She cringed on the inside and, at the same time, forced a smile at the short, rotund, bald-headed man waving a fifty in her direction, coaxing her to pay attention to him. "Com'on, honey, ignore him."

Knowing very well he couldn't afford it, but she would take what she could get, she turned away from the bum. She blew kisses at the bald-headed man a few inches above his head while snatching the fifty. She let him rub his greasy unshaven cheeks between her bounteous breasts for just a moment as she slid the bill into her boot. Then she pulled back from him in a heartbeat. He smiled.

As she looked for another mark, the bum reached far up onto the stage and grabbed her leg throwing her off balance. His first mistake. She recouped and kicked him in the chin knocking him backward with a strength that forced the onlookers to back away. "Fuck off, buddy, you're ruinin' my act!" Her loud New York accent permeated the music.

He tumbled to the floor with a bleeding gash on his chin from her pointy-toed, five-inch stiletto. He rebounded faster than she expected. In an Irish Brogue, he said, "I'm not giving up on you, Sheila!"

She smiled as his comment struck a chord deep within her, unlike the other losers, who merely whimpered away like wounded pups.

Sheila. It's better than being called "bitch."

"Try that again bud and you'll wind up on the first floor." She resumed dancing around the pole, ready to strike again at the simplest provocation from him or anyone else in the room.

A tattooed bouncer, with his biceps and six-pack outlined by his skin tight black Zodiac T-shirt, grabbed the bum by his jacket collar to drag him down the stairs. The bouncer had a firm grip on the bum, who struggled and fell over the red velvet couch against the wall. Still, held by the collar, he strained from the bouncer's strength as the glare from the swirling psychedelic lights blinded him.

"Clancy Davis. Remember the name, baby. We're gonna become real good friends, real soon."

She trembled for a moment, and stood still, but this wasn't new to her. It went with the territory, almost every time and in every club in which she worked. It made her hard and indifferent, but resilient.

She'd initiated her personal vendetta now. Nothing would thwart her. No one would stop her. Ever.

She continued to dance, swaying her body to the music faster than before, while caressing her now bare breasts. But something was different about this one. Something different, yes—the aggression in his dark brown eyes, telling her he was once someone special, who longed to find his past.

Yes, Clancy Davis, we will become friends real soon. Yes, tonight was the night. You're just the type of creep I'm looking for. Then you'll be sorry you didn't give up on me like everyone else. But you can bet I'll make you rich, before you die.

Hanging one leg around the pole and sliding up and down, she rubbed her crotch on the shiny metal, floor to ceiling rod. She feigned moaning with pleasure to entice the enthralled men.

Assessing which one would give her sugar next, she lunged

back, holding the pole with her left arm and letting her right arm taunt and playfully touch the next unwitting fool.

All the while, she pondered her next move with Clancy.

❦❦❦

Manhattan never slept even in the dead of winter, but this area in the lower west side dozed.

Pushing out the door into the snow-filled streets, Clancy staggered and onlookers moved to avoid him. "The nerve of that bitch to ignore me like that." Some young hookers on the street rushed past him. "Who are you lookin' at?"

The streetlights made round reflections in the snow, which was dirty from the traffic and pedestrians struggling their way through it. It was eerie walking here at this hour. The sleaziness. The danger. The loneliness. Clancy liked it this way. He had a lot to hide and the less people saw him, the better.

Out of breath, with frigid air coming out of his nose, he wobbled and struggled to keep himself upright. He passed a couple of vintage furniture stores, a modern art gallery, a theater, a tailor shop, and a park that closed at three a.m. He made it down the brownstone and tree-lined side street to the abandoned house on the corner. It was the perfect temporary home for him. With broken windows, doors boarded up, bricks falling down from the sides, and graffiti sprawled all over, no one would care about the non-rent-paying tenant.

Walking down the steps to the studio basement apartment, Clancy eyed two rats scrounging around the overflowing garbage pail. He threw his knapsack over them to scoop them up, taking them by surprise.

"These little cocksuckers'll be put to good use soon," he mumbled as he zipped up the sack. With his fingers trembling from the cold, he turned the key in the padlock to open the door. He plopped down on the weathered Salvation Army couch he got for twenty bucks and scanned the room. He'd developed this habit every time he returned to make sure everything was still there. The cameras—Arriflex 35 mm, and an old Mitchell along with different lenses, a stead cam, base tracking, and hand held cameras, and a photo developing tent in one corner, which had not been used in years, since the industry went from film to digital—were all he had left. Against the wall was a shelf with statues. Some Emmys and one Oscar. He picked up one of the Emmy's, read the inscription with his name, Clancy Davis, as if he needed to remember they were his. He hurled the Emmy onto a table holding a stack of Cinematography magazines. The head broke off and rolled onto the floor.

ⱷᴈⱸᴈ

In her palatial, six-room, Central Park West apartment the stripper relaxed on her six-thousand dollar royal blue, velvet, wing-arm couch in the living room. She had updated the apartment's 1950s era décor during the last twelve years since she "inherited" it. She flipped open the laptop on the mirrored glass coffee table. Lights reflected off every wall and item of furniture. She lived in a maze of glass. Fragile glass that could shatter in a moment's notice. Fragile, just like her life.

It was six a.m. She hadn't slept in over twenty-four hours.

Googling Clancy Davis, she found him on the first page.

Oh yeah. I could sure use your talents, Clancy. This is a tad dated but I'll find you. I always do. I'll find you. Use you. And dispose of you. Just like all the others. And you'll never know what hit you. Just have to make sure the cops aren't after you. Can't afford them busting in here. I'm much too precious to be in a cage. Nope. That's not even an option. Now, to make sure.

She reached for a wooden box on the coffee table. The painted eagle and the Native American woman on the top of the dark blue box peered into her eyes. She opened it and lifted a deck of tarot cards into her left hand. She asked a question. *Is Clancy the right man for this mission?*

She shuffled the deck, split it in two, revealing the Major Arcana card, The Magician, and the Nine of Cups, also known as the Genie card.

Perfect. The two most positive cards in the deck. I'm on a roll now. Thank you, Universe.

She slipped the two cards back into the deck, kissed the top card, compressed the deck to her heart, replaced it in the box, and then leaned back on the couch.

She pulled off the wig, shook her head, revealing long, highlighted blonde hair. She popped out the emerald contact lenses and then pulled off the boots, emptying the contents onto the hand-woven, sky-blue shag carpet that mimicked the color of her eyes. Out flew bills in twenties, fifties, and a few hundreds.

Last to hit the carpet with a bounce was a Charter Arms Pink Lady .38 caliber.

My closest and dearest friend. My only friend.

She embraced the mother-of-pearl, pink-marbleized grip in the palm of her hands, bringing it up to her lips. She adorned it with a long sensual kiss, running her mouth from the short handle to the end of the metallic pink barrel. She then moaned an exaggerated, long, and relaxed sigh. Coming back to the present, she removed its five bullets and put them into a heart-shaped jeweled treasure box coated in its entirety with emeralds and rubies with a diamond tiara serving as the handle. She then placed it back on the far right corner of the table—its permanent place.

She had decorated the apartment in yellows, blues, and accents in hot pink, which were very calming to her anything-but-calm life. She loved her cartoon paintings, many of them of princesses from contemporary artists. She received peace in the sense of magic, charm, and whimsy, but no child had set foot in this home.

This was her private haven, where she escaped from all of the death around her. All of the death she'd caused. All of the deaths she planned to cause.

CHAPTER 2

Chief of Forensic Psychiatry, Dr. John Trenton, PhD, MD, had a few uninterrupted hours in which to write his reports from the huge stack on his desk in his office at Manhattan Psych.

The patient follow-up treatment plans, pre-trial evaluations, and criminal profiling he had to complete for the NYPD had stringent requirements and deadlines. He hand marked every document with the date he intended to complete it. More importantly, he had to make sure his patients met the criteria for being under the umbrella of "forensic" patient. Once a treatment plan was modified, or a patient was deemed fit to stand trial, their classification changed. His mind ruminated over the few patients to whom this applied.

Those files would be on hold for just for a few minutes as he stared blankly at the title of a medical text he was writing scrawled on a yellow note pad. *Holistic Forensic Psychiatry: Making the Mind-Body Connection.* Today he had trouble making his own connection.

With his elbows on the arms of his chair and his hands clasped under his chin, he swiveled around and contemplated his framed diplomas on the wall above the couch. Encased in matching wood frames were his degrees and organizational affiliations with The National Medical Association, The United States Academy of Psychiatrists and The Law, and The United States Psychiatric Association. He was proud that these depicted his codes of ethics and standing in the forensic psychiatry community, as they were more prestigious than those just issuing licensure. At forty-five, he had achieved more than most doctors. He was the youngest department head in any New York City hospital.

And after today, his accomplishments would be all he had left.

As much as he tried to concentrate, his gaze kept going back to framed photos on his oversized colonial desk. Not a day went by that he didn't reflect on these photos. His beautiful wife Vicki, with a golden blonde ponytail, wearing a light pink T-shirt, short shorts, and flip flops sat in the bright sun on a lounge poolside. He picked up the photo and smiled at the date. Exactly a year ago. Her contagious smile and sparkling, round blue eyes showed contentment in her rural Central Florida hometown. And she was leaving him tonight on a five p.m. flight to go back home. No matter how hard she tried, she never considered New York City her home. He hadn't been able to sleep or drum up the energy to work out since she told him she was leaving two weeks ago. How could he deny the woman he loved so much her happiness? He couldn't. He was going to have to let her go. He sniffled to hold back emotions that would flood out of him had he not had control. He felt his eyes burn. He began to sweat. He loosened his shirt collar. But he was at work. He had to hold it in. He put down the photo of Vicki, put his lips to his platinum wedding band, and lifted the other photo.

Five-year-old Ricky and he had slept together, wrapped in each other's arms with Ricky's blond curly head on John's bare muscular chest. Ricky's tanned skin made John ghostlike in comparison. He noticed his hair. It was jet black then, wilder, and a little longer—a couple of inches below his neck. He ran his fingers through his hair, acknowledging the change. He'd become gray at the temples and through the crown. But he still had all of it. He couldn't believe it. Three years made such a difference. His life was so different. It had been so much better until two weeks ago. Tears welled in his eyes again, and his breathing became stifled as he went into a daydream and saw five-year-old Ricky being taken away on a September morning in Florida by Social Services. He thought about him every day. He sent out messages to the universe to bring Ricky back.

So far no answers.

ℭℨℭℨ

An arthritic left hand, with the crippled fingers of an aging man, slipped unnoticed behind the stainless steel counter in the hospital's kitchen and depressed the silver panic button.

ℭℨℭℨ

"Dr. Trenton, Code Silver, STAT!"

Hearing his page snapped John back. "How the hell did that happen? There's the word maximum before security for a reason! Damn it!"

He took a precious moment to grab a black tourmaline log from his desk, holding it in the palm of his right hand. One deep breath to ground him. That's all he allowed himself. He replaced the log on his desk. Then he took off his Rolex and secured it in a locked box in his desk drawer.

Throwing his long white lab coat over his dark gray pin striped Armani suit, he ran out of the room, preparing his mind and body for a lengthy confrontation. This would be a serious one, as serious as it could get in this facility. He had taken control of these crisis interventions with the most severe psychopathic and psychotic criminals in New York City for the past ten years, since finishing his psychiatric residency and fellowship training here. As well trained as he was, the outcomes were always uncertain.

"Dr. Trenton! Kitchen."

Kitchen? They're kidding me, right? The Kitchen? The food isn't that bad.

ℭℨℭℨ

"Yous stay in the corner." Hal, the twenty-four-year-old patient, stood blocking the exit and pointed to the far left corner in the kitchen next to the largest counter space, as he grabbed the paring knife off the prep counter. Waving the knife, he almost dropped it from his trembling hand.

Stan, the head chef for the past thirty years, and twenty-two-year-old Bobby, both wearing cooking whites and hairnets, huddled in the corner. Stan took a pill out of his pocket and popped it under his tongue. A nitro.

A burning odor permeated the space. Smoke came out of the pilot lights on the stove.

"What you lookin' at, Stan?"

"Hal, the food is burning."

Hal stared at the stove. The chicken soup for lunch boiled over in both of the two twenty-quart commercial stainless steel pots. The chicken stock, carrots, celery, onions, and the soft meat that fell off the bones, overflowed onto the stove-top and then onto the floor.

"Good. Let it burn."

Stan struggled to get up.

"Don't you think of movin', Stan." Hal crinkled his nose at the odor, too, but ignored it. He would have liked a fire. It would have been his way out.

He pulled on a locked drawer so hard that it broke and fell out, sending a bunch of different-sized knives crashing to the floor. He contemplated what else he could do, picked up a twelve-inch serrated butcher knife from the floor, and raced to the fridge holding all of the facility's food. He opened the door and scanned the fridge. Amazed at how much food was in there, he stared at it for a minute, standing in front of the door with it open while the cold draft on his body sent shivers down his spine. He was undeterred. He pulled out a large boiled ham, so weighty he almost dropped it. He hauled it to the counter and "Bam," he sliced the ham in half with the largest blade. Very proud of his accomplishment, he waved the big, now-slippery knife at his two terrified hostages.

He decided to try the smaller blade on himself. In full view of his audience, he picked up his institutional gray shirt and without any fear or hesitation ran the blade in his right hand across his emaciated chest, only stopping at the beginning to look at the initial cut. Then moment by moment, he progressed until the knife made a cut in his skin from his left side to his right. He drew blood and moaned with almost orgasmic relief. The dripping blood seeped through his shirt, but he barely paid attention. His gaze remained glued on his hostages. He put the smaller, blood-stained blade in the elastic waistband of his pants. He then waved the bigger blade to threaten and torment Stan and Bobby.

"This is sick," Bobby said as he snuck out from behind the counter.

Stan yanked Bobby away from him, grabbing his arm using a lot of his strength, which wasn't much.

"Hal, just go back to the rec room!"

"Stan, you know this creep?"

"For the past three years."

"I'm not taking this shit," Bobby said. "Ya got balls Hal, come here." Bobby cocked his head toward Stan. "I can take him easy. Just watch, old man."

Bobby lunged at Hal but Hal got the better of him. Like a wrestling pro, he wrapped himself around Bobby, knocking him with a slam to the hard concrete floor, banging his head and almost knocking him out. Hal cut Bobby right across his stomach with the smaller blade. It was barely a surface cut but Bobby screamed in terror.

⁌ↄ⁍ↄ

The four large men—Sergeant Dave Shipman, NYPD Officers Milt Browne, Jackson Maxwell, and Mike Kramer—wore bulletproof vests and exuded the power and strength of the most highly trained combat unit in the city, the Emergency Service Unit. Or as they called it ESU. Carrying a laptop and cases with their guns and ammo—Springfield Armory 1911 pistols, Colt M16A2 rifles and the Heckler and Koch UMP .45 caliber—they entered their Lenco Peacekeeper armored vehicle, fully equipped with shepherd hooks, shields, Tasers, and beanbags to annihilate the perp.

Exiting a police department garage in their headquarters in

Battery Park, this Manhattan North ESU knew their trip to Seventy-Seventh Street was going to take a while, with the traffic on the FDR and the heavy snow.

While sitting on a bench at the back of the truck, Sergeant Shipman booted up the laptop. He saw the hostage situation in the kitchen, in real time. His attention darted around the screen to get the What, Where, When, How, and Why. "All right, listen up, guys. It's thirty by sixty, no outside windows so that makes our job harder. Just air vents, ten feet apart, on the ceiling. Everything is stainless steel, counter tops, doors, closets. All drawers locked. Huge islands in the center of the space. Refrigerator is on the opposite wall. There's a communication center already on the wall so we'll be able to make contact. Looks like food is cooking on the stove, but don't expect us to stay for lunch. Mike, you're on today to take down this guy."

"Got it, Sarg. How many hostages?"

"Looks like two, food-prep workers. One guy, looks early twenties. One guy, a senior. That one's a problem. Never can tell with their health."

"That's for sure. Some precincts will send the negotiators and they might be there before us, but from the looks of this, they can talk till they're blue in the face. Just let me get in there. This is one hostage taker who's coming out in a body bag. I gotta get home, guys. The baby's keepin' us up all night."

"What did ya expect Mike? He's four weeks old! Okay, the HT is a forensic patient—Caucasian, young, thin, early twenties, if that—waving large serrated butcher knives. That's all I know now. Dr. Trenton will be there to fill us in. I'll work on the outside diverting traffic and wait for the other area teams. With this weather, and most of the teams doing rescues, manpower might be tight. We need the roofs of all surrounding buildings covered and the stairwells inside. Leave nothing to chance. This guy got in and I'm sure he can find a way out. No civilian casualties today, guys, not on our watch. And, Jackson, keep the media away. Trenton hates it."

"Will do, Sarg."

"Hey, Jackson, you two know something we don't?"

"Yeah, we do. Four years ago, before the doc got married,

the camera jockeys labeled him as one of New York City's most desirable and handsome bachelors. Since then, they're up his ass whenever he's with a woman."

"Ouch! I should be so lucky." The men laughed. "Without a doubt the paparazzi puts a crimp in his relationships, which put them on his shit list," the sergeant added.

The Lenco sped up the FDR. drive, going north, with its red lights flashing. Vehicles moved out of its way. The truck changed lanes, sometimes missing the cars they cut off by a slim margin. The three-lane highway was packed twenty-four-seven and maneuvering took skill, which Milt had until they got into bumper-to-bumper traffic.

"We got a problem, guys."

"Can't afford one, Milt. This is a serious one. The HT is attacking one of the hostages. This looks bad and it's escalating."

Their truck came to a halt in the left lane along with the other two lanes. Sergeant Shipman rolled down the window and extended his body out into the frigid air. Snow slapped his face in the gusts of wind. Fire engines and ambulances were on the scene, with an accident about one-hundred-fifty feet in front of them, blocking all three lanes. A silver Toyota Corolla lay overturned in the center lane at Thirty-Fourth Street. It was so bad that firefighters used the jaws-of-life to cut into and remove the side of the jeep and rescue a screaming and horrified pregnant woman on the passenger side. Two other cars, a red sedan and blue compact, had compressed into each other. The red sedan in the front had its windshield blown out. The passenger, who had flown out of it, lay on an ambulance stretcher with a sheet over him and was covered by the blowing snow.

"Looks like a DOA, guys, and we can't get to the exit."

They sat frustrated and restless. What were they going to do now? Shipman got on the phone to find out if there was another team close to the situation. He cursed the Lenco for not sprouting wings.

ε∽ε∽

John approached at a run, less than two minutes after the page.

Bill, Hal's attendant, rubbed his sweaty palms on his white uniform. "He's tearing the place apart, Doc. He locked himself in."

John peered through the plexi-glass windows on the closed swinging doors and confirmed the HT was his patient. He saw Hal wave the large blade through the air as if he was leading an orchestra and dancing to music. It had to be that he heard music again. John couldn't see the hostages. It was safe, for the moment.

Damn! Another setback Hal didn't need.

John's gaze remained on Hal. "Bill, he should have been in rec room now, so how did he get downstairs?" His tone conveyed he intended to nail someone for this. "Why didn't the alarm sound when the door was opened?"

"Repair techs were working on the system. It was down less than three minutes. I'm sorry, Doc, I just turned my back for a second."

"All right, I'm trying to find out what I'm up against here, Bill. Who's he with?"

Bill hesitated.

"Come on, Bill! This is not going to fly!"

"Stan."

John was distraught that Stan was in such a volatile situation. Stan was his friend, who made him sandwiches, prepared meals for him to order, and had done so for the past ten years. Stan couldn't handle this stress, not with his newly diagnosed heart condition.

"We'll talk later."

Bill got the message. "Sure, Doc, and the new kid, Bobby, is in there with him."

While Bill spoke, John didn't take his gaze off the situation in the kitchen. "Yeah, knew he was coming in today, but they were late sending his file. Stan's usually good with these kids. I had an intern interview him and bring him down here."

A female attendant Debbie, who was in her thirties, ran up and stood directly in front of John. He wanted all of the facts, fast and counted on his staff to have them on demand. He thought he was going to get more information, but instead, she zoned out, looking into his eyes.

John watched her in amazement. Obviously, she didn't perceive the people around her who stared at her, hiding their laughter. She let out a lustful sigh. It did break some tension of the situation, but that was the last thing John wanted.

He smirked, at first, at her approach, then his expression changed to an emotionless stare. He knew his effect on women. He'd had that effect on them since he was a teenager. They all swooned. He'd learned to live with it.

The clang of metal pots thrown onto the floor inside the kitchen startled Debbie. She shook her head and blurted it out. "He attacked Bobby with a knife."

John didn't stir. He watched Hal throw the pots toward the cabinets, but John responded to her comment. "How bad?"

The petite brunette didn't impress him. His heart belonged to Vicki. Not getting an answer to his question, he stared at her. He met her stagnant gaze, as he glared her down into a humiliated sweat.

He pressed the intercom button on the wall so he could hear all the conversation and ruckus inside the kitchen. He'd demand answers later.

"Everyone back please." John glared for a moment, until the staff followed his directives, then he returned his focus to his knife-wielding patient. "Hal, you hear me?" Silence. "Hal, answer me."

"Yeah."

"Hal, you know who I am, right?" The first step he wanted to take was to make sure his patient knew who he was talking to.

"Yeah, Doc Trenton."

"Good, Hal, that's right. I'm Dr. Trenton."

He stressed "doctor" to show his patient how to address him in a formal manner. His attitude and austere presence commanded respect. Unfortunately, this worked against him at times, too. He was the go-to guy in all crises in this facility, even if they weren't his own patients.

He would never say "No" to any request to assist.

"Get me outta here," Bobby screamed at the top of his lungs. "I'm bleedin' to death!"

Bill shook his head. "That's Bobby."

"The baby's not bleedin,' but he will if he don't shut up!"

"Hal, I can't hear you with Bobby screaming in there. Can you tell me what's going on? You need to clear things up for me, Hal." John glanced at Bill. "Did he have his med and supplements this morning?"

"Yes, he did."

"I'm gonna kill them!" Hal jumped up and down then ran toward Stan and Bobby, thrusting the blade a couple of inches in front of them, but not making contact.

That's not good. Man, this doesn't get any easier.

"Can you come closer to the door, I still can't hear you."

"I can hear ya just fine, Dr. Trenton," Hal said in a mocking tone.

"This is good," John told Bill. "He's responding. We can do this. Good, Hal, I just want to make sure everyone is okay. Hal, how did you get blood on yourself?"

Before Hal could respond, Bobby yelled from inside. "He cut himself across his chest and he cut me, too!"

"Shut up or I'll stab ya for real this time, asshole."

"I need you to talk to me, Hal, and no one else."

Damn! His mind still isn't off the others. But he's giving good, rational responses.

"What about you Hal? Are you still bleeding?"

"It stopped already."

John realized this was not a psychotic or schizophrenic episode. This was very deliberate and thought out, or Bobby would have been another one of Hal's kills.

Now I just have to figure out what he wants.

"All right, I want you to talk to me, Hal. You're the important one."

Bobby jumped up in his own tantrum. "No, he's not, what about us, you prick?"

John was taken aback and he almost laughed. He swallowed hard in an attempt to regain composure. He whispered to Bill, "Was prick meant for me?" He hadn't gotten back talk in years and now regretted having an intern interview Bobby, instead of himself.

"Oh, man, I think so."

"John got a glimpse of Stan grabbing onto his chest. "Bobby shut up!" Stan said.

"Up yours, old man."

"How are you doing, Stan?" John asked.

"My breathing's a little tight. But I'll be okay."

"Hal, why don't you be the good guy and let Stan out for his medication? You know what it's like when you need your meds, right?"

"No! He ain't leaving!"

Two hostage negotiator NYPD officers from Manhattan North, Larry Sutton and Jeff Wallace, pushed their way through the staff. Sutton covered the intercom speaker with his hand. "How's it going, Dr. Trenton? We can take over from here. ESU's on their way."

"What are you doing?" John demanded. "Wallace, Sutton, thanks, but I've got it. You can stay here and listen. Just don't get in my way." John received competitive glares from both of them. "Hey," he growled. "You know the drill. I start. I finish. If you guys remember, I taught the certification course on this. Look, I can't waste time debating with you. One of the hostages isn't well. Hands off."

Sutton grimaced but nodded.

"All right, Hal," John said. "What do you want me to do to help you?"

"I can't take anymore. I'm stuck in this place. I got no visitors for three years—three fuckin' years. Everybody in rec room was getting visitors today. And I get no fuckin' nuttin, no pictures, no nuttin."

"I know how you feel, Hal." John took a moment. "My parents left me alone and moved to Florida, and I don't have any brothers or sisters, either. So, help me understand, Hal, who do you want to visit you?"

"He killed everyone in his family! Who'd he expect to visit?"

"Bobby, be quiet when Dr. Trenton is talking," Stan ordered.

How does Bobby know that Hal killed his family?

John heard the raspy quality of Stan's voice. He needed to get in there. He rubbed his forehead. "Pull up Bobby's file, please. It has to be here by now," he told Debbie. "Fast. He's adding time Stan doesn't have."

Hal lunged at Bobby and grabbed him by the arm. "I've been killing since I've been fourteen, a few more won't make a difference."

John saw Bobby swing at Hal with his clenched fists. Hal let him go and pushed him away, hard and fast.

I only know about the five murders when he was twenty-one.

"Hal, don't do that. I know it isn't your fault. You didn't mean to cut Bobby. He provoked you. No one else needs to get hurt, so tell me what you want."

"Go away."

"Why do you want me to go away, Hal?"

"So I can kill 'em."

Sutton put his hand over the intercom. "Look, Dr. Trenton, you've been at it awhile and it's not working. Let us go in."

"That's not happening if I can help it. Move your hand, Sutton."

Sutton opened his palm and pulled his hand away.

John turned his back on the negotiators. "Stan, how are you holding up?"

"I'm okay, Doc."

John doubted Stan was telling him the truth but he was still able to talk. The doctor contemplated his next words before he responded, knowing he had to be very careful. "Hal, how long have we known each other?"

"Since I been fourteen."

"That's right, Hal, ten years now, and I'm the reason you're here and not in prison, right?"

"Yeah."

"So you know I can't let you do that, right?"

"Yeah."

"So how about you come out and we can talk in my office? Let's end this now."

"No, I ain't comin' out! I ain''t comin' out! You can't make me!"

John put his own hand over the intercom, this time, addressing Bill and the negotiators. "It's been over an hour. I'm not waiting anymore. I'm going in. Can't afford to make Hal any angrier. And Stan needs medical attention." He removed his hand from the mouthpiece. "Okay, Hal, okay, so let me come in and we can talk about it man to man."

"I ain't no man."

"Yeah, he ain't no man. He ain't got no balls!"

"Bobby, you and I are going to get to know each other real well when this is over."

"Yeah, yeah."

John turned to Bill. "They both sound alike." He could see there was be a very fine line for Bobby to cross over to being a patient here. "Yes, you are, Hal. You're over eighteen. That's why you're here. How about I come in?"

"You alone?"

"Just me and the hospital people. You know them all."

"No cops?" Hal whined.

The cardinal rule against lying to a patient took precedence so John modified his response. "No cops are coming in Hal, absolutely no cops. You sound disappointed."

"Yeah, they'd come in with guns blasting and it would be over—one, two, three—just like on TV."

John put his hand over the intercom and leaned toward Bill and the negotiators. "Now I know what he wants, suicide by cop, and that's not happening, not on my watch." He removed his hand and spoke directly into the intercom. "Hal, okay if I come in?"

Bill laid a hand on John's arm. "But, Dr. Trenton, with all due respect, it's against protocol."

"Believe me, Bill, I know that, but I can't risk it, not with Bobby in there. Got to make an executive decision."

Sutton shook his head. "Dr. Trenton, the lieutenant will have your head on a platter."

"I'll let him have it if I can't save Hal."

"So let one of us go in. We're armed."

"Sutton, that's exactly why you're not going in." John leaned toward the intercom mic. "Hal, may I come in?"

Hal clutched the knives to show his power, almost daring John to take him down. "Yeah."

Hal, don't make me have to get physical with you. Damn, I hate doing that.

Hal held one serrated butcher knife in each hand, ready to strike when John entered. He threatened the two huddled in a corner. "Try to warn him and you'll get dead!"

Stan and Bobby remained squatted down by the counters while Hal stood in the middle of the room in an open area.

John opened the swinging door in slow motion, so as not to startle Hal. Bobby, crouched in the corner, finally saw Dr. Trenton for the first time. John's eyes conveyed that he had zero tolerance for insubordination. Bobby keeled over, holding his stomach, and broke out into a sweat. John nodded at Bobby, satisfied that he'd gotten a reaction from him.

With dominance permeating from his inner core, John still approached Hal with caution, watching him hold the blades and getting ready to attack. "You know I'm not armed, right?"

As John's adrenalin pumped, he felt the surge of energy in every cell in his body. The rushing blood through his veins made his temperature rise. His focus and determination increased. His stamina increased. He was in power mode. He'd trained himself that way, intending to save a life. His ego thrived on his self-made energy. He'd sleep well tonight.

CHAPTER 3

"I want him taken out of the house today. Damn it. He came back to us with a broken arm!"

"Hold on, please."

Dr. Barbara Montgomery, PhD, school psychologist, heard music play. Her jaw tightened. She was ready to explode when that social worker came back on the phone.

Calm down, Barbara.

She stiffened as she sat in a plain wood chair tucked into a worn teacher's desk that had been aged with notes written on the wood, coffee and food stains. She doodled different shaped hearts on it herself as she panned her office, checking out the new paint job in her twelve foot by fifteen foot space on the third floor of an elementary school in the Sheepshead Bay section of Brooklyn.

She had been in many schools but this was the first one where the principal, Mrs. Sarah Bennett, had asked the teachers and staff what colors they wanted their rooms painted. Barbara had chosen a light blue and pale yellow for her home away from home because it had a calming effect on her students.

Even the window shades covering the massive floor-to-ceiling windows had new light blue shades. The bookcases under the windows, running the full length of the wall, had come out a darker blue than she had envisioned them, but she was stuck with it. The pale yellow walls didn't compliment the blue either. She loved matchy-matchy, but her time here would end soon enough. The thought of it made her want to get up and do a happy dance.

Hearing the voice on the other end of the line at Child Protective Services, brought Barbara out of her reflection.

"Dr. Montgomery, all right, Dr. Cohen said he spoke to you about Jeremiah in detail."

"Yes, he did. So now I expect him to carry through on what he told me he would do."

"Yes, he will. We'll take care of it this afternoon, Dr. Montgomery."

"Thank you. I have to go. I'll call you for a follow-up in a few days. Bye." She hung up smiling. She had saved another child.

Getting her clipboard and the evaluation sheets she needed for her student's observation from her desk drawer, she got up and pushed in her chair a little too hard this time, causing the roller ball on the bottom of one leg to fall off. Anger did that to her.

Damn! *Just a little while longer, Barbara. Have patience.*

She put her left hand in her jacket pocket and clutched the tumbled, rutilated-quartz stone. She needed all the strength she could muster. The stone's energy started at her feet and gushed like a stream, running north to her head. She took a deep breath, stood straight, dusted some lint off her double-breasted, navy, three-piece suit, and kicked the roller ball under her desk.

She opened her door and noticed that the black floor tiles in the hall still needed a cleaning from the paint job. Before she took a step, she mentally navigated her path. She'd never forgive herself if she got paint on her navy sneakers. She entered the down stairwell and, wincing at the rancid odor of the paint job, covered her nose and mouth.

As she descended to the second floor, she heard uncontrolled screams of anger coming from a classroom. Sounded like a major fight going on while the teacher shrieked unintelligible words. As she opened the second floor stairwell door, she realized the commotion was coming from the classroom she'd be visiting.

Standing outside the closed wooden door of room 215 and

observing through the plexi-glass windows on the top third of the door, she assessed right away that the problem in this room was not the children. Thirty six-year-olds were doing their own thing, ignoring their teacher of one year, Miss Klein, who was at her wit's end. They were running and chasing each other around the perimeter of the room. Some played a boxing video game in the corner and wrestled over whose turn it was, as one girl pulled another one's braids. Two others engaged in a knock-down-drag-out fight. Considering the screaming she heard, Barbara knew this wasn't center time or any constructive activity.

The teacher's high-pitched squeals came out as raspy screeches. "Sit down, sit down. I told you not to do that! I can't take you anymore!" It was obvious this teacher did not want to be there. Nor did she belong here wearing skintight jeans with a low V-neck sweater showing too much cleavage. And her long greasy hair was in pig tails. Seriously? Barbara crinkled her nose in disgust. Better now than in front of the class.

"He hit me in the eye with his pencil, Miss Klein," Little Treasure said. With her hair in cornbraids, held at the ends with about twenty brightly colored barrettes, she looked up at her teacher with pitiful eyes.

"Kyle, what did you do? Why are you poking her again? Can't you behave?"

Kyle, a chubby little boy wearing a striped shirt and jeans that were too small for him, just stood there crying.

Barbara had heard enough. She opened the door with caution, not wanting to be a target of books, crayons, and candy that were being thrown about the disheveled room. She surveyed the classroom. There were no colorful bulletin boards in the many possible places for them, or current children's work on display. The only colors in this classroom were on the painted walls and the alphabet carpet in the reading center at the back left corner of the room, where the children sat on the floor during reading lessons.

The bulletin boards on the closet doors, which spanned the entire left side, had their original brown corkboard showing.

The same went for the bulletin boards on the back wall. Everything had come down for the paint job last week. But a week had passed. And nothing had been replaced.

Barbara entered and proceeded to the front of the room. "Good afternoon." She addressed the children a little louder than she would prefer to speak, clasping her hands in a relaxed manner, low and in front of her. For a moment, nothing. Then one by one, the children noticed her and scrambled to their seats, without her saying another word. She maintained eye contact with them the entire time.

One group, still arguing in the corner, ignored her. She walked over to them with her signature Barbara smile, looking at them eye to eye with a warm and wide smile they couldn't resist. When they felt her presence, they looked up and realized everyone else was already stationed at their desks.

"Oops," spilled out of their little mouths as they scurried to their seats. Through a tide of little voices, Barbara heard, "Hurry up! Sit down!" "Move over," "'K, bes quiet." "Beeeeeeeeeee quiet!"

Six-year-old innocent eyes connected with hers. She smiled from where she stood by the bookcase under the window on the right side of the room. Her right arm rested on the ledge, while her left hand was in her pocket.

"Complements to table two." All eyes went to the six adorable children sitting at the table postured up in their chairs with their hands folded on their desks. "Complements to table four, table four is joining table two." Her imaginary magic wand with faerie dust worked every time in every classroom. Each child now paid attention. "My compliments to everyone now. You look wonderful, just like grown up first graders."

Miss Klein stood in the corner next to her desk with her arms folded across her chest. She tilted up her nose, tightened her mouth into a sliver, and rolled her eyes as she turned to focus her gaze out the window.

Now that all little eyes were on Barbara, she said, "This is the way you're expected to behave. And you all knew that from last year, right? I know a lot of your mommies and daddies." She gave them a sincere smile and welcomed precious smiles in response. "I'm going to be visiting for a while so I want you to show me, and Miss Klein, just how wonderful you can be."

The children, trying to be in unison, answered her with "Yes, Miss M."

"Now I'm going to sit back here and see who's paying attention so you can get a compliment."

She walked to the back of the room. "And Miss Klein is going to take over."

Miss Klein sucked in her cheeks. "Why can't you teach the lesson?"

Taken aback, Barbara glared at her. "I'm not here for that today, but perhaps another day we can arrange for that." Barbara's signature smile spurted pure malevolence.

Miss Klein trudged to the front of the room. "We're going to learn the consonant L. Who can tell me words that begin with L?"

As she waited for an answer, Miss Klein kept looking at the door.

Is she waiting for a message from God?

Not soon enough for Miss Klein, another teacher came in to relieve her for her fifty-minute preparation period and Barbara planned to take advantage of the opportunity. She got up from the chair in the back of the room and approached Miss Klein, who grabbed her jacket and worn bag to rush out. Barbara noticed the bag, a very soiled tan leather that had had years of daily wear. Just the antithesis of herself, in her expensive, conservative three-piece navy suit, carrying her Louis Vuitton tote, this woman had no concept of what was the professional attire necessary for a teacher. Or she had never looked in a mirror. And her glasses! They were so dirty, how could she see out of them?

"Where are you planning to go, Miss Klein?"

"Outside for a smoke. Do you mind, Dr. Montgomery?" she asked, imitating Barbara's tone of superiority.

"We're not allowed to leave the building on a prep, and I was hoping we could spend the period chatting about this case you sent to me."

"Can't we talk next week?"

"No, there's a specific time frame for the eval and, actually, I wasn't asking you. My office is 321." Barbara left the room and vanished into the stairwell.

e⁂

Miss Klein entered the office and slammed her plan book down on the sun-yellowed conference table. She pulled out a plain wooden chair without arms, slumped down into it, and made sucking sounds with her tongue on her teeth.

Barbara glanced at the coffee-stained plan book, then turned her attention to the expression on Miss Klein's face. *She thinks I'm a bitch? Well, surprise, surprise, I am.*

Miss Klein sat with arms crossed on her chest, revealing a tear on the right arm of her sweater.

"Glad you made it. Here." Barbara handed her a spray bottle of eyeglass cleaner and a tissue. "You probably ran out of yours."

"Thanks." While she used the cleaner, she glared at Barbara. "Why do I have to call you Dr. Montgomery and the kids call you Miss M? I should be calling you Barbara."

"Seriously?" Barbara studied her. "Children, not kids. Those are baby goats. The children address me as Miss M. because it's less threatening to them than calling me doctor. You haven't earned the right to address me by my first name. Now let's continue, shall we? I have the five pages you sent to me that I downloaded," she said, flipping through it. "But it isn't complete."

"I don't have the time to fill out this crap."

"Well, the Department of Education has specific requirements for referrals, and this is mandatory and it needs to be complete. They also help the state and me to get the child the help they so badly need. I didn't create these regs. But putting that aside, why are you referring Kyle?"

"I already wrote it in there."

Finding the page, Barbara scanned it. "You wrote, 'hits other children.'"

"You saw that today."

"Yes, I did, and he doesn't do homework, he curses, and what else?"

"That's enough."

"Miss Klein, actually, it's not enough to refer a child to special education. Okay, teacher interventions. You wrote that you called the parents. But it's not annotated here when, how many times, what the results were, and the exact verbal responses were that you got from them."

Miss Klein rolled her eyes. "You're kidding me, right?"

"Actually, I'm quite serious. What did his parents say to you when you called? Better yet, what did you say to them?"

"I don't even remember. I was so pissed, but they told me to fuck off."

"Did they verbalize that or were they pissed at the way you approached them?"

"What the hell is wrong with you? They didn't actually say fuck, but they said 'when he's in school, he's your problem,' then I got more pissed."

"More pissed? So you began the conversation angry with them, like you're being angry with me?"

"Well, yeah, I had to call them on my own time at night, since they both work during the day and you're making me lose my prep."

Barbara wasn't the least bit fazed and ignored the prep comment. "That goes with the job. Every successful teacher I know does work at home and a lot of it."

"I don't care. I'm not doing anything at home. Once I leave here at three, that's it."

"So, how's that working for you?"

Miss Klein smirked and rolled her eyes again.

"Look, you have a child who isn't behaving and, by yelling at the parents, you've made enemies so you blew any collaboration you might have had to help this child. And it was clear today that you didn't have a lesson planned, so you didn't fool me or even the children, for that matter. And they are very smart, so don't underestimate them because of their age. Even on the eval, you left out what you've done in the classroom to help him."

"How do you know I didn't have a lesson planned?"

"In this district, visual aids are mandatory to teach the alphabet and sounds. Where were yours?"

Barbara remained quiet and let it sink in.

"I don't do lesson plans, anymore, because whenever I do I can't get my plans through to them, anyway, the way this class behaves."

"How have you managed to get away without doing plans?"

"We have a choice, to do them on line or in my plan book. I chose the plan book. Then I give Bennett an excuse, and she just walks out of the room."

"That's it?"

"I have a few letters in my file, but I don't care. What can they do?"

"They can do plenty. You can get fired, for one, and leave here with a U rating. No principal will want you after that. And you're lucky to be here. Mrs. Bennett is the fairest and most caring principal I know, and I'm in a few schools."

"Well, she can't hurt me."

"Why not? You're not tenured yet."

"My uncle is the superintendent of schools in Queens, Sherman Greenberg."

"Sherman? Sherman Greenberg? He's your uncle?"

Guess I'll have to become acquainted with Sherman Greenberg.

Her face lit up as if she was now immune. "Yes, he is."

"I know him very well. I give teacher-training workshops for him. And I speak with him at least once a week."

The color in her face faded. "You do?"

"And even though he may have gotten you the job, now you have to prove you deserve to keep it."

Miss Klein rolled her lips together after Barbara's remark.

"So, what help have you gotten?"

"From whom?"

"Support staff in the school, staff developers, reading teachers."

"The staff developer said I needed to attend her meetings and that would help me with everything."

Barbara's eyes met hers. "And?"

"They're after school and I just want to get out of here."

"I'll ask you again. How's that working for you?"

She weakened, becoming teary eyed. "Horrible."

"All right, acknowledged. So why are you really not going?"

After a minute of silence, she caved. "I'm afraid that if I try really hard and commit to doing this job well, I'll fail anyway, so why bother trying? I've failed at most things I've tried in my life so I've given up."

"You bother trying because it's the little lives you're affecting, not just your own. And you can turn it around. Teaching is a learned skill, and you learn it by practicing it over and over again. Adults need to do repetitions up to twenty one times to make it a habit, so think of how long it can take little ones to grasp a concept. Winging lessons on the fly won't work. Honestly, start putting some effort in, and you will get results, but you have to want it." *Hell, it took me fourteen kills to get them right—quick and neat.* "When is the next meeting?"

"Today."

"Okay, I'll make this agreement with you. You go to all of the meetings that are offered after school and on weekends, and I won't mention to your uncle that you're not making the grade if Mrs. Bennett hasn't already."

"I'll go. I will, I promise." Looking at clock on wall, Miss Klein saw that her prep time was almost over. "Got to go. The prep teachers hate it when I'm late. Thanks."

Barbara nodded in acknowledgment but before she could reflect upon this meeting, a young female colleague charged into the room, bumping into the round children-sized table with kindergarten-height chairs around it.

"Dr. Barbara, Mrs. Bennett needs you downstairs right now. Jeremiah ran out of the building. She called ESU five minutes ago."

CHAPTER 4

In a bland and cluttered office, in a South Brooklyn precinct, with dull light green walls—and bulletin boards and posters all over them, showing pictures of New York City's most wanted—NYPD Lieutenant Paul Carlson, sat at his desk with an open file. He picked up the intercom and fingered his overgrown gray beard as he called his secretary.

"Jennifer, get Mandella and Valantino in here now!"

His gruff voice was more impatient than usual. Jennifer had to notice how cranky he'd been lately. He was surprised she hadn't said anything about it to him. Had she mentioned it to the team? He rubbed his hand over his bald head in frustration, in a vain attempt to stimulate his gray matter. He yawned, closed his eyes, and pictured himself lying in his comfortable bed at home. He really needed sleep, but his day was far from over.

"Right away, Lieutenant."

Two detective investigators, Tony Mandella and Sal Valantino, sauntered in.

Tony closed the door behind them and tossed his linen khaki sports jacket on the back of a chair. "What's up, Loo? We just got back from Coney."

"You mean to tell me you two took the fucking time to go to Nathans?" Carlson bellowed with as much force as he could muster.

Tony flipped his palms up and out. "We were starvin'."

"Hey, To," Sal scoffed. "You *were* starving, stuffing yourself with two pepper and onion dogs and a large cheese fries. That's over seventeen hundred calories, bro."

"Hey, how many times I gotta tell ya, it's To—ny. It's short enough, man. And I can afford the calories." Tony swaggered around, pulling in his stomach, showing off his physique, and turned all around. He ran his fingers through his curly dark brown mane, as if he was a stripper beginning his act. "See, I got it, just right. I got it, and, besides, I don't got no woman at home anymore to care about that shit." He pulled a chair out from the desk and flipped it around. "But I sure as hell won't let the boys eat that. You got the Italian babe at home to take care of ya. And you ate pretty damn good, too! A dog, fries. How many calories was that, Mr. Muscles? Don't play me with ya bullshit."

"Somewhere around eleven hundred." Sal flexed his biceps to show off and a New York Ranger's tattoo pulsated on his left. He then made himself as comfortable as he could on a gray metal chair with his broad shoulders extending beyond it.

Carlson's raspy voice hindered him from getting the words out. "What—are you two? In fucking junior—high school? Fifteen years together and ya still act like jerks!"

"Just foolin' around, Loo." Tony picked up one of the folders on the desk. "Hey, Loo, if ya don't mind me sayin', ya need to lay off the smokes."

"Yeah? Well, I do." Carlson gulped half a bottle of spring water. "How the fuck do you know how many calories are in that fucking stuff?"

"There are signs all over, Loo. Seriously, you're not going to be able to talk soon," Sal added, backing his partner.

"Knock it off! The both of you." Carlson started to strain and cough. "People pay attention to that fucking crap?"

"He does. How many sit ups do ya have to do to burn that off?"

"A few hours with my Angie should do the trick," Sal said.

Tony's thin eyebrows arched, and his hazel eyes popped in disbelief. "A few hours with a teenage girl in the house? You're taking a big chance."

"My little girl knows if that bedroom door is closed she doesn't dare come in unless she's bleeding to death."

"You're beginning to sound like your fucking buddy, Trenton. Where the fuck is he, anyway?"

"He's at the hospital. So?" Tony asked.

The lieutenant scowled.

"Why? What's the problem?" Tony continued.

The lieutenant jumped up, ready to throw the files on the floor. "What's the fucking problem, Tony? I'll tell you what's the fuck's the problem. I got a folder full of cases Trenton has to sign off on, a city full of weirdos he has to profile, and he's in that hospital trying to save the perps we've already caught! They belong where they are and—"

"All right, Loo," Sal interrupted. "We get the picture. Has he called in?"

"No, Sal. That's the damn point! And he hasn't called Vicki either! And that poor woman is even more aggravated than me! When the fuck is he going to follow the rules? Why are you still standing there for cryin' out loud? Go find him!"

"Right. On it, Loo."

℘℘℘

Tony and Sal entered the main lobby of Manhattan Psych. They'd already learned the drill and even though they'd been there numerous times to see Dr. Trenton, and everyone recognized them, they abided by the rules. It was maximum security for everyone the moment they stepped through the front door. Tony and Sal took off their overcoats as well as their sports jackets. They could wear only one layer of clothing inside. They should have left them in their car. The lobby guards sneered at them as if they should have known better. That slight oversight cost them time. They emptied their pockets into a tray—change, wallets, and cell phones.

Tony stopped in his tracks as a thought struck him. He removed chewing gum from his mouth and chucked it into a garbage pail. He remembered an incident years ago, about chewing gum being contraband here. He learned the hard way, when he sounded the alarm on the metal detector three times, not realizing his chewing gum wrapper was the culprit. He had to succumb to a body search, and it took two hours for someone to appear with the consent forms. It was two hours he didn't have to waste, but it was the law. He made it his business not to allow it to happen again.

The three armed security guards checked out their credentials and unloaded their Glocks, putting them in a concealed locker without taking their eyes off them. The detectives had good luck today. Neither one of them set off the alarm in the metal detector. They pocketed the receipts for their weapons, cell phones, and personal items.

☙❧

The ESU arrived and joined the other members of their team already there. The four men loaded down with equipment set up a station on one of the three tables in the hallway. The hostage negotiators from Manhattan North joined them. Ten law enforcement operatives with special tactical training readied themselves to storm in and take control. It sounded like organized chaos with each team leader shouting orders to their commands. They were just waiting for the signal and Hal would be down.

Sergeant Shipman started to get information his team needed from the negotiators that were with Trenton.

"Trenton just went in, couldn't wait, and he didn't want one of us—"

Sergeant Shipman wanted to put a bullet in the man's head. "What the fuck in the world were you thinking, Wallace? Why the hell did you two let him go in?"

"Hold on, Sarg. You know the doc. You know him as well as I do. And put a cork in the attitude. You sure as hell ain't my superior."

The sergeant took it down a notch. "All right."

"It's Trenton's sixth sense that told him he could do this, and he wanted to save his patient at all costs," Sutton said,

"Damn. We hit an accident with DOA's on East Thirty-Fourth," Shipman muttered. "Ten minutes earlier, this would be over and done with. All right, what have we got? Tell me about the HT."

"It's one of his patients, Hal Martin. Been here last three years and Trenton's been his doc on and off since he was fourteen in other hospitals. In actuality, he'll do better with someone he knows and trusts. They all do. Doc could very well talk him out of this."

The sergeant let out a deep sigh of relief. "Okay, Wallace, okay. So there's a history. I feel better about it now. I can deal with him being in. Time frame? Diagnosis?"

Bill approached them. "In and out. Schizophrenia."

"What's he in for now?"

"Five counts of murder, Sergeant."

Sutton's face reddened. "What? He failed to tell us that. Dammit, Trenton."

Sergeant Shipman fumed at Sutton's reaction. He was very close to telling his team to bust in there. "And you're so ready to defend him. I'll make sure Carlson hears about this. He's got to see his department shrink. He's got a problem, a big one. Puts himself in the face of danger too damn much. One day it'll cost him his life. Who'd the HT kill?"

"His family. Three siblings and both parents. Drug induced psychosis."

"So Doc got him here on 'settled insanity'?" Shipman asked.

"Guess so, according to the law, he's not competent to stand trial yet. Had a few court dates but Dr. Trenton won out," Bill said.

"Weapon of choice?"

"Knives."

"Shit, and he's in the kitchen! That's just fucking great. Fucking great. Doc will have to disarm him and that'll destroy any relationship." Shipman raced to the other end of the hallway to check the laptop, "What's going on in there, guys? Let me know, fast!"

❧

"Hal." John waited to get Hal's eyes focused on him. He

signaled with his two fingers, index and middle, to his own eyes to gain Hal's attention. Hal responded and John didn't have to try to get his focus again. "Remember the last, and only, time you tried to attack me when you were seventeen at the pool hall?"

Hal hesitated. He swallowed and closed his eyelids halfway.

"Tell me what happened, Hal. I see in your eyes that you remember."

"My bitch mother called you to go get me. I wasn't listenin' to her."

"What happened, Hal?"

"You stuck me in a hospital and gave me those stupid meds and kept me in a room till I would talk to ya."

Not exactly, but close enough. "Excellent, Hal, excellent."

"Yeah, well, I didn't have these." Hal waved the knives up and down with the serrated edges up and toward John, thrusting forward, but not making contact, as if he was an ace at dueling.

John backed up a bit. He glanced up through the window and saw ESU with all of their gear on, ready to bust in.

"No, you had a gun. Remember what I did?"

"Yeah, you kicked it outta my hand. How'd you do that?"

"That's excellent, Hal. You do remember. You're doing great."

"Just try it! Go ahead. Just try it," Hal said, standing his ground.

"No. Hal, how much do you weigh?"

"One thirty."

"I'm 220. Think you stand a chance? Come on. Come on, Hal. Think about it."

Hal held back tears. He lowered the knives but clutched them to preserve his last bit of dignity.

"Hal, how about we talk in private?"

"Now?" Hal's pitch raised.

John realized Hal had planned this and that was something no one else was cognizant of yet. "Sure."

"With them here?"

"Well, what do you think we can do about that?" With consistency, and expecting Hal to accept the consequences for actions, John had been able to reach him. And he would continue to be, as long as Hal continued his meds and supplements to keep him clear thinking. John knew Hal wanted the cops to end it for him. This was no psychotic episode. This was an immature attempt to end his life.

Hal still did not want to let the food prep workers go. "Well, I do need private time."

"I'm glad you asked."

John got it. He had been preparing Hal for three years to mentally stable enough to stand trial for murder, even though Hal did not know that was the end-result of his progress.

"Well, I'm here. But you first have to do something for me. Throw the knives over there."

"No, I ain't. Damn you!"

John had to be aggressive. He saw the ESU right outside the door, waiting for a signal from Sergeant Shipman. Now, the compassionate, therapeutic shrink had left the building. John assessed this side of himself very carefully before he allowed it to appear with the patients. "Excuse me?"

Hal lowered his beaten-down eyes and stared at the ground between his feet.

"I'm not backing you into a corner, Hal. Just do it. Come on, Hal, do it."

Without looking up, Hal tossed the knives to where John told him.

"Pick up your shirt, so I can see what you did to yourself."

Hal did it like a little kid, with hesitation, and stared down at the wound himself.

"All right, it's a little deeper than a surface cut. We'll take care of it."

"I'm gettin' it for this, ain't I?"

John's strong, protective aura sent out the message. He didn't have to say a word. Hal could read him after ten years.

Hal slumped down on the table. "Okay, they can go."

John signaled to Stan and Bobby that they could leave. He noticed Stan was breathing easier now. John put his arm around Hal's shoulder, in case he tried to bolt, but he didn't.

Bobby scrambled out into the lobby where Sal and Tony waited. Stan struggled to hold himself upright, looking as if he aged ten years over his sixty.

❦❦❦

"Wait here," Tony called to them.

Stan sat down on the bench. A doctor and Kramer went to him immediately. The doc helped calm him down and Kramer took the report.

Bobby paced back and forth. Tony and Sal made notes of his behavior.

Bill approached. "Doc must have done a number on him in there."

"Yeah, with just one look."

The three men laughed at their private joke.

❦❦❦

"I'm tired."

"Hal, I know you must really be exhausted. How about going to your room and lying down? You'll probably sleep for a few hours."

Hal nodded. "Okay."

"And we'll talk about this later."

"We will?"

"Come on, Hal, you know we have to."

Hal whined like a child. "Okay."

"We're coming out."

❦❦❦

John held onto Hal's arm and handed him off to Bill. "Clean up his cuts. He needs a tetanus shot and then please escort him to his room. See he gets into bed and lock the door. And he—" he said, pointing to Bobby, "—needs the tetanus, too."

Hal and Bobby cried out in unison. "I don't want no shot!"

The hostage negotiators and ESU unsuccessfully tried to conceal their laughter. Ten men split up. The negotiators escorted Hal to a table where a male doctor waited to check him out, and the ESU escorted Bobby to a table across the hall for the same. They carried on like five-year-olds.

"There's a fine line, Doc."

"Tell me about it, Sergeant."

Debbie handed him Bobby's file. "Dr. Trenton, it's not from personnel."

He already had an idea about that. "Thanks."

Tony and Sal were ready to blast John but they didn't have the chance.

"I'm going to review the observation video," John said. "And I want your complete reports in an hour. Whoever is responsible will be dealt with. Alarm or no alarm."

Sal and Tony did not say a word, knowing John had to deal with his staff and they already knew their friend was tough. Even the support teams refrained from coming over to tell him he did a nice job in there. They didn't want to give him an excuse to smile and break the tension he'd just created with his staff. Everyone knew he meant business, except for Bobby—yet.

"My office."

CHAPTER 5

Just another thing to prolong my day." Barbara jumped up and pushed the young teacher out of the way, knocking her against the wall without even thinking about it. She grabbed her Burberry coat out of her closet, threw it on, grabbed her tote, and ran out of the room.

❧❧❧

Mrs. Bennett paced the lobby, crying. Her heavy mascara ran down her cheeks and her nose was as chafed as a reindeer's. Her breathing deepened and she looked wobbly on her feet. She had been the principal here for twenty-five years and Barbara realized the handwriting was on the wall that she really needed to call it quits soon. Mrs. Bennett's high expectations took their toll on her. She had been walking with a cane the past several months. Barbara couldn't understand why she was still at it day after day, putting all of her energy into the children and staff. Barbara couldn't be upset with her. Mrs. Bennett's love and advocacy for the children was genuine, the opposite of hers.

"Barbara, Jeremiah, he just disappeared."

Barbara showed more compassion than she felt. "Which way did he go? Anyone see him?" She handed Mrs. Bennett her bag. "Please hold onto this for me, Mrs. Bennett."

"Sure, Barbara."

Frustrated, Barbara took a deep breath and ran out the door and down the ten steps to the front yard.

 espeso

ESU officers from Brooklyn South combed the playground in the front and back of the building and found nothing. The front playground had jungle gyms, benches, a small stone horse, and a wall for climbing, which was now covered with snow.

"Doc, you stay here. Can't canvas the whole neighborhood."

Barbara stood for a moment. Her gaze darted to the private attached and semi-attached houses on the tree lined side streets and the ones directly across the street from the school. She hurried to the corner to look through the window of the Burger King, to see if Jeremiah had gone in there to beg for food. He hadn't.

Diagonally across the street were large co-op apartment buildings, and two blocks down from the main entrance to the left were the low-income projects, where Jeremiah lived. About twelve buildings in the complex ran for three avenues. Looking up the avenue, Barbara didn't see any children, just some drunks, wobbling and treading in the snow.

espeso

Inside the co-op ten-year-old Jeremiah, cold and wet from the snow, with his left arm in a cast, hesitated before going up the stairs. He walked up each stairwell, leaning against the wall—not the cleanest, but he didn't care—looking up to see if anyone could see him. No one did. Up five flights, he opened the door to the rooftop. Shocked that there was no locked gate like in his building, he went onto the roof, feeling free. Walking along the ledge without a care in the world he tried doing a balancing act with his arms spread out wide, one foot in front of the other, very proud of himself.

It was windy and the snow was falling, but he didn't care.

He was in his own fantasy world where he could be free from the poverty of his life.

❧❧❧

"Doc, would he have gone home?"

Barbara looked around and up, giving the ESU officer little attention. "No, I don't think so. There he is!"

She watched Jeremiah step on some grating. The metal snapped up and grabbed his foot. He screamed and fell over the edge of the roof with the metal plate, alone, holding onto his ankle. His frayed T-shirt fell down toward his head, as his body swayed and his arms flailed.

"How the hell did he—"

The snow had slowed down the traffic on this wide four-lane avenue. Ambulances and the fire trucks blocked much of it. Barbara dashed across without looking, and cars swerved to avoid her.

"Bring the bus over there, and you stay here!" the ESU officer yelled at her.

A local TV network truck arrived and the male photographer got out of the car in the middle of the street with his camera shooting straight up at Jeremiah.

"No, he doesn't know you," she yelled, without looking back. "He'll be scared to death." She yanked open the door and vaulted up the steps, reaching the rooftop with record speed.

❧❧❧

"Stay away from me." Jeremiah saw the ESU officers, and then Barbara, so he calmed down a bit.

"Don't worry, Jeremiah. We'll get you out soon."

"Dr. Barbara, I'm sorry."

They pulled Jeremiah up. He sat on the roof, shivering, and they covered him with a blanket. He must have been in pain but he didn't show it. Barbara knew he was used to pain. He'd had a hard life in the projects with an alcoholic mom and drug-addicted older brother. Barbara was the only person he could talk to about his problems who would listen. The ESU officers examined the grate. They couldn't move it. They looked at Barbara sending her non-verbal messages to keep him talking while they worked on his release.

The lead officer whispered to another officer away from Jeremiah. "Looks like it's broken."

Barbara heard them, but the wind blew her long, straight, highlighted-blonde hair across her face so it concealed her worried eyes. "How come you left the building, Jeremiah?"

"Wanted to see the roof. It's lower than my building."

"We'll talk about it tomorrow, okay, sweetheart?"

An ESU officer loosened the grate. Another member of the team picked up Jeremiah and carried him to the waiting elevator. Outside, the officer placed Jeremiah on a stretcher. The photographer took a picture of Barbara hugging the boy before they put him into the ambulance and, with sirens blasting, they sped off to Sheepshead Medical.

"You did good, Doc."

She shook the ESU officer's hand. "Thanks."

"Gotta run, my day's just beginning."

Mrs. Bennett handed Barbara the tote. "Good luck with Reynolds."

"Thanks, Mrs. Bennett, I intend to." With the snow tapering off, she ran to her red Camaro parked around the corner.

Now to get my payback. Payback for my life. Payback for these last three miserable years. You're right, Sarah Bennett. I intend to have good luck with Reynolds. Yeah, real good luck for me, but bad for him. I finally found him and he'll get what's coming to him.

CHAPTER 6

As John sat in his ergonomic swivel chair in his office, there was a lot more on his mind than his job. He put his watch back on as Sal and Tony trailed in. He didn't look up as they made themselves comfortable in the two matching leather club chairs with gold-studded detailing opposite the desk.

Tony felt the supple leather approvingly. "What a difference from the precinct."

John ignored the accolade. "So what brings you to my haven?"

"And you really don't follow the rules," Sal reminded him.

"Give me a break, I waited long enough. I've been working with him for ten years. I know him better than anyone else does. At least, I thought I did. Check this out. He said he's been killing since he was fourteen. Only the five kills at twenty-one were on his record. Why don't we have the others?"

"I don't know. They couldn't be sealed if they were homicides."

"Well, find out, Sal. He was admitted…" John rose, walked over to file cabinet, and thumbed through to find Hal's file. "Here it is. He was admitted three times from fourteen to nineteen, and at twenty-one, three years ago. Nothing about any other homicides."

"Done, pal," Sal said. "We know you'd never send us on a wild goose chase."

"Thanks. I'll be re-evaluating Hal by the end of the week

and contacting the court. I believe he's now competent to stand trial."

"Whoa, pal! After this?" Sal asked.

"Without a doubt! This was deliberate, planned, initiated, and carried out, rational and with a motive. He didn't kill Bobby when he had the chance and he remembered an incident with me seven years ago. These are not the behaviors of a schizophrenic."

Tony tried to make light of it. "Enough. We got the point, and by the way, you got Carlson PO'd again."

"So what else is new?"

"John, we get it. He's not your favorite person, but he is head of this team," Sal said.

"Nah, it's more than that. Something's going on with him. His mood, his temper. He's antsy. Don't you guys notice anything strange about him lately?"

"Yeah, his breathin' and coughin'. He won't listen to us about his smokin'. You have to get him checked out," Tony said.

"All right but, again, it's more than that. Why did he send you here?"

"To check up on you! You're upsetting your wife, too!" Sal exclaimed, not afraid to add it.

John put up a good front. "Correction, soon to be ex-wife."

"Well, why don't you do something about it? You're not even separated yet. Not every cop has to have a failed marriage."

"I'm not a cop, Tony, and don't you think I know that? What are you doing, keeping tabs on me?"

"What are friends for? Somebody has to, or else you'd get lost. And what about this little guy?" Tony picked up the framed photo of Ricky and smiled. "Given up? You and Vicki break up, there's no chance."

"No. I haven't given up. The social workers that took him away aren't there anymore. It's a crazy system. They must have changed his name."

"Did you ever once think he was adopted, and now has a loving home?" Sal asked.

"Yeah. I have, but the loving home should have been with us."

John stared at the photo. He blamed himself. He should not have let them take Ricky away. He should have fought them with everything he had.

"Stop beating yourself up, John. You saved the little kid's life. Go on, get out of here, Maybe you can catch Vicki before she leaves."

"Can't yet, Tony, got things to take care of here. She'll still be home."

"First mistake, job over wife," Sal said.

"Listen, Mr. Playboy," Tony interjected. "Vicki is the best thing that ever happened to you. Before you met Vicki, you didn't even have the patience to have a conversation for more than two minutes, unless it was with a patient. Come on, don't go back to the old John."

John sensed a lecture coming on and he deplored lectures. "Stop, guys. Just stop."

"Oh no, I'm not going to stop." Tony said. " I'm not letting you pull this bullshit. Remember three years ago when Hal did the kills and you were visiting your folks in Florida?"

John clenched his teeth. His jaw bulged. He held his breath and his nostrils flared like an angry horse. He closed his eyes and, if he could have run out of the office, he would have. Only that would be telling his friends they had won.

"You told us, Skyping at the crime scene, that you met the woman you were going to marry. Remember that? So what the hell happened in three fucking years, man?"

Tony could get excited all he wanted, but John didn't have to listen. He ignored Tony's rampage, but he knew he was right. He missed his precious Vicki already. "Go tell the almighty lieutenant, I'll be there," he said, checking his watch, "Around six. That'll give me a couple hours to clean up the mess here," he added, holding Bobby Mitchell's file.

John watched Sal and Tony leave, very exasperated, and he knew deep down that they had his best interests at heart.

Hesitating, John opened the file and read two pages to at least get an idea of why the kid was here. Then the last line and signature on the page told him who sent him. *I knew it*! This warranted a phone call.

Taking his smartphone out of his pocket, he checked the contact list and auto dialed. Sitting back in his chair, he listened to the phone ring three times before it was picked up.

"Hello."

"Hi, Uncle Jerry, it's me."

"Ah, I see you received my gift."

"Oh, a real gem."

"I thought you'd like him."

"Excuse me, *like* him?"

"Uh oh, what did he do already?"

"Aside, from calling me a prick and making a hostage situation last longer than it should have—"

"Hostage situation? Are you all right?"

"Yes, I'm fine." John thought of another battle he wanted to avoid. "But, please, don't tell my parents. You sentenced him to five hundred hours," he said, scanning the file for more details. "And there's a B-felony drug conviction with intent to sell. So you sent him to me instead of incarcerating him?"

"Yes, I did. I used my discretion."

John knew that, by law, Bobby could have gotten jail time of at least a year. "I'd like you to increase it to one thousand, please."

"Done. I'll tell him at his next court appearance. On what grounds?"

"Give me a day to think about it. Who's his PO? Oh, I see here, Charlie Smitts. I know him well. And you already know I'll be tougher on him than lockup, right?"

"Now you know why you got him."

"Like I needed another one." John was tired of getting these community service kids. They were too easy for him and he preferred to work hard at reforming forensic patients. He appreciated the reputation he'd established for himself over the last ten years as having more patients eligible to stand trial than any other forensic psychiatrist in the city. He had the right principles and methods with the ability to put theories of therapy into practice and structure them so they were effective. He wasn't planning to stop doing what he did best anytime soon.

"Come on, John, this age group is your specialty, and every criminal court judge, including myself, in New York City knows it, and your success rate. So turn him into a functioning young adult, will you please? His next arrest gets him jail time."

"So you're putting it on me to keep him out?"

Judge Marks remained silent.

Here comes the guilt trip.

"I got it. Do my best. That's actually why I need the thousand."

"You got it. Seeing him today?"

"Tomorrow, I want him to stew awhile."

"Ah, you gave him the look."

John smiled in acknowledgement. He was famous for it and no one else could imitate his deliberate, I've-got-your-number, wide-open-eyes, intense dark stare with raised eyebrows that made even the strongest-minded people wobble in their shoes. It was enough to send quivers through the most confident, let alone the emotionally compromised. Call it being vindictive, call it a skill at getting his point across, but John did it like no one else could. "Gotta go."

"And don't forget to call your mother. It's her birthday, and before midnight. They don't keep your hours."

He hated being told what to do, but it ran in the family. "I will. Speak with you soon."

Might as well do what he could when he was there, so he picked up the phone on his desk and depressed one button to the kitchen.

"Stan, how are you doing? And tell me the truth."

"I'm fine, really, John. I am. I'm telling you the truth. Dr. Malter checked me out, pressure a little high from the tension, and he'll see me again tomorrow, so stop worrying."

"All right, but I'll be checking on you more than once a day. Tomorrow, I want to see that Bobby kid as soon as he comes in. Is that at eleven?"

"He's supposed to be here at eleven, but he's always at least forty minutes late."

"Ah, okay," John now had a starting point from which to

work with Bobby. "All right, send him to me the second he gets here."

"Will do."

"Thanks." John hung up.

Tomorrow will be the last day he's late.

CHAPTER 7

Barbara paid the five-dollar-and-forty-five-cent toll on her E-ZPass and slid on the ice into the left lane of Hugh L. Carey Tunnel. The traffic didn't ease up. It was one-point-seven miles under water in this semi-lit, two-lane tunnel with both lanes going in the same direction at this hour. Small trucks, the Express Bus, all passed her on the right as she held the steering wheel on her Camaro steady with a wide-open-eyed gaze, staring directly in front of her. She hated this drive, every time she made it into the city.

Today the payoff was worth the tremors and heavy feeling that overcame her with anxiety. She trembled. Her mouth was open, and her breathing was shallow. The beads of perspiration rolled down the sides of her face. She gingerly took her right hand off the steering wheel to wipe the sweat away. Couldn't afford to smear her makeup.

The car began to sway into the orange cones separating her from the right lane. She grabbed the steering wheel with both hands to regain her focus. It was hard. She moaned in anguish. Little girl whines escaped her throat. She couldn't stop emoting. When would she reach the other end? This ride seemed to take forever.

Her heart hammered in her chest, bouncing off her ribs, and her head pounded. Lightheadedness and dizziness made her nauseous. It was worse than a migraine, and she prayed her heart wouldn't jump out of her chest. It was as if she was in a closed MRI with her claustrophobic rating off the charts.

Fumes from the car in front of her came in through the heater. She gagged and shut it off. She couldn't breathe.

The nape of her neck was soaked with sweat. Yet she was freezing, and shivers ran through her. She couldn't find what was crawling on her skin. But this would be worth it. She had endured more suffering than this in her life. Nothing would stop her. Not today.

She got out onto the FDR, going north. The traffic eased up and, in the open air, her rampant emotions calmed down. She opened the window to allow the frigid fresh air to dry her now dampened hair.

She contemplated her moves with her prospect, Morgan Reynolds, the reckless, incompetent forty-year old multi-million-dollar-a-year-publisher whom she'd been waiting to meet since last year. She recalled three years of meetings with his father. Jacob Reynolds had been a sitting duck for her, and she paralyzed him every time with her imaginary pellet gun. Being well into his eighties, she duped him into becoming a benefactor for her adolescent therapy clinic, The Gemini Clinic for Mental Health, getting a $200,000 donation from him. She smiled, remembering that all she had needed was to be soft spoken and kind with him, to make him feel respected and worthy.

He had always looked her up and down and told her how beautiful and smart she was. He even had told her she was the daughter he wished he had, unlike the bum of a son he'd raised. He'd divulged so much to her. But she never told him she would have loved to have a father like him. The memory stung. Oh well, it wasn't her fate.

Jacob had passed on several months ago, and Morgan fell into his father's shoes. Her next angle was on her mind and she almost missed the Twenty-Third Street exit. She made it to the exit, cutting off a car to her right, almost causing an accident, which earned her the middle finger salute from the pissed-off driver.

She drove up East Twenty-Third Street to Park Avenue South and turned into the Reynolds Publishing Company's garage on the corner.

Time to get my payback.

cɔcɔ

Barbara parked inches away from the sign that said *Reserved, Morgan Reynolds*, pleased she arrived before him. She made sure not to pull all the way in so he couldn't open the back door of his limo without hitting her car. There was no room for him to get out of the passenger side, either. That was good. She'd planned it that way. But she was unsure what she'd do or how it would unfold when he arrived.

First, she needed to refresh herself. She perfected her makeup, sprayed her hairbrush with sensuous Prada cologne, ran the brush through her hair, and then dowsed herself. Satisfied that she was perfect, everything went back into her bag.

Diving into her tote again, Barbara plucked out a black velvet pouch. Slipping her fingers inside, she removed a dazzling, seven-inch pendant on a twenty-four-inch black cord, the purpose of which was to increase her psychic intuition. It was rather weighty, with each of the stones being at least one-and-a-half inches in length. After she slipped the cord over her neck, she held the pendant in her left hand.

She focused on each stone, one by one, manifesting their intent, starting with an irregular shaped chunk of purple amethyst on the top to increase her mental acuity and awareness. The amethyst had varying shades of purple, which enhanced translucency. The next one was a polished tumbled stone of labradorite, with its lines of greens, purples, and blues throughout the lustrous surface, for increasing her psychic ability. Underneath that, an opaque green aventurine tumbled stone, for manifesting her goals. At the bottom tip, a jagged edged, clear quartz point positioned downward energized all of the stones above it. She inhaled deeply to intertwine the energy of all the stones and initiate their synergy as her intent focused all around them. Her gaze followed the path of pewter of varying thickness that secured the stones, from bottom to top over the purple-glass cylinder pendant.

Barbara then removed a deck of tarot cards wrapped in a vivid paisley-print multicolored silk scarf with the colors of the seven chakras—red, orange, yellow, green, blue, indigo, and purple. Then she unwrapped the cloth around the cards. She grounded herself, placing both feet flat in front of the gas pedal and brake, took deep breaths, meditated, and asked herself a clear and concise, open-ended question, taking responsibility for herself, the way she'd always phrased them.

What do I need to do to get Morgan to do what I want?

She shuffled the deck three times. Then she picked a number from one to ten—seven—and pulled seven cards, holding the deck in her left hand. One by one, she drew each card from the top toward her heart, before flipping it over and placing it on the passenger seat.

The High Priestess, Justice, Nine of Pentacles, The Devil, King of Cups, Page of Swords, and the King of Wands were the cards she pulled. She scanned the cards and interpreted her answer.

The cards told her a story. She had to be just as unscrupulous as Morgan, and just as assertive, not giving him a chance to get the better of her.

She had to cut him off before he started to belittle her and attempted to make a mockery of her. She had to have the last word and really manipulate him to get what she wanted—another two hundred thousand—not caring at all what she said to intimidate him. His board would be there and they were men of his father's age, so they would be easy to win over.

She needed to appeal to their sense of chivalry and their willingness to help her as they had been doing in the past.

Morgan needed help from them to make the decision and they could veto whatever he said. He was barely surviving and he hadn't learned all of the ropes yet. He seemed to be trying, however, so she needed to tune into his vibes.

To Barbara, this was a slam-dunk, and she would get the donation—the first step in her payback. Satisfied that she'd gotten the answer, she put the cards back into the deck, wrapped them carefully—as they were a prized possession— and put them back into the velvet pouch, contemplating what she needed to say and how she needed to behave. She removed the pendant from around her neck, kissed it, and placed it close to her heart before replacing it in the pouch.

❧❧❧

Morgan's black Mercedes limo pulled into the garage. He was arrogant with his own attorney, Steven Katz, also around thirty-five, and good friends with him as well.

"Don't tell me how I should handle this."

"I'm your attorney, Morgan. You pay me for telling you. All I'm saying is that your father always gave with generosity and gratitude to her clinic."

"My bastard father gave with such generosity and gratitude so I'd get 200 grand less for that quarter and for no other reason. There aren't any stats and very inadequate reports submitted with her application, so I doubt she's credible, but my father, in his infinite wisdom, saw something in her. Maybe she's the daughter he never had, who knows? All I know is he didn't want me. But I'll continue to give it to her. Why, I don't know."

"Oh yeah? With how many strings attached?"

CHAPTER 8

John hesitated before he unlocked the door to his seven-room condo on the Upper East side of Manhattan, carrying a yellow Tiffany glass vase that contained eighteen, fully bloomed, long-stemmed yellow roses dusted with gold glitter. He dreaded this confrontation with Vicki. He had prepared himself for a more stressful time than he had at the hospital, earlier.

"Calm down," he repeatedly muttered under his breath. He'd do the best he could, but when Vicki made up her mind, she was as flexible as stainless steel. Then again, so was he, but with Vicki, he melted like sweet butter left out on a hot summer day. "Babe?"

"I'm in the bedroom." Vicki strolled out to greet him in a solid hot-pink velour sweat suit zipped way down low to accentuate her perfect cleavage. She was dressed for winter, except for her infamous flip-flops. "Oh, darlin', they are so beautiful. And the glitter."

She slid her delicate hands over his large ones to take the vase from him. He cherished her mere touch. He closed his eyes, not wanting to acknowledge that this might be the last time he would revel in her softness.

She positioned the vase directly in the center of the glass coffee table and stepped back to admire the placement. The glitter reflected the gold off the hand-painted art deco designs on the wall behind the couch.

"Come here. You are the sunshine of my life, Vicki, just like the glitter on the roses."

She gave him a crooked smile.

"I know. That was lame. I know, babe." He caressed her in his arms, held her close, and bent down to give her a long sensual kiss. He wasn't letting go. He kissed her lips, cheeks, all around her face, and whispered in her ear, "Babe, don't leave. Don't leave, babe. I love you."

He saw her studying him with sad eyes. "John, we talked about this. We talked about this a lot. And you did it again today, didn't you?" She pulled away, plopped down on the couch, grabbed a gray and yellow throw pillow, and crunched it in her lap.

He cozied up next to her, and wrapped his left arm around her shoulders. He wanted to avoid that conversation. "What did I do today?"

"John, don't lie to me. You always bring me roses when you do something you know I'll be mad at you for doing. Um?" She pursed her full lips and glared at him out of the corner of her eyes. She couldn't face him.

"I brought them today because I love you." He looked away to avoid the tornado that was about to impale him.

"John, you could've gotten killed again today." There was no empathy in her voice.

There was only one way to squelch the tornado. He bent over and started kissing her neck while he ran his index finger down her neck and décolleté. He whispered in her ear, "I love you babe." She shuddered under his gentle touch. "Okay. Who called you?"

His warm breath mellowed her. He knew his wife, well. She closed her eyes, inhaled deeply, and relaxed. She was in a semi-trance. "Do you want the list?"

He smiled, continued kissing her, and lowered the zipper on her jacket. "Who called you?" He slipped his warm hand into her pink lacy bra and cupped her perfect breast in his palm as his ran his thumb over her already hard nipple.

She sighed with contentment. "First Tony, then Dave from ESU, and finally Paul."

"Carlson called you?"

She lunged up, disengaging his hand from her breast, and slammed the pillow with her fist. So much for squelching the tornado. "Darn, it John! I can't take it anymore. I can't anticipate the day or night I'm going to get a call saying you got shot or killed. And that's so much more beyond your job. You don't have to do what you do."

He closed his eyes but he couldn't ignore her. "Yes, I do. It's part of who I am. Don't go. I love you so much. I don't want you to go Vick."

"Darlin', I love you too. More than life itself. But it's too much. I just can't take it in New York."

"Vicki, I've been thinking about this for a while. Please listen to me. We'll move out of the city."

"Right. You wouldn't leave this condo."

"For you, Vicki, I'll do anything. Listen to me. We'll get a house. We'll look into Scarsdale. We'll look into Westchester. We'll get you a house with the white picket fence and a big backyard. And you can make your country barbeques. We'll even get a dog, Vicki. I know how much you miss Duchess."

"A dog? You hate dogs, John!"

"I don't hate dogs. I just never had one growing up."

"You always said you'd never get a dog 'not on your white carpet,'" she taunted, mimicking a childish tone.

He laughed and tapped her turned-up nose. "We won't get white carpet. We'll get tile or wooden floors. Vicki, I will do anything for you. Please don't go."

"And how are we going to be able to afford a house, John? This condo is completely paid off and you can't sell it now in this market. The loss will be too great. It's going to be impossible."

"Nothing is impossible, babe. I never stopped you from getting a job. I never stopped you from wanting to teach. If we move into a house and have a mortgage, well then—"

"I tried teaching here. I couldn't take it. I miss my kindergartners in Florida."

"You tried for a few days. You gave up before you gave yourself a chance."

Noticing her lowered eyes and her hands wrung together,

he realized that was the wrong way to go. "We won't take that much of a loss. The market in Manhattan is still pretty good. We'll get a beautiful house, Vicki, in the country with enough bedrooms for your family to come visit. Mark and Jaimie, and Brian and Ann with the kids, your parents and my parents. We can have all the holidays here. You know how much you love to spend Thanksgiving and Christmas together. You'll finally have that white Christmas. And we'll need an extra bedroom when Ricky comes back to us."

"You live in a fantasy world. Ricky isn't coming back. You think you can manifest whatever you want just by asking. It doesn't work that way."

"Yes, he is. He most certainly is. Wait and see. It does work that way, Vicki. You have to believe."

"It's been three years! Darlin', I need to go. I need my space. I'm suffocating here. You're suffocating me. Please. Three weeks, John. That's all I need. Three weeks. Please give me three weeks."

"Babe, you can have three weeks. Take your three weeks, but don't use that break up word. Just tell me you're going to visit your parents."

"I don't know what I'm going to do. Everything you've done for me to have me like New York City. I can't. You don't understand. If I asked you to come move to Florida, you'd miss your partying, your fancy stores, the dress-up affairs, the doctors' meetings, the fancy Broadway shows. You love the bright lights, the noise, and even the traffic! Well, I miss the starlit skies, the animals in the woods behind the house, the sun, roads without any potholes, the calves nursing on their mothers on the farms, the clean air without pollution, the pitch black nights, the quiet, and I miss my guns, John!"

"Excuse me? Did I just hear what I think I heard?"

"Oh my God. That didn't come out right." Her cheeks flushed. She buried her head into his chest. "John, I'm sorry."

"Victoria Elizabeth, are you actually telling me that you'd rather be with your weapons than held in my arms every night and made love to?"

"John, that didn't come out right. I'm sorry."

He released her and propelled himself down on the other end couch. "You win. Go. Go be with your guns."

Anger built up. His heart beat faster. He swallowed to keep from blurting out words he'd regret. He needed his punching bags. Boy, he'd do a number on them. He'd never lashed out at Vicki before. Today had taken more of a toll on him than he'd thought. He didn't like himself right now and, apparently, neither did Vicki.

Sulking, she retreated to the bedroom to get her suitcase and carry-on, in the same hot pink as her sweat suit, returning with the zipper pulled up to her neck. She placed the cases by the door, turning her back on John.

John eyeballed her feet. "You're kidding me, right? You're going out into the snow in flip-flops?"

"I'll be fine."

"You're not leaving this apartment in flip-flops. Go put on socks and boots."

"I hate socks and boots!" With flaming eyes and tightened lips, she demonstrated, in no uncertain terms, that if he wanted to fight, she'd fight. She crossed her arms across her chest and stood there, egging him on.

John read her defiance and took her up on her offer, flashing his signature look with the addition of a wickedly sexy grin. "Sit down, now!"

She plunked down on the couch and folded her arms across her chest like a reprimanded little girl. Then she immediately cracked up, laughing.

He stormed into the bedroom, returning with heavy pink socks and her chocolate brown knee-high Uggs. "Lay down, babe."

He picked up her right foot and kissed each toe, lingering, as he massaged her foot with both hands. He nibbled on her toes and she giggled as she always did. He put on a sock and then lifted her left foot. He tickled each toe with his tongue. He loved the taste of her. His mind didn't want to think that this would be the last time he'd take care of her. He put on the second sock and then the boots. She deposited her flip-flops in her carry-on.

"Now, was that so difficult?"

"Okay, no."

The intercom rang from the lobby. "I've got to go."

"Babe, call me when you land. Come here. I love you."

"I'll call you when I land."

Tears flowed and she tried to contain her sobbing. Her heart-broken eyes surely mirrored his. He bundled her up in her coat—slowly buttoning each button—picked up her hood, and wrapped her scarf around her neck. He caressed her face and wiped away tears with his thumbs.

He stooped down to give her one last, gentle kiss.

CHAPTER 9

T he limo pulled into the tight spot, but before the driver could warn him, Morgan, so upset by this meeting, slammed the car door open, ramming it into the rear passenger side of Barbara's car.

"What the—" Barbara jolted as she leaned against the car with her door open, changing her sneakers for high heels.

"What did you do?" Steve asked.

"Chill out, Steve."

As Morgan squeezed out the door, Barbara was prepared to go into her act. "Look what you did!"

She smirked as Morgan gave her the once over, ending with a wink as his gaze settled on her legs.

"It's not so bad. It gives her some character, woman."

"Excuse me? Woman?"

The one thing she didn't tolerate was disrespect for her gender. She opened her eyes wide as she tilted her head, and both men had to get the message or they were dumber than dirt. Her defiance spelled confrontation.

Steve got the message all right. "Come on, you two. We'll be late for the meeting."

Barbara's plan was in action. "Yeah. Okay, I'll deal with this nonsense later."

As they walked to the elevator, side by side, Barbara saw their heads cocked toward her body. First step in her plan, working. The navy skirt that she chose accentuated her tight bottom and toned legs. Perfect.

She knew what was on their minds. The same thing as every man. Every man that she had used, abused, thrown away, or killed. She projected the same sensual vibes as she did in the strip club.

Think sexy, and you'll be sexy, and never ever be afraid to show a man you could take him on.

"Don't worry, Dr. Montgomery, he'll fix the car."

"I will?"

The elevator door opened, and executive type men and women in their thirties through fifties exited for the garage, but a few remained inside. She stood as close as she could get in front of Morgan with her back toward him. He didn't waste time and grabbed her hair between his fingers. He lowered his nose into the strands and inhaled audibly. "Um, nice."

He stretched up a bit, leaned in toward her neck, and whispered in her ear, "Done. I'll fix the car." He snuck a kiss on her neck and, to his surprise, she didn't repel his advances. He gave her another, closer down toward her shoulder.

She twitched her shoulders, pretending a chill passed through her. She smiled to herself. She hadn't felt a thing.

She pivoted around, analyzing her target, and assessed that at about five-feet-five, Morgan must use his attitude to make up for his lack of stature. The smug look on his face projected major attitude. He had lean, clean-shaven, chiseled features; high cheekbones; and deep-set, troubled brown eyes. She could tell he wanted to deceive her. Barbara considered him moderately handsome, but a well-groomed man in an expensive suit always looked desirable to her. With her long, red-painted fingernail on her index finger, she shoved him back against the wall.

She'd caught him right where she wanted him, by his balls. "Nah, I'm thinking of something better."

"Oh yeah?" he replied, matching her seductive tone.

She noticed the bulge at his zipper. "Yeah, I think I'll take a black magic marker, draw a ring around the dent, and have you autograph it, just to show the world what kind of a klutz you are."

What a downer! Morgan hadn't expected that and neither had "Little Morgan."

Morgan and Steve stood frozen. The eavesdroppers in the elevator hid their laughter. When the door opened, she strutted out in front of them and the shadow on the floor told her exactly where their gazes focused. On the sexy, deliberate wiggle of her derriere.

ৎ৩৫৩

Walking down the hall, Barbara admired the antique white marble floors and expensive hand-painted gold-and-cream embossed burnt velvet wallpaper in a floral design lining the walls in the long corridor. This was her style, too. Extravagance when it was important to impress. As they reached Morgan's office, she noticed that the sign on the door read *Morgan Reynolds, President of Reynolds Publishing Co.* From what Jacob had confided to her about his son, she guessed he'd changed the sign the day Jacob died. Probably before the funeral. There was no love lost between them and, to his father, Morgan was nothing but a money-squandering, deceitful, philandering, unaccomplished procrastinating worthless bum who lived on booze and his trust fund. She planned to use all of that against him.

ৎ৩৫৩

Carol, Morgan's attractive well-dressed secretary, opened the door for them. They followed her into the conference room where five older men in designer suits waited for them. They welcomed Barbara, as she was acquainted with them from past years. From looking at their sour pusses, their furrowed brows, blank stares, their arms crossed on their chests, Barbara knew she had it made.

One of the men had emailed her and expressed their annoyance that Morgan had called this meeting. Jacob Reynolds had given her donations for the past two years, right on schedule, mid-February of each year, and they had established no reason why this year should be any different. They didn't tell her anything else, but her tarot reading in the car told her plenty. Now she just had to wait.

Morgan signaled for them to sit. Everything in this conference room was upscale and redone the past few months to accommodate Morgan's outlandish tastes. With the three multi-layered glass chandeliers equidistant on the ceiling that spread the length of the glass oval conference table with seating for twenty, this could be a tragedy waiting to happen if someone irate or disappointed slammed down on the table. Barbara knew from Jacob's complaining about Morgan, it was his goal to intimidate. He got off on seeing other people wiggle in their seats with anxiety and discomfort. He demanded that the writers prove, beyond a shadow of doubt, that they were worthy of a contract with him. Jacob didn't think he should be so tough, but Barbara didn't fault him on this. In business, you had to be tough. She was.

Steve motioned for Barbara to sit at the other end of the table, but she took the seat closest to Morgan. She made sure pheromones worked overtime, choosing the right perfume for the job, and Morgan inhaled deeply. This time he wiggled in his seat, as if to adjust his slacks. Barbara let out a barely audible, condescending laugh.

With imperious hostility in his voice, Morgan began to address this distressed group. "Let's get this over with. Dr. Montgomery, I have examined your records, the miniscule amount you provided, and, at this time I feel it is inappropriate to continue our support of your clinic, so I am, therefore, withdrawing the $200,000 donation."

The men shot glares at each other with their mouths gaping. Barbara gave it right back to him, knowing it was payback for her rejection of him.

"Then I suggest you re-read my reports. Gentlemen, Morgan is just pissed that he smashed the rear of my car in the garage. You shouldn't mix playtime with business, Morgan."

Morgan's face reddened. "This and all future meetings are over." He got up and sauntered out, unconcerned.

CHAPTER 10

It hit John already, even though Vicki had just left a couple of hours ago. The gardenia scent, her fragrance that had enveloped his apartment and his world, had vanished. That fresh just out of the shower smell, that he'd grown to love and worship, disappeared the moment she did. She was a natural beauty inside and out, right down to her natural blonde hair. He had everything he'd always wanted and had achieved whatever he wanted. Just one person made him feel empty, creating a void no other woman would ever be able to fill. The gardenia healing scent she wore—that encased her aura and spread to his, the moment he stepped into her energy field, and diminished his anxieties and frustrations of the day—would no longer be there for him.

The condo's modern décor in black, white, and gray, with geometric splashes of yellow on the upholstery, and in the faux-wall painting, reverted the apartment back to its once-bachelor-pad feel. A feeling that he didn't want anymore, and he longed to forget. This once playboy gave up all of his philandering and partying the moment he met her, very content to settle down. The bar scene at night, the heavy hitter mentality of the ones on the Upper East Side, and coming home in the early morning hours no longer captured his interest. He had lost his taste for the women who, with one phone call, would share his bed on a moment's notice. So many women had come and gone in his place that he'd had to add extra sound-proofing to the insulation in his bedroom to cease the unwanted comments of nosey neighbors. If only the walls could talk! They would be willing to share the sexual exploits of John Trenton with the world, and he could even make the most experienced and open-minded sex therapist blush.

ഇഇഇ

John entered his office, also in ultra-modern styling with white wall-units all around the room and a marble desk with white, blacks, and gray veining coming out from the center unit. He sat in his luxury black leather chair at his desk, just staring at the phone, knowing he had to make the call. Every call had been a battle in recent weeks and increased his stress level, which he didn't need after today. His blood pressure must be through the roof. Perhaps it was because his parents didn't have grandchildren like all their friends. Perhaps they were getting ill and not telling him. Perhaps it was because he didn't see them as often and they missed him. Whatever it was, he wished there wasn't the strain. He picked up the phone, holding the handset for a few moments, then dialed. It rang twice and that voice on the other end answered, the one who'd been his consistent stand-by-his-side, unconditional role model since he came into this world forty-five years ago.

"It's about time."

His father's attitude was so obvious. It was the one that John had learned to tolerate, the last ten years since he chose his specialty. That subtle annoyance Dad gave off when he didn't approve of what his son did and, today with Vicki leaving, it would be no exception.

"Hi, Dad," he said cheerfully, trying to change the mood. "I called to wish Mom a happy birthday last night but you were out."

"We were at the country club for dinner with friends to celebrate her birthday."

"That's great. I'm glad. At least you're going out more that you did up here."

"How was your day?" His dad always cut to the chase, never beating around the bush. His father was the only one who had ever been able to intimidate him, and he still did. John reminisced about "the look." The first time he was the recipient of it he'd been two-years old. He'd practiced for years until he got it right. Till he reached fifteen.

"Fine, the usual." Sensing his father already knew, and the silence on the other end was a signal, John plunged forward. "You spoke to Uncle Jerry." More silence on the other end. "Dad, you there?"

"Yes I'm here, and no I didn't speak with Jerry. What happened at the hospital?"

That's strange. Thought he might have been told. I must be losing my intuition. Don't worry about it, John. It must be the stress.

"John, what happened, aside from Vicki moving back to Florida?"

"Dad, I can't discuss it, you know that." He could, but why cause him more distress?

"All right, doctor-patient privilege, but you can tell me what happened with Vicki."

John twirled his wedding band around his finger. "Dad she was miserable here, couldn't adjust to life in the city."

"And you're not taking any responsibility for this?"

"Dad, I don't tell you and Mom everything, anymore. Vicki and I are private people. Sometimes, when you love someone so much, you have to love them enough to let them go."

"Then why are you so angry?"

"I'm not angry!"

"Oh no? Listen to yourself."

"Dad, it's something I have to work through. Where's Mom?"

"She's out playing Mahjongg with the girls from the Temple."

"Girl's?" John found that humorous at their early-seventies age. "Okay, tell her I called," he said, getting ready to hang up.

"There's something she wants me to ask you."

"Dad, can it wait? I have to get to the precinct by six."

"Then you have plenty of time. It can't wait. She needs to reserve the date."

"What date?" John grew suspicious and felt sorry he asked.

"Everyone's adult children do it."

"Do what Dad? Dad, please just tell me. I have to get out of here."

"You're always in a rush to get off the phone when we talk."

I wonder why.

But he wouldn't dare say that, never in a million years.

"Mom wants you to come down here the weekend of your birthday to celebrate the thirty-third anniversary of your bar Mitzvah."

"Excuse me? The thirty-third anniversary of my bar Mitzvah? And what does that mean?" Knowing his father, it would be something complicated to give him more work.

All through his education, they worked with him, even proofreading papers in medical school. As confident as he was, he never wanted to go away for college so it was Columbia University in New York for him, all the way from undergraduate through his psychiatric residency and New York University for his PhD in clinical psych. If there were any imperfections in anything he did, Mom and Dad insisted he edit the complete work. That was how John maintained a 4.0 GPA.

"You'd be redoing your bar Mitzvah. And then we'd make a large Kiddush for the congregation."

"No, thank you!"

"Why not?"

"Dad, I can't believe you're asking me to do that, with everything I have on my plate now. I don't need anything else to worry about. I don't even have the time to write my book. No, it's not going to happen."

"By the way, what's happening with that, the book?"

John was relieved his father had gone onto another subject. "I'm good with a title, *Holistic Forensic Psychiatry: Making the Mind Body Connection.*"

"That's it? Just the title?"

"No. I have an outline for the six sections done, and I'm developing the one on spiritual frameworks for psychiatry."

"And what is that section going to include?"

"Well, the theories and practice of vibrational medicine, the human energy field, the seven layers of the aura, color, sound therapy, chakras, and stressors, and how they manifest as mental illness."

"So how are you planning to integrate the aura into the practice of psychiatry? That's what the book is about, the actual practice, isn't it?"

"Yes, of course, Dad. The aura changes with mood. When someone is lying, in denial, aggressive, manic-depressive, masochistic, or sadistic, easy going, and even substance abuse comes through the energy field. Psychiatrists can learn a lot about their patients when they study their auras, and it makes it easier to get to the truth."

"Yes, but you see them, day or night, light or dark, you can see them. So let me ask you this. How are you going to get your readers, presumably doctors, to understand the value of this and, taking it further, to utilizing the process?"

"Dad, I think you just gave me a hook."

Silence.

His eye caught his dad's book, *Preventing Heart Disease with Nutrition*, on the shelf behind his desk. For the last ten years, that text had been his main source on the treatment of heart disease he relied upon for his patients, in addition to the latest research.

"All right, I think I got this. Hear me through, Dad. I need to teach the readers how to develop their own psychic awareness and how they can learn to see the auras of their patients, step by step. I can't start from the premise that they already know how to do this. Although most psychiatrists are somewhat intuitive, most are not clairvoyant."

"That's right. You've been clairvoyant since you were a toddler. You can't assume anything about your readers."

"That's part of being an only child, too. We tend to see things on the physical plane or in the spiritual realm, more than most."

"No. That's not it. But something else to support that. Remember a couple of years ago you were doing rounds with interns at Sheepshead Medical Hospital?"

"Yes. Of course."

"You told me you got very aggravated because you assumed the interns knew what you thought they should, and they didn't."

"That's right. For an intern, I expected a certain level of proficiency, and professional benchmarks need to be attained."

"But remember you were also judging them on what you know with ten or more years of experience. You can't do that with your readers. The only thing you can assume is that they know nothing about this topic."

"Got it. Thanks, Dad. This really helped."

"Okay. Good. Now where are you fitting in your Orgone Therapy?"

"That's in the emotions frameworks chapter. The seven armors of Wilhelm Reich, psychosomatic therapy, bio-energetic analysis of Alexander Lowen. All of it."

"So the book is coming along and then you just need better time management to write more often. It won't be that hard. It's a three hour service, but you'll be up on the dais less than an hour."

"Oh God, Dad," John snorted. "An hour in Hebrew, wonderful. No, I can't know for sure I'll be able to come down then."

"June ninth is months away. Schedule the days now."

"Dad, I'm on call twenty-four-seven. And I don't remember any Hebrew. Plus, I don't have the time to memorize all that again. There's so much I have scheduled, Dad. I have fifty hours of profiling I'm contracted for, all due before June."

"Remember when you were in eighth grade and you brought home a B-minus on an American History exam?"

"What's that got to do with anything?" John thought his father was losing it, bringing up such an old memory. He began to worry. "Are you okay? What's going on, Dad?"

His father ignored the question. "I told you to ask the teacher what you could do to make it up."

"I remember, Dad, and he gave me a college level paper that took me a month to do and I was only twelve. So? Are you or Mom sick? What are you not telling me?"

"Nothing. We're fine. Well, you did it. You just had to give up a few things. So re-learning Hebrew is like the same thing."

"Wait a minute, Dad. I'm sure you also remember it was this teacher who turned me onto psychiatry. He was a diagnosed schizophrenic and was gone by the time the paper was due. At twelve, school was my job. And by the way, you knew he was out, but you made me do the paper, anyway."

"That's beside the point."

"Beside the point? What is the point of all this, Dad?"

"I'll tell you now, what I told you then. You're a Gemini, you can multi task. Besides, the Rabbi will send you the books and tell you verbatim what you need to do."

"I'm sure he will." John laughed, getting a kick out of that one. "Gemini? That worked when I was a kid, Dad. But you're discounting and making light of all of my obligations here, now."

"We're doing no such thing. We know you do a lot. You're a workaholic. We also know you can accomplish anything you want, and everything you take on, you do to perfection."

Here it comes—the compliment, then the zinger. How can I say no to them after all they do for me? I have no medical school loans or a mortgage. They paid for everything, and they still transfer money into my account. Even with the consulting fees I charge, it's still a pittance to them. But I'll beat him to it. What the hell? It won't be so bad. That Jewish guilt, but I am so glad I still have them in my life.

"Dad, I'm sorry. I am. Tell the Rabbi he can send me what I need."

"Good. Your mother will be very happy. Now you can go to work. Speak with you soon." His father hung up the phone.

John starred at the handset.

Damn! He did it to me again. I can never win with him. Bullshit, I did it to myself.

He threw the pen he was fiddling with onto the desk. His parents always had the knack of getting him to do what they wanted, except in his choice of forensics. Oh well, he'd make it a week, get some sun.

Changed from his suit to jeans and a fleece, he briefly checked out the kitchen to see what he needed to bring home. This ultra-modern space had everything that made an iron chef jealous. Vicki was a top chef, making very good use of every appliance in it. Opening the fridge, he saw seven, oven-to-table, two-quart hand-painted stoneware pans and trays in black and white floral designs matching the color scheme of the rest of the condo that were filled to capacity. Each pan was labeled with a blue post it for what day of the week he should eat it. The freezer held about ten more. Vicki must have cooked for over a week before she left, continuing to pamper him as she'd done since they'd gotten married. There had never been a night in those two years that dinner hadn't been on the table waiting for him when he got home. And there hadn't been a night in two years that they didn't have their dessert in the bedroom. He stood there just for a moment, contemplating what he had lost, then he grabbed his bubble jacket from the closet, and left looking like a model in *Men's Style* magazine.

CHAPTER 11

John entered the precinct conference room, looking at all of the work ahead of him. Carlson, Mandella, and Valantino fidgeted around the long table that was piled high with files. John shook his head, disgusted by the disarray. A couple of the florescent bulbs on the rectangular fixture on the ceiling blew out. It had been a month since he noticed it. He observed flecks of dust flutter in the air around the functioning bulbs, which initiated an involuntary cough. Ugh.

Carlson looked up, weary. "It's about time."

John glanced at his watch. "I'm early. What have you got for me?" He plopped down on a chair, grabbing a folder from the top of the stack, confident he'd get the job done and his mind would be off his problems.

"How are you doing?"

"I'm okay, Paul, knock it off. Not in the mood for an interrogation."

"No, you're not. No one would be okay after what you went through today. You could have gotten killed at the hospital, and your wife walked out on you all in the same day. I've known you too long, John, so stop the fucking bullshit."

If he only knew about the conversation with my father.

"Getting to work will keep my mind off it, so let's go. Time is money and I'm on the clock here."

Paul snatched the folder from his hands. "The clock can wait a minute." Paul slid a card to him on the desk. "I want you to see him."

"Who?"

"The department shrink. You're going to be debriefing your staff, you need it, too."

"I'm fine. Don't pull this on me now."

"John, it's policy and that's an order. But this one you can't fuck."

"Excuse me?" He hated orders, and he hated it when Carlson knew things about him that were personal which John hadn't intended to share. He was thrown off kilter since this had been swept under the rug years ago and got rekindled as if it happened yesterday. He eyed Tony and Sal who turned away, concentrating on a file.

"Like the last one, Joanne." John blinked, shocked Carlson would harp on this. "For Christ sake, John, ya did it in her office in the first session no less!"

John struggled to figure out what to say and fast. "It was off the record and after hours and the only session."

"That's why ya both still have ya fucking jobs. There were a lot of people working here even after midnight. And yes, everyone still remembers, even though it was four years ago. Before you met Vicki. This one is on the record and during hours. And the mandatory three sessions. And you better not fuck with me on this."

Joanne was hot. Ravishing and hot, and every cop in the precinct would have loved to get what he had, even if it was a brief, one-shot deal. It was sleazy, exciting, and rough, but he had to admit, it wasn't very satisfying—the way he'd take one on the fly, not at all like the patient, gentle, and tender lovemaking with Vicki.

As soon as he'd walked into her office at one a.m. and looked her up and down through the dimmed florescent lighting, seeing her long red hair and green eyes, he admitted she was exquisite. She wore a pleated mini skirt that did her shapely legs justice. It was obvious she was on the make. Her signals of desire were clear. He'd seen enough of them and sent enough of them himself to know. Aside from noticing her cleared desk, he'd received a distinct message with her wanton eyes and flaunting seductive body language, as she shifted toward him, showing him she was hungry and ready to be taken. Magnetic currents emanated from her aura to his. It didn't take him long to get hard.

Paul had sent him in to speak with her because he'd missed a bullet by a millimeter at a drug raid that one of his released patients orchestrated. He'd insisted on being there, even though it went against protocol. But his patients always came first and Paul had allowed it, just this once. Turned out, it became a blood bath with three dealers being blown to bits as the coke lab they were in exploded. It was their own gunfire at the cops that had caused their demise. This was the first crime scene where he'd seen bullets fly. He'd been quite shaken up since he never carried guns, as he despised them. Paul had thought that John needed to talk to someone—so he sent him to Joanne—but an exchange of dialog never occurred.

Joanne must have been walking around horny and desperate for a long time. John had come in with his charm, ruggedly handsome good looks, chiseled features, and player reputation. He knew how women saw him. She'd prepared herself for him. She knew what she craved. So did John.

As soon as she'd seen him in person for the first time, a real man's man, burning desire within her became stronger and uncontrollable. John saw through her and history repeated itself.

She yanked him toward her with his tie, started to unbuckle his belt, and unzipped his pants faster than he would have liked. The thrill of dangerous excitement ran through him, and being himself, he was always ready, willing, and able to go with the flow and accommodate a woman in need.

Taking advantage, knowing he didn't have a moment to savor, he popped open the buttons on her blouse and then ran his fingers across her smaller than he liked breasts through her skimpy bra.

He intensified his pinching on her nipples, causing her to let out short throaty gasps, and she shuddered with his touch. Just like every other woman.

He laughed because he didn't even have to work for it. That was fine with him. He wasn't thrilled with the stale remnants of her perfume, so he was pleased that it must have dissipated throughout the day. It was too citrus scented for him. He much preferred the musky sandalwood vanilla scents or the lighter florals. Getting her scent on him was the last thing he wanted.

Going under her skirt with his hands, groping every smooth, tight muscle on each thigh up to her firm bottom, causing her to moan, he realized she was sans panties. He put his hands around her small waist and lifted her up onto her desk, knocking aside a few remaining pens. They both knew there was no time for romantic emotions here and they couldn't afford to get caught.

Propping herself on the edge of the desk, she, panting, spread her legs wide without being prompted. And after putting on a condom, he penetrated her with fast and deep thrusts. They had to hide any erotic sounds, though it had been very difficult. He was standing, his hands supporting him on either side of her on her desk, not even touching her. He pounded inside of her. His body heat had made his shirt transparent and glued it to his torso.

She gasped for air, leaning back, but still gripping his rear with her fingernails digging in to keep him in deeper. It was over in a few minutes with him exploding into her with fleeting satisfaction, as the feeling of her nails diminished much of what he could enjoy. Nevertheless, he remained plugged into her until she trembled in release a few minutes after him. He sneered as he zipped up, deposited a haphazard peck on her cheek, and sauntered out of the room, leaving her with her mouth agape.

Now the bile rose in his throat and shivers permeated his body at the memory. His stomach cramped and his dinner regurgitated. John bolted out of Carlson's office into the men's room next door.

❧❧❧

John vomited, retching until every morsel of food he had eaten that day floated in the toilet bowl. The stench irritated him and he couldn't catch his breath. He gagged. He heaved. He lost control and sobbed, softly, trying to prevent the team in the other room from hearing him. He sobbed over every-thing. The stress of the hostage situation. How he could have been killed. The torment of Vicki leaving. She wouldn't be there to take care of him tonight. His overbearing father. He sat on a chair opposite the bowl and bent over to regain his composure, holding his hand over his mouth.

Oh my God. What kind of a creep was I? To treat a woman like that. Oh my God. Years and years and years I behaved that way. And I should have known better. I'm a doctor for Christ's sake. I should have known better.

He splashed water on his face at the rust stained sink. Gaz-ing into the mirror above it, he barely recognized himself. His breathing was labored. His own image disgusted him. His usu-ally neat, straight hair was unkempt and had fallen over his expressionless eyes. His complexion whitened under the ap-pearance of his five o'clock shadow. He should have shaved before going to Brooklyn. Never before had he been so ashamed of himself. He held onto the sink and looked away to avoid his reflection as it hit him. Vicki changed him. He wasn't that despicable man any longer after he met her. He had to get his Vicki back, at all costs.

He washed his face with hand soap on the ledge of the sink, combed his hair off his forehead, and popped four mints into his mouth. At least his fleece hadn't become soiled. He com-posed himself to go back into Carlson's office by standing still and regulating his breathing for a couple of minutes.

❧❦❧

Paul tapped the card on the table. "John, you're not okay."
John fingered the card and slipped it into his pocket.
Yeah, I'll call him—in my next life.
His phone rang. He answered, knowing it would get him off the hook with Carlson for a minute. It was Vicki. He sat up straighter and put on his normal tone. He didn't want to let on to her how upset he really was. "Hi, babe."
"Hi."
"How was your flight?"
"Fine. Why did you do that?"

"Do what?" He knew very well what he had done.

"Why did you put five grand into my account? I told you I didn't want any money."

"You need it. How are you planning to pay the mortgage? I stopped the automatic payments, so this is just to tide you over."

"You did?"

"Yes, what did you expect? It's your house that you're living in, so pay the mortgage this month from your account. And thanks for the dinners. They're great."

"You're welcome. Heat them at 350 in the oven. I'm going to my school tomorrow to see if I can get my job back."

"Vicki, what happened to three weeks?"

"John, I don't know what I want right now."

"Vicki, it's the middle of the school year and you've been out of there for over two years, so what teacher is going to give up their class, in kindergarten no less, for you? That's not how it works."

"You'll see, John, it'll turn out fine for me. Gotta go. Thanks for the money."

"All right, call me tomorrow and let me know what happens. Bye, babe." He hung up thinking about his wife's unrealistic expectations, and more importantly, that she might want to stay there, permanently.

"Let me get this straight. Your wife left you. You're still giving her money and she's still cooking for you?"

"That's about it, Tony. She thinks she can get her job back."

"You're the one who's lacking reality, pal. She left you and you're still supporting her. Is she your wife or your kid? 'Cause that's what you're treating her like. And did you forget who her pop is?"

"No, he wouldn't do anything like that. He always made his kids work for what they got."

"Just like you, right? Still, can't figure out how you can command five hundred bucks an hour and get it," Sal said.

He didn't want to toot his own horn but he knew he was worth every penny for his consulting with the NYPD. He was their expert for the profiling of repeat offenders, serial killers when they appeared, evaluating crime scene documentation, deciding if defendants were competent to stand trial, as well as court appearances as an expert witness. On occasion when Carlson begged, John would go to a crime scene. "I work very hard to get what I have, Sal. So let's get back to it, please. The clock starts now, seven-thirty."

Tony handed him a jacket a few inches thick. "You wanted us to look into this Martin kid. There's nothing more to look into. It's all here and the investigation three years ago was thorough. We have all the evidence we needed and all the files from juvie are in here. No additional human homicides are evident. The kills at fourteen? Animals. Lots of them. Cats. Gory, too. With knives."

"All right. That's what he meant. It starts with animals. What else?"

"There are crime scene photos, forensic pathology and autopsy reports, the history the kid had with you as a teenager, and interviews with his parents in the years before he slaughtered them. A lot of it you already have. There are pages and pages of interviews with his teachers, neighbors, employers, and adults he had contact with. And his pedigree. You have everything in detail here about him since his birth, actually since his conception. So knock yourself out. If you find something, we're on it. Unless something is hiding under a rock, we have it all. So what are you looking for?"

"Not a hundred percent sure, but there might be a connection between this kid my uncle sent me for community service and Hal. So check out his family."

"What family? He killed everyone in it!"

"Tony, that's what Bobby said so how did he know that detail? So now's who's acting like a kid?"

"Hang around perps long enough, ya know there's a fine line. When are you seeing the kid?" Tony asked.

"Tomorrow. But I'm not bringing this up yet. Have training to do first and he needs to learn the ground rules."

"He's in for a rude awakening," Sal said.

"Let's hope so. What else have you got for me?"

Paul handed him a few more cases. "These go to the top of

the pile. Directives, and what we need from you, are on the first page. When are you making the fucking call?"

John stood, took the stack of files, and shot Paul his signature look.

"John, you need to take care of that problem. I mean it, pal."

He knew very well what Paul meant and, with Vicki now out of his life, he might very well have to.

CHAPTER 12

Without warning, the heavy gray steel door to John's office at Manhattan Psych blasted open with a bang—a sound it hadn't made in years. John scowled at the entrance and shot Bobby his signature look times ten. Bobby had barged in wearing a badly soiled T-shirt and torn jeans—not the in-style tears, but the ones that came from repeated wear and lack of laundering—with the waistband of his pants below his butt.

Bobby hadn't gotten the message. "Yeah, what do you want?"

"Nothing like that. Start again. Go out and come in the way you're supposed to."

"What?"

"You heard me and I never repeat myself." John delivered a long stare in silence.

After a minute Bobby took a deep breath, went out, closed the door, and re-entered opening the door slower.

"No. What do you do before you open the door?"

"I dunno, knock?"

"Good guess. Yes, again," he said, stressing, "Please."

Noticing the word, "please," Bobbly clenched his fist, which didn't go unnoticed either. He exited the office with his clenched fists tapping his thighs.

"Come in."

"You're pissed at me right?"

"Why should I be pissed?" Venting at a patient topped his no-no list.

"From yesterday."

"Nah. I'm not pissed. Before you sit down, pull your pants up. You're an adult."

Bobby looked around as if he misunderstood what the issue was and, after an open-eyed stare from John, he followed the order and sat timidly in the luxury leather chair.

John leaned back in his chair, assessing Bobby's body language. He slouched in the chair, his thin arms rested meekly on the armrests, and his eyes had a very worried look, a look that appeared on a disturbed child's face, who was awaiting a stiff physical punishment. John was used to seeing those. Bobby saw John looking directly at him, and he lowered his eyes. After a moment, he raised his head and John saw his built-up pain. John wasn't going to let him stew, anymore. This kid had been through enough in his life. That was apparent, even without reading his file or analyzing his aura, which John saw as shattered and irregular with circular voids surrounding his body.

"Know why you're here?" John said, remaining calm, which in turn calmed Bobby.

"Yeah."

"First, no more 'yeah.'" That intimidated Bobby, but John's agenda was to teach Bobby how to treat him. "It's yes, Dr. Trenton. Got it?"

Bobby swallowed hard. "Yes, Dr. Trenton."

John realized that Bobby would rebel against giving up his personal power. And John wouldn't want him to, either. "All right," John reassured him. "All right. Why are you here?"

"That judge."

"Judge Marks?"

"Yeah," Bobby said, then catching himself, he corrected, "Yes, him."

"What happened?"

"I got busted three times."

"It says here—" John started.

Bobby stiffened his body and clenched his fists as he

moved his arms to either side of his thighs. His eyes narrowed.

This was too much for him and John would have to slow it down. "This is your file. Have you ever seen it?"

Bobby shook his head. "'No."

"It says here, auto stripping in the third degree 165.09, a misdemeanor; criminal sale of a controlled substance near school grounds 220.44, a B, non-violent, felony; and forgery in the third degree, 170.05, a misdemeanor."

Hearing it read, Bobby squirmed in his chair. "What are those numbers?"

"They're very serious offenses, so New York City assigned them reference numbers. So tell me, why did Judge Marks send you here?"

"He said this is where I can wind up if I don't turn it around."

"Turn what around?"

Bobby grimaced. He didn't seem to comprehend John's questioning. "Like the stuff ya just said."

"Well, from yesterday's behavior, it's apparent that you don't understand what Judge Marks meant."

"What behavior?"

"You thought I was pissed at you, so you have to know." John pulled up the video from yesterday. "Watch this." He turned the computer screen on his desk so Bobby could view it.

The dialog was clear. "No he's not, what about us you prick? Who the fuck is this guy? Yeah, yeah."

"I get it."

"And that behavior is going to stop, right?"

"I dunno."

"You don't know?"

"No, you ain't my father, you can't make me." Bobby snickered and looked away.

"That's getting so old. Do you realize how many times I've been told that?"

"Then maybe you should take a hint."

No way is this going to happen. This kid's becoming way too comfortable, too soon. "Well, what hint are you going to get from this, and pay attention?"

Bobby focused on him and made direct eye contact for a longer time. John nodded in approval.

"You now have one thousand hours here not five hundred."

Bobby bolted up out of the chair. "You can't do that!" He flung the chair he was sitting in onto its side. Tears welled up in his eyes. "No. That can't happen. You can't do that to me. Fuck you. I hate you!" He stomped around in circles in the room with clenched fists. "Fuck that judge. I'll get him for sending me here. Just let him wait. I'll get them after him."

His jaws tightened, he hyperventilated, and his eyes stared at John with blankness and no feeling of humanity in them.

Bobby grabbed the arm of the fallen chair with both hands. He emitted growls of intense and childlike anger as he shook the chair, vehemently back and forth. John cringed at the sight of his furniture tolerating abuse, but he didn't intervene. It was better that Bobby attacked the furniture than him. Good thing there was no glass.

Bobby breathed a little easier after his explosion, but he still stewed with anger, showing only a little more control. His trembling hands slowly became still.

"Are you finished with this tantrum?"

Bobby nodded.

Bobby had only just begun to get his negative feelings off his chest. John had a long way to go with him. "We're not done yet. Sit down."

Bobby picked up the chair, slamming it into place, tossed his body into it. His brows furrowed. He leaned forward with his hands clenched around the armrests.

"Actually, I can," John told him. "I spoke with Judge Marks yesterday and Charlie, your PO. It's a done deal. By the way, just so you know, crocodile tears don't have any effect on me. So your hours here are eleven to two?"

"Yes."

"But you come late every day."

"So what?"

"Well, here's the way it's going to work. Listening?"

Bobby nodded.

"If you come later than eleven, the day isn't going to count in the thousand. Do anything that is not acceptable to anyone that works here, profanity, attitude, the day doesn't count, either. I keep very accurate records and so does Stan."

Bobby sat up at attention in the chair.

Good. The light bulb went on.

"And for every day you come in on time and do what Stan asks of you without back talk, you'll get one hour taken off the hours you owe. Any questions?"

"You can't do that!"

"Yes I can. Trenton's Law."

"What the hell is that?"

"What I say goes, no choices given. Not yet, anyway. And you just used a profanity."

"What?"

"Hell."

"You're not that old! You never said a curse? No, I can't do that. You're crazy, man!"

"And no back talk," John said, without reacting.

"So I have to watch everything I say and do here?"

"Excellent, Bobby, that's excellent. That's spot on what you have to do."

"That sucks!"

"Well, today isn't counting so you want to keep going?"

"You didn't give me any warnings."

"You're twenty-two, not four. It's your responsibility to remember the first time."

"You're asking a lot."

"What does that mean to you?"

"No one ever told me to do nothin' like that before so I don't know if I can do it."

"So you don't know if you can talk to people without cursing or being disrespectful?"

"Yes."

"Okay, so what do you think you need to do to get into the right habit?"

"I dunno."

"I appreciate the honesty so I'll help you out."

"Okay."

"The first thing is to think before you speak or do something. Think you can do that?"

"I never did that before."

"Do you think that had anything to do with you getting arrested three times?"

"Probably."

"I think so. Judge Marks said your next arrest will get you prison time."

"You're shitt—Really?"

"Really. But I can help you avoid that."

"How?"

"By turning that behavior around while you're here. That's actually why you need the thousand hours. So we can do the work. That wasn't a punishment for yesterday's behavior. So, are you up for it?"

"You're too strict."

"No, I'm not strict at all. I'm just teaching you what you need to do to get along here and follow the rules. This is a maximum-security facility with heavy-hitter criminals. There are rules for everyone."

Bobby smirked. "Whatever you say, Dr. Trenton. Am I talkin' to you every day?"

"Maybe."

"Don't count on it."

John curled his lips down. "I have to see other patients now so you can go back to work."

Bobby got up, moping, gave John a mellow look, and slowly left the room.

As he closed the door, John smiled, content with where he'd gotten for the first session.

This kid's going to be a piece of cake. He had a few minutes, so he picked up the newspaper and became engrossed in the first page. The picture showed a woman helping to get a child into an ambulance. He read the caption under the photo.

Brooklyn School Psychologist, Dr. Barbara Montgomery, acted heroically today, helping to rescue a child from the rooftop of a nearby building.

"Nice."

CHAPTER 13

Clancy lay in bed in a drunken stupor in his sparse apartment. He awoke, agitated, tossing and turning, remembering he had to be somewhere. Then he noticed the clock, reading twelve p.m.

"Damn! Not again. Not again. Not again. I can't do nothin' right."

He had missed too many appointments lately. He'd missed all of them. He became more aggravated as he struggled to get out of the bed. Fighting with the blanket, he got his legs entangled in the bed sheets and landed on the floor, scraping his back on the bed frame.

"Damn! What that woman has done to me? I should have killed her when I had the chance. I'll find her. She'll be sorry she was there that night. Dancin' and carryin' on, that whore."

While he threw on some filthy clothes—green army-print jeans, a long-sleeved T-shirt that used to be white but was now a dingy gray, and a jacket that matched his pants—he stared at the Oscar statue on the shelf.

Melissa! Why d'ya go? Why d'ya leave me? Damn, Melissa. I want you so bad. I want our SaraLynn so bad. We had it so good, so great. God, please take me, so we can be together again.

Memories flooded him. Once an Oscar-winning cinematographer, here and abroad, he was in very high demand. The movie producers lapped up his skill, especially in animations. He'd had a long roster of A-List clients wanting him. Commanding seven grand a day on the set, he'd been living the *Life of Riley*. Everything was wonderful for him and his family, his wife of ten years, Melissa, and his precious six-year old daughter, SaraLynn, living in that fantasy dream house in LA. Then that dream was shattered in one split second when Melissa was driving SaraLynn to school and an uninsured motorist hit them sideways in an intersection. All three died at the scene.

The guilt still haunted him. In a shoot in Europe at the time, Clancy couldn't get home for almost a week. He'd had a mental breakdown, spent a year in a mental hospital, and devoured his savings. Then he lost the dream house. He couldn't live there, anyway, not with the memories. The drugs—coke; amphetamines, to keep him going; and then the valium with booze to help him sleep at night, became his daily consolation. Then all of the money disappeared from supporting a thousand-dollar-a-week habit, and no producer wanted anyone on the set with that monkey on his back. He came to New York with what was left of his money, but now everything was gone, including his dignity.

It was too late for his appointment, so what the hell? He stumbled out of the apartment onto the icy steps, padlocking the door behind him. The hazy gray clouds mimicked his mood.

He meandered to the newspaper stand on the corner. He saw a picture on the front page of a woman helping a child into an ambulance.

That's her! That's her! Now I know where to find you, Barbara. You'll be dancing for me for your life! Barbara? She didn't look like a Barbara. Not at all like a Barbara. That name is too serious for a whore. Sure looks like her, the same legs. But the hair, the makeup is all different. Is it her? I don't know now. Doesn't look like a whore. Makeup and hair could make her look different. The eyes, the eyes could be the same. Same shape. Different color? Can't tell in black and white. She was on a stage, can't tell her height. And those boots she wore, they added about five inches. No boots here. Photos make ya look ten pounds heavier. Was she that skinny? I don't remember. How fat does this one look?

In his hangover, he twisted and turned the paper into different angles.

I just don't know.

ℭℜℭℜ

John lay stark naked on his back in bed on the top of the
designer gray silk bedspread, every muscle in his gleaming
body defined and, with a BMI of about sixteen, he kept himself in the best shape he could. He thought about Vicki all day.
He just didn't want to give her the satisfaction of him calling
her first. He was still shocked that she'd left and given up their
beautiful relationship out of her own selfish needs. He'd never
tried to put his needs above hers—or had he?

She didn't call him either and she'd promised. His glamorous California King bed seemed gigantic and now, in the 24K
gold trimmed mirrored ceiling, he only saw his own lonely
reflection.

This once protective, loving haven now felt cold and un-
welcoming, with the black lacquered night tables attached to
the sides of the bed flowing into a dresser for her and, on the
other side, an armoire for him. He grabbed her soft pillow and
held it across his chest putting his face into it to inhale the
remnants of any fragrance that she had left behind. It was only
two days and he doubted he could get along with her being
1200 miles away. Wanting to hold her close he caved, picked
up the phone on the nightstand, and dialed.

"Hello."

"Hi, babe. Expected to hear from you. How did it go at
school today?" Was it his parental attitude that had turned her
away? Or maybe she just didn't want any added responsibili-
ties. He'd fought with himself all day.

"I didn't go."

John expected an excuse from her. Why should things be
different now? She'd gotten into the habit of never carrying
through, or maybe he pampered her too much. "Why not?"

"Had so much to do around the house and the fridge was
empty. And—"

He cut her off, not really wanting to hear any more excuses

and tried to tantalize her with a seductive tone. "I need you to go into bed now."

"John, I can't now," she whispered. "I have company."

"Company?"

Then he heard the cute voice on the other end of the phone.

"Hi, Uncle John. It's me, Amanda."

Relief. "Hi, sweetheart." He'd fallen in love with her when he first met her three years ago. The precocious, then five-year-old, with her blonde curls in a ponytail and light blue eyes knew how to get right through him with her warm smile and giggles.

"When are you getting your butt down here?" she asked.

"Excuse me? Since when do you speak to your uncle like that?"

"Someone has to knock some sense into that little bit of brain you have! Your wife needs you."

I sure need my wife, too.

"Are you eight going on twenty-one? How long will you be there?"

"Over night. Mommy and Daddy went to a wedding. Why?"

"Oh, uh, you'll do your favorite uncle a favor, right?"

"You're not my favorite, anymore. But give it your best shot."

Knowing he deserved that, he just laughed. "When are you going to bed?"

"It's only five o'clock. What kind of a question is that?"

"Well, go in the bedroom and read a book. I really need to speak with your Aunt Vicki in private."

"You can speak in private. Here."

"Amanda, go into the den for a minute. John, we can't now," Vicki said into the phone.

"Why not?"

"This house isn't soundproofed like yours and..."

"All right. I get it. You know, in all honesty, I'm glad we didn't have any kids to interfere."

He meant this, even if it was just to get back at her for leaving him, even if it was the selfish child within him who always wanted all of her undivided attention, even if just for the moment.

She started sobbing, "Then I'm not coming back. Ever. I'll speak to my principal about a position tomorrow when I take Amanda in. Got to go. Bye." She hung up without letting him respond.

His mind reeled. He thought about what he just said. He couldn't believe those words had left his mouth. That stung, a cruel blow below the belt, the cruelest he could give to her since she wanted children more than anything else. He went along and they hadn't used anything to prevent it. They had been trying to conceive for two years, had seen the top fertility doctors in New York City, and everything between them had been fine. Stress was to blame. She hadn't been able to cope with the momentum and fast-paced energy of Manhattan. Every day had been a struggle for her to walk the crowded and well-lit streets, take public transportation and the trains. The odor-ridden stench of the overcrowded trains made her a nervous wreck. He'd hired a private driver and a limo, but hearing the loud horns of the cabbies, buses, and other cars on the crowded avenues just gave her such stomach pains she had to see a specialist. Living with a top New York City psychiatrist, such as himself, who got high on the action of the city and craved its energy, made it all seem worse.

He wouldn't prescribe anything for Vicki, not even a small dose of Valium. He realized all of this came, not out of fear, but from the mere fact that she didn't like city life. She was a country girl, through and through.

The parties, shows, upscale restaurants were so intimidating. She felt out of place, not comfortable in her own skin, having to wear high heels and even that staple, that little black dress. Being his wife came with a price. He was well aware of it. Vicki always had to look perfect with her hair and makeup and trendy designer outfits. They never knew when the paparazzi would invade their privacy and start snapping their cameras. He had turned her into a fashion icon over the last two years, and she was now recognized as one of New York's Best Dressed Women.

He was so proud to be seen with his gorgeous wife, but

deep down he knew that she longed for her flip-flops, shorts, and tank tops, even in the dead of winter.

It was clear to him, the only ones she felt comfortable with were Tony, Sal, and the other cops. After all, Vicki came from a family of them, the only girl with two brothers, and the only one who left to go to the big city, one of the biggest of them all, New York.

Vicki had begun to isolate herself from their friends and any friend she made on her own and spent her time alone in the condo reading, cooking, and baking, which was her forte. She made lunch for him every day. She packed it with loving notes and baked enough cookies and pastries for the doctors' lounge and police precinct. John's treats grew to be expected. Everyone would stay after hours to indulge in Vicki's delights. Oh, man, was he going to miss that!

John stared into the closet. He saw that the knob on her jewelry safe was in the same position and she'd left most of her clothes. All of the exquisite Tiffany diamond jewelry, the ten-karat necklace, with hearts in diamonds and platinum, and the matching bracelet and ring he bought her—not necessarily for special occasions, but for just because—and the designer six-thousand-dollar bags and high-priced clothing were all left behind. She wouldn't need them back home.

John let the tears flow at the thought she'd be leaving him for good.

CHAPTER 14

Three Years Earlier:

John's parents had moved to Sun County, on the west coast of Florida, at the beginning of June, the day after his forty-second birthday. It had been three months since he had seen them. In New York, he would see them at least once a week. He'd thought he cut the umbilical cord. But what he was about to find out was that the cord was still wrapped just as tight and stretched over 1200 miles.

"Let us have a car pick you up at the airport. It's a long drive."

"No, Mom, I want to rent a car. I'll need it during the week anyway."

"You're coming down to spend time with us. Aren't you?"

"Yes, but you have your new friends. I don't want to disrupt your schedules. And I just want to vegetate by the pool. I'm not going to stop you and Dad from doing your thing."

"I'm not going to argue with you. Pack your Tallit and bring a few sports jackets and ties."

"Mom, I know how to dress for Temple."

"On Rosh Hashanah people get a little more dressed up. Even down here. Do you have the directions?"

"Yes. Dad gave them to me and I put them into my GPS. Mom, stop worrying, I'll see you tomorrow afternoon."

"Call us from the plane when you land."

"Yes, Mom, I will. Let me go finish packing."

"Have a great flight. I love you."

"I love you too, Mom." He hung up, amazed at how she still treated him like a little boy.

He laughed to himself.

What did she mean? Even down here?

☙❧☙❧

The pilot came on over the loudspeaker. "Welcome to Tampa. The temperature is currently ninety-three degrees. We'll be getting to the gate in approximately five minutes and will disembark at gate three. Follow the signs to the shuttle and then to the luggage carrier A1 for pick up and ground transportation. Hope you had a pleasant flight and thank you for jetting Jet Blue Airways."

☙❧☙❧

In his reserved black Cadillac Escalade, dressed in a jeans and a polo, already feeling the heat, but loving it, even with beads of perspiration on his neck dampening his shirt collar, John put the Garmin on the dash. He drove out of the lot onto Veterans Parkway North, heading toward Crystal River. He was eager to leave the chilliness and early change of season in New York behind for the warmer weather.

Getting to the first toll, his first surprise came from the toll-booth attendant, a woman in her sixties as she greeted him. "How are you, sir?"

He handed her a buck twenty-five for the toll. "Fine. Thank you. How far is it to Serento?"

"All the way to last exit, sir, about seventy-two miles. Then follow the signs."

"Thanks."

"Have a great day, sir. And make sure to stay on the highway. Keep to the right."

"Will do." Pulling out, he smiled. *This doesn't happen in New York! She would have had a conversation if I wanted.*

He received the same greeting at the next five tollbooths. He enjoyed the friendliness, for a change, and it relaxed him. The drive took longer than he expected but he'd never driven on such a barren highway. He mellowed out, went into his own thoughts, and focused on where he was going at the same time.

Finally, I can relax. I need this week badly. I hope they don't embarrass me by introducing me to all their friends. No fix ups, Mom, please, no fix ups. Ah hell, when did she ever listen to me? And her Mahjongg group, definitely not that, not her Mahjongg group. No rain, just no rain. I want sun, swimming, and relaxation. No cops. No work. No phone calls from Carlson or the team. No hospital emergencies. Nothing. Just "me time."

After an hour and fifteen minutes, he reached the end and the female Garmin voice startled him, jerking him from his thoughts. "Turn right onto Highway 98." And then, three miles later. "Turn left onto Highway 491."

All he saw were trees and more trees—big oaks mixed with palm trees, so many different ones he couldn't name them— lining the roads. And then some farms with cows and horses, lots of them. He saw many calves with their mothers and smiled to himself at how innocent they looked, so free, just grazing at their will. It was a calm and peaceful area.

All the greenery overwhelmed him. Some homes were in desperate need of repair. Some were abandoned run-down shacks. Then the trailer parks appeared at the edge of the road. Their laundry hung on lines outside the trailers, next to charcoal barbeque pits, while the smokehouse odors contaminated the supposedly clean clothes.

Where the hell did Mom and Dad move to?

He passed a community college, a high school complex, and some privately owned businesses, then trees and more trees lining this six-lane highway.

He'd had no idea that this trip he was taking was going to alter his life forever, turning it upside down and inside out. He would be kissing his playboy lifestyle goodbye for a monogamous one. His late-night partying would be over, except with the same woman in his own bedroom. His living his life only on his terms would be nonexistent. There would be a new person he worshipped and held high on a pedestal. He'd had no idea that tonight, Friday, a little before midnight, on Erev Rosh Hashanah, September eighteenth, he would be meeting the woman who would become his wife, Victoria Elizabeth Marin.

The Garmin spoke again fifteen miles later. "Turn right onto Highway 486 and drive seven miles."

Where the heck am I going? It's farther into woods? This is like the Adirondacks with palm trees.

About three miles on, he got one of the finest amusements of his adult life. A mature black and white cow broke through a farm's fence and found its way onto the now two-lane highway right in front of his SUV. He quickly came to a halt, just in time, and looked at this massive 1220-pound creature standing in front of his car, looking straight at him. A "Moo," came from the cow's mouth.

Laughing out-loud and not believing his own eyes, he squinted to make sure it was what it was in front of him. He'd always welcomed a new adventure, so he got out of the car and approached the cow that plodded toward him. Right before the cow licked him, the farm owner came through the fence and secured the cow with a rope around her neck.

In his mid-fifties, wearing overalls, with a haggard beard, baseball cap and a few missing teeth, the farmer laughed at John's amazement. "I got her, fella. The storm last night probly tore down this here plank." He sneered at John and the car. "You're not from around these parts, are ya?"

"No I'm visiting from New York." Like the guy couldn't tell.

Leading the cow back to the field, the farmer said, "Ah city folk," almost mocking John, "Come on, girl." Then he turned to John, "The next time ya see her, she'll be on your plate," he said.

"What?" John was stunned, not expecting that kind of remark.

"Yes sir, she's goin' to market next month. Just needs to gain a few more pounds in her gut here." He patted the cow on her belly. "Have a great stay in Sun County, sir."

John stood there, bewildered. He knew raising cattle was a business, but now it had become personal.

I'm becoming a vegetarian, definitely a vegetarian.

Getting in the car, still shaken by the guy's comment, he sat there contemplating the matter-of-factness of life.

Wow, that's not something I could do, but I do love my steak. Just never thought about it before I ate it, though. Wow. Maybe I ought to.

That was humbling and would stay with him for a while. Sitting in the car, reflecting, he let the traffic build up behind him with at least four cars, but no one beeped their horn. He checked the rear view mirror, saw the traffic, registered the silence, and resumed driving, while his analytical self realized this was a different style of living down here. No one was in a hurry to do anything or get anywhere. Good for his parents but not good for him.

Five miles later, he came to Bueno Terrace.

Finally, civilization.

There was a CVS, Walgreens, and a shopping center on the other side of the expanded six-lane highway with the Publix supermarket, known throughout Florida. Getting to the welcome gate of his parents' new community, he waved the pass they'd sent him and was on his way to their brand new, million-dollar home.

John had examined the pictures and layout they showed him before they moved. He thought it would be too large for them with five bedrooms, two of which were master suites, but they always appreciated grand things and were hoping for visits from John and their future grandchildren. Driving through the development and seeing its beautiful, lush, and colorful plant life; flawlessly manicured lawns and gardens; hills that encased the eighteen-hole golf courses; and the huge, elegant colonial style homes with earth tone color schemes with lots of well-kept land between them, he understood why his parents chose to move here for their retirement.

The view of his parent's house on the hill was breathtaking. He looked it over as his eyes took in the massive structure, knowing that his mother had put her heart and soul into decorating the house for a year before they moved here. Her hard work had definitely paid off. Two Corinthian columns with acanthus leaves on either side of the outer frame gave the one-story home—lavishly decorated on the outside with Gothic engravings throughout the stonework—a structured, but elegant look.

The door opened and he was thrilled to see his parents. Likewise, they missed him. His mother Esther, formerly Esther Marks, was seventy years old and had just retired from her lucrative OBGYN practice. Over the last thirty-five years, she had delivered over 2,000 babies and had loved every minute. She was both assertive and aggressive, packed into a five-foot-three inch frame, and what was on her mind came out on her tongue. Attractive, with short salt and pepper hair and azurite blue eyes, she always dressed as if she was going to meet someone important, even down here, in casual horse-and-cow country.

His father Sam, seventy-two years old and about five-foot-eleven inches tall with a medium build, had retired from his practice as a cardiac surgeon in New York two years ago. John looked just like him, no mistaking it. Sam had longed for a retirement where he could play golf as often as he liked, and now he had it. He was always consistent and predictable and everyone around him knew what to expect. To Esther, this was a tad boring. She was just the opposite, as the free spirit, spur of the moment, go-getter.

Sam firmly believed that wives should always have their way and he never said "No," regardless of whatever Esther asked of him, even this move to rural Florida.

After the usual hugs, John looked around, enthralled by how his parents had decorated. Earth-tone beiges enveloped him, but the design in the marble floor of a vase with flowers in gorgeous shades of pink, burgundy, and mauves—which accentuated the beauty of the rest of the tiling and his parents' attention to detail—captured his interest the most. The furniture was Italian Mediterranean style with scrolls of gold leaf in the woodwork. The long couches and adjacent club chairs were covered in gold and sand brocade fabric and had claw feet in rounded animal-paw-shaped bases.

He smiled in approval as he took it all in. They showed John into his master suite, and he looked around, amazed at the care they had taken to decorate this room for him. They left him to unpack and get ready for the evening. In keeping with the beige tones of the rest of the house, the king-sized bed was dressed with tan and beige jacquard bedding.

The armoire was huge with modern styling with straight lines in light wood tones.

The en-suite bathroom was massive, at twenty feet by thirty feet, and tiled with matching beige and brown marble from floor to ceiling. The walk-in shower, with eight waterspouts coming from different angles on the walls, was large enough to accommodate at least five people at the same time.

If I only had a woman to share this with, I could have a lot of fun in here!

The closet was bigger than the one he had in New York, and it was sectioned into a dresser, shoe racks, built-ins, and a wall unit for everything he used.

They don't expect me to move in here, do they?

♥♥♥

"You're going with Mom tonight. I have other plans."

"Dad, how did you get off the hook?" John demanded, since he couldn't have pulled that off. Nor would he dare try.

"It's only a forty-five-minute service tonight. I'll go with you tomorrow. Mom's not happy but she'll get over it."

"It's his Friday night poker game with his golf buddies," Mom said. "I pick my battles. Besides, I have you to show off."

"Mom, please don't. Don't do anything to embarrass me, and please don't try to fix me up."

"Well, you're not doing so well on your own."

"Mom, I'm doing just fine."

"I don't know what you didn't like about Laura. She was a beautiful and well-educated lawyer. And her parents are wonderful people."

"Mom, we weren't compatible. Let's just leave it at that."

"So you want to be single the rest of your life? I can't believe that with all of the doctors you know, there isn't one woman you can find to have a relationship with. And everything with you just goes down to the bedroom. Just remember, it'll never be truly meaningful and satisfying unless it's with the one you love."

This is going to be some week.

"Mom, believe me, when I meet the woman I love and want to marry, I'll know it and embrace it immediately."

Esther escaped for a moment into the bedroom to get a jacket. "Let's go. I don't want to be late."

oↄeↄ

John's cell phone rang as he was coming out of the Temple. He looked at the three-five-two area code and recognized it to be from here, but he didn't know who else here had this number.

"Hello, Dr. Trenton."

His mother talked to friends with the usual chick chat.

"Dr. Trenton, good. This is Deputy Haggerty. Sir, there's been a slight fender bender and your father was taken to Sunshine Memorial. He's fine, sir. I just thought it best to have him checked out. He banged his shoulder against the driver's side door. I took him to the hospital myself."

"What happened?" John was alarmed, even though the deputy reassured him.

"Apparently, he didn't turn left wide enough to avoid a pole in the island of the intersection. It was probably too dark for him to see, sir. When you get there, just go to the ER in building B."

"Thank you. We're on our way." John slipped off his jacket. "Mom, let's go. Mom, we have to go now."

"Why? Who was that?"

"A deputy," he said as he pulled off his tie. "Dad had a minor car accident and he's at the hospital. Where's Sunshine Memorial?"

"What?" Her nervousness almost made her trip on a crack and she grabbed onto John's arm for balance. "In Talmont. I'll tell you how to go. He couldn't give up that damn poker game for one night?"

ⱷⱷⱷ

In the lot, John pulled into the doctors' parking area, since he was so used to doing that, and they ran into Building B. He looked around, trying to absorb the surroundings. Everything was new, with comfortable club chairs and love seats in yellow and green-toned plaid upholstery, matching the walls, laid out in different sections in the room. Organized magazine racks lined the walls next to a sign announcing free Wi-Fi. This place was warm, inviting—a non-threatening place to be. The quiet was the most shocking. John was not used to an ER like this. He had never been in an ER like this, so quiet, so clean. He noticed a table against the wall with coffee urns, bagels, cream cheese, and doughnuts.

And, best of all, the waiting room was empty—almost empty, except for a few patients with blankets covering them waiting to be seen. He even doubted he and his mother were in the right area. He didn't waste time, but went straight to the attendant at the desk—a male in his fifties, wearing a blue uni-form.

"My father, Dr. Sam Trenton, was brought in a little while ago."

"Yes sir, he's right through there. I'll buzz your mother and you in. He's in Room 3."

"Thank you."

They both hurried in through the door into a private room. As soon as he saw his father in a hospital gown, okay, and sit-ting up, John relaxed.

"Don't say it, don't you dare say it!"

"Say what, Dad? Are you all right? What happened?"

"I'm fine. The deputy was right behind me so when I hit the pole, he stopped and insisted I come here. Had nothing better to do I guess."

"Dad, he was very nice not to have you wait for an ambu-lance. He said you banged your left shoulder?" John rolled up his sleeves before he proceeded to check his dad's deltoid muscle. It was tight and in spasm. "Does this hurt?" His father grimaced, but wouldn't admit he was in pain. John also noticed something else. "Dad, how much weight have you gained since you've been here?"

"About ten pounds!" Esther chimed in, since she was so mad at him.

"Dad, ten pounds? In three months? That would be forty in a year, Dad. Come on! You're a cardiac surgeon. What are you doing to yourself?"

"It's the southern cooking he likes."

"Everything we do here is around eating." Sam raised his arms and let them fall onto his lap. "Go out with friends, we go to eat; at poker, we eat; get together at friends' homes, we eat."

"Dad, I'm putting you on a diet."

A nurse, Kathryn, entered. She was in her sixties, with curly gray hair. "What are you doing?"

"Dad, we're not finished discussing this." John directed his attention to the nurse. "I'm checking my father's shoulder. Did you take any blood or order any workup yet?"

"Not yet."

"I'm ordering lipid profile with LDL, HGAIC and the CMF profiles."

"Excuse me? And you are?"

"His son, Dr. John Trenton."

"Dr. Trenton, are you on your father's list of contacts on his privacy form?" She thumbed through the paper work. "No you're not. Only Esther is."

"That's my mother. Dad, you didn't put me down? Oh no. That won't fly. Dad, do it now." John took the sheet from her and handed it to his father.

"If you make him add you under duress, it won't count."

"It's not under duress. Tell her, Dad."

His father nodded that it was okay and corrected the paper work.

"There it is. Now order the tests please."

"Dr. Trenton, are you licensed to practice medicine in the state of Florida?"

"No. I am not." He hadn't even thought of that but he knew she was right.

"Then I'm sorry, sir. You have no authorization to order anything in this hospital or in the state. And you have no privilege to examine a patient, even if he is your father. I didn't make this up. It's the law. Are you familiar with the law, Dr. Trenton?"

"Yes. Thoroughly."

"Good. Now that we understand each other, can I get you or your mother something to eat or drink while you're waiting for the doctor?"

"No. Thank you. I saw a table out there, I'll get some coffee. Mom, I'll leave you to argue with him."

☙❧☙

In the lounge, John approached the buffet with the coffee. They even had decaf. But he needed regular, and strong. He noticed a woman with mid-back-length natural-blonde hair, wearing tight jeans and a blue and orange University of Florida T shirt that caressed her body and accentuated her curves in all the right places. He snuck next to her to feel her aura, her energy field, and sensed her warmth and sincerity. Not a mean bone in her body, just some tension, probably from being here. He wanted to see what she looked like.

She must have sensed someone close to her and looked up at him. Her light blue eyes connected with his as waves of attraction shot through him like bolts of lightning in an out-of-control Florida storm.

CHAPTER 15

Present Day:

Page Dr. Trenton. I know he's here now." Carlson filled out a report by the welcome desk in the ER of Sheepshead Medical Center and Training Hospital in Brooklyn, New York. Meanwhile, he was pushed out of the way by people racing to sign in.

EMS staff wheeled Barbara into the ER. She was sedated, with her hands and feet bound by restraints She lay on a stretcher covered with a heavy blanket, drifting in and out of twilight sleep.

"Dr. Trenton, ER, STAT."

Carlson couldn't believe the crowd. He followed the stretcher, agitated and shaking his head, deep in thought. He hated to do this, to bring her into this environment, but she'd left him no choice. It was the closest hospital to the precinct. And he needed Trenton. He nodded a hello to the NYPD officers and security guards on duty.

The ER was maxed out at two-hundred-sixty people waiting for the three doctors and six nurses on duty to call them. It was dirty, dismal, and run down. The old plastic seats were held together with metal bars, securing them in rows, throughout the waiting room, and were attached to the floors.

The seats were all taken. Carlson would have to stand. His gaze scanned the perimeter of the room and he grimaced in disgust. The cracked gray walls left bits of plaster on the floor.

The scuffed old tile floor, in desperate need of repair, looked worse with the plaster dust near the baseboard. The exam rooms—curtained off areas with beds in a row and tattered curtains in between them—were the maximum amount of privacy afforded here. He couldn't focus on the people. He'd stare. The population of druggies, gang members, and wounded teens from gang initiations would not pass over staring, the utmost sign of disrespect. His heart broke for the infants and young children who cried inconsolably because of the intolerable noise and chaos. With all the years on the job, some things you never got used to. He turned away from the children. Patients sat with bullet wounds, knife slashes, and injuries from brawls, as well as the elderly and children with serious conditions. They heard each other screaming in pain and often saw the blood dripping from wounds. Some were homeless and the stench of stale urine permeated the air. Sitting next to someone could make one want to vomit. Another reason he'd stand.

A few minutes after the page, Trenton approached, surprised to see him.

"To what do I owe this honor?"

"I need you to do me a favor. A big one."

"Such as?"

"Take a look at this one please. She shouldn't be assigned to you. She's not a criminal by any means, but you both work with a younger population, so maybe, just maybe, she'll relate to you better. Maybe you could understand where she's coming from. We can't make heads or tails out of what she's complaining about. All I know—" Carlson handed him the file. "—she's crackin' up, Johnny Boy."

"Wasn't she in the paper a couple of weeks ago?"

Carlson nodded.

"Occupational hazard," John said. "All right." He turned toward the EMS officer. "Please wheel her into an exam room. What's with the restraints?"

"She was out of control."

"So sedated and restrained? Isn't that going a little overboard?"

"Wait before you judge," Carlson snarled at him.

"Sorry, Paul. No one deserves to be treated like that."

"Oh, really? And here's her weapon of choice." Carlson took out of a manila evidence bag a clear plastic one, which held a five-inch stiletto-heeled, black patent-leather boot, embossed with a red embroidered dragon on its outer side.

"Wow." John held the boot in the plastic shield. "These are hot! What did she use it for?"

"Kicked a cop in the ribs. And fractured two! And she fought three armed cops!"

John tried to contain himself, holding in a laugh. "Seriously?"

"Yeah! Fucking seriously! One thing before you go. You have an appointment with him at six." Carlson handed him the card.

"Who?"

"Dr. Burt Landers."

John rolled his eyes.

"You didn't make the call so I made it for you. Don't even think of missing this appointment."

John read the Manhattan address on the card. "Not at the precinct?"

"Private practice."

"All right, I'll go."

Paul looked at him with raised eyebrows.

"You have my word. Look, I know I can use it. Okay? Satisfied? Let me go deal with this gem you dumped on me."

೮ఎ೮ఎ

In the exam room, Barbara had been transferred to a bed, with restraints fastened. When Trenton entered, he dismissed the attendants who waited with her. He observed Barbara for a moment before approaching her, not at all happy about how she'd been treated.

She strained her neck, struggling to get up. "They don't believe me! They don't believe me!"

"Who, Dr. Montgomery. Who doesn't believe you?"

Barbara began to tune in. "Where am I?" She pulled at the

tight restriction of the straps. "I can't move. I can't breathe."

"All right, take it easy. I'll take these off. You can't go anywhere."

John released the Velcro wrist and ankle straps. She pulled her arms into her chest, not being able to normalize her breathing. He leaned against the bed with his right hip looking straight at her with his arms crossed over his chest. His evaluation began.

Barbara sweated, unfocused. She didn't waste time mincing words. "Who the fuck are you?"

He didn't expect this language from a peer, of sorts. "Excuse me?"

"Who in the world are you?"

"Good. I could do without the expletive. Dr. John Trenton, forensic psychiatrist. You're a brave lady."

She couldn't focus her eyes. Her teeth chattered. "Get to the point, Doc."

John saw her exaggerated reactions. She must have been shaking off the sedation. He reached out to touch her wrists. "Let me take your pulse."

She jerked her hand away. "No."

He let it drop for the moment. "I saw your picture in the paper a couple of weeks ago."

"Oh that. And it's been downhill ever since."

"Are the kid's parents trying to get even?"

"No, we've been through that already. Where the hell am I?"

"Any older student playing tricks?"

"No. Tell me where I am!"

"Anyone in your personal life less than stable?" He hit a chord. Widened pupils glared at him.

Okay.

She didn't let him in. "*No!* Where the fuck am I? Or don't you listen?"

"Look around. Where do you think you are?"

"It stinks like a hospital."

"Yes. You're in Sheepshead Medical."

"Why?"

"Says here you had an emotional breakdown with delusions

of persecution and hallucinations. Someone sent you decapitated rats? Strange pictures coming off your walls in your home?"

She screamed at the top of her lungs. "That's fucking bullshit, Doc!"

He stood up and stared at her. Shocked into having second thoughts about her, he backed off to get a better view of her outrage.

"It's not a delusion. There's a lunatic out there and, for whatever reason, he chose me as a target, so you can take those bureaucratic files and shove them!"

"Whoa. Stop screaming. I'm not deaf," he said, in his usual, low key demeanor. "Calm down. It also says you physically attacked three armed police officers." He thumbed through the file. "And fractured a couple of ribs of a cop? With a boot? I saw it by the way. It could do serious damage." He stared at her in amazement. "What's that all about?"

"They tried to get me to sit down."

He couldn't understand her over-reaction. "What were you doing?"

"Screaming at Carlson."

"I see that went well."

"What the fuck does that mean?" she demanded, lifting her head and looking down her nose at him.

"You were brought in sedated *and* with restraints. What possessed you to attack police officers—three, no less? You had to know you were going to lose."

"Stop with the lecture, Doc."

"It's Dr. Trenton, and I can, without a doubt, add here the lack of reality testing. But we have seventy-two hours to figure it out."

"What do you mean seventy-two hours? I want out of here!"

"You're here under police order, and I can definitely see you're out of control right now. Therefore, you can be a danger to yourself and others. I can't release you. It would be against the law."

"What the fuck are you going to do with me for seventy-two hours?"

"A complete mental, emotional, and physical workup. There are so many physical imbalances that cause mental distress. You, of all people, should know that."

"You are not touching me. There's nothing wrong with me. I take very good care of myself."

"Then talk to me. Tell me what's going on that pushed Carlson over the edge to send you here."

"No. Let me go, and I'll make an appointment to see you. And then we'll talk about it."

"No can do."

"Then go read my file. It's five inches thick and with Carlson. And I wrote it all, except for the parts that bastard changed so he can commit me."

She swung at him with both hands, and he immediately grabbed her forearms.

His firm grip made her pay attention. "I will. But first I have to complete all of the tests here, and I need your cooperation."

"You're getting nothing." Her spiteful gaze spit bullets at him. "Let go of me!" She struggled with all her strength but John didn't budge.

"Not with that look of terror in your eyes."

"Okay. Okay. I'll calm down." She relaxed just a bit. "Now let go of me."

"No. Not yet. Not until I feel you relaxing. Take a few deep breaths."

She closed her eyes, as if hoping he'd disappear. After a moment, she opened them. It took a few minutes of her trying to stare him down, before she gave up.

"Are you calm enough for me to let go?" She nodded. He released her arms. "Here's the way it works. Legally, I have the seventy-two hours to perform the workups. If you don't cooperate, and I can't complete them, I can extend your stay for as long as I deem necessary, even assign a long-term commitment. So it would behoove you to participate, in your own defense, I might add, so you can get out of here and resume your life."

"You are—not—getting—one—bit—of information from me."

"Well then, I'll have to find everything out on my own. Won't I? And if that's the case, every cell in your body will be thoroughly examined. A nurse will be coming in to help you change into a gown and ask you some questions."

Barbara attempted to beat up on him but she was no physical match for him. He didn't like having to be that forceful with a woman, but he had to use a lot of strength to restrain her. Out of frustration, she burst into a deluge of tears and sobs, while pounding on his chest. After several minutes, she calmed down, collapsing back onto the bed. He knew she'd have to become exhausted, eventually. John pulled open the curtain and signaled to a female psychiatric nurse, Gladys, with whom he had worked for several years.

"I don't want her left alone, even for a millisecond."

"Yes, Dr. Trenton. I'm going to do an intake now, anyway, and then she's going to her room."

"Thank you. Get as much information as you can and make a note as to whether you think it's the truth or not." *Good luck with that.*

"I will."

෴

Gladys approached Barbara, who was off the stretcher, looking in her bag for the rest of her belongings. "Dr. Montgomery, may I help you with something?"

"I can't find my boots. I need them."

"Lieutenant Carlson has them, along with your knitting bag."

"Why? He better not damage them. They cost over 1500 bucks! And my knitting bag?"

"You're not allowed anything sharp in here. Now please, here's a gown. Take off your suit and put this on with the opening to the back. Your bra, too. My name is Gladys and I'll be your nurse for now."

"Now?"

"Right now. And I'll be here with you. We need to take care of this paper work."

Barbara removed her red skirt and matching blazer, folding each of them neatly. She deposited the black camisole, bra, and suit into the bag Gladys handed her. She slipped on the gown.

"Now sit up on the stretcher and we'll talk."

Barbara sat up on the bed, rocking forward and back, with a distant look in her eyes.

Gladys sat on an armchair next to the stretcher. "I see you're very nervous. Have you ever been admitted to a hospital before?"

"No, Gladys, and I don't know why I'm here. Carlson just got pissed at me." Barbara feigned crying. "And I'm so upset. I can't believe this is happening to me."

Lie number one recorded.

"All right, dear. Dr. Trenton will find out what is happening. He's very kind and caring. And very gentle. He won't have you stay here for no reason. Is your address the same as on your driver's license, in Brooklyn?"

"Yes."

"How long have you been at your current residence?"

"Three years."

"Are you on any medications?"

"None."

"Are you being treated for any conditions?"

"None. Nothing. I'm in perfect health. I exercise and eat right."

Lie number two recorded.

"Good, then no need to go down this list." *Why waste my time with lies?*

"Have you had any surgeries?"

"No. I told you. I have never been admitted to a hospital for any reason. One of the lucky ones, I guess."

Lie number three recorded.

"Yes. You certainly are. Do you have any allergies?"

"No."

"Do you smoke?"

"No."

"Drink alcohol?"

"Socially."

"About how often would you say? Once, twice a week?"

"Twice a week."

"Illegal drugs?"

"No! Not at all," Barbara declared emphatically.

Lie number four recorded.

"What about your parents? Are they—"

Barbara cut her off. "Both deceased. My mother died of breast cancer when I was ten. And my father, we were estranged, but he died two years ago, heart attack, I think. I'm not even sure, honestly. I haven't seen in him fifteen years. His landlord called me. I must have been on his contact form or something."

Lie number five recorded.

"Where did they live, dear?"

"California, Los Angeles."

"When was your last physical?"

"Years ago."

"When was your last mammogram?"

"Years ago. I only took it because of family history. And it was perfectly normal."

"Where was that?"

"In California, actually."

"And your last internal and pap?"

"Same thing. Honestly, I'm doctor phobic. Look, Gladys, you've been very nice, but I'm feeling so dizzy and nauseous. I don't know what the EMTs gave me. Can't this wait? Please?"

"Yes, dear. Dr. Trenton will review this with you. I believe your room is ready now." Gladys recorded on the form, *I don't believe anything she told me is the truth.*

⇛

Barbara, wearing a pale green hospital gown, sat with her legs crossed on her bed in a private room with a bathroom, TV on the white wall, dresser next to the bed, and a window with a main-avenue view. A worn, green club chair was in front of the window. She removed the deck of tarot cards from her bag. She inhaled deeply to ground herself. After unwrapping the cloth around the deck, she asked a question, aloud. "What do I need to know about that Trenton Doc?" She pulled the Devil, The Emperor, King of Swords. "Oh my God. Yeah sure, right, Gladys. He's kind, caring, and gentle? Bullshit. He's going to be a problem."

❧❧

Outside at the nurse's station, the video camera showed Barbara holding the cards. Gladys and a couple of other nurses watched her. Gladys signaled for Trenton to come fast, knowing this would peak his interest.

He glanced at the screen and snickered.

"Here's the intake and, by the way, I think most of it is false," she said.

He scanned the questions and answers, nodding in agreement, and took the file with him. "Thanks, Gladys. Good to know. I'm going to set the ground rules." He exuded a quiet laugh that only he heard as he round the corner to Barbara's room.

❧❧

Barbara saw him enter and grabbed up the cards.

He pulled up the chair, smiling at her. "No. Don't put them away."

She had recovered from the sedative and now studied his commanding good looks. *He's not laying one finger on me. He's one bad boy.*

She focused on his wedding band.

He leaned toward her. "Ask them a question for me."

She humored him. "Okay, what is it?"

"What does Barbara need to know about cooperating with Dr. Trenton? And you can change Barbara to 'I' as you say it."

She did a double take and she felt the heat rise in her cheeks. "What?"

"Say it out loud. Now. Shuffle the deck." She did. "Now pick a number from one to ten."

"You know tarot?" She was flabbergasted, to put it mildly.

"I would have to say, yes. Now say it."

Intimidation prevailed and she was cognizant it was justified. Her voice trembled. "What do I need to know about cooperating with Dr. Trenton?"

"Good. Continue."

"Okay, five." She pulled The Emperor, King of Wands, King of Swords, The Moon, and The Devil. She closed her eyes and put her hand on her stomach. Three of the five cards were ones she picked previously. And she shuffled four times!

He smiled. "Now what does it all mean?"

Damn! I can't let him see his effect on me!

"In a nutshell—you're an SOB on steroids!"

"No. Not on steroids." He laughed. "I'm a self-made man. Let's break it down."

To her, he sounded as if he was reprimanding a group of interns.

"The Emperor, the law. You don't cooperate, you're in contempt of a police order, and that can mean jail time. So think about that. It also means that I'm the one in authority here, and what I say goes."

She cringed.

"King of Wands. I know what I'm doing and I carry through. So no threats, no crazy behavior. The King of Swords. I can be very assertive, even aggressive if I have to be, so don't even think of fighting me."

She gasped to prevent her tears.

"The Devil. I will find out what you're doing to be manipulative."

She looked at him with apprehension in her eyes, as she knew what the card meant as well.

"And I'll also find out about the abuse in your life, the sex abuse, and the drugs. And let's not forget about the Moon. I usually don't tell patients this. It just evolves and they realize it, but since you're intuitive you should know. I'm psychic."

She was wide eyed shocked.

"Clairvoyant."

She closed her eyes and rocked back and forth like an autistic child.

"I see auras, and the armoring in your body, and I can see when a patient is blatantly lying to me. Any questions?"

He would take everything she worked so hard to achieve away. She felt fear—the fear of the end of her life as she knew it. She was in a vulnerable weakened state. "No."

"Good. So now, pack up the cards. And move back on the bed so I can begin your physical."

CHAPTER 16

Three Years Earlier:

Wow! She was definitely his type. John found her alluring. She had sun-streaked multi shades of shiny natural blonde hair. He'd never met a natural blonde before, though he had met plenty of bottle ones. She was so natural in every way, with a gorgeous tan, needing very little makeup, just a little blue eye shadow, highlighting her big, round eyes, and pale pink lipstick. Her eyes were vibrant and her skin flawless, with the cutest little turned up nose and luscious lips, which he could savor for a long time. He measured her height against his—right at his shoulders, perfect. He was glad she wasn't a zero-sized thin. Curvaceous. A round bottom that he'd love to squeeze. Right now. He thought about a perfect C cup. A and B were too small and a D too large. The girls sagged when a woman aged. Size C perfect. And to him this woman was perfection with gardenia-scented cologne radiating through her clothing.

He smiled, warmly and seductively. "Hi there."

"Hi," she replied with a soft southern tone. She turned away as she placed a strawberry jelly doughnut on a plate.

"You're not going to eat that, are you?"

His equally soft tone told her he was being flirty, not mean. His wickedly sexy grin ensured she got the message. She gazed up at him and backed up. "Usually, no, but when I'm nervous, I go for the sugar. My father had to come in. We're hoping it's not his heart."

"Ah, sorry, mine is here too, fender bender. You know there are other ways to release the tension than eating this." He took a big chance here and opened himself up to the wrath of a smack across the face. But the message was clear, and this country girl turned every shade of pink. "I'm sorry. I didn't mean to embarrass you."

Take it slow John. This is not New York.

"Oh yes you did," she said, taunting him back.

She knew how to flirt, and he realized he might just have met his match as she returned to the doughnut on her plate. Looking straight up into his eyes, she took a big bite.

Um, spiteful. I'll fix that.

All he knew was that he would hook up right there and then if he could. He could use a diversion from his parents this week. But, right now, no go.

Before he could introduce himself, a little boy around five called to her excitedly. "Miss Marin!"

She turned and raced to him. "Ricky, what are you doing here?"

Miss, that's a good thing.

The boy was there with his early-twenty-something mother. With his shrink's hat on, John observed from a distance, but stayed close enough to hear. With washed-out, bleached-blonde hair—with a couple of inches of dark roots showing—and tattered clothing, the mother probably looked older than her years from the hard life John assumed she had. She smelled of nicotine and had the shakes as if she needed a smoke or something stronger.

"I'm havin' an asth—ma attack." Ricky struggled with tight breathing, trying to get the words out.

John didn't know how long he'd just be able to stand there and not become involved. Regardless of the law.

Vicki sat in the chair next to his mother. "What happened, sweetheart?"

Ricky cried, wiping his tears away with his chubby hand, and tried to explain the best he could. "My daddy gave—me a whuppin'. And then I—couldn't—breathe." With curly blond hair and a face like a cherub, all he needed was a quiver with bows and arrows and he could pass for cupid. A little chubby, but it was still his baby weight. John smiled as Ricky's personality shone through his discomfort. He was a real trooper. John liked that. He admired survivors.

"He's always doin' sometin' to upset his father. And I'm the one who has to sit here waitin' on the pediatrician with him, the brat. He just don't learn nothin'." His mother raised her hand to smack him across the face.

Vicki grabbed her hand, without batting an eyelash. "Miss Strathmore, you can't do that. You're going to make it worse. We talked about this yesterday. Did you and your boyfriend go to the counselor appointment I made for you?"

"No. Nothin' will work wit him."

"Miss Strathmore, the two days Ricky has been in my class, he hasn't had any asthma symptoms at all. And he's a very sensitive little boy. I don't know how else to impress upon you that you shouldn't hit him. Help me understand, please, why is this happening?"

"His father ain't workin'. He's too damn lazy to look for work and whenever he gets upset he lashes out at Ricky."

"Well, tell me, what have you done to protect your son?"

John figured, from the abrupt tone of this teacher's voice, that she seemed to be reaching her limit of what she could do for this family. Couldn't blame her.

"Nothin', he'll beat me, too."

John had heard enough. He became livid at the mom and he liked Vicki's honest approach. And how long should a child have to wait for a pediatrician? He walked assuredly over to sit down in the chair next to Ricky who wheezed, his breathing labored. "What happened, champ?"

"I—can't—breathe." Ricky shook from nervousness. His small body hunched over, struggling to exhale the accumulated oxygen from his lungs.

John placed his right hand on Ricky's back and his left hand on his chest, without even bothering to ask his mother first.

Vicki intervened, though his mother couldn't have cared

less. "Excuse me?" She had the attitude of *why are you touching this child?*

John appreciated that.

"Ssh, I'm a doctor. You'll be all right, Ricky. Listen to me, okay, champ?" The boy nodded. "This is what I want you to do. Okay?" Ricky nodded again. "Do this with your mouth." John showed him how to pucker his lips and blow out the air. "Breathe in, and then let the air out, as much as you can. It's called exhaling."

John demonstrated inhaling and exhaling deeply, modeling for him. Ricky gazed up at him with bright blue open eyes. He watched John's chest extending out and pulling in.

"Wow, y'all sure big, sir."

John laughed. He liked the little kid. "Now when you exhale say, 'Ahh,' each time."

John bellowed it out to model it for him, not at all concerned with anyone watching. It was a loud bellow. It was enough to awaken patients who were dozing, waiting for their turn to see the doctor. Vicki perked up straight at attention in her seat. Ricky's mom barely looked up. Ricky tried it, clumsily at first, but he got it after a few attempts.

"Does he use an inhaler or nebulizer?"

"I couldn't afford it this month."

"What does he use?"

Ricky followed John's directions and some of his wheezing subsided.

"Good boy," John said.

"Proventil HFA, children's size."

The warmth of John's fingers rubbing with gentle pressure on Ricky's mid-back and his chest at the chest armor eased the tension in the area and facilitated pretty close to normal respiration, in a few minutes.

"I'm all better. What did you do? And no needle!"

John smiled at him compassionately.

His mother looked shocked, but she showed no gratitude. Vicki closed her eyes for a moment and gasped a short breath. John felt the connection. And he hoped it was mutual.

"Be right back." He winked at her, and her cheeks flushed. He smiled. That was a good sign.

He headed over to the attendant and asked to speak with the nurse who had chewed him out, as if he was a doctor on staff.

"Thank you for coming out, Kathryn. What is done down here for a parent who can't afford medicine for their child?"

Kathryn noticed Ricky. "Oh, the repeat customer. Dr. Trenton, what are you doing?" She pulled him out of hearing distance into a private area around a corner. "That you know you shouldn't be? Unless you have a very short memory?"

"Come on, Kathryn." He charmed her with his sincerity, radiating warmth. "She can't afford his inhaler."

"We'll get her one."

He sensed there's was a lot more she could tell him but, by law, she couldn't.

"Now stop what you're doing!"

"Thank you." He returned to Ricky. His breathing had become somewhat easier. Again, he decided to butt in where he knew he shouldn't. "Miss Strathmore, can I speak with you privately, please? Ricky, you stay with Miss Marin."

She shrank back deeper into her seat. "Who are you?"

John wasn't going to let her escape. "Dr. John Trenton. I'm a psychiatrist."

The mother became more belligerent by the moment. "I don't need no shrink."

"I beg to differ and I'm not asking." He was used to cutting right through the covering up behavior of this age group. "Come on. I could help you."

She looked at Vicki who sat wide-eyed, but Vicki gave her a nod that she should go. The woman stumbled up, and John knew there was something extremely wrong with her as well. He supported her arm, leading her over to the other side of the lounge area.

"Sit down."

She did.

John tried to ease her trepidation. "How long have you been with him?"

"We're not married or nothin'. Just staying wit him 'cause I ain't got no place t'go."

John radiated his usual compassion, warmth, and patience

with a willingness to listen. She broke down in a deluge of tears. She had needed to vent for a long time and she let it all out. That had been the case with most of his patients. He just remained quiet, focused on her, and listened.

"He's only twenty-one and has no idea how to be a father. He'll whip him in a minute. Ricky doesn't even have to do anytin' bad. It's all the drugs, the oxy, the blow. He hasn't had a day's work in over a year. Everytin' is on me. I work at Burger King behind the counter. My folks keep tellin' me to leave him an' I can move in wit them, but I don't want to put it on them. They can't afford nothin' either."

John didn't buy her excuse. "But you're working so you can contribute."

"I guess." She turned her eyes away.

"So what's really stopping you?"

Silence overcame her. His signature look told her he expected the truth.

"My pop. He won't let me do what I want. I moved out when I was fifteen an' had Ricky a year later, 'cause I didn't wanna take their crap an' follow their damn rules."

"Um, so how might your life have been different if you did follow their rules?"

His presence and steady gaze intimidated the truth out of her.

"I wouldn't got wit Ricky's father, dats for sure. They hate 'im."

"So what must you do now to protect your son?"

"Call 'em."

"You can use the phone at the desk." He accompanied her over to the reception desk and didn't even ask to use the phone. He just picked it up and handed the receiver to her.

Hopefully, she'll stay away from that guy.

She dialed. "Mommy, it's me. I'm at da hospital wit Ricky. Can we come home?"

At the desk, Kathryn came out to get him. "Dr. Trenton, your father is ready to go." She exited as quickly as she came in, sending him a clear signal.

John smirked. He understood that vicious glare. As she trailed away, he said, "Thank you, Kathryn." He removed his card from his wallet and handed it to Vicki. In a very charming yet enticing tone, he said, "Call my cell tomorrow afternoon, and you can take me around to see the sights in the county."

She smiled, taking the card, and he winked at her.

"Ooh." For a moment, she looked disoriented. She then turned her gaze on him.

Oh yeah. I could make her feel real good.

John disappeared through the doors to his father's room before she could respond. She read the card. "Dr. John Trenton, Forensic Psychiatry. Forensics? Uh oh!"

CHAPTER 17

Present Day:

John observed Barbara cocoon herself against the headboard pulling up the two crisp, white layers of sheets until they covered her to her neck. She bent her knees into her chest with her arms wrapped around them and buried her face in her knees, as if to shield herself from him.

"You're not touching me." Her voice was almost inaudible.

Standing next to the bed, he placed, a warm, kind, left hand on her shoulder. She retaliated with remorseless wiggles to shrug it off. She stiffened, rather adamantly, so he removed it. "Tell me why not." He peered right into her soul.

"I'm doctor phobic." Her tears began to flow, along with heavier breathing, but John sensed they were just crocodile tears.

He slouched down in an armchair next to the bed, his body relaxed, but on guard. "How did that start?"

She didn't pick up her head to look at him. "I don't know, when I was a kid, I guess."

"Well, you're an adult now. And something is definitely going on inside of you. There's some imbalance somewhere."

"No, there isn't."

"No? You go from calm into a rage in less than a second. Why is that?"

"I only went into a rage—and I admit it was a rage, I do— when I couldn't penetrate that warped brain of his." She tilted her head to the right when speaking. "I just lost it, but it won't happen again."

"And what about attacking me in the ER?"

She straightened up. "I hit you. I didn't attack you."

"So that makes it acceptable?"

"I'm sorry. That must have been the sedative. I never had that before. I don't know what came over me."

He sensed something was way off base, so she wasn't getting special treatment or empathy. "So don't you think you need to exert more control over that? Let me take your blood pressure," he said, asserting himself without hesitation.

"No. No. *No!*" Her eyes spit defiance, hostility, and hatred.

Too many negative emotions cast out all at once were off putting in a supposedly well-functioning woman. It compelled him to question what he was up against here. Barbara was five years younger than he was. That was a gigantic stretch to his specialty age. He didn't think Carlson had a clue as to what her story was. Now, by law, it was up to him to figure it out in three days. There was no time to waste. This gorgeous woman was going to be a problem. He realized he had to confront her issues head on.

"You know, if you would have had a physical by your doctor within six to eight months ago, I wouldn't have to be doing much of this, maybe a few tests, but not to the extent we need to do now. You told Gladys it was a few years ago in California?"

"Yes."

"Then you're long overdue. And your mother died from breast cancer?"

"They were my adoptive parents."

'Uh huh," he said, suspicious. "Well, there are discrepancies in what you told Gladys, and I quote: You had the mammogram because of family history, so which is it?" He hitched his eyebrows and smiled.

She swallowed hard and pulled the sheet up to her chin. "Will nothing get past you?"

"No. Never. That's my job. Now straighten out your legs, and let me take your blood pressure. Come on. It doesn't hurt."

Sniffling, she condescended and stuck her arm out. He wrapped her arm in the cuff, pumped it up, and listened with his stethoscope.

"It's high, 145 over 85."

"That's because I'm as nervous as hell."

"Don't think so. Come, sit up." He assisted her and used the stethoscope to listen to her heart, pulling down the gown slightly in the front so he could put it on her skin. His left hand was on her shoulder. "No, hon. Way too fast. I'm ordering an electrocardiogram."

"What the fuck is wrong with you, Dr. Clairvoyant? It's high because you're turning me on!"

"No, you're not."

"What?"

"You're not exhibiting any signs of arousal," he said in a matter-of-fact, clinical voice.

"You're kidding me, right?"

He grinned.

"Get the hell out of here!"

John did not intend to give up his control. "No. Not happening."

"I don't need an EKG."

"Yes. You certainly do. And these are the tests I'm ordering. Relax, lay back." He guided her back onto the pillow.

"Tests as in plural?"

"Yes. We're starting with a full range of blood work."

"No blood tests. I'm afraid of needles."

"Tough. Better question, what are you afraid that I'll find out?"

She clutched her stomach. "Nothing. What are you looking for?"

"Specifically?"

She nodded a meek yes.

"We're doing a sequential multiple analyses, CBC count with differentials, blood type, thyroid function test, vitamin and mineral deficiencies, hair, heavy metal analysis, medication levels, hormone levels, liver and kidney function tests, vision, candida, allergies, tests to weed out any adrenal, cardiac, respiratory, neurological disturbances, and tox screens."

"No you're not. If you're so clairvoyant, why can't you just see everything like an X-ray, and write all that down?"

"Ah. Funny lady. That does not hold up in court. I need the medical science. That's just for starters."

"But why do you even need this?"

"Okay, fair question. For one, if I can show Carlson that you have an imbalance somewhere that triggered your rage, maybe he won't press charges for assault on the cops. You can still be arrested. He knows very well where to find you. Secondly, he's saying you had hallucinations. I want to eliminate any organic involvement. Clear enough?"

"Very. But no blood work. What other tests?"

"Yes. We have to. It's nonnegotiable, so don't even try. And also an MRI, PET, CAT of the brain, urine analysis, and I'll throw in a breast, pelvic, and rectal exam, since you haven't had that either in God knows how many years. The psych tests, as well. And whatever else presents itself to need further exploration."

"It's a big *no* to everything. No MRI, I'm claustrophobic. No internal. You're not touching me there. And as for the psych tests, I hate to burst your bubble, but I give them also and know all of the acceptable answers, so that won't be useful to you at all."

"You're just a bundle of cooperation, aren't you? I'll get you a female doctor for the internals."

"No. You can't make me. Don't I have rights? You can't do this to me."

"If you came in on your own volition and your doctor ordered tests you didn't want, you could refuse. But you're here under a different set of circumstances. We need to do this even if it's against your will. The lab techs will be in to draw your blood. You know, your lack of cooperation is speaking volumes."

"Want volumes? I'll give you volumes! Oh—" Her voice rose, louder with each word. "No—they—won't!"

"Are you going to cause a scene?"

"A scene, like you've never seen in your life."

John signaled to the observation camera in the wall with his hand to bring on the techs. Two men, as big as John, entered, wearing light blue hospital uniforms.

At first, she was startled. "You expect them to scare me?"

"So much for the promises. I'd like you to use some reality testing here. You against the three of us? Come on, think a little. But then again, you didn't with the cops. And they were armed."

John positioned himself by the right side of the bed and the techs on the other. They prepared to handle her. Before he even suspected she could do anything, she commenced fighting.

"Get the fuck away from me now! All of you! Get the fuck away from me!" She lashed out at all three of them with her arms, and then she started kicking, with violent rigid kicks. She kicked the sheets off, exposing herself with just the hospital gown on. Her body bobbed up and down so violently, they didn't know what limb to grab first. They didn't know where to look. She struck their bodies, hard. She had strong legs— strong dancer legs—and now the gown had worked its way up to her neck. "You can't do this to me!" She was fully exposed, her voluptuous breasts bared, and she was not shy at all at letting these three men see her in action, raw and in action.

"Want to give her something, Doc?" A tech had to yell over her screaming, struggling to hold onto her leg. She writhed under his control.

"Can't give her anything, not until I find out what's in her system." John had had enough. He labored to hold down her right leg and arm. She was just warming up and he wouldn't let it go any farther. He removed his stethoscope and tossed it on the chair behind him without looking, lay down on top of her, grabbed her left arm, and put on a wrist restraint attached to the side of the bed. Her body riveted under him, and it was some hot body at that.

John felt her warm breasts on his chest. It was a lot for him to ignore. He closed his eyes for a split second and swallowed while turning his attention to secure her left ankle.

She pounded on his back with her free hand. "No, I'm claustrophobic! *Stop, no!* Don't put these on me!"

He had to ignore her pleas. There was a time crunch. If his

suspicions were correct, and there was a physiological basis for her behavior, he had the methods to help her.

He rose and grabbed her right wrist, before her fist came down on his head, and secured her arm in the restraint while the techs bent over her and secured her right leg. That was some feat and one that he'd had to do before, but not on such a gorgeous woman. It was a workout. Showing his usual respect, as soon as the restraints were on, he pulled the gown back down over her.

She continued in a full panic attack, screaming, "*No! No!* Take these off me!" in a high-pitched little girl voice. "Daddy, *no*, Daddy *no*, don't, don't this to me!"

John glanced up at the techs, knowing from experience what had transpired—her transition, from defiance to psychosis. It started by her refusal to comply, probably defiant on principle, as she didn't want him to find out certain things about her—things she might have hidden for years. But then, when the restraints were put on, she went in to a severe psychotic episode. Her eyes and voice changed as she relived traumas from her past. That was the usual. Unresolved traumas from his patients' pasts always surfaced in therapy, especially when he exerted stress upon them. He decided to go with the role-play. John got into his character, the role of Daddy, as Barbara had called him. She was not much different from his other patients. He prepared to be harsh. He had to be.

"What am I doing?"

"Don't beat me. I can't take it when you beat me."

"I'm not going to beat you. You're safe. What's my name?"

She cried hysterically. "Bill. No. You're Kenny. No, Thomas. I don't know which one. Don't send me away again. Please, just don't send me away!" She sweated. Her heart palpitated. Her eyes looked frenzied—pupils bulged—but she stared coldly, blank, and non-perceptive of the present reality. She was somewhere else, somewhere in her deeply troubled past.

"What's your name, little girl?" John grasped onto his intuition and it paid off.

"Kellie."

"Kellie what?" He was not surprised the he'd gotten something.

"Kellie Wilson." She gasped for air, hyperventilating. Her body was hot, her gown saturated with her own sweat.

He had uncovered enough for now and didn't want to torture her. Surely, she'd had enough, so he'd use the snippet of information she let out, but he knew restraining her was necessary. John covered her with the sheets, leaned over her, and placed his hands on her shoulders as she still struggled to get free.

He then removed his right hand from her shoulder and held her face, forcing her to look eye-to-eye with him. "*STOP IT!*" he yelled, right into her face, and it worked.

He'd taught patients to use STOP IT therapy for panic attacks, but they said it to themselves. With an occurrence like this, he had to say it. She looked at him, quivering, with fear in her eyes. She was quiet and still, but continued to hyperventilate. At least for now it worked to bring her back to the present.

Calmly and compassionately, he moved his right hand onto her chest right over the bronchial tubes and, after a couple of minutes, the warmth from his hand slowed down and normalized her breathing.

"Barbara, look at me." She clamped her eyes shut. "Barbara, now—look—at—me. Come on, look at me."

She opened her eyes a sliver. He moved her face so they were eye to eye. She didn't fight.

"Good girl. Barbara, listen to me." She opened her eyes fully. "I not only took an oath to do no harm, but also to dare to care. So If I have to be aggressive to help you, I will. Now after they take the blood, I'll take these off, Okay?" She let out a scared moan, which he interpreted as an affirmative response. "Good, very good. Turn your left arm over and let them do their job. Take some deep breaths and look at me."

This time, she allowed him to move her arm. Exhaustion and fright had weakened her. A tech put a tourniquet around her upper arm, prepared the butterfly needle, and approached her.

"Just a little poke, a little one." She winced at the needle's insertion. "Come on," John said. "That doesn't hurt."

"Yes, it does. Is it over yet?"

"No. Don't think about it." John needed to keep her attention on him. "Tell me when were you restrained?"

"Never."

John pushed to get her to remember in the present. "No. I don't buy it. Only someone restrained under horrible conditions would react with such extreme anxiety as you did. What happened to you?"

She whined again. He stared at her with a determined look and remained silent. He would continue to stare until she had realized he wouldn't let up. He would reach the emotions she had buried deep within her core for a long time.

"Go to hell!"

Her hostile response was the confirmation he wanted, that she was, indeed, cognizant of what she shrouded.

The techs finished and removed the tourniquet.

"Thank you."

"Sure thing, Doc." They quickly left the room.

"Get these off me now."

"Not until you calm down and your vitals normalize. And I bet you can do it consciously. I'm staying with you. I'm not leaving you. Take some deep breaths. Inhale through your nose and exhale through your mouth."

After a few minutes of compliance, he used the stethoscope to check her heart rate. Still erratic.

"A little better. A little while longer to calm down. Then I'll get you a new gown, and you can take a shower. There's plenty of soap and shampoo in the bathroom, and I'll have an attendant change the sheets. You got everything soaked. Okay?"

"Yes. I'm all right now. Please take these off. See? I could never do an MRI."

"Yes, you could. I'll give you a little Valium, and it'll calm you enough. But not until I get the blood test results back. I'll take these off now, but don't you dare take a swing at me."

"I won't. I promise."

"Yeah, you told me that before. I see how good your word is. You may be in charge in school, but you're not in charge here. I mean it. It would be in your best interests to control these tantrums." He removed the left hand restraint and antici-pated an aggressive reaction. None. Then the left leg. None. Then the right leg. None. And lastly, the right arm. Also none. He relaxed and sat down on the chair. "Want to tell me any-thing?"

"Yeah. I feel sorry for your wife."

"Why is that?"

"You're one tough bastard."

"Yes. I am. And I could also do without the foul mouth. But I was thinking more in terms of what you don't want me to find in your blood."

"All right! You'll find it anyway. I used coke this morning before I met with Carlson. I've met with him about six times and have spoken and met with those other two, and they all get me so nervous. They laughed at me and treated me like an in-competent female. They have a badge, so they think it gives them balls. I needed something to calm me down. I'm not ad-dicted. I'm not going through withdrawal or anything."

"But it didn't calm you down. Did it? It put you so on edge, you went into a rage and attacked three cops. So what's the purpose?" He got up. "Look up at me." He checked her nose. "No coke residue here. Open your mouth." He checked the inside of her cheeks. "None there. So where?"

She looked away.

"Forget it. I just made it up to get you off my back. So now what? Are you going to drug me up to the gills like other shrinks until I cooperate?"

"What's been your experience with psychiatrists?"

"None personal."

Her aura shouted to him.

Big lie. Okay.

"With some of my children at school."

"Nah," he said. "Not with me. I'm the talking shrink. No chemical straightjacket from me."

"That's an interesting choice of words."

"Statistically, the drugs do more harm than good. I'll do a lot to you but without drugs."

"Bring it!"

"You have a dirty mind." He pointed to his ring. "Married. Commitment. All right. Here's the way it's going to work. If I find cocaine in the toxicology report, I'm personally giving you an internal. Enough with the lying. Now anything else you didn't want me to find out?"

"I had a hysterectomy ten years ago. That will show up with hormones, right?"

"Yes. Why a hysterectomy?"

"I had extensive fibroids and some polyps, everything was benign, and I don't want kids anyway."

"Anything else?"

"No. I just feel so filthy. I desperately need that shower."

"I'll take care of that. You'll have enough time and privacy, but if you stay in there too long, attendants will come in."

"How will they know?"

"You're in an observation room. Everything that is done, except in the bathroom, is recorded and seen at the nurse's station."

"You're kidding me?"

"No, I am not. This is a seventy-two hour observation room. Go take your shower and, while you're in there, an attendant will change your sheets and make the bed comfortable for you."

He exhaled in exhaustion, exiting the room, relieved that it was over, but knowing he hadn't scratched the surface with her. He exhaled several times to expel her negative energy and leaned against the wall, trying to regain his composure, while he contemplated the seriousness of what had just transpired. He could just imagine what she was holding onto and how much pain she'd endured. He put his hands into his lab coat pockets. His left hand wrapped around a black tourmaline log he used to deflect negativity. It had worked overtime the last hour. In his right pocket, he felt the malachite tumbled stone broken in two with parts crumbled into the lining of his pocket.

Oh, man. She really is dangerous.

He had heard of malachite breaking when the wearer was in a dangerous situation, but this was the first time it had actually happened to him. He glanced up at the ceiling.

Thanks for the heads up.

∽∾∽

Barbara sat up and stared out the window. She saw nothing though the frosted glass.

I've got to get out of here. What if he finds out? What if he doesn't stop? And from the looks of that bastard, he won't. I know. So what if I lose my job? I'm skipping the country any-way, after I get rid of that Clancy bum. I'll let him give me the internal. Force him to make me climax. Then press charges for sex abuse. When he's suspended and loses his license, I'll be out by then. I'll get out on a technicality. Improper medical procedure or something. I'll hunt him down, kill his wife and kids right in front of him, and then I'll kill him. What pleasure I'll have watching him die. It'll be so worth it for what he's putting me through.

∽∾∽

Inside his office, Morgan anxiously dialed the phone, as Steve looked over a file sitting at the luxury desk.

"Barbara, where the hell are you?" Morgan demanded when he got no answer. He turned to Steve. "I haven't been able to get through to her."

"Call her school."

"She hasn't shown up there either." Morgan stood, still holding the handset, and paced back and forth, staring out the window facing Park Avenue.

"So she took a vacation for a few days. What's the big deal?"

"No way, and leave her precious clinic?"

"I thought you didn't like her."

"I don't. But my board put through her donation at twice the amount, right after I ended the meeting. At that rate, I'll go broke! And you—you made me buy a new car!"

"Hold on. I didn't make you do anything. She told me she would go public if you didn't make good on this, and you can't afford—"

Morgan dialed again. "Any publicity, yeah, yeah. She doesn't deserve a single dime of my money."

CHAPTER 18

John dreaded having to go to therapy more than he had ever dreaded anything in his life, lately. The thought of having to open up to a stranger about issues he had under control and to give up his dominance was daunting.

His blood pressure was higher than normal. John sensed the tension around his chest. He had armored himself and deliberately shut down, and had no intention of allowing hurt feelings to surface if he could help it. This *mere* psychologist wasn't going to unravel him. He would have to do intense bodywork tonight to loosen up after what he faced now.

Hesitating, he entered the warm and welcoming light-brown, vinyl-paneled office of Dr. Burt Landers, PhD in clinical psychology. The receptionist greeted him. Right away, John focused on her personal appearance. He stared at the matronly woman who was probably in her late sixties, though she looked much older due to her ill-fitting clothing. Her blouse was a couple of sizes too big for her, and the once-vibrant colors had faded from multiple laundering. Overall, the office lacked the professionalism he respected.

"Hello, Dr. Trenton. Dr. Landers will see you now. Right through there."

"Thank you." John stopped for a moment and knocked on the door, before he changed his mind and tried to manufacture a reason to leave.

"Come in."

John opened the door and was not pleased with what he encountered, an elderly man in his late sixties, bald, short, and stout, with critical looking eyes. He realized, right then and there, from the doctor's intense look that he couldn't act foolishly or there would be repercussions from the department. But that didn't mean he wasn't going to try. Carlson had done it to him again and the anger festered.

"Come and sit down, Dr. Trenton."

Landers extended his hand, and John shook it, smirking at the rather weak grip.

"What can I help you with Dr. Trenton?"

John sat back in the chair, stiff and on guard. "Did Lieutenant Carlson tell you anything?"

I'll be out of here in a minute. This guy's a wimp.

"No, why don't you?"

"I don't know why he wants me to see you. I'm fine, really. We had a hostage situation at the hospital. The hostage-taker is a patient of mine, and I knew I'd be able to handle it." John was overconfident. "I knew he wouldn't hurt me, so I refused to let the ESU go in. I don't know why Carlson is making such a big deal over it. I've debriefed my staff. They know not to let this happen again. The patient is locked away at Rikers' mental health building, awaiting indictment for five counts of murder, as he should. I've done this in more dangerous situations before, and I've never had to see someone, so I really do not need to waste anymore of your time." He prepared to leave, bolstering himself up with his arms on the chair.

Landers gave him a stern look. "Sit down, John."

John shot him an unappreciative glare in return.

Landers didn't back down. "This is a mandatory hour."

John complied and sat back down.

"Now what else is going on?" Landers asked.

"Nothing I can't handle." After two minutes of silence, John caved. None of his self-armoring protected him now. He did have a lot to get off his chest. He'd admitted it to Carlson. Slumping back in the chair, he swallowed hard. "My wife left me and went back to Florida. It was the same day as the hostage situation."

"That's a lot of stress for one day."

"Yes, it sure is. And I haven't spoken to Vicki in two weeks. I'm worried. She won't answer my texts, or calls. I spoke with my mother who told me she was okay but depressed. And that I should give her some time."

"So how are you handling it?"

"I'm worried about her but managing."

"You don't look like you're managing," Landers observed. "You look like a man who's gone through a battle with himself and lost. The wrinkles in your forehead probably deepened the last couple of weeks."

John looked away from Landers for a moment and groaned.

Landers sighed. "I'm sure you tell your patients that if they're not honest, they're not going to get what they should out of a session. Same goes for you."

"Not so. My patients are sociopaths, psychopaths, and psychotics. They haven't had an honest thought in years."

"All the more reason for you to be honest with yourself. Why did she leave?"

"Vicki didn't like the city life."

"Maybe on the surface. What goes deeper?" More silence. "John, if you're going to be successful in your marriage you need to confront your own demons, too."

John felt his inner wall cracking. "I pushed her away."

"How did you push her away?"

John hated talking about this. It was painful to acknowledge his part in it, and he became anxious. He twisted his wedding band around his finger and fidgeted in the seat. "I acted like a child the day after she left, and I told her I didn't want children which is the furthest thing from the truth. I was just so upset that she'd left. I was always the rock, and she'd never seen me so vulnerable. She must've thought I was just mean-spirited, which I'm not."

"What else pushed her away? Your blow up was the culmination. What led to it?"

"I made too many demands and had too many expectations. I expected her to like my life style, the parties, going out, my social sphere."

"And you got disappointed when she didn't?"

"Yes."

"What do you miss?"

"The way she took care of me, the way she stood up to me, the dinners, the camaraderie, someone to go home to at night, the sex—the sex was fabulous. I love everything about her."

"Tell me about the sex."

"Now that's personal."

"You brought it up. I don't mean the details. What made her better than the others?"

"The doctors, lawyers, were stiff, rigid, no energy flow. There wasn't that wild excitement, that willingness for new exploration."

"I didn't ask you about the others. I asked you about Vicki."

"You really want me to address this, don't you?" John was silent for a minute. "Why?" He was silent for a longer minute. "Sex is a very important part of my life. I knew I was going to marry her our first night together. I'd been looking for this a long time. Her warmth, her innocence, her energy, her nurturance, openness, even her stubbornness—we were both in sync. She didn't have any armors built up. We could go on for hours. She and I consumed each other. Our libidos were completely satisfied with each other."

"Armors. That's right. Now I know where I heard your name before. You're the forensic psychiatrist who uses Orgone Therapy with schizophrenics."

"It's Medical Orgone Therapy and that's right. And quite successfully at times, without having to resort to medication. That, in combination with proper nutrition, enables the body to do wonders healing itself."

"Impressive. And now that you let her go, what are you going to do?"

"With what?"

"You said sex is a very important part of your life. So how are you going to release your tensions now?"

"I don't know. I've had so many women, looking for the right one, but there was always something missing, and I didn't see them again."

"You just described yourself as a sex addict."

"Excuse me? I've never thought of myself as a sex addict. I've been monogamous with Vicki since we met. No! I am absolutely not a sex addict."

"How often do you need sex?"

"Uh, Vicki and I made love almost every night." Landers did a double take. "Look, I have a frustrating job, tense and dangerous at times. Sex and the gym are my release."

"That's not what I asked you. Sex for release is not the same thing as making love. You said completely satiated, so sex every night? You, more than anyone, should know that. Orgone Therapy is all about the full orgasm."

"Primarily. But it's a lot more than that. It's about freeing up the blockages in the body so one can feel the flow of energy, be more fulfilled and sexually satiated, and deal with buried traumas from childhood. All of that which inhibits a productive life. And I said almost every night. But we always had some physical contact before we went to sleep, even if it was just talking and holding each other close. Perhaps I need sex more than most, but I've never had a woman say 'No.'"

"You're drawn to women who say 'yes.'"

"I'm not a sex addict. I was raised in a home where my parents were always demonstrative. Do you even know what behaviors describe a sex addict?"

"How long were they married?"

"Forty-six years. Answer my question."

"That's different from you."

John became more irate with this doctor by the moment. "I was single until I was forty-two. I wasn't going to lead a celibate life. You still didn't answer my question."

"Okay, then. You tell me what describes a sex addict," Landers demanded.

"Multiple affairs, one night stands." Landers hiked his eyebrows. John glared right back. "Don't look at me like that. The list is far from complete. Consistent use of porn, unsafe sex, cybersex, use of prostitutes, exhibitionism, obsessive dating through personal ads, voyeurism, sexual harassment, molestation, failure to resist sexual impulses, public sex, mood swings, irritability, headaches when the need is there and it's not satisfied, and history of sexual abuse. These people are armored, emotionally blocked. Shall I continue?"

"And you can't pick a few out of that list that pertain to you?"

"Absolutely not! It isn't like a Chinese menu. It's not just one item. It's a composite. I told you I've been monogamous with Vicki since our first night together. Even when I came back to New York and she stayed in Florida, I didn't go with another woman. Even now the past two weeks, I haven't sought out another woman," John shouted. "I don't have to justify myself to you!"

He caught himself and shook his head. He hadn't raised his voice this much in years.

"You're very angry."

"You're damn straight, I'm angry. I'm livid! You're accusing me of something I'm not. So this is going nowhere. And you're wasting my time. I left a new patient to come here and she could have benefited from more time with me."

Landers ignored John's outburst. "And you never had a long-term relationship before Vicki?"

"On and off. Why do you only want to talk about sex?"

"That's my specialty."

"Are you serious? So that's why Carlson sent me to you?" John was still louder than usual but a tad more subdued.

"Guess so. Why did you think?"

"The age difference. You're older than me so he knew I'd respect you more." Now John spoke in a normal tone.

"So a young therapist couldn't be effective?"

"I'd turn them into mincemeat."

"That's angry. You seem to be full of anger today. Is that the way you treat women?"

John knew damn well he was angry. He didn't need Landers to tell him that. "No. Not at all. Where did that come from?"

"Well, the main problem you're having is with a woman. In your professional life, you're on top of your game. No need to talk about that."

John hesitated a moment before speaking. "Look I thoroughly enjoy sex and making women happy. And being made happy as well."

"Even your friends know it's a problem. Lieutenant Carlson sent you here."

"He conned me. Said it was for debriefing the hostage situation."

"Why should he have to con you? You're a psychiatrist. You know the importance and impact therapy can have."

"Guess I didn't want to talk about personal things."

"And you're still resisting. Afraid to give up control?"

John shot him an *I've-got-to-get-out-of-here* look. This mere psychologist not only hit the target, he hit the bull's eye.

"All right, the hour is up. You have two more mandatory hours. Shall I see you next week, same time?"

John took a deep breath and let out a long deliberate sigh before answering. "Definitely. I don't know why, but yes. Thank you."

They shook hands. Landers smiled. "Anything else you want to say?"

John was irritated and couldn't wait to leave. "Like what?"

"An apology for your aggressive outburst would be appropriate."

John was angry at himself for misreading this guy. Still, he wanted to get even. "No way. You're a therapist. Deal with it." He snatched open the door, wanting to break off the knob.

"Sit down, John. You're not leaving yet."

John couldn't believe he was being spoken to like this. "What?"

"I never let patients leave in such an angry state. And I don't have anyone after you today, so consider this session two."

"Oh, come on. I can't take any more of this today," John muttered as he slumped back down in the chair.

The comment whizzed straight into Lander's catcher's mitt. "What's going on with that?"

John clenched his fists and gritted his teeth. "I feel like I'm being disciplined, that's what's going on. And I had more than enough of that growing up."

"Tell me more about that."

Damn! Why did I let that slip out?

Feelings began to surface that John had not had in years. "My parents were very strict. I never got my way with them. When my father was reprimanding me, shivers went through me."

"Is that happening now?"

"Yes," John admitted, although unwillingly.

"How did they discipline you?"

John shifted in the chair to a more prone position. "I was never spanked or hit. They believe hands are only meant to hug. So do I. I could never hit a child—or anyone for that matter. Theirs was mental. I was a very early talker and loved to be with them. They encouraged talking, so no pacifier for me. So the biggest punishment was being sent to my room, away from them. I'd be grounded, couldn't go out. They'd take away Tae Kwon Do which is a passion of mine, and I couldn't go to workouts. They gave me extra work assignments. That kind of stuff."

"What happened when you got out of control and raised your voice?"

"Like I did before?"

"Uh uh."

"That really didn't happen. They didn't blow up and they didn't push my buttons so I'd blow. I didn't see it in my family," John reminisced. "But I was still getting punishments into my teens."

"Give me an example of one."

John inhaled deeply before he spoke. "Okay. I had three exams that day, eleventh grade. I was ahead a grade, and I knew I'd aced them. I got straight A's all the time and I worked very hard for them. But I came home tired and just wanted to vegetate in front of the TV. I'd been watching for about an hour, and my dad said, 'Okay, enough relaxing. Start your homework before dinner.' And I said, 'No.' I just wanted to relax. We went back and forth a few times. He just casually took the remote, shut off the TV, and ordered me to my room. I got up, sulking, but I went."

"And that was the end of it?"

"No such luck. He came into my room, and I said, 'Dad, I'm sorry.' He responded—and this is verbatim, 'In medical school, you'll have no time to relax so you better get used to it.' And, boy, was he ever right. He looked at the historical novel I had to read over the weekend. I had just the first hundred fifty pages to read, which was half, and then answer five essay questions in in the back of the book. It was for an AP English lit course. He told me that since I was grounded for the weekend—which took me by surprise, but punishments were always more than one—he wanted me to read the entire novel and answer the ten questions in the back of the book. I tried to get out of it by saying that it wouldn't be following my teacher's instructions, but that didn't fly. I spent the entire weekend in my room doing that assignment. And I didn't complain at all about it."

"What did your teacher say?"

"Ah, this one you'll like."

"Why?"

"My teacher was about twenty-three, on the petite side, and a knock out. Wow, Melody Smythe—every boy in the class had a crush on her. We all fantasized what it would be like to do it with her. And my imagination was really vivid. I handed in the paper, and she saw immediately that it was longer than she'd assigned. She said, 'John, you didn't follow my instructions.' I told her I knew that, but my dad gave it to me as a punishment. And she was like, 'What did you do?' I told her that I mouthed off. And she told me to come to her office after school so I could delineate where her assignment left off, and then she said she'd count the rest for next week's assignment."

"Don't tell me you—"

John nodded his head and smiled. "Yeah, we had an affair that lasted over eight months."

"Eight months? How did that evolve?"

"At fifteen, I was already built. Not as tall as I am now, but big. I was already shaving. Very sexually mature. Not a virgin. When I went into her office, Melody told me to sit down and I saw that the buttons on her blouse were undone. She took out her ponytail band and her long blonde hair was so sensual. She seduced me and I was quite willing. This woman taught me everything on how to treat a woman. What a woman likes, erogenous zones, cunnilingus, fellatio, how to undress a woman to arouse them more, different kinds of foreplay, that a traditional bed can be boring, every position imaginable, and we were young and very flexible. Everything. She had a couch in the office, but after the first time I went to her apartment, two, sometimes three times a week."

Dr. Landers leaned back. "How did you get away with it for so long?"

"I never bragged about it to my friends. Never told anyone. There was no texting or Facebook back then. We never called each other. We kept it completely to ourselves. I told my parents that I was going to the library after school to do research. I only came home an hour or two late. Then we started on Saturdays, after Tae Kwon Do. I told my mom I had to go to the library. The library worked for a long time. Then a neighbor of hers, a crabby senior, who Melody had told she was tutoring me, saw us. Melody opened the door and we kissed as I was entering the apartment. The neighbor called the police with an incident of child abuse. The cops came and arrested Melody, for child abuse by a person in position of trust, and brought us down to the precinct. It was the only time I was ever handcuffed, and I'll tell you, it was scary."

"And then what?"

"I tried to convince the cops I wasn't abused. I actually told the cops in a real cocky tone, 'Do I look abused?' I went on to say we were close in age and we were simply enjoying each other. That didn't go over too well. Melody pled guilty. They'd caught us in bed, naked, with me on top of her and her arms wrapped around me with us kissing. No argument there. She got her teaching license revoked and three years jail time, but she only did about a year. And I got a two-week, in-house suspension. That way, it wouldn't go on my record. And it led to a of couple months of being grounded. I never went to see her. They told me I wouldn't be allowed in and my parents forbade it. My parents couldn't believe that I had gone along with it, and they were so embarrassed, but they met her, and they did realize she was the type I'd go for. And it still is. I only go for blondes. And about twelve years ago, during my psychiatric residency, Melody was institutionalized for schizophrenia, and she became one of my patients. She had moved around the country, teaching in private schools where she didn't need the state certification, and she had been doing the same thing until she came back to New York where she had a breakdown."

"Did she recognize you?"

"No she didn't. And that actually hurt my feelings a bit. 'We had so much fun, and you don't remember me?' But I got over it. Melody was so incoherent and non-functioning that she didn't recognize herself when looking in a mirror. I did recuse myself as her physician because of our history, so I don't know of her status now."

"Are you feeling any calmer now?"

"Actually, yes. Going through painful memories does that, calms the anger when you let it come out into the open."

"Okay then, I'll see you next week."

"Thank you, and sorry about the outburst."

They shook hands and John left the office, letting out a sigh of relief.

Damn! What made me hash up all that now? Man, my parents still have a hold on me. I'm forty-five, and they still have the same hold on me as when I was fifteen. How in hell do I change that? I'm the most important person in the world to them.

CHAPTER 19

Three Years Earlier:

John propelled himself across the luxury outdoor seventy-five-foot-by forty-foot kidney-shaped pool in Bueno Terrace without missing a breath. The sun was shining and not a cloud was in sight.

He enjoyed the elegance and high-end construction of the surroundings. The ninety lounge chairs with strong and supportive cushions, lining the perimeter of the pool on the hexagon shaped tiles, interspersed with tables and umbrellas, presented the utmost in relaxation. Palm trees and red sisters alternated in sections with huge, flat leaf philodendrons in oversized dark green pots, surrounding the perimeter of the gated area. It was truly a tropical resort paradise, dressed up to the max.

In the lap lane, he was not at all concerned with his hard kicks splashing anyone else in the pool, especially the three sixty-something women in the middle, holding on to their three foot long, Styrofoam noodles which allowed them to float effortlessly. He didn't care if he made them scatter like pins in a bowling alley. He was in his own little world as he swam lap after lap in perfect swimmer's-body formation.

After about ten laps, John stood up and faced the stares of the women. He sauntered out of the pool with a snide smile on his face, knowing everyone ogled him from all directions.

He had heard the women yelling at him, but he did what he

did best, ignored them. After he moseyed over to his lounge and grabbed a towel, he made himself comfortable and prepared to relish the sun.

A few moments later, his cell phone rang.

"Dr. Trenton."

"Hi, it's Vicki. How are ya, darlin'?"

I didn't even know her first name. Vicki, that's cute.

"I'm doing just fine. I'm at the pool in Bueno. Do you come here?"

"Yes, actually I do, darlin'. I can be there in twenty."

Oh man! That southern voice. She could melt me with that voice.

"Great, looking forward to it. See you soon." He hung up, grinning.

She called. Now let the games begin.

Right on schedule, he felt Vicki's presence in front of him as he savored the rays. "You're blocking my sun."

"You better be careful, darlin'. Florida sun is strong." Taking the lounge next to him, she tossed down her bag and removed her top and shorts, revealing a conservative two-piece girly pink bathing suit showing very little cleavage.

He turned on his side and looked at her, quite impressed that she didn't throw herself at him in a skimpy G-string. He appreciated the modesty for a change. He had to respect this one. "How's the little guy?"

"I won't see him till Monday. But I can assure you he's going to have a lot of problems."

"I bet. And your father?"

"He's good, too. It was indigestion, not his heart."

"That's great." He motioned for her to sit on the lounge and moved his legs over to accommodate her. "Come here."

She sat on the edge of the lounge, leaning in toward him. Her long, sensuous, sweet-smelling hair fell onto his chest.

"So where are you taking me to show me the sights?"

"How about I take you to a country restaurant to show you how the natives have dinner, and then we can go back to my house for dessert." He ran his fingers through her hair. "I make a great apple pie," she said.

He pulled her down on him and whispered in her ear. "I

was thinking of something sweeter, that's simpler with a lot less calories."

She giggled like a shy little girl. He sensed her innocence, and again she turned a shade of pink. "Don't start now, darlin'. My goodness. You *are* a dangerous man."

Blushing again? He contemplated what they'd be doing later. "Acknowledged and agreed. But every woman needs at least one dangerous man in her life. So give me a good reason not to start."

"My father is watching us."

"You're kidding?"

"Nope. He's probably walking over here right now."

"There is a guy, about sixty-five, medium build, shorts, and T shirt, coming our way." *What? She is an adult, isn't she?*

"That's him." She turned around in the nick of time. "Hi, Daddy."

He extended his hand to shake. "Sheriff Marin."

John met the firm hand shake. "John Trenton, nice to meet you."

Marin cut right to the point, not mincing words. "You better be a gentleman with my daughter. I put the bad guys in jail."

"That's why I'm still single, by the way," she said.

Good to know. "Well, I keep the bad guys out of jail and put them in mental hospitals."

"You a lawyer?"

"Forensic psychiatrist."

"Ah. Consider yourself warned. Have fun, but not too much." Marin walked off before John could respond.

"So he drives around in those Dodge Chargers marked Sheriff? Isn't he getting a little too old for that?"

"Those are his deputies."

"Deputies? What is this, the Wild West?"

She was insulted. "My father is an elected official, the top elected position in the county."

"Highest official? Like a police commissioner?"

"Yup. Top cop."

Damn, I just can't get away from it. "In New York, the police commissioner is selected by the mayor."

"It's still top cop. And my father doesn't appreciate being talked to like that, so you're on thin ice already."

"So what else is new? I'm not going to worry about it." *He can't watch us all the time.* "You really care about those little kids don't you? I liked the way you spoke to his mother."

"Thank you, darlin'."

⸎⸎⸎

John and Vicki, both wearing shorts and tank tops, entered The Country Ranch, the rustic country restaurant that prepared all of the regional southern favorites with Willie Nelson music playing to enhance the country atmosphere. The rustic feel resonated with John. It was completely wood paneled with comfortable booth seating and wrought iron light fixtures on the walls. Expired license plates for decoration, and art and crafts for sale by local artisans added to the rustic feel. They were escorted to a booth by the hostess, who wore jeans and the restaurant's T-shirt. "Enjoy ya dinner, folks."

Their gazes cascaded over each other's bodies and Vicki's baby blues sparkled when she examined his biceps and pecs. He interpreted that to mean she wanted his arms wrapped around her. And he—he wanted to caress "the girls." She giggled when she noticed where his eyes settled.

To prevent her blushing again, John turned away and examined their surroundings. He stared at piled-high plates of food brought to the tables and fixated on one particular plate set down in front of a forty-something guy. "What's that?" He grimaced. "That looks disgusting."

"Sausage gravy over biscuits and cheese fries. It's delish. Want to try it?" she asked, teasingly.

"No! That's a heart attack waiting to happen." He stiffened as he read the menu and dismissed the county favorites, reading them one by one. "Louisiana creole shrimp and grits; fried chicken and waffles with heavy syrup; turkey with corn bread stuffing, garlic mashed potatoes, and string beans sautéed in bacon fat; sausage meat loaf; coconut fried shrimp over creole rice; eighteen ounce chopped steak with fried onion straws, stack of onion rings; country fried steak." He scowled at it all. "What are you having?"

"The AUCE ribs. They're amazing here."

"AUCE?"

"All you can eat. Want to share?"

"Don't think so," he answered without missing a beat.

The server, a gal in her twenties, appeared. "What can I start y'all off with to drink?"

"An unsweet ice tea, light ice, no lemon."

"And for you, sir?"

"The same thing but with ice and extra lemon, thanks, and I think we're ready to order."

"Okay, what will it be?"

"I'm having the AUCE ribs, garlic mashed with bacon, and salad, ranch dressing on the side. And the sweet rolls, please," Vicki said.

John scowled at her for her choice.

She scowled back. "And extra cinnamon butter, please." She pursed her lips and gave him a corner of the eye stare.

"And for you, sir?"

"Rotisserie chicken, baked yam, salad with Italian on the side."

"Thank y'all."

She returned moments later with their drinks and a basket of fresh, right out of the oven, piping-hot, steaming sweet rolls, and two-ounce cups of cinnamon butter. "Enjoy, y'all."

"Thank you. They make them from scratch here." Vicki helped herself to one, almost dropping it. "Yikes, that's hot." She tore the soft, fragrant roll apart, gently collapsing it in her fingers, and spread a tiny amount of cinnamon butter on a small piece. Then, with the smile of a temptress, she slipped it into her mouth, enticing him. "That's so good."

"Now who's starting?" He enjoyed her playfulness. He adored her softness and innocence. She was angelic. He grabbed a roll, ripped it apart, spread it with the butter, and popped it into his mouth. "Oh God, this is good. Really good." He downed the remaining part of the roll in less than a minute.

He could relax with her, not be on edge. He could just be a man with Vicki without the tough upscale image he had to uphold in New York.

Their dinners arrived and her plate overflowed with the ribs and enough mashed potatoes for a few heavy-weight Sumo wrestlers. "You're going to eat all that? Don't you even think it. And you needed the extra bacon? Really?"

"John, I didn't start yet, and the calories only count if you consume them. And I just like a little of the bacon for flavor. And—who died and left you my boss?"

"We'll see how much of it you eat."

"So you only eat healthfully all the time?"

"Ninety-five percent. I work too hard in the gym, but I'm sure tempted to make an exception down here."

He dove into the chicken while she teased him with the ribs. She broke one apart from the rack on her plate. The meat fell apart with her touch, and the tangy and sweet sauce spread onto her fingers and around her lips. She nibbled on a rib, moaning with satisfaction. Bite by bite, the meat came off the bone as she devoured it. Then she slowly licked it down to its barren white core with her saucy tongue and held the bone by her teeth as it dangled from her lips, giving him the distinct signal that she was ready to be consumed by him, tonight. He didn't need to be psychic to understand that one.

Laughing, he dug into her plate with his fork and helped himself to two ribs. "You better feel honored. I don't play 'Have Fork Will Travel' with just any woman."

The owner of the restaurant, a woman in her forties, approached the table. "Hi, Miss Vicki! How are y'all enjoying dinner? Everything yummy?"

"It's very yummy, Sally, thank you."

"And you, sir?"

"Very good. Thank you."

"Good. Send my regards to your father." Sally walked off to another table.

"I will. Thanks."

"Do you come here often?"

"Yes, but everyone here in the county knows me."

"Ah, the sheriff's daughter. Okay."

"Does that bother you?"

"No. Not at all." But deep down inside, he was knocked off his throne.

"Betcha just can't eat just those two. These are addicting."

He chomped on the ribs without taking his enraptured eyes off her. "Oh man, these are good. Order more. I can see how my father gained so much weight down here." He winked at her and she blushed again. "You really have to tell me what that's all about later."

"What what's all about?" She knew darn well. She stopped dead in the middle of salivating on a rib, receiving his signature look.

CHAPTER 20

Present Day:

How's my girl?" John asked Gladys as he approached the nurse's station, knowing today would be a rough one, based on what he planned. Gladys had been observing Barbara who was reading an issue of *Glamour Magazine*. Another nurse, Mary, late fifties, was with Gladys doing paperwork at the desk. Otherwise, the unit was quiet. Barbara was the only patient in an observation room.

"She's calm today, Dr. Trenton. She let the techs take blood this morning without incident, and both results are in her file. And the Valium you prescribed got her through the MRI, PET, and CAT without too much difficulty. The results didn't come up yet, though."

"Too much difficulty?"

"A lot of whining, but she was too relaxed for an aggressive outburst. They managed to keep her still for the scans." Gladys handed the file to him. "And she's been asking for you all morning."

"Thank you. Did she say why?" He sat down, eager to learn the results. Opening the file, he read every detail, nodding his head as his expectations were confirmed. He had a lot more on his hands than he'd bargained for. Some small favor Carlson had asked of him. The additional information he wanted was on the second page. As he turned the page, Gladys pointed out the item he had specifically asked for.

"No. She didn't tell me why. You know what you have to do now, don't you?"

"Believe me, I know very well. How late will you and Mary be here?"

"Four."

"I want you both on stand-by."

"Yes, Dr. Trenton."

"Okay, here we go."

CC

John stood at the door of Barbara's room, taking a moment to reflect upon what he wanted to accomplish today. He wondered what kind of battle he'd encounter. She was one dame he didn't understand yet. "Good afternoon."

"It's about time you got here."

"It's only noon and I have other patients to see as well. Why the rush?"

"I want to do what we have to do so I can get out of here tomorrow."

He walked to the chair on the window side of the room. "Correction, the day after tomorrow. Today is the second day. And, yes, we have a lot to do. So are you telling me you're going to cooperate?"

"Yes."

"Good. Because this afternoon I'm meeting with Lieutenant Carlson and the team, and we're going over everything. And what we do here, I'm bringing with me, so if we can make sense of it, that will mean an expedient release for you on Thursday."

"And if you can't make sense of it?"

"I'm hoping we can, so let's cross that bridge when we get to it. Okay? I'll share everything with you tomorrow." She agreed. "I want to go over your blood tests results." He sat in the chair and made himself comfortable.

She propped herself up, with her legs crossed, facing him. "What's wrong?"

"Actually, there are several imbalances we need to address and take care of."

"But I take very good care of myself."

"You think you do." He scanned the file as he talked to her. "Your serotonin level is very low, much lower than the normal range of 101-282. That could be why you go into aggressive behavior so quickly along with the anxiety attacks. You're low in Tyrosine, GABA, Taurine, Inositol, Choline, all the B vitamins, zinc, Omega-3 fatty acids, magnesium. There are trace mineral imbalances and toxic metals. You have high blood histamine and lead. Your blood glucose is elevated, as are your triglycerides. You're just below diabetic, but if you don't watch your carb intake, you can progress into that. And your blood sugar can drop too low as well."

Her temper soared. "You're kidding me, right? You've seen my body! Do I look like I need to lose weight?"

"Angry already? Noted. And for what reason? See what I mean?" He stared her down. Barbara gasped and lowered her eyes. "It has nothing to do with weight, not in your case, anyway. No, you don't need to lose weight, but I'm going to teach you the carbohydrate exchange system so you'll know how many carb units you need to maintain your weight without spiking your blood sugar. Okay? And I'm going to add nutritional supplementation. I'd prefer to do it through an IV if you'd allow it."

She commenced her little-girl-whining routine. "I exercise like crazy. I don't need to do all that."

"Would you rather I start you on anti-psychotic medications?"

"No!"

"Didn't think so. What do you eat? Do you cook yourself well-balanced meals?"

"Honestly, no. I'm so busy, I eat a lot of fast food. Chinese. Italian. I figure I burn off the calories."

"Fried, greasy, empty calories? Come on, you're an intelligent woman. Just go with me here. When was the last time you had a panic attack? Aside from with me?"

She lowered her guard and finally admitted a truth. Her aura lightened. "A couple of weeks ago. I had a meeting in the city for a grant, and driving through the Hugh L. Carey Tunnel always gives them to me."

"What do you feel?"

"Breathing is hard. I perspire. I get dizzy, headaches, heart palpitations, stomach cramps, jittery, nausea. You name it. I get it."

"Apprehension?" Nod. "Confusion?" Nod. "Anger?" Nod. "Lightheadedness? Leg cramps?"

"That's a big one! While driving, that's no fun."

"That's your magnesium deficiency. What time was this?"

"Around four."

"When did you eat lunch?"

"Around noon."

"Your blood sugar dropped. Your fear caused an out poring of adrenalin, which caused sugar in your body to pour into your blood to give you energy. Very simply put, you used it up. Too much adrenalin can bring on the attack. And you needed to eat to balance the insulin that's being produced, or blood sugar drops too low. Next time, eat healthful foods before you go. Nothing white." Her confused look forced him to explain. "No white flour, no sugar, no milk, no white rice, try to eliminate dairy. Understand?"

"Nothing white? That's too hard. No."

"You have to do it. Sugar imbalance does create mood swings and you've got them. I've seen that first hand. And serotonin is a major factor in aggression responses. Something physiological is causing your erratic behavior. And you should be happy about that because it's an easy fix. Well, only easy if you follow it. I'm ordering a low carb, high in fiber, and low fat diet for you while you're here, and I want you to continue this when you leave. We'll check your sugar a few times a day. So how about it? Can I start an IV?"

"No IV, but I will take supplements orally."

"Okay, I'll give you that one. Only because I wouldn't want you to pull it out if you go into a rage. What do you do for exercise?"

"I dance a lot."

"What kind?" He wrote everything down in her file, verbatim.

"Ballet and modern dance."

"Where?"

"At a dance studio near my apartment."

"For how long and how many sessions a week?"

"A couple of hours and two to three times a week."

"Did you tell Carlson this?"

"Yes. He thought this might have originated from there."

"Did he check it out?"

"I don't think he checked out a damn thing!"

Her defiant attitude struck an unpleasant chord within him, but he remained official-sounding and spoke in a monotone voice. "What's the name of the studio?"

"Marigolds Dance Studio. I bring my own music and pay monthly for the use of the room, consistent times and days."

"Good. Very good. Now…" He smiled at her, knowing she hid more than she let out. "Where else do you dance?"

"Excuse me?"

"I'm guessing you dance somewhere else, too."

"What?"

"Come on. Honesty, here. You're cooperating, remember?"

He just glowered at her, observing a change in breathing, nervousness setting in. She looked away in avoidance.

"Okay, Dr. Clairvoyant. Where do you think I dance?"

"You really want me to answer that?"

"Yes. I do. Because you'll be wrong"

"You asked for it. Judging from the way you weren't shy being all exposed in your tantrum when the blood techs were here yesterday and those uh…" He had to think of a way to keep it professional. "…extravagant boots, your toned legs, and your guarded behavior, I'd say you're an exotic dancer in a strip club on the lower west side. Can't be the east because of zoning laws. How did I do? And I didn't even need to be clairvoyant."

"Oh, my God!" She flipped over on her stomach on the bed. "Go away. I'm not talking to you anymore."

"Cooperation lasted less than fifteen minutes. Just what I expected. What's the name of the club?"

"John, I can lose my job."

"First, I didn't give you permission to address me by my first name. Second, you should have thought of that before."

He approached her and untied the top of the hospital gown.

"What are you doing?"

"Relax. You're a bundle of tension. Let me work some of this out." He applied pressure to her shoulders and the base of her neck, focusing on the upper and middle trapezius fibers and splenius capitis in the neck.

"Oh God, that feels so good."

John pressed harder on the cervical armor area to get her to emote. "Breathe, inhale, and exhale deeply. Got to break up this tension. This is the anger center. All gets lodged in here." She breathed deeply and seemed to be relaxing. "What's the name of the club?" he asked again.

"Do we have doctor patient privilege?"

"Not in this case. Look, Barbara, the nut you say is chasing you could have come from there."

"I can't tell you. That hurts!"

He bent down closer to her while he continued to press on the points in her neck. "I know. I have to work deep. Look, Carlson and his team are experts. They know what they're doing. All they have to do is take that boot to a few clubs, and they'll find it. May take them a day, but they'll find it. So if you tell me now, it's less work for them, and Thursday's release won't have to be delayed because they didn't get the information they need."

She began to whimper. Then she cried, which turned into sobbing.

He knew it was from the pain caused by his deep touch—the point of the therapy. "That's all right, cry. Let it out." After a minute of crying, he asked, "What's coming to mind now?"

"I don't want to be here. I don't want to be here. But I have to. Stop you're killing me!" She thrashed her legs and tried to wiggle herself free. "Ow, that hurts! Stop!"

He moved out of the way to avoid getting kicked.

She bounced violently up, trying to get out of his grip. Emotions flooded out of her with screaming, "Stop it, stop it!

You fucking bastard!" She attempted to prop herself up on her elbows to get him to stop, but he prevented her, holding her down on the bed. She emitted real tears and then, after a moment, collapsed deeper into the bedding.

John remained calm while struggling with her. "Nope. You're not going anywhere." As strong as she was, he was much stronger. "Where's here?"

"There, at Zodiac!"

He got it. The name of the club. "Now why do you have to be at Zodiac?"

She sobbed. Her armor weakened and buried emotions, whatever she had been repressing, poured out. "To get even."

"Get even with whom?"

"Everyone!" Intense sobbing. "Everyone! Everyone who hurt me They all hurt me. Just like you! You're hurting me. You're all bastards. All men are bastards!" She remained inconsolable.

"Who hurt you?"

"All those men hurt me, all those men. Just like you," she sobbed.

"What men?"

"The men when I was young, the men that hurt me."

"What did the men do?"

She gasped for air. "They tied me up and beat me. They raped me."

"How old were you?"

"I don't remember. It kept on happening. Over and over and over." Fatigue closed her down.

John accepted that she'd had enough for this first session. He slowly removed his hands from her shoulders and lower neck, tapping the areas lightly.

She turned over and immediately pounded on his chest. "What did you do to me?"

He held her close. She sobbed into his chest and then it slowly decreased. She had a hard time breathing, gasping. He could tell all seven armors were blocked and he'd barely opened one.

"You have so much anger, Barbara. You need to release it. Holding it in will just make you sick."

She calmed down and he gently laid her down on the pillow. She whimpered. "Breathe, Barbara, inhale fully and exhale fully. You have to do this. Come on, full breathing. I'm here with you. I'm staying with you. I'm not leaving you." Drained, she listened. "Look at me," he cajoled. "Come on, direct eye contact."

She couldn't do it. She attempted but then looked away. She tried again but couldn't focus on his eyes.

"Barbara, follow my finger with your eyes but keep your head facing forward. Come on, follow my finger. Just move your eyes." He moved his finger around, up, down, to the right, to the left. Barbara couldn't do this simple exercise without moving her head. "Barbara, keep your head still, move just your eyes." She still couldn't do it on the second round. "Okay, now without moving your head, roll your eyes to look at the four corners of the room. Look to the upper left." Couldn't do it. "The upper right." Couldn't. "The lower left." Couldn't. "The lower right." Couldn't.

Her head moved with her each time.

She'd calmed down just a bit. "What's wrong with me?"

John sat on the bed, cupping her right hand in both of his to comfort her. "Well, we have seven armors in our body," he explained calmly and compassionately. "Parts of the musculature that hold tension and traumas, and when they're blocked, you can't enjoy life to its fullest. And you're pretty blocked. Your eyes aren't moving freely and it's called the ocular armor. And your neck and shoulders armor, the cervical armor, is blocked, too. I haven't checked your others. But my guess is they're blocked as well."

"What does that mean?"

"Well, our eyes see things, our life, our behavior. Our eyes hold our past. When the ocular armor is blocked, there are usually traumas in our life that we don't want to resolve or that we're hiding from. Unresolved traumas from our past impact our present-day lives. And the neck armor holds angers from the past. Does this resonate with you? What past traumas don't you want to let go of? What angers?"

"None."

"Not so, Barbara. That's not the truth. Continue to breathe. Inhale deeply, exhale completely. Come on." That she did. "Do you feel any energy flowing through your body? Heat? Cold? Tingling?"

"No," she whined.

"That's because you're blocked. You're blocking out pleasure, a painful past, blocking anyone from getting close to you. Do you remember anything you told me when you were sobbing, while I was pressing on your neck?"

"Nothing. What did I say?"

"You told me, now listen carefully. You told me you're at Zodiac to get even with all of the men who hurt you, beat you, and raped you when you were young."

"I told you all that? Oh, my God!"

"Come on, Barbara, stop. I know you remember what you said. So do you want to tell me about this?"

"No, absolutely not."

"But did it all happen?"

She cried softly, avoiding eye contact.

"That tells me yes, and I know it did. Okay, well that's why we have to do this. You're not telling me anything to help you. Nurses are coming in to talk to you when I'm not here to do evals. You're not answering any of their questions. You refuse to cooperate with the psychologists I sent in to do tests. Telling them nothing about your past. You won't speak honestly. This work is painful. I'm not going to lie to you. But we have to do it. I'll do anything within my power to get to the truth. Ordinarily, I wouldn't do so much in one day. It may not even be appropriate, but I need answers now. I know there's a lot you're hiding. Whether you've been through traumas you're still repressing, or you've done things in your past you don't want discovered—"

Her eyes shifted. Beads of perspiration trickled down her hairline to the base of her chin.

He realized he'd hit on something. Now tell me, who's Kellie Wilson?"

"Who?"

"Was that your name when you were a little girl?"

She became more agitated.

"Barbara, I listen to everything. Now tell me." He had expected her to let it out when he stressed her. He had also expected her to deny everything she had said.

"When did I say Kellie Wilson?"

"When I had to restrain you for the blood tests. You called me Daddy and yelled I shouldn't do this to you. I asked you what your name was and you told me Kellie Wilson."

"Oh, my God!" She jerked her hand out of his. "Dr. Trenton, I need a couple hours break. I'm so tired." She turned her back on him.

He pulled her back. "No, Barbara. You just want a couple of hours so you'll have some time to fabricate a story you think I'll believe. That's not happening."

She removed the sheet. "I have to pee."

"Go ahead."

She disappeared into the bathroom, did her business, came out stark naked, and strutted over to him.

John gazed at her dynamite body. "What's this?"

"You can't deny you want me."

She positioned herself right up against his chest and tried to throw her arms around his neck but he grabbed her wrists to stop her. She jerked her hand out of his grip so she could try to unzip his pants, but he stopped her again. The only woman he wanted was his Vicki.

"Not appropriate, get back into bed." He led her there.

"You coming in with me?" She lay down on the bed, protruding her breasts toward him. "I want your hands all over me."

"That you'll have. Lay back."

He covered her with the sheet and blanket—no new gown to give her—and placed his hands on her solar plexus in her midriff area. "I just want to check your energy flow. Relax, this doesn't hurt. It's called Reiki, energy healing. Now I'm going to ask you a very personal question, Barbara. Very personal. It's probably the most personal question you can ask a woman."

She bit her lip. He sighed.

"I know I won't get an honest answer from you, but your

body will tell me." She flung a you're-damn-straight-you're-not-getting-the-truth look. "When you orgasm, where do you feel it?" he asked.

"Excuse me? What kind of a question is that to ask? You're perverted!"

"No, I'm not. Do you feel it near your pelvis?" His hand hovered about three inches above the blanket in her pelvic region. "By your navel?" He moved his hand to the sacral center keeping the same distance. "At the solar plexus? Or near your heart?" He moved his hand over her chest. "Do you feel it up to your throat or through the top of your head? Where do you feel it, Barbara?"

She cried softly.

"Do you feel the wonderful, intense ripple of sensations taking over your body from head to toes?"

Her crying intensified.

"No, you don't, do you? You don't feel anything."

She cried real tears.

He clasped her hands in his. "Barbara, you're missing out on wonderful, natural feelings with what you're doing. Talk to me, tell me what you're afraid of me finding out."

She broke down, minimally. "I had a horrible childhood and I still can't deal with it."

"Tell me. I'm listening to you."

She feigned sobbing, more glycerin tears. "My mother gave me up at birth, and I was adopted. But my adoptive mother died when I was four, and my father shot himself in the head right in front of me six months later. I went from foster home to foster home, where the abuse in some was more than in others, and then at eighteen I aged out of the system. I was alone on the streets. I became a prostitute to get money to pay for college and support myself. I swore that I wanted to help children, so they wouldn't have to endure the same pain I did."

"So is Kellie Wilson your birth name or your adopted name?"

"It was my prostitute name. I don't know my birth name. My adoptive parents named me Barbara and their surname was Montgomery."

This was only the partial truth, if at all. "You told me Kellie was your childhood name."

"I must have gotten confused."

"What state was this in?"

"California, Los Angeles. It was the prostitution I didn't want you to find out about. I could lose my license. Then everything I worked for will be for nothing."

He understood her story was just beginning. "Anything else?"

"Don't you think I had enough for today?"

"No. We have that other issue. But yes. You did. We'll take care of that another time."

CHAPTER 21

Three Years Earlier:

Exiting the restaurant, Vicki rushed off ahead of John, fighting tears and sniffling. She was in shock from his look that sent electrical waves of energy through her from head to toe. She didn't know what to make of it, other than the fact that it was to chastise her.

Silent tension filled the walk to his car, though it was a short one, just ten yards into the crowded parking lot.

Should she just tell him to take her home and leave? Was her flirting with him a mistake? What was her infatuation with him all about? What was she thinking? This New York City doctor, would he settle for the likes of her, the county girl? Or did he just want to use her for his vacation thrill? He'd bruised her ego and it just brought up the more-than-painful memories from a failed and hurtful relationship that had damaged her self-esteem and made her swear off men. But that was years ago, fifteen to be exact.

Now she was feeling different. At thirty-seven, she'd become desperate. Her biological clock ticked, and she didn't want to spend the rest of her life alone. She needed warmth and comfort in a man's arms.

She needed him.

Getting in, starting the car, driving out of the lot was done in silence. She fidgeted, staring out the window into pitch-blackness. When they reached the main road, he drove about five miles in the darkness, except for the high beams on his car, in nerve-racking silence. All that they heard as he maneuvered down a narrow county road was the low hum of the engine and the rustling of leaves from the huge trees lining the sides of the road swiping against the sides of the car. "Now tell me, what is the blushing all about?" he asked.

She didn't expect him to get right down to it after being silent for so long. "Excuse me?" She shot him a none-of-your-business glare. "Now you tell me, what was that look all about? The one that sent shivers down my spine?"

"Good. It's supposed to."

"What?" She couldn't believe his punitive response.

"Send shivers down your spine. It show's you're receptive and open to energy, plus you weren't being forthcoming with me and I let you know that's not acceptable."

"How in the world am I to respond to that? Do you take a parental role with all the women you date? Well, not with me, John. I'm not one you can control. I've been on my own since I was eighteen, and I do things on my own terms. And I only give out personal information when I'm good and ready."

"Really? First, I'm not acting parental at all. I just expect honesty." He took his eyes off the road for a brief moment to look at her. "I will never be dishonest with you, ever, and I expect the same. What's wrong with that? And second, if I can't control you—control is actually the wrong word. I don't do that to women, but whatever—you wouldn't have had that reaction. You would have thrown the look back at me. Or given me a kick under the table or something to retaliate. Even tossed a rib at me, but something."

She laughed. "Throw a rib at you? Oh, so you like to fight?"

"No. I like to play. I even like to argue, playfully. But I've got to admit you've got spunk. I like that. I really like that. In your own innocent way, you've got spunk."

"I can't help the blushing. I'm kind of shy. I'm not used to your New York City manner." He did a double take.

"Your upfrontness."

"Well, you're not shy. You have an answer for everything."

"I'm not shy in conversation, just in—" She paused to say it without embarrassing herself. "—in getting close to some-one, in trusting. It's the southern way."

"I don't buy that for a second. But tell me more about that."

"Sorry, Doc, not in the mood for therapy right now. Been there. Done that. Turn left at this corner."

"Okay, for now."

She jumped out of the car before he shut the engine off. "Are you coming?"

"Not yet, but I'm sure I can," he said, shooting her a wick-ed grin.

"What?" She caught on and laughed. "Oh my God, John!"

He stayed in the driver's seat with the window open. "Ah, you mean trusting as in…"

She felt her stomach drop. He'd nailed it, but she didn't ex-pect him to be so blatant. Was he always going to be this open, and honest? Could she handle that?

"You do realize that if I come in, you'll most likely be fac-ing those trusting issues, right?"

"Yes, I do." She had thought she was ready for this but, now, she wasn't quite sure.

"Okay. We'll see."

ↄ◠ↄ

They entered her modestly decorated, eclectic-style house. John headed straight out to the lanai. It was about thirty feet by thirty feet, enclosed with a screen canopy on top and on all sides, with doors on either side leading out to the yard. As soon as he entered, a large motion detector turned on lighting that illuminated the area. He looked around at the length and depth of the space and inhaled the fresh, cooling air. Wow, this was an awesome place to be right now.

The lush plant life cleansed his aura and John basked in the intensity of the energy emanating from them. It was a sheltered cocoon just for the two of them. There were no other houses on either side of hers or in the front and back. She had the only isolated house in the woods, like in "Little Red Riding Hood." It was just trimmed grass, in the yard outside the lanai, and lots and lots of trees. The Flowering Dogwoods, with white petals; acacia, with wide spreading leaves; red Florida maple, with thick dense trunks; weeping willows; and oaks, mixed in with palm trees, filled the woods behind the lanai. All he heard were the mating calls of the frogs, crickets, and birds.

John relaxed as all the tension from his job left him under the starlit sky. The stars were visible and striking, not hidden by pollution. It was content and serene, and he realized he could get used to this.

John took everything in. Vicki had huge plants on the lanai—a few stick or pencil plants that were so full and irregularly shaped and so tall they reached the ceiling of the lanai, just under ten feet. There were two large philodendrons in twenty-four inch pots. She had an oval table that seated eight, with other groups of chairs and smaller tables around the area. He appreciated her style.

Vicki watched the family of deer that played in her yard. "Come here. You have to see this."

He encapsulated her in his muscular arms. With his physical and emotional strength, her back melded into his chest and, closing her eyes for a moment, she kept her swooning to herself.

John felt the same way. She needed him as much as he needed her.

"Look it's a mommy, daddy, and baby," she said.

The deer pranced around in the back yard and just stopped to look at them, not at all fearful. John admired their agility at running and playing. They scampered off into the deeper woods after a couple of minutes, having enough of being observed.

"Mommy, Daddy, and baby? How long have you taught kindergarten?" He gave her a tight squeeze and a tender kiss on her cheek, and then placed his on hers from behind.

"Fifteen years."

"I think it's about time you went up a few grades." He pecked her cheek again to show her he wasn't being critical of her, just teasing.

"Nope. Kindergarten is where I stay."

He pivoted her around and their eyes met. "That could be part of your problem. You act like you're five."

"I do not!"

"Well, that you'll have to prove to me." He knew what he desired, but he was unsure if he'd get it. He led her to the lounge built for two.

"Can I get you a drink or something?"

"No, I'm good, thanks. I'm stuffed."

"Anything hard?"

"I think I'll take care of that."

She laughed. "Does everything boil down to sex with you?"

John cocked his head and grinned. He reclined on the left side of the lounge in a prone position, taping the spot on his right. "Come here." Vicki cozied up next to him and brought her legs up onto the lounge. He drew in a deep breath and re-laxed on the lounge. "This is really great out here, so relaxing, peaceful under the stars. Can't find this in New York."

"I know. I love it."

"How long are you living in this house?"

"Twelve years."

"Alone?"

"Just me and Duchess." He glanced at her. "My German Shepherd," she clarified. "I had to put her down just last week. It was cancer. And I'm still not over it. I never cried so hard in my life."

He hugged her tighter. "Oh, Vicki, I'm sorry. I truly am. How old was she?"

"Twelve. She was a K-9 but flunked out of the academy. That's how I got her."

"How did that happen?"

"She was too hesitant. When they were trying to train her, she didn't focus right away. They want a dog that will follow directions immediately. So I took her at four months. Believe me, John, putting her down was the hardest thing I ever had to do in my life, but I couldn't let her suffer."

"I know she had a wonderful life with you," he said, hug-ging her. "You made the right decision."

She glanced up at him. "I know."

He caressed her face and lifted it slightly so he could deposit a tender kiss on her lips. She turned on her side and reciprocated with a longer, but still gentle, kiss.

His protectiveness extended through his energy field and radiated through hers. Right away, he felt her tense muscles relax.

His left hand slipped under the lounge, and he managed to find the lever that made it flip down into a bed. They both flopped down, but he secured her in his arms to brace the impact, though it was light. "Oops, I wonder how that happened."

She giggled. "You know the thing that made me so attracted to Duchess?"

He caressed her with his arms around her, twirling her hair between his fingers. "What was that?"

"We had the same birthday. March twenty-third. What's yours?"

"Really? June ninth, Gemini. And you're an Aries. March twenty-third. You know, that's Artemis' Festival Day."

"Who's Artemis?"

"That's right, you don't teach Greek Mythology in kindergarten. She's the Goddess of the Moon and the Hunt and the protectress of children. She loved being out in the woods and the wilderness and she traveled with the deer."

"Ooh—Just like me. Wait a minute, now I remember her from an English Lit course. Wasn't she a virgin goddess? Uh oh," she cooed, teasing him. She tickled him on his waist.

Content that she'd loosened up, he hugged her, tighter. "Not virginity as we know it. Psychologically virginity means autonomy. The woman could take care of herself without a man. Like, you're still single."

"Very funny! So are you! But didn't she also take a vow of chastity?"

"No, not at all." He kissed her neck gently and then more aggressively in between talking to her. "The virginity thing was political. The Greeks wanted to dominate women. They told them myths." His lips explored her skin down to her cleavage. She relaxed giving out little sighs of contentment as his breath touched her body. "If they did that, there would have been total male control. There was never any monogamy," he added.

She was aroused to the point he wanted her at, for now. He let her hands wander down his muscular chest. She raised her body up, leaned over, and pulled off his tank top, letting it fall to the ground. That was the go ahead he was waiting for.

"Then she was promiscuous?" she asked. "That's not me."

"Well, the women of Sparta were wild." He slipped off her tank top as she talked, flipped open the clasps on her bra, and slid it off, ogling her. "They are perfect. You are perfect." He cupped her right breast in his hand and lowered his head to suckle her.

She arched her back and breathed heavily as she quivered and moaned with delight. He sucked a little more forcefully on her breasts, declaring them his.

He was still testing the waters on how far he could go without intimidating her. He'd done enough of that at dinner. Now he wanted her to feel like a woman, a very much-desired woman. Amidst her soft gasps and hungry moans, he removed her shorts and dropped them on the ground. Then he removed his own.

"And they're all mine, if I might add," she teased as he fondled her breasts.

"Affirmative. I can tell." His mouth salivated as his tongue teased the pink skin around her nipples, making them pebble and then peak. Intermittently, as he talked, his lips and teeth took turns gently tugging at her hardened buds. "They had sex in the streets. When an Artemis woman is in sync with her libido, her lovemaking is well…uh, ferocious, like gorillas making love."

He imitated growling sounds on her midriff and stomach with his warm breath, feeling her tingle and quiver with excitement beneath him. At this moment, he was thankful that he could feel a woman's energy. With his tongue, he tasted the deliciousness of her clean fragrant skin. His hands caressed her legs as she let out soft involuntary moans, and then her body moved rhythmically toward him as he reached her tight, round bottom, letting his fingers roam on the small of her back.

Vicki couldn't get enough. "Oh my God."

He wanted to make sure she knew he was the one man who could make her feel wonderful—like a treasured woman— taking the time to find out what pleasured her most. He wanted her to float toward the heavens. "So now, my Artemis woman, you can trash those trusting issues," he whispered in her ear, causing her to gasp. He picked up on that and kissed her again, stronger, wetter, from her ear down to her neck, until he felt her tremble underneath him. He loved that a woman could climax this way.

She turned over onto his chest, breathless. Her satiny, smooth body lay directly on top of his defined muscles, and she wanted to kiss him. He gently opened his mouth and eased his tongue between her lips. He was welcomed with fervor.

Their passion increased and the rapture of that kiss propelled them both to another galaxy. Their breathing intensified and they clutched onto each other tighter. Even with his eyes closed, he envisioned the stars. He was never letting her go. His hands glided up and down her body, faster and with more pressure, squeezing her bottom. Then he grasped her hand, wedged it between them, and placed it on his hard length.

Her breath hitched when she first touched him, but her intimidation was gone. She caressed him, her palm sliding up and down. Her thumb lingered on his tip, causing him to moan, shudder, and release pre-cum. He felt as if they had known each other a long time and he relished in her gentle, but confident touch. She fondled him and her fingers encased him as she intermittently and gently scratched his underside with her fingernails.

He rolled her over onto her back, still savoring her lips, and ran his warm hand down her stomach. She spread her legs, giving him permission to explore her. She was so wet and so excited, her moaning so uninhibited, she held nothing back and neither did he, both uttering sounds of pure pleasure, and he loved her for it.

"I want you in me," she whimpered.

He slipped two fingers into her and glided them up and down, over her G-spot. She moaned, louder than before, as if uncontrolled, and her juices enveloped his fingers. Her mound swelled. He slipped his fingers from her entrance and slid them up and over her clit, knowing that she was more than ready for him.

She let out multiple short gasps. "Oh, God, John."

Her quivering told him she was close to the apex. After putting on a condom, he mounted her and held her hips. She spread wide and high for him as he penetrated her, pausing to wait for her signals to continue. She was so warm, wet, and welcoming as he thrust into her, pumping slowly at first. She gasped with pleasure, and when he felt her body responding by moving beneath him, in-sync with his rhythm, he thrust harder and faster. Her arms wrapped around him and glued to his slick, shiny with sweat torso. He wanted her in his arms forever. He felt her sheath contracting around his length and, a couple of minutes later, at the same moment, they both trembled with a rich spontaneous release, the intensity of which neither of them expected.

Their hearts pounded, their bodies quivered. Their emotions were drained, their senses heightened. For the first time, he had been truly satiated. She was the woman he had been waiting for. He embraced her and had no intention of letting her go.

This innocent country girl had captured this free-spirited playboy's heart.

He collapsed on top of her, wiped out and drenched from his own body heat. Taking some time to recover, but not too much, he rolled onto his side. "You're good, kid. Real good. And you smell so darn good." He hugged her in appreciation, his pleasuring her still on the agenda.

"You're not so bad yourself. And yes, Doctor, I would say that you cured what ailed me. That was wonderful, darlin'. Thank you."

He laughed. "You're welcome. Come here." He coaxed her to lie on top of him again.

She rested her head on his pecs, moaned, and snuggled with him. "Where did you learn to kiss like that?"

"I only give out personal information when I'm good and ready. Isn't that what I was told by a feisty miss?"

"I want you to keep kissing me forever."

I will be kissing you forever.

His hand slid through her hair to the back of her head, pulling her close so their lips interlocked in passion again. Her sleek, warm body molded into his muscular frame, and they both sizzled from the moisture emanating from each other.

Then drop by drop, they sensed it. He wasn't sure what it was. She shielded him. The drops came faster. Then they heard it, the thunder. And the lightning.

"Oh my God, it's lightning. Let's go inside."

"No, it feels too good."

"John, it's going to pour."

"No, I'm not letting you move. I'm way too comfortable. No way, kiddo." He devoured her, kissing her neck and shoulders. The rain poured harder. She laughed and pulled away from him.

"John, Florida rainstorms are heavy and sudden, and there'll be a downpour any second. The thunder and lightning can be deadly. Come on."

"No." Then it happened. The downpour. "Oh, man! You weren't kidding."

They became drenched, cooled down but drenched! The rain was strong, constant, and the thunder was not to be taken lightly. She jumped up off him and grabbed her soaked clothes off the ground. He did the same, both laughing, as the thunder and lightning continued. He had never been in such a torrential rainstorm like this, naked no less. The bushes and trees trembled in the wind. Some huge branches on the trees in her yard made horrific sounds as they crashed down, just missing the lanai frame. The impending danger startled him. The lightning flashes pierced the sky, illuminating the woods as if it was daylight behind them. They made it into the house, splashing through puddles on the lanai with the rain running off their bodies and dripping onto her tile floor.

❧❧❧

She darted to her bathroom, grabbed towels, and tossed one to him.

"Here. Let me do it," he said. He was only concerned with her. He wrapped her up and dried her off, rustling her hair and rubbing her down from head to toe before taking care of himself. From that moment, he hoped he would be pampering her and taking care of her forever.

ഏഇ

They made it into her adjoining bedroom with light gold tone walls and Colonial furniture. Teal carpeting added to the warmth of the welcoming room. John was in awe of a hand-painted mural on the wall behind the bed—a wild stallion with a flamboyant mane and tail, running in a field. The rich vibrant colors of the greens and teals created the pasture and leaves going through a trellis. Multi-shades of brown, which were used to create the image of a life-like stud, made a perfect backdrop for her headboard. The wrought iron headboard was like a fence and, on the wall, painted in the same spiral pattern, was an archway over the horse. Gold and silver threads of paint were wisped through the mane and tail, giving it the three dimensional appearance of the stud jumping off the wall.

"This is amazing. Who did this?" He glided his fingers over the mane. "Really nice."

"Thank you. A local artist."

Laughing, she plopped down on her back on the bed, still nude. He felt as if nothing in the world could disrupt this tranquility, not even the thunder and lightning outside. He lay down on his stomach very close to her, his right arm across her body, and cuddled with her. He kissed her stomach and she giggled. When he picked up his head he saw it, the flashing red dot on the wall through the spiral pattern in the headboard. He almost missed it with the complicated design and colorations on the mural. Was that deliberate? Without hesitation, he threw the blanket over them.

"Stay under the covers."

"Why? What?"

He reached down and put on his soaked briefs.

Oh, man! That's cold! Brutal!

"Just do as I say." He sat up, snatched his NYPD consultant

ID out of the pocket of his shorts, and stared up at the wall in front of the bed. Inside an antiqued gold picture frame was a red light flashing. He got out of bed, opened his ID folder, and held it up to the light. "Dr. John Trenton, NYPD consultant. I expect a call within thirty seconds on the house phone." The phone on her night table rang. He picked it up on the second. "Who is this?"

"Commander Mark Marin, Sun County SWAT. I'm Vicki's twin brother."

"You've been watching us?"

"The entire house is wired, inside and out."

John felt a mixture of fury and embarrassment.

What the hell is going on here? What kind of invasion of privacy is this?

"So you've been watching us all evening?"

"No. We shut it down on the lanai."

"And exactly when did you do that?"

"When you were watching the deer. You triggered the system again when you went into the bedroom."

"And the house is wired because?"

"Look, it's to protect Vicki. Our father is an elected official. She can be a target anytime for anyone's revenge. We knew you were safe. The lanai was clear. She didn't have her weapon with her."

"Weapon? She's armed?" He looked at her with arched eyebrows. "You're armed?"

She smiled and shrugged.

"Have a good night, Doc." The call disconnected without warning.

"Why do you carry?" He sat on the bed, wanting the answer to this one. He removed his uncomfortable briefs and then got under the snuggly blanket already warmed by Vicki.

"It's a right to carry state, and I carry because I can," she said in between more kisses. "And my dad is top cop. You think he's going to let me go unarmed?"

"So I'm assuming you have more than one?"

"This house is an arsenal."

He was astonished. "What do you have?"

"A couple of Glocks, .38 caliber, Smith & Wesson, a 357 Mag stainless pistol with a six-inch barrel, a Ruger lightweight .38 special, and a 9mm Luger. I'm exhausted. You wiped me out. Let's get some shut eye."

John didn't know what to think. What would this do to their relationship? He hated guns and wouldn't have carried even if he could.

Yet his future wife was Annie Oakley. But then again, she wouldn't be able to carry in New York.

CHAPTER 22

Present Day:

Clancy looked around at the destruction he'd just created in Barbara's modest living room in her apartment in the Manhattan Beach section of Brooklyn. Just enough. Just what he wanted. And he was smart enough to wear latex gloves and put surgical booties over his shoes.

Smashed glass landed everywhere. An imported French chandelier ripped down from the ceiling, which left the live electrical wires dangling, exaggerated the statement he wanted to make. That was the most exorbitant item in the room. Very fitting where he hurt her. With the money. He sliced the matching fabrics on the couches and chairs, causing the foam stuffing to spill out onto the furniture. He knocked pictures off the wall and threw them on the floor. He stomped on them to crack the glass. He smashed nick-knacks from shelves with a hammer. The sound of the extra loud ring startled him. It transferred to voice mail. "Hi. This is Barbara. You know what to do and you know when to do it."

"Come on, Barbara. It's Morgan. You still can't be pissed off at me. How about dinner? And you can give me some return on all the money I gave you."

Clancy stewed. "I sure do know what to do. I'll get rid of you too, fella." He slipped a transmitter for an explosive device out of his pocket as if he caressed a fine timepiece. He depressed the shiny red button. The light flashed with a very subtle blink. It was set. The bomb would only affect the surrounding three hundred square feet. He meandered around to find a spot to station it and saw the ideal location under a silk pillow still left on the couch. After placing it for maximum effect, he escaped the apartment.

In his apartment, Clancy checked his clock. 3:30. "It's that time. Boom!" He gave a vulgar laugh.

⁂

Carlson sat at his desk, quite annoyed he had to bother with this. It was nothing but a nuisance case.

John scanned the five-inch thick folder. "What is all this?"

"Papers to fucking nowhere."

"Come on, she thinks someone made her a target."

"We checked everything out. Drew a big zero."

"She thinks you didn't bother to check anything out."

"Well, she fucking lied to you," Carlson snarled. "What a fucking shock. Look, no one hates this woman enough to torment her, yet alone want her dead. She started calling and we just laughed at her. I'll admit it. We did, at first. The only reason we started to investigate was because neighbors started calling, little old grandma types, reporting commotions in her apartment more than once. Now she's milking it. Don't know why."

"What kind of commotions?"

"Montgomery yelling, shouting, 'Stop that!' 'What are you?' 'Ugh. That's disgusting!' There were no responses. It was as if she was yelling to herself."

John rose and walked to the window, peering out as if wanted to find clues in thin air, just to avoid Carlson's bantering. "What about surveillance? Phone taps?"

"Are you kidding me? With all the crime in New York City you expect me to waste tax-payers money on a woman who calls every day, claiming someone is after her, but leaves not one shred of evidence? My detectives would die of boredom. Then she doesn't want to investigate. Then she does. Come on. As far as I'm concerned after what you found out, which is a hell of a lot more than I ever expected, the case is closed and she belongs where she is. And you are now her official doctor on record."

"Close the case? You can't be serious! Too much is going on here, from her moving around a lot and a clinic after only three years residency in New York? Her psychotic episodes interspersed with lucid conversation? Prostitution when she was eighteen and now being a stripper at forty? No, it doesn't make sense. How can she manage a normal life? No, Paul. This case is not closed, far from it."

"Hold on a minute. So she has a vice. Big fucking deal."

"A vice? It's not that simple, for Christ's sake."

"Yeah? When did you start having sex?"

"What does that have to do with it?"

"Answer me."

"Fourteen, now—"

"Prostitution at eighteen, stripper at forty, and you're seeing Landers for—"

"It's not the same thing."

"You're pretty similar in my book. The only difference is that she had an abusive family and you had a loving one. There's a fine line, John, and you know it. If you weren't so fucking lucky you'd be pushed over the edge, too, and could have wound up where she is."

"I can't believe we're having this conversation. It's not luck. It's called conscience. And you're not addressing the case here."

"Goes back to family. She's mentally ill, yes. And that's your job. This is not a criminal case. I'm only going through this again to entertain you, our almighty shrink."

John turned around and addressed Carlson with a tone the man couldn't ignore. "So entertain me. Doesn't this double life of hers bother you? What did she say? Let's just suppose there is a person. What did he or she do?"

"Phone calls, presents. And no, her double life doesn't bother me any more than yours does. But it might now that you let Vicki go if you start acting stupid again."

"Focus, Paul, focus. Says here decapitated rats. So where are they?"

"She said she was so repulsed she threw them away. We searched tons of apartment building garbage. Nothing."

"What about the pictures on the walls?"

"Said they were written in disappearing ink. Then messages under her door. We saw blank paper. Disappearing ink again. And then get this one, holograms."

"Holograms? Of what?"

"Now don't start. We don't have any direct evidence. Just face the fact that this fellow shrink of yours can't hack it anymore."

John slammed the file down on the desk. "Holograms of what?"

Carlson's right hand started to tremble. He dropped his pen. "Ghosts, skeletons, rainbows," Paul said. "And only she sees them. See? I told you she was crazy. Look, based on all of the abuse in her life, wouldn't she escape it with hallucinations?"

"Very true. But she's been a functioning and contributing member of society for many years. So why now? What made her snap? There's a lot more to this."

Carlson's phone rang. "Lieutenant Carlson. Yeah. What? When? Are you sure? Montgomery is still in the hospital, isn't she?" he asked John.

"Yes, I just left her."

To the caller, Carlson said, "We're leaving now." He slammed down the phone. "Let's go. Her place has been tossed."

സരസ

Outside Barbara's apartment building—a four story, sixteen-unit complex two blocks off the beach in a cul-de-sac—police cars and ambulances had been stationed as the first responders cordoned off the front and two sides of the building from the street access points. John and Carlson drove up to the barricade in an unmarked jeep. The crowds of boisterous bystanders who formed outside the building and across the street were ushered behind police barriers.

Inside the apartment, ESU officers and crime scene techs searched for the trigger in the living room, the room closest to the front door. Right now, there were more people in here then there was room to hold them. This room had been the only one assaulted.

Crime scene techs measured and contained one hundred feet beyond the exterior perimeter of the area where the bomb hit. They also set up the path where the investigators could enter or leave. There was one way in and one way out. The outer perimeter of the three hundred square feet of debris had been roped off.

John had never witnessed a crime scene being set up so expediently.

Okay, so now they're damn serious.

All the other rooms were intact, which surprised John, but he kept that to himself for now. Camera lights flashed, as crime scene photos took the maximum amount of time and primary importance.

Tony and Sal explored the mess, stepping over glass, while John analyzed the surroundings.

Gemini posters lay on the floor. Gemini sculptures had been smashed. The Ouija board left on the table, the tarot cards on a shelf, plus psychology and education textbooks all added to the multidimensionality of his patient. Carlson joined him, picking up a Gemini statue without first putting on gloves.

"Hey, Loo! Lay off, huh?" Sal called. "They already have enough prints here to keep us busy for a decade!"

"Yeah sure, Sal, sorry. Find anything?"

Sal stood by the phone. "Yeah. Listen to this."

"Come on, Barbara. It's Morgan. You still can't be pissed off at me. How about dinner? And you can give me some return on all the money I gave you."

Carlson looked away, distracted. Tony and John noticed.

"Know him, Loo? Who is this guy?" Tony asked.

"No, I don't. Just trying to put pieces together. That's all."

John's annoyance flared that it was he who had to direct the detective. "Tony, check the caller ID."

"Smart man. Reynolds Publishing. 212-555-6200."

John recorded the number on his pad. "Thanks."

"It's been two weeks and I see you still haven't taken off your ring," Tony said.

"I don't intend to. Keeps me grounded. And, Tony, that's your business because?"

"We're friends. That's why. And I'm glad you're not ready to let go."

John ignored his assumption, though it was spot-on. He missed Vicki to no end. He turned toward Carlson. "Still think she did this by herself?"

"Not convinced yet, but she's your patient, so you figure it out. This stuff is…weird, like you with your psychosis."

"Psychosis?"

"You know what I mean, your psychic stuff."

John accepted this humorously. He was aware that Carlson didn't understand the spirit realm at all. He'd been working with John for five years and still hadn't grasped it. Carlson was a mainstream conservative guy through and through. Black or white, good or evil, criminal or law abiding. Nothing in between. Even Carlson's wife, Maria, complained to him about her husband's inflexibility. "Well, it stands to reason she couldn't do this herself. She's been with us two days."

Tony and Sal examined the couch. They found the transmitter.

"Let Arson figure out when this was set and find out who this fucking Morgan character is." Carlson turned toward John. "Check her for suicidal quirks."

⟡⟡⟡

John left them and went to inspect the bedroom. It was a conservative bachelorette room, nothing fancy, nothing to raise a red flag. No personality. It was boring and depressing, with monotone shades of yellow on the walls without any patterns or depth, solid dark yellow comforter on the bed, butterscotch yellow sheets with one pillow.

This is telling. All yellow. The color of Gemini. And who sleeps with only one pillow on their bed?

There were no accessories on the night tables, which were a plain, light-toned wood. There was nothing to show that a vibrant, energetic, successful woman lived here. John began to take deep breaths. He focused and stared at the bed, embracing one of his clairvoyant visions. He shivered and felt his spirit guide, Max, jump into his crown chakra and travel through his body on the right side, his psychic side. The energy flowed from the top of his head through his body to his toes. His channels to the unseen opened. He concentrated his focus.

He tuned in psychically to Barbara who was wearing a long, sleeveless, black nightgown with ruffles around the neckline, tossing and turning. This appeared to be rough nightmare. He heard her screaming and crying with painful emotions that had overtaken her entire being. Real tears. This was more than a nightmare. This illustrated her life. She rolled from side to side on the bed then curled into the fetal position. Her screams of "No! Stop!" vibrated through him as if they arose from him. He felt the heat, sweating in the middle of February. He envisioned a muddy gray irregular chord of ragged-edged light, three inches in diameter, coming from her solar plexus and going down to the floor, attaching itself to the carpet.

He perceived blood on her hands, dripping onto the floor where the gray light landed as she callously laughed over her victim and then cried.

Who is that on the floor?

He couldn't decipher if it was a man or woman, child or adult. Where was a weapon? How old was Barbara then? At that moment, she looked younger. He couldn't tell how much younger.

It was just a hazy cloud. Less than two minutes. That was all Max gave him.

Carlson, who'd watched him from the doorway the entire time, awakened him. "Hey! psychic boy, wake up!"

John re-entered reality, so stunned it took a moment to recover. "Paul, you don't do that to someone. Not when they're not ready to come back."

"Care to share where you went?"

"No. I need proof first." John went to her dresser and was about to open the top drawer.

He still needed to shake off the uneasy feeling from Carlson's abrupt awakening. He forced himself to open and shut his eyes repeatedly to refocus to the present.

"Stop. We don't have a warrant," Carlson shouted.

"Don't need one for this. This is an emergency situation."

"Yeah, you do. This is beyond the crime scene parameters. Her place. She doesn't know we're here and she expects a reasonable amount of privacy."

"Look, Paul. I have to bring her clothes anyway. Tomorrow I have to move her. The seventy-two hours are up. Between tonight and tomorrow, I have to find a way to delay any release. She can't wear a hospital gown in gen pop. I'm doing her a favor here. See if you can find an overnight bag in her closet."

Carlson tossed him a fresh pair of gloves and a big paisley overnight bag. "You can only take the clothes you need and not look under or in things."

John studied the disorganized top drawer and pulled out a couple of bras and several panties. In the second drawer, he pulled out socks and some T-shirts. In the third drawer, he found it, the long, sleeveless, black nightgown with ruffles.

He felt a tingling initiate through his crown chakra and flow through his body.

"Thanks, Max." He chose a couple of others to take instead.

"Who you talking to now?"

"What?"

"Who's Max? In the fucking five years we've been working together, I never heard you mention a Max."

John was upset that he'd said it audibly and not in thought language. "Just something I was thinking about, never mind." At the closet, he pulled out sweat pants. Everything had been strewn in without any semblance of order. "She's a mess."

"Hire a housekeeper. Done yet?"

"No. Come on, Paul. You know a person's closet is an indication of the structure of their life."

"I don't fucking psychoanalyze everything. Or anything. What else do you need?"

"Toiletries."

❦

John returned to his office at the hospital and examined Barbara's file. The MRI, CAT, and PET results were still not in there. He picked up the phone and dialed an extension.

"Imaging."

"This is Dr. Trenton. I'm waiting for the three scans of my patient, Barbara Montgomery. Taken this morning."

"Dr. Trenton, I'm sorry, the radiologist hasn't looked at them yet. It takes at least twenty-four hours."

"I need them ASAP."

"I'll pass that along."

"Thank you." John hung up, irritated. He needed them to put the pieces of the puzzle together. He wanted his intuition to be wrong for once. He prayed for it, counted on it. If what he thought was correct, they would have a monumental problem on their hands and this nuisance case would become a major one, spanning decades.

The phone rang. "Yeah, Paul, what is it?"

"The transmitter was set for three-thirty."

"When was it set?"

"Can't tell. No prints. Whoever set it wore gloves. I'm not sure of anything right now so get her into a safe house."

"She's already in one."

❧❦❧

John toted a large bag of Chinese food into Barbara's room. "Um, that smells good."

"Don't get so excited. It's all steamed. Brown sauce on the side."

"Oh, ugh, but why the special treatment?"

He leveled the serving tray over her bed and removed the containers. "Just want to give you the update on my meeting with Carlson."

"Ah, a man of his word. And why the special treatment? I know the drill. This isn't the usual food."

"Nah, I brought you something special. Professional courtesy."

"That's pushing it. Okay, so why the generosity?"

"Well, it's nice to find someone like myself who still cares about people." He didn't trust her one bit. But, with Barbara, he had to be manipulative to get anywhere. So he played her game.

"What do you mean?"

"You're not money hungry, trying to sap everyone for what they have."

"My clinic is free."

Barbara attempted to conceal her true thoughts on that matter. Her aura shouted a black outline at him. *She actually thinks I can't tell when she's lying? Short memory.*

He lied, too, a bit. "I know. Now who's Morgan?"

"Morgan?"

"Yeah, he called you yesterday."

"Wait a minute. How do you know?"

"I was at your place."

"Get to the point."

"Okay. You want it blunt. Here is blunt. Your apartment was hit."

"Hit as in blown up? Torn up? Well now, do you believe me? I've got to get out of here."

Blown up? Torn up? Knowledge of this?

"No, sorry. That's not possible now. You're under police protection. Here is where you'll stay. At least, until we catch him."

Barbara was so enraged she almost tossed a container of food at him.

He grabbed her arm in time. "Oh no, you don't. Eat."

To his surprise, she accepted the reprimand. She dove into the container of chicken and vegetables using a plastic spork.

"Who's Morgan?"

"My clinic is free for patients, but I pay my counselors."

"Okay and…"

"Look, my counselors have masters and doctorate degrees. They're not doing this just for community service."

"Who's Morgan?"

"His publishing company gives me a donation every February from a grant I wrote. I told you about that yesterday. All of it goes to salaries."

"You just told me about your drive into Manhattan."

"That's what it was for. No, Morgan wouldn't do this. He wants me in bed, not to scare me to death. Besides, he's not smart enough to think of this."

"One more thing. There were so many Gemini artifacts around. Why only that sign?"

"Oh yes. Dr. Psychic. Of course, you'd notice. I'm a Gemini. May thirtieth."

"That's it?"

"Yes. It's good energy for me."

"What does Gemini mean to you?"

"Sorry, Doc. You won't get free associations from me."

"Of course not. Silly of me to try." He focused on her, without changing his gaze, to perceive what she wouldn't tell him verbally.

❧❦❧

"If the stock went down, buy ten thousand more shares!" Morgan yelled into a phone, sitting at his desk and being his usual irate self.

"That's taking too big a risk."

"I don't care what the risk is. Take it!"

Carol waited in the doorway for him to complete his tirade.

After he slammed down the phone, he turned to her. "Yes, Carol, what is it?"

She carried a white box with a huge black bow wrapped around it. "A special messenger brought this over."

He took it. "Thanks." She waited for him to open the box. "That will be all, Carol."

She sauntered out. He was amused at the thought that he could have her anytime he wanted. He expected something glamorous or exciting.

He almost passed out when he inspected the contents—a condom over the carcass of a rat. Nausea overwhelmed him as he ripped open the card, which read, *Stay away from my woman.*

He slumped into his chair and pushed it away from his

desk. He called on the intercom, "Carol, call Mr. Katz. I need for him to come here immediately."

"He's already here, Mr. Reynolds."

Morgan's body shook. With trembling hands, he pushed the box to the end of the desk as Steve approached. Steve stared at it and then jumped back as if the odor of death appalled him.

"I know you're not liked. But isn't this pushing it?"

"I'm not in the mood for your sour jokes."

"All right, what do you want to do?"

"Calling the cops for this nonsense is out of the question."

"Morgan, this isn't kid stuff."

"It isn't so serious, either. Just some crack pot. I'll ignore him and he'll go away."

"Yeah, sure. Then how come you panicked?"

"I didn't panic. I was just surprised. A dead rat as a present? That's too creative, even for me. You can go now. Just stop at Carol's desk and sign off on the new contract we negotiated."

Steve read the card. "What woman?"

"Haven't a clue."

"Could Montgomery have done this to send a message to back off?"

"Nah. This is sick."

❧❧❧

John hunched over his desk in his home office with Barbara's file. He had a lot to tackle. His mind had bent out of shape on this one. He had stopped off at Imaging and begged for her brain scan reports. He got them. Now he separated the blood work, MRI, PET, and CAT into piles.

Serotonin 50. Major clue here. Tyrosine, GABA, Taurine, Inositol, Choline, B vitamins, Pantothenic acid, zinc, Omega-3, trace minerals, toxic metals, lead. Where did she get lead from? Could be here since childhood. I'll ask her if she ate pica off walls as a kid. Blood histamine, glucose. Everything is out of normal range here. All right the PET. She let them inject her. That's a surprise.

He continued reading.

Ah, no its not. They needed to do a full-body restraint, and with the ten mg Valium, she was too relaxed to put up much resistance. Okay. At least they got it. Um, lower glucose metabolism in the prefrontal cortex. Could be why her eyes are so armored. It's right there. Not exactly poor, but somewhat below normal functioning. The corpus callosum, also functions poorly. So her thinking left hemisphere can't communicate with her right hemisphere or emotional side. Could be why she becomes so aggressive. She can't rationalize herself out of it. The MRI. Brain cells within the prefrontal cortex region are eleven percent smaller than normal. She does break conventional rules, shows no remorse, and she's very hostile. Let me look at the amygdala, hypothalamus, and periaqueductal gray matter. All dysfunctional. Premeditated acts of violence? Reduced glucose metabolism in prefrontal cortex and reduced glucose metabolism in corpus callosum, left angular gyrus and abnormal asymmetries in amygdala, hippocampus and thalamus. Oh no, Barbara, what have you done? The orbitofrontal cortex and middle frontal gyrus compromised. Greater volume of white matter in prefrontal cortex. Got that. She's a pro at deception. Oh man! Why couldn't I be wrong on this one?

He picked up the phone and dialed.

A groggy voice answered. "Hello."

"Paul, it's John."

"Do you realize what time it is?"

"Uh…"

"It's three a.m., damn it."

"It's important."

"What's so important it couldn't wait till tomorrow?"

"Barbara is a murderer."

CHAPTER 23

Three Years Earlier:

John opened his eyes, awakened by the sounds of forceful-ly running water from the shower. Vicki had taken care not to wake him. The closed blinds prevented any hint of the morning Florida sun from disturbing his peaceful sleep. Tossing, turning, and stretching to get back to reality, he glanced at the clock on the night table. Seven-fifteen. What a night. He hadn't slept so soundly in a long time. He'd needed it.

In the bathroom, he scrutinized himself in the mirror above the double sink. He felt unkempt with his disheveled hair and coarse beard growing in. Vicki had left him a toothbrush and toothpaste, which he thankfully used. He opened the shower door, without hesitation or contemplating what reaction she might have, and joined her.

"Oh my God! Do you mind?"

"Guess not." He snatched her bath sponge, a fluffy pink ribbony round one saturated with her favorite scent of bath gel, gardenia. "Let me." He washed her down with tender, loving care, from her neck to her toes, treasuring every part of her body as he inhaled the scent he grew to worship, all the while, passionately kissing her lips through the suds.

Her hands caressed his face. "Oh God, you look like a caveman! I have to go to work. Don't start now."

"Work? It's Sunday."

"I teach Sunday School."

She gazed up into his eyes as the water cascaded down her bounteous breasts.

He craved more of her. He embraced her and rubbed his belly against her body, wanting her to enjoy the moment. In between soft gentle kisses on her breast, he said. "You've got plenty of time."

"I have to make my lunch."

"I'll make your lunch."

Her pleading look made him give in. They rinsed off. He shut off the water, dried her, and lifted her in both arms. Then he carried her into the bedroom.

She laughed. "John, I have to dry my hair. I have to go."

"What time do you have to be there?"

"Eight-thirty."

"You have over an hour." He plopped her down on the bed and kissed her neck down to her breasts. "You're going to go to work very happy."

"You're so scratchy! You're tickling me. And I'm happy already!"

He continued down to her stomach and lower, with gentle pecks of his lips.

She gasped. "John if you're going where I think you're going, stop."

He did, the moment she said to. "Really?" He lay down next to her. "Why?"

"The thought of it makes me nervous. Please, don't be mad."

"No, not at all. I'll never push you to do something you're not ready for, but I will tell you, you don't know what you're missing."

"How about I cook you a delicious dinner tonight to make up for it?"

"Ooh, that sounds great."

"What—"

"Anything you make is fine, just low carb and not fried."

"I can do that. I've got to get ready for work."

"I'll be at the pool this afternoon. Meet me there?"

"Sure, darlin'."

❦

He opened the door to his parent's house at eight, hoping they weren't up yet, but, no such luck. They sat around a table for six in the nook adjoining the kitchen.

"John?"

"Yes, Mom." He peeked into the nook, his beard matured and his hair protruding out in all directions.

"You look barbaric."

"I've been told that already this morning, thank you."

"You had to sleep with her on the first date?"

"Mom, let me get myself together and then you can give me the third degree. What time are we leaving?"

"Nine."

"Give me a half hour."

Esther and Sam had finished with breakfast of rolled oatmeal, bagels with cream cheese, and coffee. John appeared all cleaned up; clean-shaven; and dressed in navy blue slacks, light blue shirt, navy tie, and light-blue Versace jacket. He'd adorned himself with his signature sexy Jean Paul Gaultier cologne that even his mother loved. He held his arms out so they could inspect their son. "Better?"

"Much. Now tell us about this woman."

"That's right to the point, Mom."

"So?"

"I'll match you. She's the woman I'm going to marry." He escaped to the blender in the kitchen to make a protein drink.

"What?" his parents yelled in unison.

"I think you heard me." He poured in milk, banana, raw egg, a vanilla protein powder and wheat germ.

"What do you know about this woman other than who her father is?" his father demanded, lashing out.

"She's thirty-seven, a kindergarten teacher. And she has a twin brother." He wouldn't dare tell them about her affinity for weaponry. The blender whirled. After he poured a large glass, he joined them.

"That's it?"

He made himself comfortable, unbuttoning his jacket. "Well, Dad, her dog died last week."

"What do you know about her?" his father asked.

"Uh…"

"What's her favorite color?" his mother asked.

"Don't know."

"Where did she go to college?"

"Don't know, Mom."

"What's her favorite food?"

"Don't know, Dad."

"When's her birthday?"

"That one I do know, March twenty-third."

"You do not know enough about her to say you're going to marry her," his mother said emphatically.

"I thought you'd both be happy I found someone."

"Not from a first date, not from down here, and not someone who's just a teacher."

"Mom, come on."

"Does she have a master's degree at least?"

"I honestly don't know."

"Don't let your little head control the big one."

Getting embarrassed, he shrugged. "I think I had enough of this line of interrogation for now, don't you think?"

"We'll discuss it again when his highness is ready to divulge more, his mother said. "Shall we make plans to go to the country club for dinner?"

"I'm sorry, Mom, Vicki is cooking dinner for me tonight."

"Play it your way. Let's go."

❧❦❧

At three p.m., John drove into the country club's parking lot. While walking to the pool, he noticed the SWAT black hummer with the letters SWAT written across the driver's side. Laughing, he took a picture of it with his smartphone.

Wait till the guys see this.

He made himself comfortable on a lounge chair in the sun to the far right of the entrance and didn't notice he was being observed. He relaxed, wanting to catch some rays, and the least he expected was a confrontation. Within a few minutes, a take-charge-looking guy strode over to him. About six feet tall, built—but not like him—with blond hair and blue eyes, wearing shorts and a short-sleeved shirt revealing muscular arms and legs, he resembled Vicki. He extended his hand to shake, and John reluctantly acknowledged the extremely firm grip.

He grabbed a chair from a round glass table next to the lounge. "Mark Marin. Sorry about last night."

"Still don't know what to make of it."

"Nothing for you to make of it." Mark said, his tone unapologetic.

"Must put a crimp in her social life."

"Nah, we shut it down when it's someone she knows."

"Isn't that going to an extreme?"

"No, in the one instance we may need it to save her life one day, it'll be worth it. And you got me into trouble with my wife."

"How's that?"

"Vicki told Jaimie everything. They're best friends. From the moment they met, they became like sisters, not sisters-in-law. They tell each other everything, every minutest detail. And then Jaimie told me."

John smiled in embarrassment. "So what's the problem?"

"The problem is who has time to spend so much time? And on the lanai? Sure, it's romantic. I'll give you that, but we need more privacy than that with three kids."

"Well, you make the time. Your wife is supposed to be the most precious person in your life and you need to show her that. Women love pampering. Find a time when the kids—"

"Hey. For fourteen years Jaimie and I have had a great—"

A high-pitched, sweet little voice interrupted them. "Daddy, Daddy!"

She sprinted over and jumped into her father's arms. She was five, precocious, adorable with natural blonde hair in a ponytail and banana curls, big round light blue eyes like Vicki and Mark. The dimples on her cheeks accentuated when she giggled, hugging her Daddy.

"This is the most precious person in my life and this is

what's it's all about." Mark squeezed her tight and kissed her on her cheeks. "This princess and her two brothers. Amanda, say hello to Dr. John."

"Ooooh, you're Aunt Vicki's new boyfriend."

John cringed. He had already fallen in love with Amanda. "No."

"Oh yes you are, don't fib."

Mark laughed. His daughter had John's number. And John knew it, too.

Mark received a beep on his pager, as did his two, team members on lounges on the opposite side of the pool. "Got to go to work. See you later, Doc." They dashed off with urgency before John could respond.

John recognized a situation. He had experienced this reaction so many times before. Furrowed brows, distant eyes on their faces replacing smiles, stiffened body language, the forewarning, that signaled death could be an outcome today.

"Can I—tell—you a secret?" Amanda whispered.

Oh, man, she already has me wrapped around her little finger. "If it's a secret, you can't tell anyone."

"Yes, I can. Please?"

"Nope."

She jumped up and down and John melted.

"Please? Pretty please?"

He rolled over onto his stomach. "I'm taking a nap."

She bounced up and down impatiently and patted him on his back. "No, you can't. Not till I tell you the secret."

His parents came over and made themselves comfortable on the two lounges next to John. "Amanda, say hello to Dr. Sam and Dr. Esther. They're my parents."

"Hi."

"Hello, sweetheart."

John smiled at his mother's loving voice. She longed for one of her own, as she constantly reminded him.

"I'm telling Dr. John a secret and you can't hear."

"Yes, they can."

"No, just you."

"Okay, tell me already so I can take my nap."

She cupped her delicate hands around his ear and whispered, "Aunt Vicki told Mommy she met the man she's going to marry." She giggled as if she'd told him the secret of the universe.

John laughed deeply. "Really?"

She giggled. "Yes."

In the distance, her mother called her and she scampered off. John looked after her and waved to Vicki who was talking to Jaimie.

Okay at least we're on the same page. That's good. Damn good.

Vicki waved back, and then joined him, wearing shorts, a tank, and her signature flip-flops. She strode toward his parents, extending her hand with a big smile. "Hello. I'm Vicki."

She shook hands with both of them. His father wore that shit-eating grin that always meant he was charmed. She sat on the edge of John's lounge chair with her right leg crossed over her left.

John didn't know what to think. Were they pleasantly surprised at her casual elegance and confident presence, or did they expect the down-home country girl? To him, Vicki was the perfect combination.

"Hello, dear."

Esther wore her probing GYN look. The glare she absorbed from her son wouldn't deter her from the in-depth Trenton interrogation. John knew that look all too well. Every woman he dared to introduce them to receive the same treatment. Many, it chased away.

"Your niece is precious."

"Yes, she is. Thank you."

"Is she the only grandchild?"

"No. The only girl, though. She's my twin brother Mark's daughter and he has two sons, eight and eleven. And my older brother Brian has two sons, six and ten."

"Your parents are very fortunate."

"Yes. Thank you. We are blessed."

"John tells us you teach kindergarten."

"Yes. I love the little ones."

John sensed Vicki didn't like his mother's inquisitiveness

and hoped she'd tell her some things but just enough for her to be liked by them. She must have been used to interrogations. Her father gave her plenty. John knew he should relax and just keep his mouth shut.

"So tell us, Vicki, where did you go to college?"

"UF at Gainesville."

"So you dormed?"

"Yes, I loved it."

John and his father cringed, but let Esther conduct this examination. They understood how Mom operated and it wasn't always pretty.

"Did you decide on teaching early on?"

"I knew in high school I wanted to teach. I volunteered at a group home and I realized after being there a week I wanted to help these children. These are the kids who had no families to take them in. Did you know that fifty-five percent of the children here in Sun County are being raised by grandparents?"

"No, I had no idea."

Even John picked his head up for that one.

"It's a staggering amount," Vicki continued. "And very often, their teacher is the only positive role model they have."

"They're very lucky to have you, Vicki."

Wow! She can handle my parents. That's a first. If my mom likes her, that's a go.

"Thank you. I just wanted to come over to say hello. I'm going home to prepare dinner now."

"He's a very picky eater."

John laughed.

"Yes, his highness already told me the restrictions, and I shall abide." She patted him on the shoulder. "Come around six."

He turned over. "Sure thing." He didn't want to be demonstrative and kiss her in front of his parents. "What do you want me to bring?"

"Nothing. Just yourself. Nice to meet you." She smiled and walked away.

"Same here, sweetheart."

When she was out of hearing distance, John turned to his parents. "So?"

"She seems like…a lovely girl."

"That's a start." He pretended to nap and listened to his parent's conversation.

Esther whispered to her husband, "She called him his highness. Only I can call him that."

"I think you may need to get used the fact that you're not the only permanent woman in his life now."

CHAPTER 24

Present Day:

Clancy, clean-shaven and well dressed in ironed slacks and a light-green button-down shirt under a heavy fleece, pulled up in a rented dirty white van. He parked across the street from Barbara's school at eight-fifteen in the morning on this clear and sunny, but brisk, day. He was lucky to find a parking spot, as most of the street space was for bus stops.

The newspaper article and photos of Jeremiah's rescue with a small photo of the principal in the lower right corner of the article lay on the passenger seat. He recognized Mrs. Bennett in the front yard eagerly waving lower-grade children onto the front steps and into the building, welcoming them to their school day.

He grinned.

Clancy approached behind Mrs. Bennett with a casual gait, not wanting to startle her. She turned around, giving him a warm smile. Other teachers and parents in the front yard ignored him as he blended in with the regulars.

"Mrs. Bennett?"

"May I help you, sir?"

"Yes I hope so. I'm worried about my son, Roger Miller."

"Have you spoken with his teacher?"

"It's nothing she could help with."

She hesitated. "Please come into my office and we'll talk."

He followed her up the steps with his fingers over his mouth to conceal his nefarious grin.

❧

Mrs. Bennett's desk stood catty-cornered so she could see directly into the main office. Bookshelves, filled to capacity with current education journals and the teacher's guides in every curriculum area for every grade, hugged the wall adjacent to her desk.

A large conference table with chairs surrounding it accommodated most of the space in the center of the room. She sat behind her desk and motioned for him to take a chair opposite her. "I don't believe we've met before, Mr. Miller. How may I help you?"

"No. We haven't met, Mrs. Bennett. Roger came to live with me, this past summer, after his mother re-married. You see, he's one of Dr. Montgomery's cases and he's telling me that she hasn't seen him in over a week."

"Yes, Dr. Montgomery is home ill."

"But she lives in my apartment complex. I haven't seen her coming or going. Even her car is gone. Did she leave for good?"

"No never. But tell me, Mr. Miller, how come your son is still attending here? Dr. Montgomery doesn't live in this immediate vicinity."

His pale cheeks reddened. "I didn't realize a change of address would make a change of schools mandatory. I've been driving him here."

"Yes, it would. Unless you get a variance from the district office and they are difficult to obtain. Now what class is he in? I'll start the paperwork. It will be easier for you in the long run."

His jaw twitched. "Ah, thank you, Mrs. Bennett. As long as I am reassured that nothing is wrong." He rushed out, sweating.

Mrs. Bennett observed him from her desk, but let him go without further confrontation. In an instant, she called to her secretary. "Get me Barbara's case file, please."

ↁↁↁ

Tony and Sal entered Mrs. Bennett's office after three p.m. With them was a sketch artist, Matt, a nerdy looking guy, in his thirties wearing thick, black-rimmed glasses.

"Hello, Detectives. Please have a seat. I've checked all records. This parent and child do not exist in this school. He said he lived in Barbara's complex. But that area is all Russian. Barbara is the only American living in that building."

"We'll investigate this, Mrs. Bennett. We're glad you called us. This could be a lead as to the hit on her home. Can you give Matt a composite?"

"Yes, of course, and I'm so glad you apprised me of what happened to her apartment so I knew who to call. I was more aware of irregularities than usual. But, in all honesty—now please don't take offense—I expected you here earlier."

Matt readied his pad and charcoals.

She caught the we've-been-nailed look that Tony and Sal shot each other.

"We were waiting for crime scene results to put this together," Sal said.

Mrs. Bennett read them well. "I hope you're giving this case the appropriate attention." She had their number, and her brazen tone conveyed that. "Ready, Matt?" He nodded. "Caucasian," she continued. "Clean shaven. Bald on top, longish blond hair from the back of his head to over his collar. Bleached blond and a poor job at that. Too much peroxide. Dark brown roots with some gray, about a two-inch growth."

Sal grinned.

"It's something a woman would notice," she explained. "Dark brown eyes, oval shaped, but not almond. His eyelids had folds. He has an intense look but full of anguish. Very dark looking soul."

Matt worked diligently at composing the primary sketch.

"Dark pupils, oh, and a squared jaw," she added. "Wrinkles on his forehead. Ruddy cheeks, very pale complexion. Needs to get out into the sun more."

"That's very observant, Mrs. Bennett. You don't even need any prompting."

"It's my job to be observant, Matt."

Tony smiled while nodding in agreement.

"Irish, but didn't speak with much of a brogue. Wrinkles on his face, too, deep ones, like he's a smoker. About mid-forties, small straight nose, medium build. High cheekbones. And dark brown eyebrows, thick, bushy, with a very small arch. Like his eyebrows couldn't hike, even if he tried."

Tony scribbled notes. "Any scars or distinguishing marks?"

"None that I could see. He was dressed in slacks and a fleece, bundled up. His hands had brown spots though, but he was too young for age spots. Maybe it was a chemical burn."

"I'm very impressed, Mrs. Bennett." Sal pursed his lips. "Chemical burn? What makes you say that?"

"My niece studies photography and once she didn't wear the protective gloves. Something she was working with, I don't even know for sure what, got on her hand and left her with a brown spot. Sort of looked like that."

Matt showed her the composite. "Close, Mrs. Bennett?"

"Oh my, young man. That is him. A little narrower on the nose, and eyes closer set, though. If you ever need to change jobs, we can sure use an art teacher."

"Sorry, we're not letting him go." Sal handed her his card. "Thank you very much Mrs. Bennett. If you think of anything else, please call us."

"Yes I will. Thank you, Detectives, Matt."

They got up to leave, nodding a sincere thank you.

"Matt, get that into the database, ASAP," Sal ordered.

ের

Carlson slouched at his desk frowning, as Tony and Sal entered with Matt's composite of the suspect.

"We got it, Loo," Tony said. "Mrs. Bennett nailed it to a T. Real name is Clancy Davis. DUI arrest ten years ago put him into the system. Cinematographer. Real big ten to fifteen years ago. Get this. Even won an Oscar. The photography shit would explain what Montgomery was complaining about."

John barged in, interrupting them. His intense presence forced them to stop mid-conversation.

"Wait a minute. What he's got tops even this." Carlson turned his attention to John. "And what makes you think I care enough about this to want to be bothered by a phone call at three a.m.?"

"Nice to see you too, Paul. Glad I'm appreciated." John tossed his jacket onto a couch and then extracted the medical files from his attaché.

"What's going on?" Sal asked.

"This medical genius here now thinks Montgomery is a murderer," Carlson explained.

Sal straightened his posture. "Yeah?"

"Before you start," Carlson warned. "Don't give us fucking psychobabble or medical jargon, and don't tell me parts of the brain I don't even know I have. Just give me the behavior and what she did, and no psychic crap."

John contemplated for a moment, thinking how he could water this down for a layman. "All right. There's excessive damage in the parts of her brain that control impulses, rational thinking, deception, acting on right and wrong, and inhibiting aggression. She has chemical imbalances and toxins in her blood that combine with this and trigger her aggression and impulse to kill without remorse. There are impulse murderers, like serial killers, and predatory murderers that go after a target for a goal. Do I need to name who they are specifically?" Carlson glared at him. "Didn't think so," John continued. "She's the latter. Simple enough?"

"And you know this how?"

"Sal, studies have been conducted after murderers have been incarcerated, both impulse and predator types, and their brain and blood profiles have been compared. These are the common elements. Since Montgomery didn't tell me anything truthful, I had to examine her more thoroughly than I would have had to with a cooperative patient. She has the same profile."

"Can't someone who's not a murderer have the same brain dysfunctions?" Sal asked.

"Yes and no. It's still inconclusive. But with these abnormalities, she's incapable of making sane choices. It's all in sync with an abusive childhood. The abusive childhood added into the mix makes it plausible. She's a psychopath. She can be sane and functioning, when she wants to be, and a killer when it suits her. A killer without remorse, who kills anyone who gets in her way. The psychopathic personality fits her. Superficial charm, absence of nervousness, specific loss of insight, lack of remorse or shame, no empathy, sex life impersonal and—"

"How do you know about her sex life, bro?" Tony interrupted. "Don't tell me you—"

"No way! Through energy work. She's blocked. No warm and fuzzy feelings in her."

"Now, hotshot, who did she fucking murder?" Carlson demanded.

"That's for you to investigate. But I think it has to do with money. That's her objective and this Morgan character gave her a huge donation to cover the salaries of her staff at her clinic. She even coped with a panic attack going through the tunnel to meet with him. Most people would avoid it, but she didn't, so I know the objective of getting the funds was stronger. Right now, I only have today to keep her in observation. Tomorrow I have to move her to a less-restrictive environment, even though she's in protective custody. I'm not telling her about what I concluded, but I want to move her to Manhattan Psych."

"You bet, you're not," Carlson argued. "'Oh by the way, Dr. Montgomery, I discovered you're a murderer so I'm moving you to be with the criminally insane.' That will open us up for a major lawsuit. And I'm in charge, so I'll get the heat."

"Give me a break. She belongs in Manhattan."

"That's not less restrictive!" Carlson exploded.

"She'll have some more freedom to roam around but she won't be able to escape. She'll be watched by armed guards 24/7. Hey, you two know what it's like going through security there. Just last week a female rookie got detained for two hours. She couldn't pass through the metal detector. She had to endure a strip and cavity search because she was unaware she couldn't wear a bra with an underwire. At Manhattan Psych, Barbara will be away from TV, cell phone, and computer access. If I keep her at Sheepshead, which is minimum security, and has volunteer admissions, with people coming and going all day, she'll find a way to make contact with the outside."

"He's right, Loo. John, take a look at this." Tony deposited the photo of Clancy in front of him. "Mrs. Bennett got a visit from him inquiring about Montgomery. A photographer."

John connected the dots. "Okay, is he her predator or accomplice? And where does Reynolds fit in? Talk to him yet?"

Carlson balked. "No. We didn't talk to him, yet."

"Damn it, Paul! Why are you dragging your feet on this? Even if you think this is nonsense, a woman's home was hit. That's a crime."

"Yes, a fucking crime against her. Why do you say accomplice?"

"Only her living room, one room, was destroyed. Everything is easily replaceable. Ever hear of someone setting themselves up as a victim, so they can take the onus off them as a suspect when they commit the major criminal act?"

"It happens all the time, John, but in this case it doesn't distance her from the investigation. It brings her fucking into it."

"Well, I don't think she considered the possibility of you incarcerating her." John paused to think. "Exactly. This fits. That's why I need to keep a hold on her in a secure location. I need to move her."

"Absolutely not. We'll need her for questioning, and I'm not sending my guys to make a fucking trek into Manhattan, when she's five fucking minutes away now."

"Tony, knock some sense into him."

Carlson didn't give Tony a chance to respond. "No, John. Not happening. Get us a lead to show that she murdered someone in her past or she plans to murder someone in the future and we'll investigate that. And what you saw or heard from your fucking imaginary friend Max in la-la land won't cut it. We will bring in this Clancy guy, though, and see where it goes."

"Who's Max?"

"Never mind that, Sal. When you spoke to Mrs. Bennett, what did she tell you about Barbara?"

"We didn't ask her about Montgomery."

"Why the hell not?" John's frustration level mounted. "What exactly did you tell Mrs. Bennett about the situation?"

"Nothing to alarm her." Tony trod carefully. "We told her we had to place Dr. Montgomery into police custody because she reported someone stalking her, and a couple days later her apartment was ransacked. That's all. Nothing about her mental state or observation."

"All right. Good. At least I'll know what direction to take. So tell me, am I all alone here? Is that it? Paul, I mean it. This one will come back to bite you in the ass."

"John, you're not alone," Tony said. "What do you need me to do?"

"I fucking don't like you sucking Tony in," Carlson snarled. "But, then again, I know damn well he's your best friend."

"Thanks," John said to Tony, ignoring Carlson. "Here's what I need. I need to know everything about her educational background, degrees, schooling, and adoption at birth if that's the truth, her entire pedigree. Start with the last three years at this school. And I don't care if you have to hack into the Department of Education's personnel files to do it." He deliberately didn't mention her Gemini obsession. They already thought he was nuts, so that one he'd tackle on this own.

"What are you going to do now?" Sal asked.

"First, I'm telling her we didn't get enough info from her for her assault case, so I'm not releasing her, which is sort of the truth. Because she was uncooperative, I can legally delay her release and keep her housed here, instead of moving her to an actual safe house. So that will give me more time to prove my theories. I'll show her the picture of Clancy Davis and see what I get, and then I'll speak with Mrs. Bennett. And you guys pay a visit to Reynolds. His address is in the Yellow Pages, if you don't want to bother finding it online." He didn't mistake Carlson's glare. "Then prove to me you don't need to be spoon-fed on this one. Call me when you get what I need."

John prepared to leave and compiled all of the paperwork

he'd brought in, without saying another word, but his annoyance with Carlson had reached an intolerable level. As he looked at him, with Carlson avoiding direct eye contact, John perceived that something else was going on which Carlson was hiding. That added another level of inconvenience to this case. Carlson had never been so lax or disagreeable before, or hesitant to investigate.

John's only ally in this was Tony, but would he go against his lieutenant or behind his back? John's gut churned with nervousness about what he might have to uncover, not only with Barbara. That was his job. Now his friend was involved. Carlson knew Reynolds for sure. John's instincts told him that. But how? John's motive for finding out the truth was now clouded, and his unconscious sent him confusing messages that he didn't know whether to accept or repress. What was Carlson into that he was afraid John would find out? Max would be working overtime on this one, helping him sort out all of the inconsistencies. John departed without even saying goodbye.

෧෧෧

Barbara napped out of sheer boredom. She tossed, turned, and moaned while having a nightmare…

Nineteen-seventy-nine. Kellie, aka Barbara, was four years old wearing a white dress with pink and lime-green dots throughout, with the cutest white sandals on her feet. She was holding her daddy's hand. But Daddy didn't say a word. Her blue eyes sparkled and her warm light brown hair flowed down her back. She was happy here with the semblance of a normal childhood.

Her father Ralph Wilson—late-thirties, stocky, wearing a cheap polyester suit—walked his adorable Kellie down a poorly lit basement corridor in a city hospital. He concealed the tears in his eyes from her with sniffles. He dreaded what was to come and what he'd have to do. They strode down the long empty hallway to a room with the door closed. He winced at the odors of formaldehyde and disinfectants. Kellie didn't notice. Ralph picked up Kellie, seated her on a wooden bench outside the door, and motioned for her to stay there.

He hesitantly entered the morgue.

A solemn-looking doctor approached him and shook his hand then escorted him over to a table that held a body covered by a white sheet. He nodded to the doctor, who pulled the sheet down to the woman's neck revealing her identity. Ralph collapsed in tears and anguish over the body of his once beautiful Sandra, who had been mangled and disfigured after being mowed down in a hit and run in downtown Brooklyn earlier that morning.

Now Ralph snuggled next to Kellie on the bench. He told her Mommy went to heaven to be with God. Kellie didn't understand that Mommy wouldn't be holding her and loving her anymore, but she knew Mommy wouldn't be coming home today. She cried as a reaction to seeing Daddy so distraught, but not because she comprehended what had just happened. All that concerned her was who would do her hair?

Barbara cried in her sleep but still didn't awaken...

It was six months later. Kellie and her daddy walked, in the middle of the night, down a dark alley in between two large apartment buildings. Garbage pails were filled to capacity without covers and dark black torn garbage bags surrounded them, so the rats had a glorious feast. He let go of her hand and motioned for her to stay there. Barbara heard herself screaming, "Daddy. No, Daddy, don't leave me!"

He pulled away from her, pushing her down onto some garbage bags. She landed hard.

Barbara wrenched in bed, screamed out loud, "Daddy, don't leave me!" In the distance around the corner, four-and-a-half-year-old Kellie heard a gunshot. She ran to where the sound came from and discovered her daddy with a gun in his hand and a bullet hole in the side of his head. She attempted to waken him, pushing and pulling on him. His blood smeared all over her.

A female officer lifted her off him and removed her to the side, isolating her from the chaos.

"Don't come near me! Kellie screamed, You'll get dead, too!"

⌘⌘⌘

Police and ambulance sirens roared in her dream and on the main avenue of the hospital.

John entered her room, stood by the doorway, and observed her heart-wrenching pain.

She screamed out loud. "Death to all those who come near me! Death to all those who come near me!"

CHAPTER 25

Three Years Earlier:

John opened the door to Vicki's house. "Wow, smells good in here. You had the door unlocked. What would your brother think of that?"

"I just unlocked it. Dinner's ready. Come in, darlin'."

"What did you make?" He made himself comfortable at the kitchen table. The soft suede like fabric on the oversized chairs conformed to his body perfectly. He relaxed on the armrests, glad they weren't narrow feminine chairs.

"You'll have to wait and see." Vicki placed a salad on the table with fresh green lettuces, home grown grape tomatoes, cucumbers, green and yellow peppers, sprouts, avocado, red onions, topped with croutons, and tossed with light homemade fat-free Italian vinaigrette.

She served the salad with tongs matching the stoneware. All of the dishes, serving pieces, and platters coordinated in the varying shades of green, gold, and with a hint of red in the same geometric pattern.

John noticed and appreciated the visual effects. This woman knew how to put things together. "This looks great."

"Thank you," she said. "Please start. I just want to take the rest out."

"You're doing all the work. Need any help?" He plucked a piece of green pepper from the salad and tossed it into his mouth.

"No, sit there, please. It's my kitchen. I like to do it myself."

He laughed at her possessiveness, studying her every move, quite impressed with his wife to be. Vicki pulled a tray of oversized orange-brown pumpkin muffins with crispy tops out of the oven. The aroma filled the air with sweet cinnamon and nutmeg. She gingerly placed them on a matching platter and put them onto the table. She scooped mashed cauliflower and spaghetti squash from pots on the stove, and put them into a two-in-one sectioned serving stoneware, topping both of them with a pat of butter. Then the main course, a sizzling almond-crusted baked tilapia, came out of the oven.

"This is amazing. And you cooked all of this in an hour?"

"Yes, darlin.' I love, love, love to cook."

"Ah domesticated? I can get used to that." He enjoyed the salad. "And this stoneware pattern, it's nice."

"I love everything to match. That's why I need so much cabinet space. I extended the kitchen into here." There were eight feet more of cabinets, top and bottom with a counter in the middle, extending one foot out from the wall right in the dining nook.

"I'd like this stoneware for my place. But in a different color," he said, delving into a muffin. "Wow, these are amazing," he moaned with delight. "Oh man! You can spoil me with dinners like this."

"That'll be my pleasure. What are the colors you'd want?"

"Black, gray, with yellow."

"It does come in that."

"Really?

"Yes, darlin' and if you're a good boy, you'll get this set for Christmas."

"Chanukah."

Her eyes widened.

"Is that a problem?"

"Not at all. Jaimie's Jewish. With your last name it didn't sound…" She served him the fish and veggies. "It's cauliflower, not potatoes."

"Never had that before. My dad converted after he and my

mom got married. Are the boys going to be bar Mitzvah?"

"I honestly don't know. They do celebrate both holidays though. Does it matter to you that I'm not Jewish?"

"No, not at all. This is fabulous. Thank you."

"You're very welcome."

He devoured everything on his plate. "I'm going to need to do twenty laps to burn this off."

"No, you won't. It's low carb. But save room for dessert later."

"Dessert has no calories but burns over three hundred an hour."

She scowled at him. "You actually know the statistics?"

He hiked his eyebrows, winked, and shot her a wickedly sexy grin. "Yeah. So you do know the kind of dessert I'm talking about."

"John! Well, I'm talking about apple pie. But I made it with sugar replacement."

"Sounds great. How late is the pool open?"

"You want to go swimming now?" Finished eating, she cleared the table.

"Let me help you. Yes, why not?"

"Okay." As she put dishes in the dishwasher, he noticed there was much more food on the stove.

"You made so much."

"Actually, on the way to the pool we can drop this at your parent's house, and they can have dinner, too."

"You cooked for my parents? Trying to score points are you?" He hugged her.

"Absolutely, why not? I'll show them one of my many talents." She packed the food up in stoneware with pop on lids.

"Many talents?"

"Well, the others are personal. But you know about them already."

"Ah, yes, do not tell them about those."

"Does your mom cook?"

"Yes, she's an excellent cook. But I think she's met her match with you. If her fangs come out, it's because she approves."

"Ah, jealousy. Let's go before it gets cold. I hope they haven't eaten already."

"They usually eat about now, so I don't know."

"Let me put on a suit."

He held her around her waist. "Do you have a real sexy one?"

"As a matter of fact, I do."

☙❧☙

John and Vicki carried in the trays to Esther and Sam's house, to find his father standing in front of the immense refrigerator with the door open. Vicki took it all in with envy. It was a huge modern space with rich dark mahogany cabinets and a luxurious expensive brown-grained granite island in the galley style kitchen. There was every up to date appliance.

"Dad, what are you doing?"

"You didn't want to go to the country club for dinner, so I'm trying to figure out what Mom should make."

"Problem solved. Vicki made you dinner. Where's Mom?"

Esther entered from another room. "What smells so good?"

"Vicki made you dinner, too. I'm going to get a suit and towel. We're going to the pool." John dashed into his master suite.

"Oh, how thoughtful, sweetheart. Thank you."

His father set the table and Esther examined Vicki's every move. Vicki positioned everything on the table carefully and removed the lids.

"Oh, my! This looks wonderful. You better not be as good a cook as I am."

So that's what John meant by fangs coming out. No, Esther darlin', I'm definitely a better cook than y'all.

"Enjoy." Vicki laughed at Esther's comment as if she accepted it teasingly. She already knew she had his father where she wanted him, now she had to work on his mother.

John called her from the door. "Vicki, I'm ready."

"I'm coming. Bye, see you soon." She scooted off to John, but not fast enough.

"It's a very nice salad."

"Yes, it is and these biscuits are fabulous. Melt in your mouth delicious. Try one." Sam urged.

She accepted begrudgingly. "Oh, my God. These are wonderful." She tasted the cauliflower and squash. Then the fish. "This is very, very good. Okay, so she's a *balabusta*. I'll give her that. John needs someone who's a fine homemaker too."

❧❧❧

The pool area was empty. Perfect. It was dark and there were very few lighting fixtures around the pool. John was confident no one else would show up this late. He couldn't have asked for anything better. They strolled hand in hand over to the lounges on the far corner, away from the main entrance, so they could enjoy the serene peacefulness and privacy.

"That was a brilliant move."

"What?"

"Dinner for my parents." At a lounge, he flipped down the back to make it flat and took off his tank and shorts. "Now, show me. What do you think that I think is sexy?"

"Okay." Swaying her body to excite him, she performed a belly dance for an audience of one. She removed her shorts to reveal a skimpy black bottom, an inch more coverage than a G-string. Then she removed her tank, revealing a black-lace, strapless top with a lot of cleavage showing, and her firm breasts held up just the way he liked them. She spun around for his approval. "Well?"

"That passes with flying colors." He lay down on the lounge. "Come here, lie on top of me."

"Here?"

"We're the only ones here. Come on. And I got us coverage." He unfolded the oversized towel. She lay down on top of him, giggling, and he threw the towel over them covering them from head to toes.

"Oh, my God, you're crazy. But it's so comfortable." She laid her head on his chest. His warm hands caressed her back and slid down to her bottom.

"Come here." He scooted her up a little, and their lips interlocked in utter passion, with him showing her how much he was enamored with her. He unfastened the back of her top and then slid down her bottoms. She pulled her feet out of them. Next, he removed his trunks. Her arms wrapped around his neck. They were sucked into each other and couldn't be pried apart. The moans and groans of intense arousal emanated from the both of them.

He squeezed her bottom. "Just go with me here."

"Whatever you say, your highness. Oh, my God. Your hands are so warm."

He adjusted her hips and raised her up. She spread her legs. He was hard and warm. She was satiny soft and wet.

He repositioned her hips, sliding forward and back while he massaged and tickled her bottom and base of her spine. "Just slide, just like that."

"Oh, my God. Oh, my God. Oh, my God. Oh, John…"

"Ssh. Now imagine what it would feel like if my tongue was there."

Her body quivered against him from head to toe. He breathed deeply, squeezing her tighter as waves of trembling spiraled through her. In response, he felt himself explode with energy, from his core up to his head.

"Oh my God, what are you doing to me?"

He slid her harder and faster and faster.

"I'm going to, uh, so fast. Oh my God!"

He breathed harder. "Oh, yeah, oh, Vicki…"

Their passion reached its peak as they attempted to contain their moans. Sensations still rippled through them. He felt her climax, again, as her head collapsed onto his chest, her messy hair going in different directions across her face. He let go. The warmth of his discharge came between them on their stomachs. They were both breathing heavily. Suddenly, without a moment to recoup and without any warning, the towel was yanked off from their heads down to their necks.

"What the—" John demanded.

"Daddy!"

CHAPTER 26

Present Day:

That's nice, real nice. Should I be forewarned?" John approached Barbara with caution watching her come back to reality. He focused, looking right through her to her very empty core. What a disturbed and tormented woman. He almost felt sympathy for her, but just for a fleeting moment. Feeling sorry didn't do his patients any good. Being tough was a necessity to push them forward. No enabling from him. No empathy. Not for this murderer, he reminded himself.

Barbara jerked up, terrified. She wrung her trembling hands together and hyperventilated as she stared at him with vacant eyes. "What did I say now?"

"Death to all those who come near me. Repeatedly."

"Oh my God." She shuddered and clutched her throat. "How much am I going to reveal to you?"

"Well, your unconscious is telling me a lot. Maybe it's telling you it's time to confront your demons. Now what does that mean?" He sat on the chair next to her bed, leaned in toward her, and cupped her hand in his. "What does that mean?" He expected, or rather hoped for, a truthful answer.

"What?"

"Barbara…"

She took a few moments. "Everyone that I get close to, everyone who I have feelings for, dies. My mother gave me up for adoption and I don't know why. I tried to find her, but couldn't. My adoptive mother died—"

"From cancer."

"No, that wasn't the truth. Sorry."

He sneered, letting her know he knew that already.

"From a hit and run when I was four. They never found the driver. Then my father went ahead and shot himself in the head six months later, dumping me on a pile of trash in an alley." She sniffled. "I never found out why."

John assessed her aura and tone the entire time and noticed a change when she spoke the last sentence. Her aura sent out jagged waves of a grayish color. That was a definite lie. She did know why and this could be a major clue. A clue he'd investigate with fervor.

"How about telling me something new."

She averted her eyes.

"Everything you divulged sounds like a rehearsed scenario and you told me this already. You have it down to a science. How about something spontaneous, from your gut?"

No response. Not making a dent.

"You never found out why?"

"No."

"What did you do to find out?"

"I hired a private investigator."

"Name?"

"It was eighteen to twenty years ago. He passed away."

"Name?"

"I don't remember."

"How did he die?" He looked at her with focus and intensity, trying to read her response.

She became frustrated. "For Christ sake! I don't know!"

She killed him. Got to be it. Max, give me a signal.

At that moment, he felt Max jumping into his crown chakra.

Damn! Now to prove it.

"Why are you looking at me like that, Dr. Clairvoyant?"

"I haven't gotten a straight answer from you in three days."

"Too fucking bad."

He was immune to the expletive. "Who else does that refer to? Sounds aggressive, like you're warning people to stay away."

"I'm not. But isn't that enough?"

"No, actually, it isn't." John stared her down but she wasn't budging. He knew she was cognizant of what she was hiding and he'd collected more information than she realized.

"What's in the envelope?"

"Changing the subject? Okay, I'll play. Let's see what you tell me about this. Truth or lie." He pulled out the photo of Clancy and placed it on her lap.

Barbara looked down to her left, took a deep breath, and swallowed, her tell that she was about to lie.

"Who is he?" He smiled because he'd caught her. "Don't recognize him?"

She stared at him, wide-eyed. "No."

"Clancy Davis. Visited your school this morning looking for you. Mrs. Bennett gave the detectives a composite. She was so observant and detailed it took the department less than sixty seconds to identify him. So who is he? Your stalker or partner?"

"Partner? Partner? You actually think I'm involved in something sinister?"

He laughed at her naiveté.

"Just tell me already. When am I getting out of here?"

"You're not."

"What? The seventy-two hours are up, you bastard!"

"Quiet! Yes, the seventy-two hours are up, but I can keep you longer since you've been uncooperative, and you're in protective custody until we find him."

"Dr. Trenton, okay, I admit it. I know him. Not personally—" She looked down to the left. "But I've seen him before. He came onto me at Zodiac. He's not a serial killer or anything. He's just obsessed with me. His tormenting is an obsession of something he can't have. He's just like any of the other losers that go there."

"Yes, you do know him personally. You look down to your left when you lie."

"I'll just have to change that, won't I? Okay, so I know him, but he's still a creep."

"How do you know him?"

"None of your business."

"Really? Come on here. You're in a mess. Do you realize that? You're not letting me help you at all."

"You really piss me off. Do you realize that? I met him for drinks once. He creeped me out."

He was pleased he had that effect on her. He was forcing her to be more cunning and deceitful. Deceitful people took careless actions. The more careless she was, the faster he'd catch her.

"What about him creeped you out?"

"He just wasn't my type."

Do you even have a type?

"Well, he *is* dangerous. What time do you get home from school?"

"About three-thirty. Why?"

"The timer on the amateur bomb he made was set for that time. Right in your living room. The room you first enter and, by the way, it was the only room damaged."

"Everything is replaceable."

"That's exactly what I thought. Interesting that you had the same bland reaction to your own personal belongings being destroyed. And you didn't ask how we know he was the one to set it. Interesting. So you already knew it was him."

She closed her eyes.

What does she think she is? An ostrich? Closing her eyes so I'll disappear?

"Actually, you just confirmed it. I really didn't know."

So Clancy is her partner.

"I can't talk to you. I feel everything I say is being analyzed."

"That's correct. And, I would add, everything you don't say, as well."

"So every conversation has a hidden agenda?"

He shrugged with an affirmative smile.

"So what happens now?"

"Good question. I'll get back to you. First thing tomorrow morning." He stood up, exhaled out of frustration, and exited the room, invoking Max as he crossed the threshold of the door.

❦

In his office, after taking off his jacket and tie, and hanging both on his coat rack, John sat behind his desk, placed his feet flat on the floor, and breathed deeply to ground himself. Then he called his secretary through the intercom. "Marissa, please hold all phone calls and visitors for at least twenty minutes."

"Yes, Dr. Trenton."

He closed his eyes, inhaling and exhaling ten times, and crossed his feet at the ankles to prevent negative energy from penetrating his energy field from the floor. Next, he visualized a golden sun centered above his head, his crown chakra. He drew down, concentrating intently, the warm energy of the sun's rays all around him—a foot and a half in front of him, a foot and a half behind him, a foot and a half on top of his head, and a foot and a half underneath him. He visualized bright golden rays of the sun encapsulating his aura so Max could enter a purified, cleansed, and whole energy field. No doubt, Barbara's toxic energy from her sick behavior had put unhealthy debris into his auric field and he had to get rid of any toxic residue for Max to consider coming to him when summoned.

Then using his psychic vision, he created a smooth golden chord, about three inches in diameter, extending out from between his eyes, his psychic center or third eye, and pushed it out the window of the room, penetrating the glass without cracking it, through the sky, and up to the universe. John concentrated to increase the length of the chord, to reach out to Max, all the while maintaining diaphragmatic breathing. Oxygen penetrated deep into his gut and his stomach extended in and out in a consistent rhythm.

Max, grab onto your home base.

That was the other end of the chord. John talked to him in thought language. Max, who had been with him since he was three, was called by his parents, "the imaginary friend." John didn't know if Max was his real name or not, but John's little buddy got a puppy and named him Max. John's parents said "No" to a dog, but John wanted a Max, too. So Max it was.

Max always wore clothing and styles depicting what John's interests were. When John commenced Tae Kwon Do, Max wore a dobok, the typical white uniform with the white belt. As John progressed in rank and wore different colored belts, so did Max. Now Max wore the dobok with a black belt, knowing John was past his third.

If Max didn't enter John's energy field on his own, to confirm when John's intuitions were correct, John could invoke him when he needed the help. Max had been with him through every exam from kindergarten through medical school, through every hostage situation, work related crisis, and through every turbulent part of his life.

John experienced a tug, and psychically using his hands, he pulled the chord toward him, one hand after the other in a concentrated slow movement until Max was in view and right in front of his third eye. Max hadn't come voluntarily. What was up with that?

Max. I need your help on this one. I see you. I know you're there. What's the Gemini obsession about? What's Paul's relationship to Reynolds? What's going on here, Max? Am I right about Barbara murdering?

John received affirmation on the last question. Max sent chills through John body, on his right side, from head to toes.

Okay. Good, Max. Thanks.

Confirmations were always of a physical nature for John. He either experienced a change in his body or saw a change in his environment. When John was studying late and his parents were about to enter his room to tell him to go to bed, Max would flash the light on his lamp on his desk to forewarn him Mom or Dad was on the approach.

What can you tell me to put all of this together?

He kept his body still with his mind blank. No thoughts about patients, dinner, doing laundry, nothing—a blank slate.

The only message that transpired was Castor and Pollux. Max broke the contact. The golden chord evaporated.

Max? Castor and Pollux? Can you tell me more?

No Max.

He wants me to do this alone. Why? Is he pissed off at me for letting Vicki go? I'm pissed off at myself. Don't need him to tell me that. Damn! Castor and Pollux. I will make sense of this, and then I'll throw it all in Carlson's face.

John recorded the message in caps on a pad so he didn't forget it. Channeled information was not meant to be remembered and he couldn't afford to forget this one.

CASTOR AND POLLUX

CHAPTER 27

Three Years Earlier:

John stared wide-eyed as the sheriff detonated. "When are you going back to New York?"

The sheriff was as vicious as a lion protecting his young and no one would survive taking advantage of Vicki. The roar of fresh water pumped into the pool that began at this instant, matched his intensity and it resembled a warning from the universe, which this New Yorker should heed.

"Next Monday. Why?"

"Maybe a few days in the slammer will do you some good."

"Daddy!"

John snuggled her head close to him. Her messed up hair covered her tears. "Ssh, let me handle it. Why?"

"Lewd and indecent exposure in a public place. I believe this qualifies."

"Come on. There's no one here. We were under wraps. And its pitch black now."

"I saw enough of you bobbing up and down. You, young lady, get up and go onto a lounge over there." He pointed to a lounge at the far end of the pool.

"She can't get up right now. How did you find us?"

"GPS on her phone."

"What's with all the invasion of privacy?"

"Let Vicki tell you about that. But bottom line, I don't trust you."

Looking at John's expression, Vicki didn't have to be a shrink to know what he expected. "I'll tell you later. I promise."

John wanted to respond, but the ring from Vicki's cell interrupted them. "You might as well answer it."

Her bare arm extended from under the towel trying not to expose herself in front of her father. "Hello."

"Vicki, it's me. Is John close by?"

John heard the question and hoisted the phone from her grip. "Yes, Mark. I'm very close by."

Vicki hid her head in his chest.

Mark hesitated for a moment. "Oh crap. I'm sorry."

"Don't worry about it. Your father beat you to it."

Mark cracked up, laughing. "What?"

Holding the phone between his ear and shoulder, John managed to hook Vicki's top. "What's going on?" Then he resumed holding the phone in his hand.

She murmured in his ear. "Where are my bottoms?"

Mark heard anyway. "Thanks, pal. You're getting me into deeper shit with my wife. Remember the Dunn boy from the ER?"

John laughed. And first, to answer Vicki, he said, "I don't know." He looked around and saw her bottoms on the ground. He snatched them up under the stares of death from her father and assisted Vicki in getting her feet into them under the towel while talking to Mark. The two of them moved and coordinated their efforts. Their arms entangled and John felt Vicki's knees plunge into his abs. "Ow! Of course."

The sheriff looked baffled.

"His father took him, the mother, and her parents hostage. And he's demanding to see the doc that made his girlfriend leave him."

"Damn! I'll be there. Where?"

"Trailer park in Coconut Crossing. Down the main road outside Bueno Terrace. About eight miles. Go to very end and make a right for a mile. You'll see us."

"You put them on backward," she whispered, again in John's ear.

Mark couldn't control his laughing. John's frustration rose like lava from a volcano. "Thanks, Mark. You're not helping. Vicki will—"

"Oh no, she won't," the sheriff bellowed. "She's not going in there, That's a crack area. I'll take you."

"I'll be there ASAP. Sheriff, why don't you go elsewhere, so we can get ourselves together?"

"Where are you?" Mark wasn't making heads or tails of this.

"At the pool."

"At—the—pool? Don't you believe in a bedroom, like most normal people?"

"Bor—ing. Now if your father would give us some space."

"All right, I'll meet you in the lobby."

"I'll be there soon."

೮೨೮೨

"You go home and I'll call you."

"Let me go, please. I can help with Ricky."

"*No!*" her father and John yelled in unison.

"I'll drive," John said. "I can get there faster."

"I have a siren on the police car."

"As do I." John secured the red-cupped siren from his back seat, that his intuition had told him to bring from New York, and attached it to the roof. "Get in."

He wasn't happy with her father at all. And that was mutual. This was going to be a battle of the egos—two very strong, unbending, uncompromising egos.

John intended to win.

Driving out and getting to the main road—a three-lane highway bordered by trees and more trees—the tension inside the SUV mounted. They were driving deeper into the woods and stuck with each other.

"What are your intentions with my daughter?"

John retorted as if there wasn't any other option and the decision had been made. "I'm going to marry your daughter."

The sheriff did a quick double take. "Oh no, you're not."

"Why not?"

"I googled you. You're a player. New York's most eligible bachelor? Come on. I saw pictures of you with at least twenty different women. All blondes. You're not for my daughter. She's not in your league. She's a cracker."

"She's a what?"

"See? You don't even speak our language. She's a country girl, through and through. Never lived any place other than here. Except when she went to that high-fallutin' school in Gainesville. Fifth generation Sun County. I won't allow my daughter to be added to your trophy list."

"Any more derogatory comments?"

"Plenty. I'm just getting started. And don't think I'm not doing a full investigation of you already, doctor hot shot."

"I'll save you the trouble. I'm a medical doctor with a Ph.D., three residencies, a fellowship in forensics, and enough degrees, certifications, and affiliations to make your head spin. So what's wrong with that?"

"That's not what concerns me. Your accomplishments don't define who you are. Not to me anyway. Nor to my daughter."

John's train of thought halted dead in its tracks. His accomplishments defined him, his entire life. It was how his parents defined him. And his colleagues. And his past women. Everyone in his sphere of influence, and anyone who wanted to be included within it, envied his power and prestige.

He began to realize there were different values down here. Now he had to be different. His point of view about himself would have to change. His belief system about what made him a worthy man would have to change. He'd have to look deeper within himself for the answers. "Then what?"

"You're too experienced for her."

"Experienced?" John knew what he meant but he was going to make him sweat. "I see that as a good thing."

"She leads a very simple lifestyle down here, nothing fancy."

"What? I don't think we're talking about the same thing."

"Yes, we are, and you're too non-traditional for her. That can lead to other things. Now what's your three—"

"No, I'm not letting you off the hook. What do you mean?" Silence. "Have difficulty talking about sex?"

"When it's about my daughter, yes."

"We're not talking about Vicki. We're talking about me. Now what do you mean?"

"Just drive, hot shot."

"Uh-uh, finish what you started. What do you mean? Because I don't want you hanging onto any thoughts that aren't valid."

"Do you always play shrink?" The sheriff received the signature look. "The New York swinger type stuff."

"Go on."

"Ah, come on!"

"No you have to say it. Or has Vicki made some poor choices?"

"Do you realize who you're talking to?" the sheriff thundered.

John accepted the reprimand. "Yes, I do. I don't mean any disrespect, Sheriff, but I want you to feel secure about me being with your daughter, so explain what you mean and tell me what you're afraid of that she'll do. Then maybe the surveillance will stop."

"The kinky alternative lifestyle stuff."

"No, I'm straight."

"That's not what I meant. Damn, you're difficult. You know. The kind of…where you…inflict pain on each other. There, I said it. Happy?"

"Yes. S and M?"

The sheriff shuddered in the seat.

John acknowledged his discomfort. "That will never happen. It's not my style. I'll never do anything to inflict pain on Vicki, ever. Okay? Now what did she become involved in? No. Don't answer that. That's something she has to tell me."

"That's right. So end of discussion. Three residencies? In what?"

"Psychiatry, gynecology, and orgonomy."

"Gynecology?"

"Yes."

"Ever deliver a baby?"

"Several. My mother is an OBGYN. I worked in her office for a while."

"And how many little John babies are there running around in New York?"

"I'm assuming you mean personal ones?" John asked with a snide look.

The sheriff stared at him, wide-eyed.

"None, I'm careful."

"So when did you finish school? Last week? You sound like a student lifer."

John smiled at the analogy. "I loved being in school. I loved learning. When did I finish formally? About seven years ago."

"Hospital or private practice?"

"Hospital for now. Maximum security psychiatric center. Criminals only."

"You're kidding?"

"Nope. Young adult psychopaths and schizophrenics are my specialty."

"So you always put yourself in harm's way?"

"Not deliberately. But I don't back down either. Look, I'm with you now."

"Very funny. A comedian, too. Do you realize what you're getting yourself into now? Ever work with the police?"

"Yes, I do. And all the time. Consulting."

"Doing what?"

"Profiling, assessing whether perps are mentally fit to stand trial, crime scene investigations, court appearances. Hostage negotiations when I can get there faster than the precincts."

"What do you mean, precincts? Here we have SWAT and the CNT—Crisis Negotiation Team—for hostage negotiations."

"In New York City, SWAT is called ESU. They encompass all the rescue situations, criminal or not. Hostage negotiators come out of the precincts. They send two to the various situations, depending upon who's closest in the boroughs."

"New York City's a big place. So your SWAT—ESU—don't know the negotiators?"

"Exactly. And there are battles of the egos to boot."

"Not here. Small team. They all know each other. Success is built on cooperation. My son Mark—"

"I met him."

"You know he's the Commander of the SWAT?"

"He made it clear."

"Glad he did, hot shot. He'll be called in by the negotiators or vice versa, but it's his call what happens and how long he'll let them negotiate. And mind you, he won't let a New Yorker get in his way."

"Hey, he called me."

"You're the negotiating leverage. That's it."

We'll see about that.

"And as a consultant you charge—"

"Hourly, five hundred bucks per."

"Five hundred bucks per hour?"

"I'm worth every penny."

"Y'all too gussied up an' high cotton with a big yapper, an' y'all make her mad as a hornet and ah reckon she'll high tail it outta dere in munts."

John did a double take. "What did you just say?"

"You even need a translator, son. I said you're cocky and arrogant and rich. Vicki will not be able to keep up with your lifestyle. She'll get hurt in the end and run back home."

"Well, don't underestimate her. We'll make each other very happy. And I can support her very well."

"There's more to marriage then the bedroom. You're arrogant, cocky, think you're God's gift to the world, so forget about it."

"No. I'm not. You called me that already. You'll come around. You're like my mother."

"Oh yeah? How?"

"You need to accept the fact that you're not the only man in Vicki's life now."

CHAPTER 28

Present Day:

John, forced by law, had to do what he realized was the worst thing he could do. He was a stickler for the law. Barbara had to be moved to a less restrictive environment even though he suspected her of murder. Carlson's team had been less than cooperative, so John carried Barbara's belongings in her paisley case into her room to make the transfer. He had the items he took from her apartment for her daily wear and the suit she was wearing at admittance. Carlson even gave John back her boots and knitting bag.

She was shocked when she saw him carrying in her things. "You're letting me go?"

"I'm good, but not that good. You're being moved to a private room on the twelfth floor."

"Twelfth floor? Afraid I'll jump?"

"Nope. Got that covered. I hate to tell you this, but it's also volunteer admissions floor. People come and go but you can't."

"What?"

"Let me finish."

"Okay. Do finish."

"There's a rec room and you're free to lounge there. Also a dining room with set meal times. I took the liberty of bringing you casual workout clothes and what I think you'd need from your apartment."

She examined the bag. Everything she would need was in there, from toothpaste to shampoo and conditioners and body treatments, as well as the appropriate undergarments. She lifted a pair of panties, full briefs.

"Didn't bring the bikini ones. Didn't think you'd want a pantie line to show. I know my wife wouldn't."

"You went into my drawers and closets? Without a warrant?"

"That I did. So you'd rather wear a hospital gown with no undergarments in public when everyone else is in street clothes?"

She crossed her arms across her chest spewing defiance.

"A 'thank you' would be nice, but those two words don't seem to enter your vocabulary."

"No, they don't."

No wonder she's still single.

And here's your knitting bag."

She smiled.

"But you can only knit in your room. You cannot take the needles into an area with the general population. Agreed? I need your word on this. Staff will be watching you and they'll follow my orders. Oh, and, I took the liberty of removing the metal needles. I replaced them with plastic children's ones. And I got you a pair of children's scissors, too."

"How would you even—"

"I stopped off at a yarn store. I don't know about this stuff. So, agreed?"

"Definitely, agreed. You have my word on this."

"What is this anyway?"

"A sweater, when I finish it."

"For me?"

"A Barbara Montgomery original? No way. You haven't done anything to earn it yet."

"And what do I need to do for that? No sexual innuendos intended."

"No sexual innuendos taken. Let me go on my own recognizance. I'll stay in New York City and be available to meet with you and Carlson."

"No. Can't do that."

She rummaged through her tote. "Look, you see how the supplements you're giving me are working. And it's only been a couple of days. I'm taking everything the nurses give me and they have helped. You see? I'm not getting so angry anymore and not attacking you. You see that I'm calmer. I even slept better last night, and only had that nightmare when I was napping when you came in. Dr. Trenton, you can trust me now."

"What you're showing me is that your aggression is under your own control unless you have an emotional trigger. The supplementation takes much longer to kick in and work on the brain. Up to ninety days in some cases, sometimes more. Some do help you sleep better though. You're a long way from fully functioning, in my opinion."

"Thanks for the confidence. You'll see. I'll be much better when I have some freedoms. I promise. I won't get crazy or have any outbursts. But when will I be free to leave?"

"Honestly, I don't know. Not until we catch this Clancy character, at the very least. Ready? Go into the bathroom and change, and I'll take you upstairs."

He noticed an on-guard look in her eyes and realized he and Tony needed to act fast. Her hands raced through her bag.

"By the way, I have your cell phone if that's what you're looking for. And your coat."

She threw her hands up in the air. "Yes. Of course, you do."

❧❧

John walked down the twelfth floor corridor to the nurse's station with Barbara. The nurse, Callie, welcomed them.

"Callie, this is Barbara Montgomery, your new admit. I'll get her settled, and then I'll come back and give you the charts."

"Yes, Dr. Trenton."

John escorted Barbara to the room down at the far end of the corridor as she scanned the names on the wall plates outside the doors. "Looking for someone?"

"Uh, no. I'm just very nervous right now."

"Uh-huh." *Who does she know here from when was she a patient?*

Max sent him an affirmative jolt. *Yes!* "Get settled. Lunch is at noon, so you have a half hour. The dining room is straight down the corridor."

"Okay. When will you be back?"

"I'll surprise you." He closed the door and left with his mind reeling.

What is she up to? Paul, if something happens, your head will roll. I'm not taking heat on this one.

An armed guard approached. "Right here, Doc."

John craned his neck to address him. "Thanks, Jake. Got the directives?"

"Yes, sir. This chick and I will be attached at the hip."

"That's the idea." John smiled as he walked away.

He removed his smartphone from his pocket and sent a text. *Vicki, I miss you, babe. Come on. You haven't text me back or returned my calls in two weeks. I need to know you're okay, babe. I didn't mean what I said. I want children as much as you do. You have to believe me, babe.*

ℰ⁓ℰ⁓

Jake stood at-ease in front of Barbara's door, facing it.

She opened the door. "Oops!"

Instantly her memory brought up a vision of when she was ten in 1985, held tightly by a guard as tall and wide as he was mean, as a doctor gave her a sedative with a needle. She remembered herself biting and kicking him the entire time. The guard had wrestled her with his big arms wrapped around her so tightly he almost suffocated her. He laughed continuously at her before she succumbed to the drug.

She remained dazed for a few minutes and unresponsive.

"Hi, doll." Silence. "Doc, you okay?" He reached out and gently touched her arm to awaken her from the daydream.

She trembled, but became alert. "Ooh, yeah, yeah. And you are?"

"Your guardian, Jake."

"Excuse me?" she asked as she peered up at him.

"Your escort."

"What? Dr. Trenton said I'm free to walk around the building."

"Building? I doubt that. The floor, yes. And I go with you."

"I knew I couldn't trust that bastard. It was too good to be true. It wouldn't pay for me to fight you, huh?"

"How many Black Belts do you have?"

"Ah. Got it. By the way, there are no windows in the room."

"Plan to jump?" He laughed. "This is an interior room. The rooms on the outer side have the windows. Guess the doc wants you real well protected. Lunch in twenty minutes."

"I'll see you in twenty, Jake." She slammed the door.

ॐ

In her room, Barbara searched all around for the recording light on the wall. Even though she didn't see one, she carried her knitting bag into the bathroom. She put the needles, twenty skeins of yarn in various shades of greens and browns, and the instruction book on top of the closed toilet seat. She fiddled around in the bottom of the bag until she found it. Even the zipper was paisley. She unzipped the hidden compartment and retrieved a disposable phone.

Yes, you jack-ass. You have one of my phones. I'm always prepared. Thank God for minimum security. Obviously, he doesn't have anything concrete or he wouldn't have brought me here. And, obviously, Carlson was too damn lazy to check. But I knew that already. That's good. I'll take advantage of that. God. I must have had such good karma from a previous life that I'm getting away with such shit in this one. Damn. Life is good.

Barbara pressed a number on her phone.

"Yeah?"

"You took a big chance going to my school. My whole set-up could have been blown."

"Why are you whispering?"

She shot a quick glance toward the door. "I have to be quiet."

"I thought you skipped town."

"I was tied up for a few days. Listen, I didn't put in three years at that lousy Department of Ed job to not get what I want."

"Why sacrifice that much to get to Reynolds?"

"I'll tell you about it sometime. Very long story. And don't make any more stupid moves. The police are looking for you. Don't go near my Brooklyn or Manhattan apartments. Did you deliver a present to Reynolds?"

"Yeah. It went as expected."

"When's the next phase?"

"I'll do the filming this afternoon when they leave early for the long weekend. Then I'll give him the surprise of his life tonight."

"Good. All right. I can't afford to risk staying here. That shrink is way too smart."

"What are you going to do?"

"I'll find a way out. I know this place like it's my own home. Proceed as planned. First Reynolds and then—" she added with a wolfish grin, "—that shrink and anyone close to him will have their day in hell."

CHAPTER 29

Three Years Earlier:

Johan pulled over to the side of the road and saw the SWAT Hummer. The entire area was illuminated by huge strobes, powered by a generator. It was irregular terrain, more loose dirt and mud holes than grass, with several dilapidated trailers, stationed about ten feet apart and raised on huge tires with unstable wooden planks leading to the front doors.

There was a lot of garbage strewn about, and unsanitary living conditions promoted a feeding frenzy to the insects flying around and on the ground. John jumped out of the car and sprinted to Mark and his team, who were stationed about five hundred feet from the trailer door. The stench of stale food along with human and animal wastes overwhelmed him. His dinner came up into his throat during his approach. He swallowed the acid as he stumbled in dog poop, a big dog's poop. It was warm, squishy, and odoriferous. This was one unhealthy dog. Wearing sandals had not been the smartest move. John would have to toss them before he went home. He was in work mode, even though on vacation, so he struggled to ignore the mess.

The situations at home had been indoors, in air-conditioned buildings with electricity. He'd never been in the woods before now. Roughing it, camping, had never been his thing. He'd never been called to a scene on vacation. But then again, he hadn't taken many vacations. He never had to work with a team he didn't know or who didn't know of him. His reputation made sure of that. He'd never had to succeed to impress someone other than himself. This situation agitated him.

The men—wearing vests, boots, gloves, and Kevlar-3 helmets, with their side arms, the Glock 23, .40-caliber drawn—took cover behind three police cars and the SWAT Hummer. Their gear covered every inch of them. When John approached in sandals, shorts, and a tank top, without a signal from Mark, a kid grabbed his arm.

"Loose the sandals, sir."

John obliged willingly. The kid blasted water from the hose, powered by their own on-scene generator, onto John's feet, then poured a generous amount of antibacterial detergent on them, and handed him a rag on a pole. "In these woods we have to come prepared. And you sure as hell ain't dressed for it, sir."

"This was unexpected." John appreciatively washed his feet off. "Thank you."

"No problem, sir. Here put these on. We prepare for the unexpected. Even havin' to take care of big city folk like you."

He wasn't kidding. John knew it. The kid handed John socks and a pair of size thirteen boots, sweat pants, and a sweat shirt. "Ya gotta keep covered. If the red ants don't bite ya ta death, the 'squitos will." He also handed him a can of bug spray. "You'll use it if ya smart, sir."

This kid sure has an attitude. Guess that happens when you're demoted to clothing duty. Wonder what he did to earn this privilege.

"Got it. Thanks." After he dressed, John dashed over to the communication center Mark and his five-man team had set up.

"Better."

John started to apologize for the delay but Mark cut him off.

"No problem. We take care of our own, first. If we're not optimum, we can't do our best."

"This is optimum, huh?"

"Yeah, fifty pounds of gear on in ninety-three degree heat. That's as optimum as it gets, Doc."

John had just gotten a dose of humility. "When was the last time you made contact?"

"About forty minutes ago after I spoke to you. He refused to answer the phone again until you got here. We already announced to the residents to remain in their trailers until they're notified. So far, so good."

"Was I the only demand?"

"Yes. We've been trying to get him to come out for two hours. He won't release any of the hostages, but he swears they're unharmed. And as far as we can see, they are. An hour and a half ago he demanded to see you."

"It looked like you left the pool this afternoon for an opp."

"Yeah. Great. Right? Two in one day. Earned blood money today."

"It looks so calm and peaceful down here."

"Definitely for the retirees, but among the locals? Not so much. Mainly the young ones. Drugs."

Enough with the chit chat. "Okay. Call him on the phone. Let's do this."

"Hold on, sir," said another man. "This is our negotiation. I've been talking to him the entire time. Lieutenant Randy Leigh, chief negotiator."

John could tell that without the intro. Leigh sported the black, squared-off vest, with negotiator in white block letters on the front and back. The presence of this thirty-year-old guy that permeated through the vest earned him the title.

John was impressed. He hesitated. He knew the lieutenant was right. But he wasn't familiar with this guy, nor any of them. The only one he trusted was himself, and his concern for Ricky forced him to override the protocol. "I know the little kid in there and he knows me. We can use that."

"Doesn't matter, sir. You're the reward. He doesn't get to you until he releases the hostages unharmed."

John was aware of the procedure. "What do you know?"

"I know we're wasting time now, if I have to share the details, sir."

John nodded. "All right. Make the call and tell him I'm here."

Randy picked up the receiver on the box phone they had

placed at the front door. John realized there was no landline in the trailer so this was their only mode of communication, and, the good thing was, this kind of box recorded every bit of conversation. John nodded. Good move. While they were at it, they had drawn a line up to the windowsill to record what was happening inside, in real time, now seen on the computer screen next to the phone. John observed Ricky, crying, cuddled in his grandma's arms, sitting at a square wooden table in the kitchen area. There were two wooden chairs around it. The computer image was so clear John recognized cigarette burns in the wood on the tabletop. Ricky's grandpa was lying down, apparently asleep, on a torn up floral print couch, while Denise, smoked a cigarette, slumped down on the floor, leaning against a faux-wood paneled wall opposite the door. From what John could see, there was no other furniture in the room. Not even a toy or book in sight. Ricky's dad was out of view.

Randy picked up the phone.

"Yeah."

"Rick, it's Lieutenant Leigh. Dr. Trenton is here."

"Good, I wanna blow his dang head off."

"That was fast and to the point," John whispered to the lieutenant. "Okay, this may be over with soon."

"Yeah? How do you figure that, Doc?" the lieutenant whispered back, putting the phone on mute.

"Give me a while."

"No, sir." The lieutenant moved the phone out of John's reach and unmuted it. "Rick, Lieutenant Leigh again. Rick, listen to me. We don't want anyone hurt, inside or out. We can work this out."

"Ah don't give a dayum. Ah hate y'all PO-leece! Ah ain't listen' to y'all PO-leece no more. An' ah hate dis ol' lady here. She hates my guts, too. Ah just fixin' to blow 'er dang head off."

The sheriff intervened. "Doc needs a translator."

John was perturbed and not afraid to show it. "I got the gist. Lieutenant, I'm not a cop. Use me."

John understood what they were thinking and they were right. But going against protocol had never intimidated him.

They wanted to end this, too. Peacefully. They all understood that the repercussions of this could be deadly if John messed up. The legalities alone would destroy all of their careers. After a long minute, the sheriff signaled to Randy, and the lieutenant handed John the phone.

"Mr. Dunn. This is Dr. Trenton. Okay if I call you that?"

"Yeah."

"What's going on?"

"Ain't dey tell you nuttin'?"

Dunn wasn't that much different from his patients. "I want to hear it from you."

"It's y'all fault."

"What is?"

"Denise left 'cause a you."

"How about you come out and we talk about it?"

"No way, Doc. Dey'll blow me away out dere."

John put the phone on mute and addressed Mark and Randy. "That's good. He's not prepared to die. That's something."

Mark acknowledged with a nod. He transmitted the gear up signal to the kid.

John watched him with surprise. The kid got his gear on. The vest, helmet, fingerless gloves, mic, earwig. "That kid's the sharpshooter?"

"Yup. Why? What's the problem?"

The shooter readied his FNP90 assault rifle. He checked the wind, temperature, and humidity. It was humid, but no wind, not even over five hundred yards away at the trailer. It was all part of the job. John nodded. Definitely. The mental part took precedence over the mere pulling of the trigger. The kid sniper surveyed the area for the best vantage point and found it.

John stared at Mark and then at the kid sniper. The sniper had found a large steady branch on an oak tree that protruded out toward the trailer, twenty feet in the air, with just enough leaves to camouflage him, but not hamper his vision or aim. He climbed up, grabbing onto branches and stepping on nodules in the tree trunk, with his rifle behind his back on a shoulder harness. He reached the branch and straddled it. His only obstacle was the bird's nest he had to dislodge. He didn't look as it tumbled to the ground. He had his priorities straight.

John nodded again in approval. The kid looked ready. Appropriate gear. Appropriate stance. He did what John expected him to do, expertly. What threw John was his age. The kid didn't look old enough to have completed even one tour of duty. The snipers John had worked with had been in Special Forces. Could he trust this kid to shoot the target and not him from over five hundred feet away? He hadn't a clue.

For Ricky, he would risk it.

"Mr. Dunn. What do you want me to do to help you?"

Vicki pulled up in her jeep and parked behind John's. They were too preoccupied to notice her.

"Git in here."

"I will. But first you have to do something for me."

"You're not going in there, John. Don't even think about it."

Mark received a nasty glare in return. John didn't appreciate any interruptions to the process.

"What'ya want?"

"Let Ricky go. He doesn't have to see his dad so upset."

"Ain't doin' dat, Doc."

"We met your demand. Now you have to meet one of ours. I came in good faith, Mr. Dunn. I came as soon as I was called."

"Why should ah?"

Instead of bantering back and forth about what the police wanted, John put it on him. "Because I think you have some feelings for your son." Some feelings? Better than saying he loved him, which was the farthest from the truth. "That's why you're doing this."

"Den you come in?"

"Yes." John fought the team with his eyes.

Mark received the signature look, but retaliated with one equally intimidating. Mark was the commander. His team. His decisions. No New York outsider was going to take over, even if he might be family one day. John interpreted that message clearly. It was understandable.

Ricky appeared on the top step, wobbling, startled, and crying, standing with his little body frozen, almost catatonic, at the trailer door, staring at all the cops pointing guns in his direction.

Vicki ran out of cover and crouched down to coax him over. "Ricky, come here. Come to me, sweetheart."

Ricky looked around and, after recognizing her voice, ran down the three steps, behind the police cars, and into her arms. She looked at John and her father. John waved at her to take Ricky into the car. She complied without hesitation.

"Can't let you in, Doc. It's not an option!"

Seeing Ricky crying out of control in Vicki's arms pushed John to the limit. "Got to. I can handle it. Just suit me up."

"No!"

"Listen, Mark. He's only five years old. Amanda's age."

"He's out safe. I couldn't care less about the others."

"His grandparents are in there, too. Who's going to take care of him? Look, I can handle this. I've done it before. If a cop approaches, he'll kill the grandmother. Listen to me, Mark. I've been doing hostage negotiations for over eight years in worse situations. I even teach it in a master's program. I know what I'm doing."

After a nod from the sheriff, Mark yielded. John dressed in a full vest like the one Randy wore with a mic and earwig.

"Give me a pair of cuffs." They handed him a pair of metal cuffs and he put them in the pocket of his sweats. "Mr. Dunn, I'm coming in and, I must tell you, I'm not armed." He still hadn't moved past the truck.

"Y'all shitten me!"

"No, I'm not. Keep the door open." John signaled to the kid sniper. "If I move to the right, you'll have a clear shot. But give me a chance first."

The kid with the assault rifle in the tree acknowledged John with a serious nod.

"Don't worry about him," Mark said, referring to the sniper. "He's not human. He's a machine. One shot right below the ear or in the cheek, Dunn's a goner."

John closed his eyes for a moment at the dismal thought and Mark's metaphor, but then he pulled himself together. He walked, taking one-step at a time, pausing after a few, with his arms extended out. He made the five-hundred-yard walk take about fifteen minutes. He wanted the man inside to sweat it out. He wanted him to become so nervous he would be easier to take down. All John knew about him was that he was twenty-one and a user. He knew nothing about his size, strength, or fighting ability. It was not nearly enough.

John would risk it all for Ricky.

The door opened. Mr. Dunn was a scrawny, tattooed, five-foot-ten-inches tall kid, holding an assault rifle pointed at him. Every inch of skin, from his neck down, was detailed with dragons, skeletons, bats flying and coming right out at the person staring at them, cemetery plots—all gory and unattractive, with red and black being the primary colors. His clothes were tattered, his tank top filthy, and the waist on his oversized trousers hung below his butt, revealing very soiled briefs. His curly straggly blond hair covered his eyes and shoulders.

John's strategies cajoled, not agitated, so he didn't demand. "Come on," he coaxed. "Put the rifle down."

Dunn blinked his eyes and squinted. John guessed having someone approach him in a mature way threw him. He stood his ground. "No. Ah ain't."

"Put the rifle down."

"No! Ah ain't. Git in here."

"Not till you put the rifle down."

"No! Ah ain't." Dunn's voice became louder.

John's slowed speech demonstrated that he was in control. He knew the procedure of three repetitions and then action, but he extended it for a fourth attempt. "The—door—stays—open—until—you—put—the—rifle—down."

After Dunn realized John wasn't budging, he began to lower the rifle, but John wasn't taking any chances. In a swift Tae Kwon Do move, *Naranhi Sogi*, with his feet pointed forward, shoulders' width apart, and his arms slightly bent with clenched fists, he punched Dunn just under the navel and disarmed him, kicking the rifle out of his hand. He flipped Dunn over, hand cuffed him, and yelled for the others to leave. It went down in less than two minutes. Mutual goals achieved. No shots were fired.

Denise and her parents ran for their lives out the door and down the three steps. The team rushed in and John handed Dunn over to Mark.

As he walked over to the car, he wanted to dig it into the sheriff more. "I forgot to mention I also hold a Third Degree Black Belt."

"You're—not—marrying—my daughter."

As John stood by the open passenger door of Vicki's car, a white Jeep Liberty, Ricky launched himself at John and wrapped his arms around his neck, crying. Vicki, her father, and John melted. Ricky and John looked into each other's eyes, left eye to left eye. That eye position created their connection, for life. Ricky and John became one and their energy fields intertwined. Something in John awakened. It was a feeling that filled a void. It was a feeling he thought he never had time for—the paternal one. At this moment, John wanted Ricky as his own, even knowing this wasn't feasible.

John hugged him and kissed him on top of his head. "It's all right, Ricky. No one will hurt you anymore."

"I want to live with you and Miss Marin."

"Miss Marin and I don't live together. We just met."

Ricky was disappointed. "I thought you were married."

The sheriff let out a deep breath and shook his head.

"No. We're not. But you have your mommy."

"My mommy hurts me, too."

John stiffened so did the sheriff. "What about Grandma and Grandpa?"

"They're nice to me."

John removed Ricky's arms from around his neck and placed him back onto the seat. "You stay with Vicki and Sheriff Marin."

✐✐✐

John sprinted to the area where Ricky's mom and her parents gave verbal reports. He was steamed. He grabbed the mother, who was smoking a cigarette, by her arm, pulled the cigarette out of her mouth, and tossed it to the ground. "You're under arrest for child endangerment and aggravated child abuse. And that's for starters."

The cops paid attention fast.

"What did that little bastard tell you?"

"Take them both to the precinct and I'll meet you there."

"John, you don't have to. You did great in there."

"Yes, Mark I do. Where am I going?"

"EOC, Lardo. Emergency ops center."

"Let Ricky's grandparents take him inside and find out if they can keep him."

Ricky's grandparents took him inside the trailer.

Vicki cried by her car. "I feel so badly for him."

"I know. No child should live like this and I wanted to keep you from this. You've got to listen. You're not trained for this. I am."

"But you're not even armed and I am."

"You carry all the time?"

"Yes, she does," the sheriff said. "Now get in the car, I'll direct you there, John, and you, Vicki, go home."

CHAPTER 30

Present Day:

Clancy double-parked his van across the street from Reynolds Publishing at the beginning of the rush hour. He moved back to let a truck driver creep out. After taking the spot, he removed his equipment from his knapsack. First, a Nikon digital camera he placed on the passenger seat. Next the Fujifilm Finepix. "Thank you, Barbara, for financing my new life. This is the best 5000 bucks you ever spent."

Professionally dressed people exited the office buildings at the sound of the 4:30 p.m. bell, eager to begin their three day, President's Day weekend. The crowds, traffic noise, and impending winter darkness complicated things for Clancy, as he wanted clarity to accomplish the next step of their plan. Light was his main concern. He always visualized the light like a camera, not like the human eye. He adjusted the Nikon's lens for the environmental light. The streetlights casted unwelcomed shadows and glare. He'd have to eliminate them. He struggled to make the contrast ranges perfect, as his editing software could not fix a mistake. The look he aspired to achieve demanded perfection if they were to con Morgan.

Clancy needed Morgan without any extraneous features. Just Morgan, moving, down to his minutest facial expressions, so the real Morgan would be scared stiff by seeing himself.

Morgan, two men Clancy didn't recognize, Steve, and Carol whom Clancy had seen in photos with his target—all dressed to the hilt of Park Avenue fashion—exited the building. Clancy commenced filming immediately. The men, much larger than Reynolds, appeared to be bodyguards. They walked toward a limo parked in front of the building.

A large truck and black and yellow taxi impeded the view. Clancy, unnoticed, zoomed in closer in between the vehicles. He carefully framed the scene to eliminate any parts of the driver's side window of his van.

"I can tell you liked my little gift. Well, there's more where that came from. Come on, move over, just a little to the right. Your pictures in *Money Magazine* certainly do ya justice, ya bloke. But I need ya moving. Come on, Morgan. Don't be so stiff. I can tell ya not a fan of the camera. And you won't be a fan of life when I get through with ya."

As the driver opened the passenger door of the limo, Reynolds moved away from his guards and Clancy had a clear shot.

"Ah, today is my jammy day." Clancy muttered and fine-tuned the mike.

"Stay home tonight, Mr. Reynolds. Nothing adventurous. Stay off the porn sites," one of the guards ordered.

Morgan shot him a glare.

"Perfect, Morgan," Clancy nasalized. "Perfect. An angry expression. Com'on, guard. Dig inta him more."

"Morgan, what's with the look?" Steve demanded. "He's right. Don't need anyone tracking any questionable behavior now."

Morgan sighed. "I get it, Steve. Believe me, I get it."

"Questionable behavior?" Clancy whispered. "Morgan, you idiot. What are you into that Barbara and I can use against you?"

"Just do what we say for once. Okay, Mr. Reynolds?" the guard asked.

"Okay, I'll stay home and veg in front of the TV. Want to know what time I'll hit the sack, too?"

"That'll work for the record," the second guard added.

"It'll be lights out around eleven. Have to be in early tomorrow for a meeting with a new writer. Some of us don't take the three day weekend. That good enough for you?"

"Very good," the first guard replied.

"Very good indeed," Clancy agreed. "Expect an unwelcome visitor before eleven tonight Morgan. A very unwelcome visitor. A life changing visitor." He was thrilled he'd captured what he needed.

The guards ushered Morgan into the back seat, slammed the door, and hit the hood.

❧❧❧

John worked in his Sheepshead Medical Center office, organizing Barbara's files and his additional notes into neat piles all over his desk.

All right, forget Paul for a moment. What have I got here? Death to All Those Who Come Near Me. Stripper. Who does she know at Sheepshead? When was she a patient? Clancy, partner. That she confirmed. Unknowingly, but she confirmed it. Restrained, sexually abused as a child. Foster homes. Brain scan indicated murderer. What does she want from Reynolds? Why Reynolds, not someone else? Were there others?

He sat for a moment staring at a blank sheet of paper.

So it's personal. Never found out why her father shot himself. Definite lie. Private investigator eighteen to twenty years ago. She killed the investigator. I'll have to prove that. Makes her twenty-twenty-two. Start with Kellie Wilson as alias. Or is Barbara Montgomery the alias? Now Castor and Pollux. Castor and Pollux. Wait a minute. I know this. I definitely know this. And Max knew I knew this or he wouldn't have said it. That's right. Barbara is a Gemini, like me.

John focused his eyes on the paper.

In Greek Mythology, Gemini is dominated by the twin brothers Castor and Pollux, two bright stars. Castor was killed in a battle and Pollux gave up his own life to join him, so their father Jupiter united them in the heavens. Castor killed, Pollux gave up his life. Father. Her father committed suicide. Maybe, maybe not. Gave up her life as a stripper to become psychologist? That's a stretch. Could it be? So she's a Gemini literally and figuratively. Max, far-fetched but possible, did Barbara kill her actual twin? Did she then assume her identity? Max, tell me! Now, Max!

An affirmative bolt of energy permeated his body. His body swayed in his chair from the invisible force.

Whoa, Thanks for the confirmation. I deducted as much. Now how in hell am I going to prove this? Damn! Paul will never believe this. Max, you're not his favorite entity.

All of a sudden, the ceiling lights went out in his office.

Come on, Max. I'll convince him. Turn the lights back on. I have work to do.

After a few moments, the lights returned. John rubbed his forehead with his fingers.

I'll go to the precinct now and see what the guys found out about Reynolds. Then give Mrs. Bennett a call. She'll see me tonight. She likes Barbara.

℘℘

In the conference room at the precinct, John, Carlson, Tony, and Sal had Reynolds's files in triplicate between them.

"Here's the profile on Reynolds. Clean as a whistle. Nothing out of whack."

"Okay, Paul. How long has he had the company?"

"He inherited it three months ago from his father, Jacob, who passed away." Carlson looked through the file. Tony and Sal followed in their copy. "He's had the publishing company since 1960," Carlson continued. "Eighty-five when he died. The father first donated to Barbara's clinic two years ago. This was the third."

"Yes. She told me she wrote a grant."

"Okay. Did she say what the donation was?" Tony asked.

"No. I didn't ask," John said.

"The senior Reynolds fucking donated $200,000," Carlson said. "Mid-February. But Morgan donated twice that. And bought her a fucking new car."

John stared at the wall, deep in thought. "Okay, so our perp isn't him. Why would he donate so much money if he wanted her to crack up?"

"What do you have in your head you're not telling us yet?" Tony demanded.

"I have a lot, Tony, believe me, a lot but it's in chunks. Doesn't make sense yet. First, we're underestimating her. If she accepted that much from Reynolds, she's not that altruistic like the newspaper made her out to be. What does she know about Reynolds that we don't know?"

Carlson tapped on the table, looking out the window.

That registered with John. "All right, I gave Mrs. Bennett a call. She said I could come over. I'll keep you posted."

"Two hour call in time," Carlson said.

"Yeah." John left with a lot more on his mind then the call in time.

оъеъо

John and Mrs. Bennett relaxed on the couch in the living room of her modest one-family home in Marine Park, Brooklyn. She served him some much-needed coffee and a piece of homemade pound cake topped with warm compote.

"Thank you for meeting me on a Friday evening, "Mrs. Bennett." John equated her to a matronly school marm in *Little House on the Prairie* with her salt and pepper hair up in a bun. He smiled at the recollection of his favorite series as a child.

"It's my pleasure, Dr. Trenton. I'd much rather speak to you than those other two detectives. I felt that they were humoring me. It's the beginning of President's Day week-long vacation. So I'm available all next week to speak with you again, if you need me."

He attempted to relax her by laughing. "Thank you. They do that to me sometimes, too. Mind if I record this? It's easier than taking notes."

"No. Not at all, please do."

John positioned a small recorder on the coffee table. "Can you tell me about Barbara? School and uh, socially?"

Mrs. Bennett smiled. "Barbara loves the club scene. Swinging bachelorette." She rolled her eyes. "She told me she vowed never to get married or have children. What a pity. I wanted to bear a child so badly but I guess it wasn't in God's plans."

She sighed, folding her hands on her lap.

John urged her out of her reflection to put her back on track. "Mrs. Bennett—" He paused. "Know where she goes?"

"Oh, yes, sorry about my digression."

He smiled warmly, but he needed to get back to business now.

"Upper East Side clubs are her thing. Where the wealthy men hang out. Keeps an apartment in Manhattan so she doesn't have to commute on the weekend."

While she talked, John analyzed her words as he played with the stewed fruit on his plate with a fork. "Have an address?"

"Mid-sixties, Sixty-Fourth Street right off Seventh Avenue."

"Thank you. And where is her clinic?"

"Not far from here, off Nostrand Avenue, and Avenue Y, above a thrift store."

"Do you know the names of her staff and other counselors?"

"Dr. Trenton, you haven't spoken to her much have you?"

"What makes you say that, Mrs. Bennett?"

"Barbara is a staff of one. She wants to expand but not yet. Needs to commit to staying put, I think. Where are you getting your facts?"

"That's why I'm speaking with you, Mrs. Bennett, to straighten me out."

"That I will do for sure."

You certainly are doing that, for sure.

"Did she ever mention a Morgan Reynolds to you?"

"Yes. She wrote a grant, applying to publishing houses for donations for an adolescent clinic she was setting up. Actually, that was before she started working with us, this time around. In order to get the funds, she needed to work in the same capacity for a city organization. She was already in education, so that qualified. She reinstated her license and came to work at my school again."

John had a sudden spark of light. "Reinstated?"

"Yes, she started working in New York City twelve years

ago when she first got her license and then moved to Connecticut, and then California. Then came back three years ago."

"Do you know how long she worked in New York the first time?"

"Yes. One year in my school. About four years, total, now."

"Help me clarify, please. So she came to New York from LA twelve years ago?"

"California? No, what makes you say that, Dr. Trenton?"

"More misinformation. Go on please." He didn't want to reveal too much.

"Barbara is a New York City woman. Born and raised here. That's the correct information, Dr. Trenton. Went to CCNY for her PhD in school psychology. I went to her induction ceremony, June 2003. It was lovely. Her parents were wonderful people. Both MDs. They were so proud of her. Their only daughter. Adopted at birth. They tried to conceive for many years and then wonderful little Barbara came into their lives. It was a fairy tale family."

John's head spun putting it all together. Was that the Barbara he knew? Obviously not.

"It's so sad what happened. Devastatingly sad."

"What, Mrs. Bennett?"

"They were both killed instantly a few days after Barbara officially received her license in the mail. At twenty-eight to lose both parents so suddenly. At a turning point in her life. What a traumatic time. A restaurant delivery van went out of control and over a construction divider on Central Park West, right near their apartment building. Blew up right into their Mercedes, taking their car and them down with it. A tragic accident. A gas tank leak on the van made the car explode on impact. Barbara's been devastated. She misses them so much. What are you thinking about, Dr. Trenton? You look like you're far away somewhere else."

"Trust me. I'm here, Mrs. Bennett, and taking in everything. You've given me very valuable information. So you've known Barbara from before she received her doctorate?"

"Yes. When she was a doctoral candidate. She did a full year internship here and I loved her so much, I requested her when she formerly got her license. I liked her better than the regularly assigned psychologist."

"What made her better?"

"Her compassion, love for the children, always their advocate, no matter whom she had to fight. It's so terrible this is happening to her. I can't imagine anyone who would want to hurt her."

"Okay. I'm asking you to really think about this because I'm going to ask you to go back all those years."

"Sure, Dr. Trenton. What is it?"

"Did you ever notice a change in Barbara, be it ever so slight, from before she received her doctorate to after?"

"Um, you know? Yes, yes I did. Several things."

John straightened up and leaned toward her.

"She seemed stronger, mentally and emotionally. Said it was because she started taking Tae Kwon Do. She said it gave her confidence. She did have to go into bad areas at times, so it's a good thing she knew how to defend herself."

"Yes, it is. Anything else?"

"Oh, yes. And I approached her about it. But, for one, she went blonde. From a warm brown to highlighted blonde. But that's a woman for you. The one thing that did stand out was…"

"What is it, Mrs. Bennett? And this is really important."

"I noticed a change in her accent, her tone of voice. She lost her New York accent after she got her license. She told me she was taking voice and speech lessons to get rid of it. She said that now that she was a doctor, she had to speak and sound professional, as well. Couldn't argue with that. She must have practiced endlessly on those speech lessons."

"Why do you say that?"

"She never once faltered. Not once. How is that possible? If I didn't know better, I'd think she was a different person."

You certainly are correct on that.

CHAPTER 31

Three Years Earlier:

John stormed into the interrogation room at the EOC in Lardo, where Rick Dunn supported himself against the wall in a corner. Restraints, wide leather bands with lobster claw clasps, dangled in John's hands. "You're being way too easy on him."

Detective Brian Marin, Vicki's forty-year old brother, who looked like Mark's twin, had just met the man who was sleeping with his sister. "Well, he's about to get deeper in trouble unless he starts telling me what I need to know. And he told me he doesn't want to lawyer up."

"Ah don't need no lawyer. Y'all can't pit dose on me."

"If you're a danger to yourself and others, I most certainly can," John said. "Maybe he needs to be coerced."

Brian glanced up at the recorder on the ceiling. John's gaze followed his. He understood it wouldn't be protocol to let him intervene. Brian didn't say a word. A few moments later, a message appeared on his monitor. *Let him.*

"Ya know what, Doc? You're right. Maybe I was being too easy on him, and I had enough of his lying. He's all yours now."

"Fine with me. Leave me the jacket."

Brian exited the room, smiling. The challenge was about to begin. For a very high price. Vicki.

"No! Don't leave me wit 'im!"

"Now sit down or I'll put these on. And you don't want to test me."

As John slammed the restraints down on a metal table, the buckles clanged in an uncomfortable, unsettling, vibrating echo that sent shrills through Rick's already damaged body. He jumped back, startled, but he sat.

"Ah ain't tellin' ya nuttin', neither."

"That's fine. I'll just hang out here until they're ready to take you to booking." John scanned the file. He nodded as he read it. He needed to get Rick's addresses, present and former, his history with Denise, his drug contacts, drug history, and story of abuse. They also required his cell phone records, real name, any aliases, and any friends or associates. The usual. He was used to the usual.

"Fa what?"

"What you did tonight. You're going to jail."

"Jail? Ah don't wanna go ta jail!" Rick screamed like a baby. He ran his fingers through his grimy matted hair, holding his head in his hands.

"I don't know anyone who wants to go to jail, but you should have thought about that before."

"Why? Ah didn't hurt no body."

"Excuse me? You had SWAT and CNT at bay with weapons for two hours," John growled, trying to intimidate him. "You took your son, girlfriend, and her parents hostage. In New York, that's a felony and I'm sure it is here, too. I don't know what you're trying to pull, but it stops now. Got it?"

"Ah took 'em wat?"

"You held them against their will. Know what that means?"

"Yeah," Rick whined. "Ah only went ta the trailer ta bard the keys ta ours. Denise took 'em wit her. Den some neighbor called da PO-leece 'cause a all the yellin' an' screamin'. Ah got no otha place ta live. Ah can't go back ta my folks like dat hussy."

"How come?"

"Dey ain't in Florida."

"Where are they?"

"Jawjuh."

"Georgia?"

Rick nodded.

"And you just wanted to borrow the keys?"

"Yeah."

"How long have you been living in Florida?"

"Since ah been fifteen. Den ah met Denise at the county festival. She was livin' alone, too, an' she took me in an' den she had dat little bastard."

"Who did you come to Florida with?"

"No one. My pop was always lay'n a hurtin' on me with that dang hickory stick an' he said if ah ain't like it ah should get out an' ah left an' never saw 'im again."

"What's the address of the trailer park you and Denise live in? Maybe we can get you in."

"It's in Park Villa Trailer Park. Unit sixteen. That hussy. She hadda go get pregnant."

"You stay with her."

"She gives good pussy. Where she at?"

"She's with detectives being questioned."

"She ain't gonna tell dem nuttin', either."

"You're wrong, Rick. She's telling them plenty."

"How'd y'all know?"

"She told me things already."

"What tings?"

"That's confidential. I probably shouldn't have mentioned that, but she's telling them her side. And for us to do what's right, we need to know your story, too."

"Ah ain't tellin' you nuttin 'bout us."

This was going nowhere. John switched gears. "Okay. Then tell me about little Ricky. He seems like a good little boy."

"He's a pain in da ass. If ah could git rida him, ah would. Denise won't let me 'cause he's makin' us some good dough.

John tossed a look toward the cameras. He had secured information he hoped was not reality. "How's that?"

Rick hesitated, closed his eyes, and ran his hand over his mouth. "We git money from social service fa his inhalers fa da asthma."

"But that money doesn't go for the inhalers, does it?"

"How'd y'all know?"

"Denise, at the hospital, said she couldn't afford it this month."

"Ah git what ah need."

"Like what?"

"Ah ain't tellin'."

"Denise said you're on oxy and coke."

"Dat bitch! Dat fuckin' bitch!" Rick stampeded off on a tangent and couldn't seem to stop. "She is, too! She uses more dan me! Takes the whole lot den when ah go fa a hit, dere ain't any left. Dat fuckin' hussy! Wait till ah git hold a her! Ah'll get Slingger ta tan her hide. Yeah! Dat's what ah'll do. Den she'll be sorry! An' ah'll git him ta lay a hurtin' on Ricky too!"

John's stomach dropped and he became nauseous. He felt the blood drain from his face. "So Ricky gets beaten by you and Slingger?" It was painful for him to say those words, but he had to clarify for the record.

"Yeah." Rick sounded proud.

"And Denise allows it?"

"Yeah. She gets off on it."

"She gets off on seeing Ricky hit?"

Rick nodded.

"Who's Slingger?"

"A friend."

"So you let your friend beat your girlfriend and son."

"Ah ain't sayin'."

"You already did. Looks like you're getting yourself in deep here, so you might as well come clean."

"What you mean?"

"You'll be facing more charges unless we can understand what's going on."

Rick crashed. "Git me sometin', man!"

"Not till you tell me what I need to know."

"Come on. Ah'm hurtin'."

John was immune to his pleading. "What is Slingger like?" When Rick just blinked at him in confusion, John tapped his own lips with his fist as he thought of what to say. "How would you describe him?"

"Big, tough, lots of tats like me. Rich though. Real rich. He knows people. He'll git me outta here. Ah'm one a his good customers. He likes doin' Denise and Ricky. So he'll git me outta here."

"So he has sex with Denise?"

"Yeah, an' she gits paid real good from him an' he gits us real good product, if ya know what ah mean."

"Yeah I do. And what about Ricky?"

"We git double fa him." Rick sounded so proud of getting money.

John closed his eyes for a moment. The nausea returned, double.

Damn! *I've got to save that little kid.*

ೲ

Mark paced impatiently, wanting to put his fist through the wall. He couldn't imagine anything like that happening to Amanda.

The sheriff was impressed with John. Maybe he would join their team. There were plenty of young adults in trouble down here with no forensic psychiatrist. Not now, but maybe in the future. Still not sure about him being his son-in-law, though.

ೲ

"Does Slingger get other customers for Denise?" John swallowed hard. "And Ricky?"

"Yeah bot'."

"You said Slingger will get you out of here?"

"Yeah, dat's right."

"We'll need to call him to post your bail. Have a number?"

"Yeah, 352-555-1737. But he won't ansa a call from a Yankee."

"That makes sense."

"Yeah, he's smart, too. Real smart. You'll have ta call 'im from my cell. He knows da number so he'll pick up." Rick retrieved his phone from his pocket and handed it to John.

"Thanks. Be right back." John confidently left the room.

He joined the others, distraught about Ricky.

The sheriff approached him as he handed the cell over to Brian. "Are you all right?"

"No, I'm not. And I didn't even need a translator."

Mark stared at him. And then at his father.

"Your father and I bonded," John explained. "We already have a private joke."

Mark shook his head.

"Did Vicki go home?"

"Yes," the sheriff responded.

"Get me Dr. Ali on the phone," John ordered. "The pediatrician at the hospital. A nurse told me that he would be seeing Ricky Friday night. I can't believe he didn't know anything was wrong with that family."

Vicki raced into the observation room, spotted John and ran to him.

"What are you doing here? It's two a.m. I told you—"

"I spoke to Jaime and she spoke to Mark. I wanted to find out what's going on."

John let out a deep breath. "You just don't listen. This isn't civilian business!"

"He's in my class."

"Okay then, as long as you're here, help me out. When did school start?" John asked.

"August ninth."

"And you didn't suspect anything?"

"Wait a minute, John. He's a new admit. Just in my class a couple of days. I saw something the second day, when he couldn't sit. He said his Daddy gave him a whipping. I reported it to the counselor and spoke with the mother. You heard what I said to her at the hospital that night. They must have kept him home from school so they wouldn't be found out. He doesn't even know the alphabet song and he can't recognize any letters, not even those in his name."

Deputies, a male and female, held Ricky's hand. His eyes darted to Vicki and he escaped to her, hyperventilating in between uncontrollable sobs.

"What happened?" the sheriff asked.

"His grandma called. Said they couldn't afford to keep him. They packed a bag for him and said they didn't care if he goes into the system."

There wasn't a word to reflect how they all felt. John shot Vicki a warning glare, but she did what she wanted and stepped up to the plate. "He can live with me," she said as she hugged him.

"Really, Miss Marin?," Ricky said with glee. "I told you I wanted to."

"Ricky, you stay with the sheriff and the deputies a minute," John ordered. "Vicki, over here." He led her into a private area. "Do you realize what you're getting yourself into? Yes, he's a precious little boy, but he's going to be troubled and have problems you can't even imagine."

"He'll be fine."

"Vicki, you can't talk to him or treat him like a regular kid."

"What does that mean?"

"For one, he's so physically abused. You'll have to watch everything you say and do—and how you give consequences when he does deserve it. He'll need a consistent behavior modification plan and—"

She cut him off. "I understand. John, I've been working with this age group for fifteen years. It'll just be a little while until they can find a relative."

"Yes. But you haven't dealt with them as a parent. I'll stay with you and let's see how he adjusts."

They went back to the team and John scooped Ricky up into his arms. "Come on, champ. We're going to Vicki's house."

Ricky held him around his neck for dear life. The warmth of John's body calmed him. John put his hand on the back of Ricky's head, as the boy nestled on his shoulder. John was more ready to be in a parental role than he'd ever thought. Not having any nieces or nephews, he was never around little ones much, but it was evident that little Ricky had embedded himself into his heart. And John wanted him.

He tossed Vicki his signature look. "And then you and I need to have a long talk."

CHAPTER 32

Present Day:

John played the tape of his interview with Mrs. Bennett in Carlson's office—to Paul, Tony, and Sal. "And you couldn't find any of this out?"

"Hey, don't you dare put any of this fucking case on us," Carlson growled. "You're the profiler and getting the big bucks. The department hired your fucking analytical brain to put things like this together for us. You're just doing your fucking job."

"All right then, Paul. Then why are you fighting me and impeding any progress by not doing the investigations I've asked of you?"

"We're not going to anymore. Okay? Just don't bring up your fucking Max."

All of a sudden, the lights flickered.

"What the—"

"You offended him."

"So he's here now? Give me a break!"

The lights flickered and turned off.

"Any other explanation?"

Carlson surrendered. "All right, Max, I give up. I'll listen to you from now on. For Christ's sake, I can't believe I'm talking to this, this, whatever he is. Max, turn the damn lights back on. Now!"

The lights glowed.

Tony and Sal laughed, wide-eyed, probably out of nervousness because they didn't understand what they'd just observed. Very few people did.

"So you really think she offed her twin?"

"Yeah, Tony, I do. Possibly separated at birth, mother gave her up. She had hell. The twin had a great life. Could be her adoptive parents did die just as she said, then foster homes or institutions. Still putting that together. She found out she was a twin, looked for her, and wanted the normalcy."

"All right, we buy it. How do you prove it?" Sal asked.

"That part is easy. Identical twins have the same blood types, but different fingerprints. The Department of Education would have them from the real Barbara, yes?"

They acquiesced.

"And no," Tony replied. "We didn't get them from this one."

"I'll get them from something she touched at the hospital," John said. "In the meantime, bring up all the files from the accident twelve years ago. We'll call her Kellie, for now. But I have a feeling, she has more aliases."

"When are you going back to the hospital?" Carlson asked without an expletive, for once.

"Have a staff meeting at Manhattan Psych in less than an hour. Otherwise, I'd go there now. Probably tonight."

৩৩৩

At his apartment, Clancy positioned himself in front of a well-equipped laptop that Barbara had bought for him. He found the exact address of Morgan Reynolds, his apartment number, and detailed street maps.

"Jaysus, you're a dope. You put yourself so out there, even your apartment number is listed, 3B, with an outside balcony, and it looks like, from the map, that there's fire escapes on your line. You must be gone in the head. I wouldn't go near an apartment like that with a hundred-foot pole. Hope you got a bloody good deal on that one."

He downloaded the photos he'd taken of Morgan and accessed graphics of religious figures. Then he discovered it. The perfect monk. He superimposed the head of Morgan onto the monk's outfit. Yes! He liked what he'd created.

He set up the projector component and flashed Morgan, in the monk's outfit, onto his wall. Very proud of his accomplishments, Clancy gave a hearty laugh. A few more clicks of the keyboard, he had Morgan dancing like a marionette. He found additional color palettes and graphics, he needed for effect, and saved them. "This is going to be such fun. I feel like I'm on a set again. A real-life, state-of-the-art set."

၆၁၆၁

Barbara, dressed in a T-shirt, squishy sweat pants, and sneakers, jogged down the hospital corridor away from Jake. He stood there laughing at her. "Hey, Doc, where ya think ya going?"

Jogging backward, she smiled at him. "I haven't moved in three days. I'm all edgy."

Other patients walked slowly, arm in arm with attendants and visitors. She looked both ways to avoid bumping into them.

"Can't run in the halls, back here. Now."

He actually thinks I'm going to obey? Just look at them. They're laughing that this giant can't control me and I'm less than half his size.

She jogged in place. "You're kidding, right?"

"No. I'm sure as hell not. Get back here now or you're confined to your room."

"You can't do that to me."

"Yeah, I can. Dr. Trenton told me I can do whatever is necessary to make you behave."

"Ooh, that bastard!"

"I'll be sure to relay the message."

"Won't be necessary." She jogged back. "Want to hold my hand so I'll be the good little girl?" She gazed up at him like a three year old and batted her eyelashes.

"Don't be a smart ass. Let's go."

As they walked down the hall, Barbara read all the name

plates on the doors, counted, and memorized the number of patients and their names in each room. At the end of the hall, she turned the corner to go around to the other side.

"Hey, where ya goin'?"

"Jake, I need to move, please. My legs feel like rubber after being in bed for three days. You look like a gym rat. You've got to understand."

"Okay, once around and then to the dining hall."

"Thank you." Barbara observed everything. The nurse's station. The erase board with the shift changes.

8:00 p.m., staff due at 7:40. Jake's leaving, too. No telling what kind of monster I'll get. Now it's 5 p.m. I have to move tonight. No telling what Trenton is finding out. Can't risk it. I thought I was good at deception but he's better than me. What a criminal mastermind he would make. Nah. Never happen.

The nameplates on the door, and the recollection of one of them, stopped her dead in her tracks. But she moved to the right, a room over. She stared for a moment in disbelief.

Oh, my God! Today is my lucky day.

Then as they continued to walk, they passed the elevator. "Okay, done now. Ready for dinner. I'm starved."

"Who did you recognize?"

Damn. He's too observant.

"No one. Just surprised they have two men on a floor with all women."

"Yeah, that happens sometimes if the men's floors are full."

She had maneuvered out of that one gracefully.

ↄ⌘ↄ

Clancy unclasped the latch on the terrace gate and walked in from the fire escape. The three-story walk-up to the terrace had winded him. He needed to be in better shape. In taking a moment to recoup, he reminded himself to be cautious and not make a stupid mistake. There were no lights and the winter darkness now shielded him. He didn't see a soul in any bedroom. This was Manhattan and way too early for anyone to be in bed, asleep anyway. He crouched behind a huge planter with an artificial white palm tree so large it concealed him and the equipment he removed from his knapsack. He peered through the sheer curtains into Morgan's bedroom.

White walls, perfect.

Clancy moved over on the balcony to examine the adjoining room. He spotted Morgan, who was mixing himself a scotch and ginger ale at his bar in the living room. Then Clancy watched him move to a club chair, where he put his bare feet on an ottoman and used the remote to turn on the TV to watch the news. Clancy disliked this apartment in bone, off-white, and stark white. The walls and furniture were without contrast, without boundaries, and projected a very uneasy feeling into Clancy. Very sterile. Even the massive paintings from modern artists didn't waiver from the monotone color scheme.

Morgan, munching chips and drinking, was an easy target.

Clancy returned to the section of balcony outside Morgan's bedroom. All of a sudden, there was a spiritually spooky voice.

"Morgan, Morgan."

Clancy created a combination of feminine pitches alternating with masculine guttural tones to throw Morgan off balance.

Morgan was startled, drunk to boot, and perked up so rapidly on the chair that he spilled his drink on the ottoman. "What the—"

"Morgan, in here, Morgan."

Morgan couldn't shake the sudden fear. "Who's there?" He trembled, attempting to stand.

"In here Morgan. In your bedroom."

Morgan tumbled over a love seat, wobbled, and staggered into the bedroom, grabbing onto the pole at the footboard of the queen size bed.

のがく

A hologram of a gold Samurai sword was on the white bedspread. "Who's in here?"

Noticing the shiny, curved sword, Morgan leaned over to grab the ornate handle, but he couldn't.

The sword penetrated right through his hand and then disappeared.

In his awkward drunken state, he vomited on his designer bedspread. He keeled over. "Who's there?"

"Sorry, Morgan, not just yet."

"Where the hell are you? Tell me now!"

"Okay, if you insist. Turn around."

Morgan's image was reflected on the wall, wearing monk's attire. The hologram depicted him in 3-D and about Morgan's actual height, five feet, five.

"You're not going to get to me. If this is a joke, Steve, you're fired."

"No, Morgan, it's you. In your next life."

"Next life? Yeah right. Who the hell are you?" Morgan lunged toward the hologram, slammed into the wall, banged his forehead, and collapsed on the floor. He curled into the fetal position, taking deep breaths, trying to compose himself. The hologram spun like a tornado in front of his eyes. The different shades of brown in the outfit became darker and darker and, as it landed, standing on its hands on the bed, Morgan lost bowel control. Waste oozed through his pants and onto his white carpet.

Morgan covered his nose and mouth. "Oh my God. Oh, no!"

Clancy grimaced as the odor seeped through the bedroom window, which was open a crack. "Your dump sure stinks. Come on, Morgan. Do some jumping jacks." The hologram performed jumping jacks on the bed. "Arms out and down, legs together, come on, Morgan!"

"I abhor exercise!"

A wicked-looking hand, with crooked fingers and bulging joints with hair on the skin between the knuckles, clutched the samurai sword and lunged it through Morgan, still crouched against the wall with his knees bent into his chest. He moved his hands rapidly around his body searching for blood as the blade gored him. Not one drop. His screams radiated around the room. The monk then reappeared in front of the bed and clenched the sword, committing Hari-kari on himself. Images of blood poured onto the bed over Morgan's vomit and flowed down onto the off-white carpet.

Morgan reached out to touch the blood, but none spread onto his fingers. He bent back on his knees as the color drained from his face.

Clancy made the hologram spin, turn into a rainbow, and disappear out the window.

On the terrace, he set a timer device for two hours, projecting the blood splatter into the room. He placed it inside the planter. It was just enough time for others to see it. Clancy packed up and climbed, in the blackness, down the fire escape without incident.

♥♥♥

Inside the precinct, Jennifer took a message.

"This is Steven Katz, Mr. Reynolds's lawyer. I need a team here immediately."

"Mr. Katz, you're in Manhattan-Midtown South. This is Brooklyn South."

"Yes, I know, but Mr. Reynolds is Lieutenant Carlson's cousin and he trusts him."

"Okay, I'll get him the message immediately. He's here now." She disconnected and ran to Carlson's office, handing him the note as he opened the door.

"Call Mandella and Valantino," he ordered. "Tell them to come here immediately. And call Dr. Trenton. He's in Manhattan now. Give him the address and tell him to meet us there. He's got to leave immediately. Tell him it's a crime scene."

"Yes, Lieutenant." She departed without hesitation.

"Damn. I didn't need this."

♥♥♥

John rang the bell to Morgan's apartment repeatedly. Steve opened the door and three badges were flashed at him.

"I'm Dr. Trenton."

"Steve Katz. Mr. Reynolds's attorney."

"Why do you feel he needs an attorney?" John inquired.

"I'm his friend, too. This time, I wouldn't let him talk me out of calling you guys."

"This happened before?" Tony asked.

"Yes, Detective Mandella, last week. Got a present of a condom over the carcass of a rat. Delivered by messenger to his office." The men stared at each other in recognition. "Come in here."

The blood looked authentic, wet and three-dimensional. Morgan stumbled in, still intoxicated, but cleaned up. His odor wasn't that offensive, but John still wrinkled his nose with disgust.

"Mr. Reynolds, what did the hologram look like?" Sal asked.

"Me in a brown, shit-brown, monk's outfit. He said it was me in my next life."

"The hologram talked?" Sal asked.

"Mr. Reynolds didn't make this up. How do you explain all this blood?"

John understood it. He walked into a blood puddle that bubbled, laughing like a little kid.

"Doc, what are you doing?" Tony asked.

John continued laughing. He kicked his feet through it and not one drop spread onto him. The blood stains mysteriously disappeared, leaving the room spotless. John guessed where the hologram could have originated. He led Sal out to the terrace. John looked around at the stunning Manhattan view, but his gaze kept coming back to the planter.

Sal lifted up the silk leaves and, bingo, there was the projector. Sal took out a small evidence bag and put the device into it. He carried it into the bedroom. "This is where the blood came from. We'll analyze it and see what comes up. In the meantime, Mr. Reynolds, have another place to stay?"

"He'll stay with me for a few days," Steve said.

"Good, we'll be in touch." Tony opened the door to the apartment.

In the hall going to the elevator, John asked, "Where's Paul?"

"Said he couldn't make it. What are you putting together, John?"

"Got to get that Clancy guy. He has the skills to pull this off. Maybe he heard the machine tape. Morgan called when Clancy was setting up the bomb in her apartment. Maybe he figured Reynolds is the boyfriend, though I seriously doubt that. Something doesn't feel right."

"No known address on this Clancy guy. No credit cards, no utility bills," Tony said.

"Keep looking, Tony," John demanded. "He exists."

❧❧❧

Inside the apartment Morgan was still shaken. "Don't know why you involved Carlson. This can open up—"

"I wasn't thinking. Call him and make sure he shreds all the files. He owes me, so he better do it. He's got as much on the line as us."

CHAPTER 33

The clock on the wall opposite the bed inside Barbara's hospital room read 8:10. She stared up at it while sitting on the edge of the bed. Waves of agitation gyrated through her as she rocked back and forth in a slow motion daze in an effort to calm down. Her sweaty hands lay palm down on either side of her on the bed.

Her eyes were locked wide open. The blood had drained from her face and her mind had gone to another place and time, long ago, to somewhere she'd rather not be. She longed to be cuddling with her old blankie right now. That was a lifetime ago, a lost lifetime. It was crocheted, pink and lime green, like her room, with her name in yellow, embroidered on top by her adoptive mommy, and it got carelessly and inconsiderately cast-off the night social services brought her, at four and a half, to her first foster home.

There were six kids in that home. She was the youngest and they all bullied her. They tore her clothes, pulled her hair, held her down, and punched her. No one came to her rescue.

She was the little girly girl with five rough and tumble boys. She envisioned it now. She saw herself on that first night raped by the seventeen-year-old boy, just when she thought she was safely tucked into bed. The rapes happened night after night, until she became so disturbed and acting out the family wouldn't keep her. Then it was family after family.

She was a beautiful little angel with a turned up nose and big round blue eyes who lost her innocence and childhood that first night. Doubt and fear toward anyone who entered her life had replaced her innocence. Anxieties and anger, that no child should know, replaced her childhood. She yelled incessantly "Don't come near me!" if anyone came within two feet of her. She would bite, kick, scream, and scratch. She wouldn't let anyone bathe her, wash her hair, or change her clothes. The little princess, who once had matching barrettes and socks for every outfit, had the stench of urine and filth, and no one cared enough to do anything about it. She remembered it all now as if it were yesterday.

No adult would believe her when she told them what was happening. They just got rid of her to sweep it under the rug. She learned very early on to trust no one and to fear everyone. To become stronger, meaner, crueler, smarter, and acting without remorse, became her defense.

A black fly circled the room, landed on her left arm. She swatted it with her right hand, but the fly escaped. It was enough to give her a wakeup call to return to the present. She blinked her eyes rapidly to erase the wretched memory that cut so deeply into her soul.

Sniffling and feeling weighed down from the pain, she breathed heavily and lifted herself up from the edge of the bed, approaching the closed door while wiping away tears with the back of her hand. She felt all alone, again. Just as she had when she was that lost little angel.

She opened the door to her room and, to her surprise, Jake's replacement for the night, another uniformed NYPD officer, stood there grinning at her with his muscular arms folded across his chest. Bald, he doubled for Mr. Clean. He was big as Jake and armed, as well, with a Glock .40-caliber. She snuck a glimpse of it and then refocused her attention on him, looking up, way up into his shrewd eyes.

He noticed her take notice. "Hi, Doc. Can I get you something?"

Don't think I can take this one either.

"Where's Jake?" Like she didn't know.

"Shift change. Phil."

"Well, Phil, can you get me a Diet Coke or something?"

"Not on your life. But they do come around with snacks later."

"What time?"

"It varies. Why? Planning to go somewhere, Doc?"

"Yeah, tough guy. Right through the walls, just like a ghost." She wanted to convince him she had resigned herself to staying put.

"Good. As long as we understand each other. And in case you didn't know, you're in your room for the evening."

"That's fine. I'll spend my time knitting. Have a lot to catch up on."

"Good girl." He closed the door slowly, stopping when he reached her, forcing her to move back.

She was insulted that he cut off conversation and that he asserted himself as the boss, but the less communication she had with this hulk the better. It seemed more than mutual. He probably wanted to do as much as he could to avoid her.

Barbara surveyed the room, discouraged. She dropped down on the bed and stared at the ceiling.

Damn! Damn! Damn! Fuck him! Fuck him! Fuck himmmmm!

Real tears swelled up in her eyes.

Trenton pulled a fast one. Now what am I going to do? He didn't miss a fucking beat. He knows about me. He knows everything about me. I'm stuck in this fucking vanilla box, no windows, air vents on the ceiling, disgusting, just look at them so dirty with crud and dust I'd get asphyxiated if I went near them. I can't reach the fucking ceiling, anyway. Those twelve-inch panels are too small to get through, even for me. And no telling where they lead to. There's nothing to climb on, anyway. And the only way out is guarded by a fucking behemoth, armed no less. He could do fucking damage to me before I went for his gun.

She rolled onto her side into a fetal position.

I'm doomed. Life without parole. Maybe if I tell him some stuff at least, I'll be eligible for parole. I'll turn on Clancy. That's it. I'll turn on them, all of them. Shit. Can't do that either. They're all dead and buried where no one will find them. Maybe he'd confine me to a state institution instead of jail. I couldn't do prison. No way could I do prison. Heck, I spent eight years here. I'm doomed. I can't be doomed. Now I know how a lioness feels pacing back and forth in her cage with no freedom in sight.

Maybe I should talk to him. He wanted to listen but I shut him out like everyone else. What the hell am I going to say to him? Dr. Trenton, I've been revenge killing since I was eighteen. That would go over big. Then he'd want the details. Who remembers them all? I should remember them. I read once that murderers remember their kills. Me, I just do it and block it out, like it was someone else doing the killing. But it was me. It was me, with all of them. He seemed like he wanted to help me for real, not like I do with those damn kids.

She sobbed real tears as she managed her way to the door and opened it.

"Barbara, what's the matter?" Phil kept her at arms distance, holding out his left arm with his palm facing her. "You okay?"

Crying, she asked, "Do I look okay? No, I'm not. Don't look at me like that. I'm not going to go for your gun."

"Go inside." He closed the door behind him. "Go sit on the bed and tell me what's going on."

She followed his directives. "Is Dr. Trenton coming back tonight?"

He stood rigid with his arms folded across his chest a few feet away from her.

"I don't know. Why?"

"Can you please call him? I really need to talk to him."

"It's late, already."

"I don't care. Please. I'm falling apart here."

"Sure." He dialed John's number, not taking his eyes off her.

"Dr. Trenton."

"Yeah. Doc. Phil. Montgomery wants to talk to you."

"Really?"

"Yup." He handed her the phone.

The crying had eased up but her breathing was still strained. "Dr. Trenton, I really need to talk to you."

"Okay."

"Are you coming back here tonight? I feel like I'm dying here. And isn't it illegal to keep me in seclusion?"

"You're not in solitary confinement. Phil will keep you company. I can have a nurse stay and talk with you. You're not in seclusion, by any means."

"No. That's okay. I'm knitting. I'll be okay alone. Can you come back?"

"Actually, I was on my way back but got called to a crime scene in Manhattan. We're just finishing up. I can be there in about an hour. Okay?"

"I have a lot to tell you."

"Good. I will listen."

"Thank you." She handed the phone back to Phil and plopped down on the bed again, very depressed. Tears cascaded down her cheeks.

৩৩৩

John, Sal, and Tony walked to their cars. Parking was not attainable at this hour on a Friday evening in the partying club area of Chelsea, so they double parked in front of Morgan's building. John acknowledged the fact that she'd said "Thank you," contemplating the conversation for a few moments, staring into space with his hands in his pockets, before taking out his car keys.

"What was that all about? Was that Montgomery?"

John ignored Tony.

"Hey! John. Is that your head or did your neck grow a bubble?"

That startled John back to reality. "Yeah. She wants to talk to me."

"You're kidding?"

"No. Guess she doesn't see a way out for herself."

"Where can she possibly go?" Sal teased.

"Can't. Got all the bases covered. Every nurse knows her face. I made sure of it."

❧❧❧

Inside her room, Barbara lay on the bed on top of the blanket, staring up at the moveable panels on the ceiling. Her knitting bag was next to her, but she couldn't focus on that now. She closed her eyes for a moment in desperation as childhood anxieties set in, drifting her mind into another daydream…

❧❧❧

An ambulance with sirens blaring pulled into the emergency entrance early afternoon on a summer day in 1985. Two drivers ran to the rear, opened the doors, and pulled out little ten-year-old Kellie, on a stretcher, wrapped in a straitjacket, screaming uncontrollably. She wore a tattered yellow dress and her beautiful dark blonde hair, carelessly done in a ponytail, was half falling out. Her eyes were reddened from crying and her face was dirty from smearing her hands across it.

She was locked in a room like this one, all alone and very scared, but pretended to be tough as she ventured into the bathroom out of curiosity. She was cautious, looking all around her. She didn't know if she was being watched, but she knew there would be consequences. They'd made that clear enough.

She studied a hole in the wall where the medicine cabinet should have been, climbed up onto the toilet bowl, and then onto the dirty and rust stained sink to look inside the hole. It led to an adjoining bathroom.

A matronly nurse, wearing a white-skirted uniform and sailor type hat, startled Kellie, by grabbing her from behind. Then she was tied down on her bed with her arms and feet in Velcro restraints.

She lay screaming and struggling to wiggle out of them in the oversized bed, as the nurse yelled at her to be quiet. She distinctly heard, 'Be quiet you little brat, or I'll give you something to cry about!'

Five hours of restraint passed with screaming, and naps, screaming and nightmares, and not once did a doctor check in on her. The five hours led into a year and then another and then another until she was eighteen.

⁓∽⁓

She was awakened by present-day sirens outside. Always something to cry about. That was her entire life. Real tears streamed down her face, again. Several psychiatrists declared her too psychologically damaged for placement in a foster home or for consideration as an adoption candidate. The screaming at adults, the physically attacking anyone who tried to touch her, her rabid anger, her violent eyes, then her depression where she wouldn't say a word rendered her untreatable and, at that time—at ten—to be given up on, to be thought of as a hopeless case, that was unthinkable. Kellie had endured the unthinkable.

Barbara had had to admit children from her schools for short-term hospitalization. She was happy that rules about their treatment had changed. She'd educated herself on the law. Since the late 1990s, children could only be restrained for a maximum of an hour at a time. They had to be monitored by a doctor constantly and only restrained when they presented a danger to themselves or others. She constantly made unannounced visits whenever she had a break in her school day. Just to make sure the caregivers followed the rules.

He's crazy if he thinks I'm staying here. I can't. I just can't. Eight years here were enough. I can't handle anymore. I have to get out of here if it kills me. And I'm prepared to kill my way out.

Then it hit her—like a ton of bricks. She sat up rapidly, looking around.

Unannounced, a nurse, Jada, opened the door and walked into the room. She wore a casual light blue uniform with different colored lollipops on it. "How are you doing, Barbara? Dr. Trenton told me to check in on you. In the mood for some company?"

He sure is good at telling people what to do.

"Thanks, Jada, but I'm just getting ready to sort out these directions." Barbara removed the instruction booklet from the bag, opened to the page that showed diagrams and graphs and three full-length columns of directions. "And this is a complicated one. I need to concentrate."

"Wow, I love those colors. Greens and browns are my favs," Jada exclaimed. "What's it going to look like?" Barbara showed her the picture on the cover, as if it would make a difference. "That's gorgeous. I wish I could knit."

"My grandma taught me when I was eight. Jada, really, I'll be fine until Dr. Trenton comes back, now that I know I'll be able to talk to him tonight. And knitting has always relaxed me."

"Okay, Barbara, but please feel free to buzz if you need me."

"Thank you."

Jada left smiling.

The medicine cabinet in the bathroom. Yes!

In the bathroom, she checked the corners of the medicine cabinets—first, the bottom two edges, then the top two. Ugh, coated with dust. Most people here didn't use them, anyway. They wiggled from the edge and there were cracks in the plasterboard surrounding it.

They're loose. Got it! *I could pull it out if I had the right tool.*

Her mind sparkled with the answer.

And I do. No one in their right mind would think of this. No one in any mind.

She dressed in her corporate business suit. Luckily, the fabric didn't wrinkle and it still looked fresh. Her undergarments were perfect for this suit. Even the fresh bra and panties that she pulled from the duffle bag matched just the way she liked them!

Thank you, Dr. Trenton. You brought me everything I need.

She put on makeup she always had, with her foundation, blue shadow, mascara, blush, and neutral tone beige glossed lipstick. After all, she had to look like the professional she pretended to be.

She quickly chose what to take. Sneakers. Perfect. The high-heeled boots that lay on the bed would just slow her down and wouldn't fit into her tote. She turned on the shower so Phil would think she was taking care of personal business. She held up a clean towel against her and then pulled the shower curtain fully across the tub, being careful not to spray water on her suit. Then she took one size-seven plastic knitting needle out of her knitting bag with the first ten inches of sweater hanging on it. She dropped that one onto the tiled bathroom floor. She retrieved the second needle.

Baby plastic, but all I need is the very tip. And if I push it with my gelled finger nail, that should do the trick.

She removed the toiletries and placed them softly on the floor. She levered the tip of the knitting needle around the edge of the cabinet to pry it loose. Very squeaky. Couldn't afford that. She picked up the tube of shea-butter moisturizer that Trenton had brought her and squeezed it all around the cabinet, making sure it penetrated between the cabinet and the wall. She picked out a Q-Tip from a baggie.

Thank you again, Dr. Stupid.

She moved the Q-Tip around the perimeter of the cabinet, pressing the lubricant in to ease the noise. Rust oozed from behind the cabinet onto the wall and drops splattered on the floor. What a mess she made! But who cared?

First, the bottom. She stopped periodically to listen for voices coming from the adjoining room. So far, none. Now the left side pried loose. She stopped again to listen. Then the right side. Listened. Listened. Listened. She had to be very careful. It was heavy and, if it dropped, the noise would alert some-one—Phil, a nurse. It was sixteen by twenty-two inches and three inches deep on each side, so six inches deep all together. At five feet eight and size four, she could easily slip through the hole. She knew for sure there was a big risk here, but what the hell? Her entire life had been a risk. So what if they caught her? She had nothing to lose.

With much effort, wiggling it by sections, she pried the cabinet out. She clutched it on either side with both hands over some towels, making sure not to allow it to fall forward and hit her on the head. She placed it gently on the floor. There were no toiletries in it from the other room.

Thank God they still haven't made these permanent.

From the hidden compartment in the knitting bag, she pulled out another phony ID tag, Dr. Pauline Jones, Chief Psychologist, Malloytone Center and clipped it on the collar of her suit jacket. She glanced back at the boots. *Damn, I love them. But can't risk taking them. Threw out 1500 bucks. I hope I can do this. I know I can do this.*

She wiped off the greasy rust on the wall, around the cabinet space, with a towel. Couldn't get any on her thousand-dollar suit. She used three towels and left them carelessly on the floor, wrapping the grimy knitting needle in them.

One last thing. She almost forgot. She put her hand deep into the knitting bag into the false bottom and pulled out a shoulder-length, professional-style, black wig. She pulled back and clipped her hair up, then slipped on the very natural looking, human hairpiece that could easily be taken as her own. She examined herself in the plastic mirror on the cabinet door to adjust it and she was ready to go. As if were an afterthought, she tossed the knitting bag onto the bed, next to the boots and duffle.

She shut off the shower, shimmied up onto the sink, and peered into the bathroom of the adjoining room. No one, yet. The bathroom door was shut. It was too quiet.

⌘

She climbed through head first, with her hands grasping each side of the ledge of the sink on the other side. She propelled herself off into a standing position, giving a silent thank you to herself for taking those gymnastic lessons. She straightened her suit, which had hiked up her legs, and then pulled though her tote that she left on the sink in her room. So far, so good.

Within a few seconds, she heard a nurse enter. "How are you doing tonight, ladies?" No answer. Not even a grunt, sigh or unintelligible sound of communication. "That's good. I'm glad you're both doing well. Here to give you your meds for the evening. Charlotte, first yours, honey." There was a pause.

"Here ya go. Drink all the water, hon." Another pause. "Good girl."

I never had a nurse so nice. Too bad, she's retiring—permanently.

Barbara flushed the toilet, delayed a few seconds, then opened the bathroom door leading into the room and saw the cute, twenty-something nurse who greeted her with a smile.

"Oh, hello there." She read her nametag. "Dr. Jones. I don't believe we've met. I'm Valerie. Charlotte and Julie's night nurse. And you're here to see…"

"Nice to meet you, Valerie. I'm sorry, neither of them is my patient. I just got off the elevator and had to use a restroom so badly that I ran into the first room. They've seen me before, so I knew I wouldn't upset them. Sorry if it's against protocol, but I drank too much coffee and got stuck in traffic coming from Manhattan."

"Not a problem, Dr. Jones. Then I assume you didn't sign in yet?"

"No I didn't. I will now." Barbara approached her as if she was leaving the room.

"Dr. Jones, who is your patient?"

Damn. People just ask too many questions. Psychiatrists ask too many questions. Colleagues ask too many questions.

"Dr. Jones?"

"I'm not at liberty to say. It's a criminal case."

"Excuse me? Dr. Jones, we still have to know who you're seeing."

"That won't matter much to you, Valerie."

Valerie attempted to back away, bumping into an IV pole. She dropped Julie's meds, that were in a one-ounce white paper cup, onto the floor, probably envisioning her life flash before her eyes. She watched the pills scatter. That was enough time for Barbara to grab Valerie in a chokehold, turning her around so her back leaned against Barbara's chest. In one swift jerk of the crook of her left arm, Barbara pulled Valerie's neck to her side and fractured it, killing the nurse before she knew what had hit her. Barbara laid Valerie on the floor, her eyes bulging. The two patients stared, without any reaction, at Barbara. "Sorry, ladies, your night nurse retired." Without taking a second look at Valerie, Barbara stuck her hand into her tote and pulled out a pair of designer glasses. She held them up to the light to check for dirt before she put them on.

She opened the door, looked down the hall, and saw staff, but no one looked in her direction. She left the room and, even though the elevator was right there, she bypassed it as the room next door drew her in. She slipped in to the room where two women—around forty, wearing hospital night gowns—silently paced back and forth, from the window to the door, in a slow rhythmical pace, as if they were listening to "Pomp and Circumstance" running through their fried brains. She focused on one woman, wearing a nametag of Lois Carrolls, and smiled in recognition.

Little Kellie, at ten, had approached little Lois, also ten, and poked her. Kellie was in a vengeful rage. Lois was schizo-phrenic. Kellie heard herself say, "Come on, Lois, come on Lois, betcha can't catch me." She'd pummeled Lois, poked her in her eyes with her index and middle fingers, and punched her nose so severely she bled. A nurse ran over and pulled her off Lois. Two attendants, assisting the nurse, dragged Kellie over to a bed and restrained her unmercifully.

Timing brought her back to reality. She had to move. After composing herself, she opened the door, only to bump full body into a nurse. "Oh." She scanned the nametag. "Karen, I'm sorry."

"Who the hell are you, lady?" Karen was so wide she blocked Barbara's way out.

"I'm Dr. Jones. I just stopped in to visit one of my former patients. Lois. How is she doing?"

"Prognosis isn't good. Wait a minute, honey. Did you ar-range this with her doctor?" Karen remained with her flabby arms out, holding each side of the door with a nasty grin on her face. "Did you sign in?"

"No, to both, Karen. Just got off the elevator."

"When did you work with her?"

"Two-thousand-two, during my internship."

Karen gave her the up and down. "Wait here and don't you dare move your lily-white butt."

"Yes, ma'am."

Out of sorts already and it's the beginning of the shift. Definitely needs a career change.

Barbara understood Karen's suspicious glare. However, the nurse was too out of shape to make it to the nurse's station, that was all the way down the hall and around the corner, quickly. Barbara took advantage, snuck to the stairwell at the end of the hall, and vanished.

Good thing you're slow. That just saved your life. On the other hand, I think she wanted me to disappear. Less work for her.

❧❧❧

Barbara was used to stairwells like this. The handrails were double parallel bars about four inches in diameter that ran down on both sides of the fifteen step flights. Chunks of paint had fallen off, revealing years of layering with poor paint jobs. She held onto both sides with her tote over her shoulder and propelled herself without hesitation down the flight, only touching ground twice. The same with the next flight and the next. She met no one.

I could kick myself for wasting time. I could have avoided that last bitch altogether. Don't think she's smart enough to identify me.

Ninth floor.

Can't worry about that now. Why was I so drawn to see Lois? Why? I don't know. Why did I want to see anyone from my past?

Seventh floor.

Maybe I needed a reminder. Maybe I needed a reminder of why I'm doing all of this. That's right. What I'm about to do is right.

She sprinted down two more flights without thinking. Fifth floor.

I have to get even with all of them for the betrayal. Focus, Barbara, focus.

She made it to the ground floor hardly winded. She straightened her suit, her wig.

She opened the stairwell door carefully. The lobby bustled with people coming and going. Visiting hours at the hospital ran late. She was casual, but alert, and walked through the lobby, cognizant of everyone around her. Nothing suspicious. No one gave her a second thought.

She got into a turnstile to exit the building in the main lobby and saw John entering through another door.

Outside, in the service lane, yellow and black cabs lined the curb. She dashed to the first cab in line and jumped in.

He pulled away. "Hello, Doctor."

"Two stops in Brooklyn and then upper west side, Manhattan."

CHAPTER 34

Three Years Earlier:

John parked behind Vicki in her driveway and hoisted Ricky, sound asleep, out of the back seat. The only light illuminating the pavers to the house was the row of garden strobes. The eerie darkness in the woods behind them and the natural quietness rattled Ricky. He awakened, looked around, still clinging to John's neck.

John could only imagine what went through his little mind. Whom should he trust? Who would calm him? Who would soothe his hurt and pain? His little brain must be falling apart in his head. From the way he expressed himself, his feelings and emotions were more developed than any five year old's should be. He had lost his innocent childhood. How was he going to get that back?

What could John and Vicki do, in just two short days, until Ricky's aunt and uncle arrived from Miami? How would he be able to let the boy go after he'd fallen so in love with him? The thought made John's heart break. Right now, his heart was embraced in his arms.

"Have a good nap?"

Ricky rubbed his eyes. "Where are we?"

"At Vicki's house. Did you eat dinner?"

"No."

"Are you hungry?"

"Very."

John put Ricky down in the entryway to the great room. The little guy looked around with wide, open eyes.

"Okay, I am going to give you a bath and Vicki will make you some dinner."

Ricky's expression changed and he shot John a serious frown. John smiled, not knowing what Ricky meant, yet.

"Sounds like a plan," Vicki said. "What do you want to eat Ricky? It's late so how about some cereal and milk?"

"What kind of cereal? I only eat Fruit Loops."

"Um, don't have that here. How about Cheerios? Every kid likes Cheerios."

Ricky looked down at the tile floor. "Okay. If that's all you have."

"Do you want soft boiled or scrambled eggs with toast?"

"Egh!" He crinkled his nose. John got a kick out of this and laughed.

"Just Cheerios and toast with lots of butter," Ricky said.

"Not so much butter. Come on, bath time, and Vicki will make the bed for you. Come on, champ." John grasped his hand and Ricky pulled away, fast.

"I don't wanna bath."

John couldn't believe the challenge. "What?"

Vicki paid attention with her hand over her mouth, concealing a laugh. John smirked at her.

"I don't wanna a bath!" Ricky shouted.

"Why not?" At first, John found this humorous.

"I hate it!"

"Why? Tell me, champ."

Ricky stomped around the space. "I hate cold water!"

John took his concern seriously. "It's okay. Vicki has warm water."

"No, she don't! Nobody has hot water where we live."

"We'll make it as warm as you want. I promise. Come on, champ. You have to."

"*No*! I don't!"

John applied the rational approach. "Vicki has nice clean sheets, blankets, and pillows for you. You don't want to get them dirty do you?"

Ricky pursed his lips. "I don't care!"

"This isn't happening." Dealing with a tantrum wasn't his thing. John scooped him up in his arms and carried him into the guest bathroom, despite Ricky's loud protests and attempts to wriggle out of his arms.

"Let go a me!"

John didn't comprehend this at all, and nearly missed getting socked in the nose. "I'll let you feel the water and we'll make it as warm as you want, okay?"

"I'm too tired for a bath," Ricky cried.

John held him close and patted his back. "Okay, champ. It's okay. Come on." For whatever reason, be it John's strong presence or his warmth, or his own fatigue, Ricky yielded.

Without saying a word and, with no additional confrontation, John removed Ricky's dirty T-shirt and shorts, then his underwear. John barely wanted to touch the foul smelling clothing, so he held it with his thumb and forefinger behind Ricky's back. The crying lessened to whining and then subsided. "It's okay, Ricky. I'm doing all the work. You'll feel better and then you'll eat. And then you'll get a good night's sleep, okay?"

Then John noticed some remaining red handprints on Ricky's bottom from his latest spanking. He cuddled him in his arms to comfort him as he poured in some bath cream and adjusted the temperature in the bath.

I hope they get life.

"Here, champ. Put your hand in and feel it. Warm enough?"

"Yes, but—" Ricky crinkled his nose. "It smells like flowers. I'll smell like a girl!"

"It's gardenia, and you won't smell like a girl. I use Vicki's bath creams when I'm here, too."

"An' you don't pass the pew test, neither."

John laughed. "Pew test? What's that, champ?"

"Grandma says Mommy doesn't pass the pew test when she smells from cigarettes. I don't like that smell, neither. It makes my asthma come."

"You won't have that smell here, champ. And I'm going to shower with this bath cream when you're having something to eat. So in ya go."

In the tub, John splashed him with some suds and Ricky, for the first time, giggled and splashed him back. That play John permitted. He won the first battle. He came out of it soaked but at least Ricky was clean. John pulled short-sleeved PJs from the bag Ricky's grandmother had packed. Ricky put them on himself.

ᏆᏆᏆ

"Up ya go Ricky, onto the nice, soft bed." John lifted him up and tucked him under the oversized comforter. He sat on the bed with one arm over Ricky. "Comfy?" Ricky tried to hide tears. "What's the matter, champ?"

"Where are you and Vicki going to sleep?"

"In Vicki's room."

"I don't want to sleep alone. I'm scared."

"Oh, Ricky, I know. It's a new bed in a new house. But you'll be fine."

"But the bad people come at night an' wake me up an' give me bad dreams."

"Well, they won't come tonight, because the bad people don't know where you are and they can't find you. And Vicki and I will stop anyone bad. Okay?"

"But how can you stop them? They're in my head."

John was shocked he comprehended this. *This is way too mature for a five year old.* "You're such a smart little kid. You know that?"

Ricky giggled. "Yes."

"Here's what you do. Tell the bad people not to come any more and you won't let them in. Say it, go ahead."

"Bad people don't come anymore! I mean it!"

"Very good. Here's one of Vicki's teddy bears to cuddle and he wants to sleep with you, too. I have to go to sleep also. I'm very tired. And you should be, too." John planted kisses on his cheeks.

Vicki appeared with an American Indian Dream Catcher. "Here Ricky, I'm putting this over the bed and it will catch any bad dreams, so you don't have them. Okay?" She fastened it to the headboard.

"Wow, will it work?" Ricky handled the feathers and looked mesmerized by their texture and rich colorations.

"Yes, it will. An Indian chief at a reservation here in Florida told me so and I believe him."

"Okay, then I'll believe him, too."

"Sleep tight, sweetheart." Vicki kissed him. "Let's go, he's a big boy and he'll be fine." She was a lot more confident than John was.

John kissed him on top of his head and rustled his damp hair.

In the bedroom, John slowly began to undress, removing his tank, as he waited for Vicki to do the same. She grabbed a not-so-sexy beige cotton oversized nightgown from her drawer and tossed it onto the bed while he surprised her with I-hope-you're-not-wearing-that look.

"Not tonight. I'm exhausted. So should you be. You worked hard tonight. And I shouldn't have to remind you that creep could have shot you." She sat on the bed with her back toward him and raised her arms above her head so he could remove her tank top. Then he unclasped her bra.

"At least you came home to change."

She turned and looked up at him adoringly.

"I am tired," he said. "But I just want to hold you close and that doesn't do it for me. Lose the nightgown."

"Ignoring that?"

"Ignoring what?"

"That Dunn guy could have killed you!"

"Loose the nightgown."

"John, do you always put yourself into danger like that?"

"Only when I know I can handle it. And I've done it before. Don't worry. It's my job. Just like it's your brothers'. I'm sure their wives worry, too. Occupational hazard. But believe me we're all as careful as we can be. And that kid sniper in the tree had my back." Staring at the nightgown, he picked it up, held it out, and dropped it like vermin. "I'm not going to say it again, lose this schmatta."

She laughed. John knew she got the drift.

"Oooooh, tough guy, and if I don't?"

"I'll tackle it off you."

She laughed and put the gown back in the drawer. Taking off her shorts and panties, she joined him as he was already under the comforter. He cuddled her close, lying on his stomach with his right arm over her breasts. Her body warmed his skin. He deposited soft pecks with his lips on her neck.

"Um, cuddly. You feel so nice and warm. And you smell like gardenia. Yummy. Always sleep raw?"

"No. Usually just briefs, but I'll manage for a few hours," he said. "Tell me what you got yourself into." He propped himself up on his elbows on his left side, facing her, and gave her his undivided attention.

"What?"

"What? Come on. The reason why your father and brother are so overprotective. What did you do?"

"John, it was years ago and I'm over it."

"Well, obviously, they're not."

"That's their problem."

"No, it's our problem, too. I don't appreciate being monitored."

"So tell me about your failed relationships."

"I've had my share. Believe me. If you're over it, then you should be able to talk about it."

"Playing shrink, are you?"

"It's who I am. I always need answers, relentlessly."

"Can't this wait till tomorrow? I'm exhausted."

"No. It can't wait."

"I was in a lousy marriage fifteen years ago. I was twenty-two, very young, and infatuated with this guy. It only lasted three months. There, ya happy?"

"No. What did he do?"

"You want the gory details?"

"Every one."

"Why?"

"Because I, uh, want you in my life and I want to know what makes you happy and sad, and I want to know more about you."

"Want me in your life—"

John cut her off. "Vicki, I'm in love with you."

"John." She embraced him with a warm, long loving kiss. "I'm in love with you, too."

He held her in a tight embrace. It was what he wanted to hear. Exhausted, but still in the mood to caress and hug, they were interrupted by Ricky, who sauntered in rubbing his eyes.

Weary, they looked up at him.

"That Indian Chief made a boo-boo. I want to sleep with you."

John was ready to pick him up and bring him into the bed, but he received soft tap on the hand from Vicki. "Ricky, turn around and put your hands over your eyes for a minute," she said. "We're playing a game."

Ricky laughed. "Okay, why?"

"Just do it, Ricky." She jumped out of bed, grabbed the dreaded nightgown and a pair of panties from her drawer, and slipped them on as John pulled on his shorts. "John, this isn't a good—"

"Just for tonight, right, Ricky?"

"Right."

John lifted him up onto the bed and Ricky plopped his head down on John's chest with their arms wrapped around each other. They both fell asleep in a millisecond. Vicki didn't want to lose this moment so she captured it on her smartphone, smiling.

"He'd make a great dad," she whispered softly.

಄಄಄

Esther and Sam were in the kitchen, having a light lunch of tuna salad sandwiches. John, Vicki, and Ricky entered their house around noon. Esther wondered what had happened to their son, having not seen him in over twenty-four hours.

"And who is this?"

"Mom, Dad, this is Ricky."

Vicki has a son. Looks like her. He doesn't need this. Deal with an ex-husband.

"Hi, Ricky. Hungry?"

"No, ma'am. Vicki made breakfast."

He calls his mommy by her name? "What did Vicki make?"

"Oatmeal pancakes with strawberries an' bananas and scrambled eggs."

"Wow! That sounds yummy."

"It was. At first John looked at it an' said 'I don't eat pancakes, too many carbs, whatever that is.'"

John laughed at the way Ricky expressed himself using his hands as he talked.

"An' then Vicki looked up at him an' said, 'Hush!'"

"Really? Vicki told John to 'hush?'" Esther looked at Sam in bewilderment. Their son was knocked off his throne? Couldn't be. Not their son.

"Then he looked at her like you two are looking at each other now."

They removed the shocked expressions and poker faces replaced them.

"And then what?" Esther asked.

"Vicki told John what was in them an' he said, 'Okay then,' an' he ate them. Three biggggg ones. I ate only one 'cause my tummy is smaller, but when I'm big like John, I'll eat three, too. Want to know something?"

"Sure. What is it, sweetheart?" Esther couldn't imagine what was to come.

"John an' Vicki are my new mommy an' daddy."

His mother, feeling faint, nearly fell off the chair and his father gasped. John disappeared real fast into his suite, laughing.

His mother strived to be so compassionate, hiding her shock. "What happened to your old mommy and daddy?"

Vicki smiled. "Go ahead, Ricky. You can tell the whole story."

Ricky sat up straight in the chair. Vicki took the chair next to him. Folding their hands on the table, John's parents waited attentively for Ricky to begin. "John put Mommy an' Daddy in jail last night."

"Oh?" Esther was stunned. What had her son gotten into?

Sam tried to remain staid. "What happened, Ricky?"

"I was at Grandma an' Grandpa's house with Mommy

when Daddy came in with a rifle an' some guns an' kept us there 'cause he was mad at Mommy for taking me to Grandma's house, an' then the policemans came an' they couldn't get Daddy out an' Daddy said he wanted to talk to John 'cause John made Mommy leave him."

"When was that?" Sam asked.

"At the hospital. Friday night. I had an asthma attack an' John spoke to Mommy an' Vicki."

Esther shot Sam a glare.

He couldn't skip that damn poker game.

Sam attempted, unsuccessfully, to escape his wife's wrath. "And then what happened?"

"John came to Grandma's house an' Daddy said 'I want to blow your head off, Doc.'"

Vicki placed her hand over her mouth and gasped.

Ricky noticed Vicki's reaction. "Yes, I heard him say that," he continued. "'I want to blow your head off, Doc.' Really I did.'" He bobbed his head up and down.

Esther clutched Sam's hand.

"Then John wanted Daddy to let me go first before he went into the house an' Daddy did an' I ran into Vicki's car. Then John went to the house with Daddy pointing a rifle at him an' John kicked the rifle out of Daddy's hand an' put handcuffs on him. An' the policemans took him away. An' I told John an' Vicki that Mommy hurts me, too, so John put Mommy in jail, too. An' then Grandma an' Grandpa said they can't keep me so the policemans took me to the police station an' Vicki said I can stay with her an' John. So that's what happened." Ricky breathed a sigh of relief that he finished the entire story.

"Oh my! That is some story, Ricky. You expressed that so well."

"I know!"

John reappeared. His parents were infuriated and not afraid to let him know.

"Come on, Ricky," John said. "We're going to the pool. Did you three get acquainted?"

"More than necessary. You could have been—"

"Dad—"

"Come on let's go. After you swim with John, Ricky, we'll read a Clifford book."

Ricky stared at Vicki with eyes wide open for a minute then, with anxiety overcoming him, collapsed on the floor shaking, screaming and thrashing his arms and legs in fear. "No! No books! I *hate* books! No books!" He thrashed and bobbed up and down on the hard tile floor, leaving the four adults staring in amazement.

Esther and Sam looked at John to see how he would handle this one. His mother dared him to stop the tantrum with a smug grin, wanting him to suffer for taking this on.

Vicki let him take over, too. John got the clear signal from the three of them that it was on him, but he was up for the challenge, even if just to prove his parents wrong. They always challenged him with dares. It was the family games they played and he had always accomplished them.

John wasn't tolerating this. He squatted and yelled right in Ricky's face. "STOP IT!"

Ricky ceased mid-scream, holding his breath and looking scared. John lifted him up and held him tight against him. Ricky rested his head on John's shoulder, whimpering. John patted his back.

"It's okay. I'm not mad at you, champ. But no more temper tantrums. Got it? You're a big boy and you can talk. So you tell us what's bothering you. Okay?" Ricky whimpered but squeezed John close. John massaged his back. "It's all right. We'll talk about it. Why don't you like books?"

"I don't like to read."

"Reading is fun for me and Vicki and my parents. I couldn't become a doctor without reading books and Vicki couldn't become a teacher."

"I don't want to become a doctor or a teacher."

"What do you want to be?"

"Six."

CHAPTER 35

Present Day:

Where's the first stop, ma'am?" The taxi driver drove down the street in front of the hospital to the corner. The streetlights were so bright, it appeared to be daytime in Brooklyn. The cabbie waited at the corner for Barbara's directives.

"My clinic, Nostrand Avenue between X and Y."

The cabbie made a right and drove through the residential area, passing through four main intersections, and caught every light.

Barbara sweated in the back seat, aggravated that this cabbie couldn't time his driving. She fidgeted, and he took notice through the rear view mirror.

"Everytin' all right, ma'am?" he asked, in his thick Creole accent.

"Oh, yes. Just a very long day and my paper work is just beginning tonight. A lot of cases on my mind."

The cabbie turned onto Nostrand.

"Stop between X and Y and stay on this side. The next stop is going in this direction."

"Yes, ma'am."

❧

Inside the elevator, John hit the twelfth floor button multiple times. He anticipated a breakthrough and he'd prepared himself for an intense meeting. "Come on, come on, come on." He paced, not being able to contain himself. The elevator bypassed the twelfth floor and proceeded to the thirteenth. "What the—" he wondered. "Oh crap. Something must have happened." He depressed the button again for the twelfth and it stopped at the eleventh. He darted out and into the stairwell.

Holding onto the railing with his right hand midway up the flight, his hand landed in a greasy substance. He examined his palm and fingers and spotted a rust colored residue. He stared at it for a moment, and then his eyes traveled to the step parallel to the handprint. He noticed sneaker treads in the same consistency pointing downward.

"What the hell is this?" He smelled it, but there was no distinct odor. He was cautious not to touch the handrail again and discerned two more footprints over the next seven steps. He stiffened his fingers and extended his palm straight up, knowing this wasn't negligent cleaning.

He grabbed a glove out of his pocket with his fingertips and put it on his left hand. When he reached the eleventh floor, he couldn't open the door, despite loud banging and pushing on the handle.

He heard the signs of trouble inside. Loud feminine screaming. He texted Phil. *Open the damn door!*

Phil squeezed past the bystanders outside the death room, marked off with stretched yellow tape, and opened the door just wide enough for John to slither through.

Phil bombarded John with the news of Barbara's escape and murder of the nurse. "Dr. Trenton, I don't know what happened or even how she knew of this," he said when he'd finished. "After we called you, Jada went in to be with her, too. Barbara took a shower and I thought she'd settled down and was knitting."

"What time?"

"Nine fifteen or so. I finished barricading the perimeter of the scene and I have to start interviewing."

"Hold on a few minutes. I need you here." John pushed his way to the door of the room, but didn't go under the barricade.

"Everyone, back to the nurse's station, but do not leave the floor." Some hesitated. "I mean, now!"

"Dr. Trenton, I'm Sergeant McDonald." John was bewildered. "She somehow figured out the bathroom medicine cabinet could be removed. No one could possibly think of that and accomplish it. She apparently came into the adjoining room, saw the nurse, and broke her neck."

"Anyone move her?"

"No, Dr. Trenton. That's the way she was found."

From outside the door, John analyzed the position of Valerie's body. He set his smartphone on record. "From this distance, it looks like the spinal cord is transfected. Barbara's definitely strong enough to tear it like this. Died instantly from spinal shock. I did not enter the room for closer look of the body. Who was the first one here? Sergeant, you're being recorded."

"That's fine, Dr. Trenton. Jada and Valerie were going to be on break at the same time. When Valerie didn't get to the staff room, Jada went to find her and check her patients' rooms. She saw this door open and the patients in the hall. Then she immediately ran to get Phil. He was the only NYPD officer on this floor. He secured the scene. No one has entered this room or Montgomery's. Crime scene is about an hour away. Everyone has the instructions not to leave the floor and no one will enter the perimeters. We closed access to the floor. Phil knows exactly what to do."

"Tell them to work the stairwell to the ground floor. That was her exit. I need to swab my hand and shoes to see what this is."

"I know exactly what that is. Take off your shoes. Bring Dr. Trenton surgical boots."

"Hold on." John photographed the shoes on his feet with them flat on the floor. He handed the phone to the sergeant as Phil returned with the boots. "McDonald, take pictures of my soles. Then see if there're any tread marks going to the stairwell. You'll see a difference between mine and what she wore. I'm a size thirteen wide shoe. She's an eight medium, at most. And they should be pointing in a different direction."

McDonald followed all of John's directions to the T. "Yes, Dr. Trenton, there are some treads visible."

"Zoom in. It's the closest you can get now. Take pics of every angle and relationship of the prints to the door."

McDonald shot about twenty.

"Take pictures of my feet in relationship to the room. The room number. Take pics of every angle, of my feet. I haven't moved except when I raised my foot."

McDonald clicked away. John removed his shoes with his gloved hand.

The sergeant handed John back his phone, then wrapped his shoes in sterile white paper, and placed them in a manila evidence bag. He recorded John's name on it as the owner and wearer of the shoes, initialed it, dated it, and wrote the exact location and time.

John put the surgical booties on. "Now you can show me. Anyone see anything?"

"No one saw a Barbara Montgomery."

"Who did they see?"

"A doc in a red suit with black shoulder-length hair."

"I'm checking out her room, then the nurse's station. Sergeant, call Carlson and our team to get here."

"On the way."

John reached her room and leaned over the barricade tape without touching it.

The boots were lying on the bed with her duffle and knitting bag, and skeins of yarn strewn all over.

Wow. She left these. Must have really thought about this one.

He put the phone on record. "Okay. Dr. John Trenton, NYPD consultant and Barbara Montgomery's psychiatrist. I see the paisley lining of the knitting bag pulled inside out." He zoomed in. "At the top, I see a zipper. I see the lining. It's a paisley zipper to a hidden compartment—I'm guessing hidden. I see a black hair in the zipper. Suspect it's a wig. Montgomery's hair is highlighted-blonde. I also see a nametag lying on the bed to the right of the bag, facing the door in plain sight. Reads Dr. Barbara Montgomery, Chief Psychologist, Gemini

Park Clinic. She must have another ID. I'll speak to the nurses to see what tag she had on."

Paul, didn't you even check this thing? Why is she being so careless? It's almost like she's toying with me. What does she want? Does she want this to be over with? How did she get away with all that she did being so blatant? Max, I'll need you later. You'd better come when I call you tonight.

The affirmative bolt hit him.

The bathroom was at an angle to the door. A knitting needle with the rusted tip on the floor lay wrapped in a rust-ridden towel. "She pried it out with this."

Damn, Barbara, how did you know?

"That stuff on your hand is the rust and some grease she used," Sergeant McDonald said.

"Damn, shea-butter body cream."

"Excuse me?"

"Moisturizer. I gave it to her. Brought it from her apartment. Damn!"

❧❧❧

"I'll be back in less than ten," Barbara informed the cabbie.

"Take your time, Doc. The meter's running."

There were some vagrants setting down for the night, keeping sharp eyes on their stolen supermarket wagons in the courtyard of the apartment complex.

Some teens drank beer hidden in brown paper bags, leaning against the building. She delivered a saccharin-sweet smile to the cabbie, exited the cab on the driver's side, and raced across the street, stopping in the middle to dodge cars before getting to the other side.

The cabbie closed the bulletproof windows and made sure the doors were locked.

❧❧❧

Barbara removed the keys from her tote, opened the door, and vaulted up a flight of stairs to the waiting room of the clinic. She was on a mission and on another plane, right now, in a world she assumed would end soon.

But if her end was near, she planned to take a lot of people along with her.

Barbara opened the window, attempting to substitute polluted Brooklyn winter air for the moldy smell.

No doubt they'll be here. It's the first reasonable place they'd look. Can't come across as the façade that it is. So what if they discover it's a façade? As long as they don't find me.

She entered her office that had two chairs opposite the modest desk. On the wall was a poster of the star constellation of Castor and Pollux. It was a diagram of H.A. Rey's depiction, connecting the stars in the constellation, Gemini, with two stick figures of the twins holding hands. Pollux's left hand held Castor's right.

The door key she clutched slipped out of her hand onto the carpet, forcing her gaze to catch the footprint stains as she bent down to pick it up.

"Oh my God! Why didn't I see this? All this street shit? How in the hell am I going to remove this fucking crap? I don't have time for this. How could I have been so stupid? Focus, Barbara, focus. I have to work even faster now. Fuck. I led them right to this. I might as well wait here until they pick me up. Fucking damn. I'm losing it. I'm *losing* it!"

She ripped the lithograph from the tiny picture hooks and chucked it hard as she could, toward her desk.

"Yeah, that's not going to happen!"

Behind the lithograph hid a safe. She punched in the code, 1993, the year that signified her first kill when she was eighteen. She removed a fully charged cell phone and a Charter Arms Pink Lady 38-caliber revolver and loaded it with five bullets, its capacity. With its two-inch barrel and light twelve-ounce weight, it was the right choice to carry in her bag. She was so proficient, she didn't need to use the fixed sights, but she looked through the V-shaped opening aiming at the wall. Smiling, she continued what she started tonight. She closed the safe, picked up the lithograph, cracked glass and all, and returned it to its place.

She grabbed a long faux fur coat out of the closet before she left her office. Then she made a beeline out of her office into the waiting room and down the stairs. She ran across the street and hopped into the cab. "Next stop, East Thirty-First Street, between Avenues R and S."

ᏒᎧᏒᎧ

At the nurse's station, the three nurses, one of them Karen, were inconsolable. John had no patience and he made that more than clear. "Stop the tears now. We need your help."

Two of the three glanced up at him. Karen avoided eye contact.

"And you are?"

She didn't respond.

"Hey."

She looked up meekly and he read her tag.

"Karen, what did you see? You're being recorded."

"Okay. I already told Phil. A woman stepped into a room and told me she was there to see a former patient. And I got suspicious 'cause I didn't have it in the files. I read everythin' before my shift, Dr. Trenton. I saw what you wrote describing her. And I didn't think it was this woman. I got a new admit just before, a real seriously ill one, and their family stressed me out. I wasn't thinkin'. Oh, my God. I was so wrong. I'm so sorry. If she's the killer, how would I have stopped her, anyway?"

"Okay. Calm down. What was her name?"

"Dr. Pauline Jones."

"Can you describe her?"

"Red business suit, black hair, looked like she had a good figure. Long bangs covered her eyes and she was wearin' tinted glasses. They looked designer, but I sure as hell couldn't tell which one. I don't know the color of her eyes but she was wearin' sneakers."

"What color were they? The sneakers."

"White and pink."

"Let the record show, those are the sneakers I gave to Barbara Montgomery from her Brooklyn apartment this morning at eleven a.m. when I moved her from observation to her room on this floor. What else did her name tag say?"

"Chief psychologist of some center."

"Gemini Clinic?"

"No, no. That I'd remember. I saw it in the file. This was a name that no one would recall. And doctors come and go here."

"Who was the patient?"

"Lois Carrolls."

"Did you talk to her?"

"Just what I said. I told her to wait by the room and not move, then I went to check the file at the station."

"How long did it take you?"

"Look at me. I can barely walk, yet alone run. She took off as soon as I turned my back. But I did notice she didn't have a coat and she wasn't wearin' stockings. Bare legs in February? But I didn't say anythin'. I figured maybe she had left her coat in her car."

"Tonight was your lucky night, Karen. That saved your life. Thanks. We'll be asking you more questions."

John led Sergeant McDonald to a private area. "Dig up the records on Lois Carrolls. Find out when she was admitted and if a Kellie Wilson was here at the same time. It's probably archived and on microfiche. I doubt if they computerized patient files from years ago. You're going back—if I did the math correctly— twenty-two years and more, 1980s. If yes, I want everything on Kellie, every transcript, every treatment plan, every time she was disciplined, sedated, and restrained, what led up to her admission here, and how long she stayed. I want every note of what happened here. She knew those cabinets came out and they connected to another room. I want to know what triggered the memory and how far back it was."

"You're asking a lot, Dr. Trenton. Could be thousands of screens. That's gonna take a long time."

"Sergeant McDonald, I don't care if you have to go through ten thousand pages. Think about it as if your job depends upon it. It was your responsibility to make sure these guards are on top of things. You let a murderer go free. I didn't have concrete proof before that she was, but now unfortunately, I do. And her murdering spree in New York is just beginning."

❧❧❧

"Park here to your right," Barbara told the cabbie.

The cabbie pulled into a spot in front of semi-attached homes.

"Wait here for me. I'm going around the corner. I'll be back in fifteen minutes."

She got out the driver's side with the thirty-degree winter air hitting her. She was so preoccupied she ignored the frost coming out of her nose and mouth. She casually strolled to the corner of Avenue R. After rounding the corner, she sprinted the two blocks to Mrs. Bennett's house. She glanced at her watch, eleven-oh-five.

Perfect, she's watching the News now before bed.

She surveyed the neighboring houses. All was dark in the Tudor-style homes on either side. No TVs on. No lights in the dens. There was no one to hear the bell that was about to be rung.

Barbara tiptoed up the steps to the house and rang the sing-song bell. Looking through the window, Barbara saw Mrs. Bennett rise cautiously from the couch. "Who's there?"

"Sarah, it's me, Barbara," she said very softly.

"Oh my God!" Mrs. Bennett raced to the door and opened it, wearing a full-length jacquard velvet robe, and embraced Barbara as she entered. "Oh my, sweetheart. How are you?" She inspected Barbara, shocked at the wig.

"They released me if I promised to wear this. They're close to catching the guy and I'll stay at my Manhattan apartment. Don't think the creep knows about this one."

"Oh my. Can I get you something? You must be starving. Come sit down, sweetheart."

They convened on the couch in the den overlooking the front porch. "I'm so sorry to come over so late, Sarah, but I knew you'd be up and so worried about me. I was just now released, so I figured I stop by on the way home."

"I am so glad you did. I'm so relieved. You know you're

like a daughter to me. How did you get here? I don't see a cab's light outside?"

"He's waiting around the corner. Didn't want to implicate you if anyone followed me, but I checked. No one did. And you know what that guy looks like, Sarah. So promise me, you'll call Detective Mandella the moment, and I mean the moment, you see him again."

"You can be sure of that, sweetheart. We have the week off so he won't find me at school. I'll be fine. I'm so worried about you. The thought of anyone wanting to hurt you." Mrs. Bennett shook her head and cringed. "I can't bear the thought. You know that Dr. Trenton, he's such a nice man, but he didn't speak to you much, did he?"

"You spoke to Dr. Trenton?" Barbara seethed.

"Yes, he came by this afternoon. He wanted to know about you. He's so concerned. We spent an hour, chatting."

"Chatting? About me?"

"Yes, my sweetheart."

"Really? Oh, Sarah. What did you tell him?"

"Well, he wanted to know how long we'd known each other. I told him about your parents' accident. You know, background stuff. How I love you so much and I requested you. Our history. Before and after you got your doctorate. What I know about your life after school. How you like, well, uh, the club scene. I told him as much as I could. He wants to find out who did this to you. He really had a sense of urgency. Didn't want any small talk."

And neither do I, Sarah, sweetheart.

Barbara wedged her hand into her bag and slid the gun to the top of it. "I really must be going, Sarah. I'm exhausted."

"Sure, sweetheart, I understand." A pillow was braced between them as Mrs. Bennett gave Barbara a final embrace.

Three shots were fired, silenced by the pillow, and pierced Mrs. Bennett's chest. She collapsed back onto the couch with wide-open eyes, killed instantly.

"You talk too much, Sarah, sweetheart."

Never did like you much, anyway. You're way too maternal for my blood.

CHAPTER 36

Three Years Earlier:

Dr. Trenton, I don't care how prominent you are in New York City," the social worker said. "I don't care that you're chief of forensic psychiatry. I know all about you, Dr. Trenton. You're not taking the child out of Florida."

John wanted to throw the phone against the wall. He leaned back on the earth-toned contemporary couch in Vicki's great room, overlooking the lanai, trying to remain rational and calm. "Mrs. Williamson, I'll be able to give Ricky a very good life and take care of all the problems he's having. And you can rest assured he has problems."

"That doesn't matter, Dr. Trenton. It's the law. His parents were just brought into custody two days ago—"

"I know. I was there. I facilitated that."

"Whatever. There has to be a full investigation and the child is the key witness."

"Ricky, his name is Ricky."

"I know what *his name* is, Dr. Trenton. Ricky's great aunt and uncle, Mr. and Mrs. Morris will be coming up from Miami this afternoon to get him."

"What do you know about them?"

"They're the maternal grandmother's sister and brother-in-law and they have three grown children."

"That's it? Ricky told me that much."

"Their children are not in jail. No signs of alcohol or substance abuse."

"Their kids are not in jail? That's a low benchmark criteria. Don't you think?"

"It's better than being in the system. Look, I've been doing this over thirty years and I follow the book. It's less complicated and more efficient that way. And better for the child in the long run."

"How about if I adopt him?"

"Now?"

"Right now!"

"That's impossible. His parents have to go through the process and give up parental rights."

"I can convince them to do that. From what I already know, they don't want him."

"Not possible. It takes a few years and many court appearances. And you're going back to New York on Monday?"

How does she know so much? Ah, yes. The sheriff. Sheriff Marin doesn't want me hanging around either.

"How about if I get an attorney?"

"They'll tell you the same thing. It's Florida law. The child, uh Ricky, cannot be taken out of the state. Even if you were to move in with Miss Marin and get married, you still can't be the guardians. There is a blood relative willing to have him. And the court won't let Miss Marin have him either, a single woman." She made it sound like it was a crime for Vicki not to be married at thirty-seven. "They would only assign a foster child to a couple, an intact married couple, even if they are in a lower socio-economic bracket than you or Miss Marin."

"Come on, single men and women become foster parents."

"We're very conservative down here. Forget it. Won't happen. Not without a lot of effort."

"If things don't work out with the aunt and uncle, then can I have him?"

"As a guardian, if you're married and live in Florida as your primary residence, maybe. You're not even licensed to practice medicine in Florida, are you?"

Again, he ignored the question. "What about adoption?"

"I told you that it takes years."

He blew out a deep breath in frustration. "All right then, will I be able to talk to the aunt and uncle, to tell them what they need to do?"

"Absolutely not. This has nothing to do with you. A social worker, Miss Angeletti, will be picking him up at noon at Miss Marin's home and he'll wait at our offices for the Morrises to arrive. So have him ready, Dr. Trenton."

"Mrs. Williamson, he needs so much medical and psychological attention. From his behavior I can see he's so deficient in many areas, including his health."

"Dr. Trenton, I appreciate your concern but, in a nutshell, it's not your business. It's between Ricky's family and the courts here in Sun County. Have you prepared him that he's not staying with you? Or did you give him false hope?"

It was I who had the false hope.

"Yes, we told him his aunt and uncle are coming from Miami to get him. He knows them and says he likes them. At first, he thought he was staying with us. And that's what he said he wanted. But he accepted it, too easily in my professional opinion. Who's the judge handling the case?"

"Good day, Dr. Trenton. Have him ready at noon." The phone disconnected.

Noon? That's in fifteen minutes! Crap! What the hell am I going to do? We love that little kid. We could give him more love than anyone else can. We could make up for the five years of hell he went through.

Vicki opened the door and Ricky ran to John.

"John, here. Vicki took this when we were sleeping. One is for you an' one is for me."

They were the pictures Vicki took of him sleeping on John's bare chest. Their arms were around each other as if crazy glue pasted them together. John tried to conceal his pain, looking at the photo. "Wow, that's great, champ. Really great! Thanks!" He ruffled Ricky's curls affectionately.

"I am going to carry it in my pocket all the time." Ricky slipped the photo into his shorts pocket.

"Me too."

"Why do you look so sad, John?"

John embraced him. Vicki noticed his eyes well up with tears and she began to flow too, so much that she had to leave the room. "I'll miss you, and so will Vicki."

"I will miss you, too, but I like Miami."

"You've been there?"

"Yes. Mommy an' me lived there when I was three. Then we came back here. I dunno why but I liked Miami better."

Before John had a chance to question him, the doorbell rang. Vicki answered, blowing her nose and sniffling. Miss Angeletti spent a moment to scan the home.

John knew she could tell they were both distraught, but it didn't faze her in the least. She barely made direct eye contact with either of them. Even at the young age of thirty, she appeared hardened by the system. Mrs. Williamson had trained her well.

"Ricky. It's time to go."

Vicki handed the woman his bag.

John released him. "Go ahead, champ."

Ricky skipped to the door, not looking back at either of them, showing no emotional attachment. "Bye." He waved haphazardly and left, holding Miss Angeletti's hand.

John grabbed Vicki in his arms and they let the tears flow freely, holding each other tightly. He kissed her neck as he whispered, "We'll get him back, Vick. He's coming back, to us."

Vicki looked up into his eyes wiping the tears away with her gentle touch.

"I need some time alone, babe." He released her and walked slowly with his head down into the bedroom where he threw himself down on her bed with his face buried in the pillow, just like he did when he was a little kid.

She stood in the great room, staring after him.

❧❧

Vicki arrived at the pool and forgot how empty she felt when she saw Amanda and her two brothers Mark, age eleven, and Evan, age eight, laughing and splashing, as their dad played the Marco Polo game with them in the pool. The kids took turns screaming Marco or Polo. Then the one who was Marco had to tag someone who yelled Polo. The goal was to move away so you didn't get tagged. To Vicki, it was boisterous, aggressive, and quite annoying to seniors craving tranquility around the pool. When parents played, especially such a big and strong guy like Mark, any observer would just want to scream. Obviously, her brother didn't care about the noise. She knew this was his first day off in weeks. Jaimie constantly complained to her about it. After this last case, he needed it.

Mark jumped out of the pool. "Watch your sister," he told the boys.

Vicki tried to relax on a lounge, but she was restless. "Hi. It's been a rough morning. John's taking it hard."

Mark adjusted his lounge to face the sun. "What did he expect? A fairy tale ending?"

"He really expected to be able to keep him."

"And you and Ricky move to New York? Just like that? You better watch it. This guy doesn't live in the same reality as we do."

"And listen to this, Mark. He said and I quote, 'We'll get him back. He's coming back to us.'"

"What is he, a fortune teller?"

Vicki shrugged.

"Ya never know, Vick. Maybe he's got some political connections you don't know about."

John appeared from behind them, carrying a knapsack over his shoulder, wearing a white tank top and shorts. "Actually I do, Mark."

Mark looked up at him and laughed.

"I'm directly connected to a higher authority."

Mark laughed harder.

John's cell rang. "Dr. Trenton."

"It's Sal. Near your laptop?"

"Actually, I have it with me. Wanted to check in."

"Go somewhere private. It's major."

"What happened?"

"Log in with your NYPD access code."

"Give me a minute." John walked over to a round table and

opened the umbrella for shade. He opened the laptop, got it up and running, put in his code, and saw Sal through Skype. "What's going on?"

"What happened to you? You look like shit. Don't look like you've been on vacation." Sal sounded alarmed.

John knew that even his Versace sunglasses wouldn't hide the expression on his face. "It's been a rough couple of days."

"Your folks okay?"

"My father had a fender bender as soon as I got down here and it's been downhill ever since."

"What else is goin' on?"

"I'll tell you about it when I get back. What have ya got?"

"Remember a teen patient of yours, Hal Martin?"

"Yes, of course."

"He slaughtered his family five hours ago. A neighbor called in a disturbance. We got here when he was still at the scene. He was plungin' and extractin' a twelve-inch serrated butcher knife numerous times into his mother. She was the last kill, but don't know order of rest. ME says it looks like over twenty times as far as a visual count. Same weapon for each kill."

John rubbed his face in despair. "Oh, man."

"We have him in custody, but what can you tell us?" Sal panned the camera.

"Where are you at now?"

"We have teams interviewing neighbors who called in the disturbance. We'll get their supps before we leave here. Probably not till tomorrow. Hello overtime."

"Who did you assign?"

"Martinson and Valore."

"Great. Those reports are covered. What else?"

"Positions of the bodies haven't been changed. They needed three crime scene techs per body. So we have twelve here now on the vics alone. It took them over an hour and a half to bring up all of the gear and tarps to set it up. The entire area is cross-contaminated from the blood of the vics and perp. The ME can't tell yet where it all came from, or which were the fatal blows. The guys you see in the background in their PPEs are first doing visuals of the bodies. Those ALS bulbs sure are hot. It must be over ninety degrees in here."

"Hey, that protective gear is a necessary evil. So no chemicals or fuming yet," a crime scene tech chimed in.

"Nooo. No fuming. When that goes down, we're outta here."

The tech came into view. "No fuming for about another five hours, Detective Valantino. How ya doing, Doc?"

"Better than you guys."

"Real mess here. Won't finish for at least another twenty hours," the tech responded.

"Seriously?"

"Seriously, Doc. This is a complicated one. More than most. I figure three to five hours per body to catch everything. The blood, hairs, fibers, transference, and did I forget to mention the blood? Yeah, at least. And that's not including the fuming and app of powders. Then we got the rooms, photographs, markers. Yeah, maybe more than twenty. Figure you'll have over nine hundred photos to profile, Doc. So you better enjoy the rest of your vaca." He returned to the body of the mother behind him.

"Thanks a lot," John said. "Okay. Here goes. Just dictating for the record. Crime scene techs are everywhere, taking a limitless number of photos and putting down markers. Number to be determined. Can't see details. Too many people in room. Blood is everywhere, clouding up the boundaries between the murder victims and the furniture. Five hours ago. Nine a.m. They were such easy targets. Were they asleep?"

Sal zoomed in very close to adults. The ME moved out of the way so John could analyze the scene. "Thanks, Ikrahm. Two adults, one male, one female, in living room. Is that what I think it is, Sal?"

"Unfortunately, yes it is."

"Wow. That's a…ooh, what rage. Okay, male is castrated."

"Now look at this." Sal zoomed in close to mother.

"Oh, damn. Female has both breasts cut off. Both? Most kills like this are just one. Just to make a statement. Something about her maternal nature, or not. Had to be post mortem. Hal isn't strong enough to hold them down to do this when they were alive. Okay, what statement is he trying to make? Whom does he want revenge on? Sal, just an idea off the cuff. But I won't know for sure until I compile all the data. This might be a sexual revenge murder spree. Mother not maternal and didn't protect kids. Find out if there was sexual abuse with the kids. Need rape kits on them."

"Will do. The kids were just stabbed once each, John. They were two girls, eight and twelve. The adult vics were their parents. Same mother different father for the Martin kid."

"Yes. I know that. Hal's twenty-one now. When I started seeing him at fourteen, the youngest was one. The other, five. I didn't suspect any abuse then, and it's something I always look for, especially when an older sibling is institutionalized for schizophrenia. He could have killed the kids to prevent them from enduring future abuse. That's happened before."

"Then why kill the kids at all? He did the parents."

"That's part of his illness. He wouldn't trust anyone to treat them differently, so they'd be better off dead in his mind. So do background checks on the parent's friends and find out if there are known abusers among them. Where is he?"

Sal panned the camera to Hal, who was all bloodied and had a blank facial expression.

"Is he talking?"

"Not a word. Just staring at all the blood splatter as if he's amazed at the designs they make. Almost as if they're one of those psych tests you give."

"Yeah. The Rorschach. He looks catatonic or he's pretending to be. Need me to come back?"

"No. We have him. Monday is early enough. We're goin' to need the six days to compile any data for you so you'll have a skeletal report. If he was on his meds, would he do this?"

"Trick question. Can't tell. He could have been planning to do this for a long time and the meds made him stable enough to carry through. Or the meds, with the drugs induced the psychosis, or he stopped taking the meds and substituted drugs. Won't venture to make a guess, but the blood tests don't lie."

"What do you need?"

"Incarcerate him at Manhattan Psych. Get me tox screens,

MRI, CAT, PET. You know what? Just tell them I'm request-ing the full range of tests and blood work. They'll know what I need. From looking at him, I would guess chemically induced psychosis. The last time I saw him he was using. And I need to know if he's still on his meds. I'll give him a thorough workup on Tuesday. And if it is drugs, see what detoxing they can do by then. I need specifics. Time is crucial. They know the drill."

The three ladies from the pool the other day passed with their noodles, behind John's back. They caught a glimpse of the computer screen and started screaming. John and Sal got scared out of their wits. John jumped up out of the chair with an exaggerated startle response. He was winded from jumping up. His heart fluttered.

"What the hell are those things?" Sal couldn't believe his eyes. Tony heard the commotion and joined him.

"Noodles," John said.

"What the hell are noodles?"

"Hi, Tony. Exercise and float things for the pool."

"Where are you?"

"At the pool."

The women screamed at John. "You're a sicko, looking at those disgusting pictures!"

They slammed him on his torso and legs with the noodles, making whopping sounds. One woman after the other slammed him. He stood and tried to grab the three neon-colored noodles from the women. Sal and Tony watched them, laughing.

"Hey, knock it off, I'm working here," John bellowed.

Mark ran to the rescue and intervened between John and the women, who were still on the attack. "Stop it." He looked at the gruesome scene. "You okay, Dr. Trenton?"

"Thanks, Commander Marin."

"It's not your business. Go," Mark said to the women. They departed, giving Mark and John distasteful looks. "Go. Now. Whoa. That's what you deal with every day?"

"Not every day. But when it's bad, it's bad. Sal, Tony, this is Commander Mark Marin. Detectives Tony Mandella and Sal Valantino."

"Detectives."

"Commander, infantry?" Tony asked.

"No, SWAT," Mark corrected.

"Totally different down here, Tony," John said.

Amanda dashed over and snuck a peak. "Ooh, a crime scene."

Sal shut the scene off fast.

"Daddy looks at those on the computer, too."

"This is Amanda."

"Hi Amanda," Tony and Sal both said in unison.

"We'll let you guys work," Mark said. "Come on, Amanda."

"In a minute, Daddy." She turned her attention to Sal and Tony on the computer, "You know what?"

"What?"

"Dr. John is going to marry my Aunt Vicki."

Tony was shocked. "Did you just say marry?"

"Yes. And he was working with Daddy and Grandpa and he almost got shot. And he's supposed to be on vacation."

"Did you just say shot? No wonder you look the way you do," Sal said.

"Yeah, with a rifle."

"I'll tell them about it later. Go back to your mommy."

"But you're supposed to be on vacation."

"Amanda, now." She unwittingly received the look.

"What's that?" She tried to imitate him, crinkling her nose and squinting her eyes so her blonde eyebrows furrowed. She caught the look again. "That won't work on me." After a harsher stare from John, she sighed. "All right, already. I'll go back in the pool." She sauntered off, frowning. "You're supposed to be on vacation."

Tony hiked his eyebrows. "You almost got shot and you're getting married? John the player?"

"I told you, rough couple of days."

"What were you doing with SWAT?" Sal asked.

"Who's the woman?" Tony geared up for an interrogation. "What's with almost getting shot?"

Bombarded with questions he didn't want to answer, John snapped, "Enough, guys! All right. Yes. This might be the one.

But let's focus on this for now. Access Hal's teen files and have everything compiled for me. Send me the crime scene photos and I'll see what I can put together over the next couple of days."

"Why don't you just get some sleep?" Sal asked.

"Haven't had too much of that, either."

CHAPTER 37

Present Day:

Apollo, Barbara's hairstyling magician, spun her around in the chair to face the mirror in Artisans, an upscale salon on Ninety-Third Street in Central Park West's Historic District.

In Manhattan's high-class salons, stylists retained nicknames so they were unique. There were thousands of Tommy's, but when he chose Apollo twenty years ago, he was the first. Now it was on the list of "tag names already in use." Known throughout Manhattan, Apollo was the best with short cuts. He was a mid-forties straight guy wearing large black framed Gucci glasses as his signature, who was at the top of his game. All of the elite in New York had sat in his chair and Barbara only frequented the best. She had been going to Apollo, well, since she became Barbara. New life. New stylist. He was probably one of the few tattoo free stylists in New York City. In this upper crust area, patrons demanded a professional attitude rather than a laid back one, a sophisticated atmosphere, rather than artsy. Exactly what Barbara wanted.

For a Saturday morning, though it was early at seven a.m., the salon bustled with middle-aged women bedecked with diamonds. However, Barbara didn't wear hers today. She looked like an out of place plain Jane in worn jeans and a plain white T-shirt.

"There ya go, gorgeous." New short cut, and back to the color you were born with."

"Thanks, Apollo, it's great." She admired her new chin-length, warm-brown doo with bangs.

"I still like ya better as a blonde, gorgeous. But it's your head."

"I think I do too, Apollo, but I desperately needed a new look. See you soon, sweetie."

"Don't forget. A trim every four weeks."

ⱷᴐⱷᴐ

After Mrs. Bennett had given John the approximate address, it didn't take the team too long to find the exact building. With the warrant, the superintendent had no recourse but to allow John in. Good thing they had a judge who would sign it early on a Saturday.

He searched around for any disturbance around the door and, finding none, he let himself in. He put on gloves and entered the kitchen. The style wasn't one John could label. The antiquated space, with painted charcoal gray cabinets and gray marbleized Formica countertops, was probably the original when the building went co-op in the 1960s. The walls in the kitchen loosely held panels in a laminate gray wood design that had yellowed from years of grease stains.

All she'd need is a little elbow grease or a great cleaning lady. This is Barbara's apartment? The same one with the $2100 bag and 1500-bucks boots? Doesn't make sense.

The only thing that caught his eye was the 1920s Anderson stove with four burners, a griddle on the left side over the broiler, and the huge chef's oven. He opened the door under the broiler and discovered a warming compartment with three metal buckets with snap on lids that were triangular and formed a circle when inserted into place. He tugged one out.

Wow, a real Anderson! These were the best stoves ever made. What I would give for one of these for Vicki.

He opened the door. Clean inside. It didn't look used. He tried the gas burners. They all worked. One burner emitted a popping sound and he snapped back to reality, letting go of the nostalgia.

He opened the old cabinets and located one aluminum pot and one cheap pan. Upon opening another, he discovered two paper plates, a few plastic forks and spoons, and bag of white napkins.

"She can afford a place in the city but she can't afford a set of dishes?" He opened the refrigerator and it was empty. "I wouldn't want to be her dinner guest. Mrs. Bennett said she stayed here on weekends so she didn't have to make the commute into the city. This place isn't lived in. And there's no evidence she was here recently. She didn't come back here last night."

He stopped at the linen closet in the hall. Inside, he retrieved one towel and one queen size set of one-hundred-thread-count sheets crumpled and thrown in. He grimaced at the poor quality. "No, absolutely not. Then where did she go? Not her Brooklyn apartment. Not the clinic. Barbara, where did you go? Bet she has another Manhattan apartment that no one else knows about."

In the bedroom, he quickly opened all of the drawers. In one drawer, he uncovered erotic paraphernalia—dildos, chains, whips, handcuffs, and a negligee. The black lace negligee sent his mind to his precious wife.

He called but it went to voicemail. "Vicki, please call me. I miss you so much, babe. I swear I'll change, Vicki. I realize I smothered you. I realize I wouldn't let you breathe and that it had to be my way. I even started therapy, Vicki. You wanted me to go. Right? Please, babe, give me another chance. You'll see it'll be different. I want a baby, too, Vicki. I was just so upset that you left. Vicki, I love you."

∽∾∽∾

Clancy's mood had changed. He sported new clothing, thanks to Barbara, and he enjoyed being clean-shaven. He put blocks of cash wrapped in tin foil into the freezer, compiling fifty hundreds into each stack, totaling one hundred grand. The doorbell rang and he answered it whistling. "Come in, my love."

Barbara strolled in, in tight designer jeans, with embroidered floral arrangements in greens, yellow, and pinks up both legs, and a yellow knit T-shirt.

They kissed passionately. He meant it.

"I see you got my present. A very well-earned present, I might add."

"Late, but still very much appreciated."

"Yeah, well. I got tied up."

"What did you do to your gorgeous hair?"

"Don't like it? I think it's cute."

I would never use cute as an adjective to describe you. I'd be signing my death warrant. He smiled, while thinking how to respond. "It looks great."

"Thought so. Got another job for you, angel." She ushered him into the bedroom area, kissing all the way.

"Same bloke?" They collapsed onto his unmade bed.

"Yeah."

"What's with you and Reynolds? Aside from his money, that is." He lay on top of her, both of them still clothed.

"If he cracks up, he's more vulnerable, angel. Besides I have a strong distaste for publishing companies."

"Is that all? You're more screwed up than me."

"And don't you forget it. I can kill."

"Oh yeah? I prefer cutlery."

"I prefer bullets," she one-upped him.

He rolled on his back, laughing. "Oh, yeah? When we met, who knew we'd have such a prosperous relationship? And I thought you were nothing but a brasser."

"A hooker? Sweet little me? Never, angel. I'm a Gemini. We can multi-task. Aren't you glad I rejected you the way I did? Even if I did lose a few days of my life. You really had my neighbors thinking I was going crazy."

"Sure did spark my creative flow."

"Wake up. You were an easy mark. You wanted money and I needed a partner."

"You know what I love about you?"

"What, angel?"

"You didn't freak out at the holograms like Reynolds did."

"Are you kidding? That kind of stuff turns me on. The more bizarre the better. And I have another one I need you to create. One with me and that miserable shrink, Trenton."

He smiled. "Done, I have an idea already. But what about your apartment? It's a crime scene now."

"It's all for the cause, angel."

"Cause?"

"You have to take risks to make money. Even if you have to sacrifice by getting a real job. And it's time you did, too."

"Pardon me?"

"We've only just begun with Morgan Reynolds. Wait until you start working for him."

"What are you getting me into now?"

"Honey, I learned very early in life what is real and what isn't. The only things that are real are money and revenge."

♋♋♋

Sal, Tony, and six crime scene techs inspected different areas in Barbara's Brooklyn clinic. Wind blew in from the open window in the seating area, that faced the avenue.

Sal closed it, shivering. "She was here, probably after she left the hospital. Wanted to air it out. Guess she knew we would be here. This place gives me the creeps. I wouldn't want to bring my daughter here for therapy if she needed it," he said.

"Why do you say that?"

"Look around, Tony. There's nothin' here to welcome an adolescent. No paintings, no teen mags, no display racks with brochures for parents. All doctors have that stuff now. Resources in a shrink's office should be visible. There's absolutely nothin' here. Hell, no. Barren walls with chipped gray paint. Reminds me of the precinct."

Tony walked around, looking at the legs of the chairs. "Take a look at this." He moved a worn armchair. "These indentations are too shallow. Watch." He sat in the chair and then checked the carpet. Much deeper. He lifted the chairs.

"No one has ever sat in these chairs. I bet this clinic is a—front," they both said in unison.

A tech signaled to them to come into her office. They glanced at her degrees, credentials, and affiliations on the walls.

"We need to take those. John will know if they're authentic," Sal said.

"Detectives, over here. We followed the sneaker prints. Same as the hospital and down the stairwell but now with street debris." A tech stood by the lithograph of Castor and Pollux with the cracked glass on the frame that he had pulled away from the wall. "This was recently opened. We got solid prints."

"Great. Can you tell how old they are?" Tony asked.

"From the depth and clarity, maybe late last night. And it doesn't look like anyone touched it since."

"Okay. She's getting careless, no gloves. ID them ASAP. Can you open it?" Tony asked.

"This sure can." The tech attached an electronic safe opening device to the knob on the safe. It turned the dial and beeped, showing the number on a screen. "One…nine…nine…three. 1993. Usually a significant number. The year?"

"We'll get on it. What's in there?" Sal inquired.

The tech unlatched the door revealing a box of .38-caliber bullets and the standard black case to a Pink Lady.

Sal handled the case. "Wow. She can't go back to her apartment, so I guess she keeps a stash here. Get what you can, guys, and tape it up. Want to limit her resources."

As they walked to their car, Sal figured they'd get some more information. "Let's go check on Mrs. Bennett. See if Barbara contacted her. She's five minutes from here."

eↄeↄ

A ten-year-old Buick was parked in Mrs. Bennett's driveway. "Maybe she's home." They skipped up the steps and rang the bell. No answer. Sal peeked through the bay window on her front porch. The blinds were raised. He compressed his lips and shook his head. "Oh, no. Tony, come here."

"No. Damn it! No!" Tony ran both hands through his hair and rested them on his head.

They pushed in the open door and entered the house with guns drawn, but deep down inside they knew it was clear. Sal immediately saw Mrs. Bennett. He approached the body with the "silencer" pillow still on her chest. Her eyes stared at the ceiling. She rested flat on her back on the sofa with her right leg outstretched and her left on the couch. Riga mortis had already set in. Sal couldn't close her eyes. The now-dried blood attached the pillow to her bathrobe. Sal didn't attempt to remove it. He didn't bother to check for a pulse. He just froze there with his hand over his mouth, shaking his head in dismay. "Call it in."

Tony did, as he eyed the shell casings.

Barbara had put three bullets into Mrs. Bennett, leaving the remaining two for another victim.

☙☙☙

"Why did she have to kill Mrs. Bennett?" John was inconsolable. He paced in Carlson's office, so agitated he wanted to put his fist through the wall. He kicked a trash pail across the room, sending it into flight like the kicker at the beginning of a football game. He narrowly missed Carlson's head. On purpose. "That should been your head, you son-of-a-bitch!"

Carlson jumped back. John knew for sure that Carlson was in way over his head, but he also knew that the lieutenant wouldn't retaliate. Carlson wouldn't stand a chance against him

John went face to face with him. Tony and Sal seized John and thrust him against the opposite wall. They were equally as strong as him with their pumping adrenalin. "John, John, stop! Get a grip, man. We'll find her! Stop! Control yourself."

John struggled to push them away. He drained a lot of strength, coming back at Tony and Sal with his shoulders but no leg Tae Kwon Do moves.

A psychiatrist attacking detectives? That wouldn't bode well. And he could wind up in jail. He breathed hard and resisted, but the two of them grabbing him by the arms, finally saddled him into a chair.

"Calm down, we have work to do. Case first, emotions later, Okay, buddy?" Sal pushed John's shoulders steadily down into the chair, looking straight into his crazed eyes. His hair was a mess, wild and all over his face, and he wasn't ready to focus yet. "Look at me, John! Look at me. Damn it!"

John glanced up and sent Sal a succumbing look. He got it. Sal exhaled hard and released John's shoulders. John leaned forward with his head in his hands, trying to calm down. He exhaled deeply for a few minutes and then contained himself. Sal handed him a bottle of water, which he accepted. John twisted off the top, threw it onto the floor, and consumed the entire bottle, practically in one gulp, without uttering a word.

"Okay, okay." John endeavored to get a handle on it. "Okay, so both the clinic and the Manhattan apartments are fronts. The licenses look legit and they probably belong to the real Barbara Montgomery. The real Barbara is in good standing with the APA."

"That's right. All of her creds check out," Sal confirmed.

"Okay, so Barbara became a school psychologist right before Kellie killed her in June 2003. Make sense?" They nodded in agreement. "The perfect identity was already created. Did you find her client list?"

"Get this, John, crime scene found folders with names, addresses, socials, and the amount of money their session cost. But they're all bogus. Kids do not exist. They never existed. She just fabricated names. These are current and for this year."

John couldn't understand such creative bookkeeping. "How did she get away with it? Didn't she have to be accountable to the Department of Education?"

Sal eyeballed another folder. "No. The Department of Ed didn't sponsor the grant. It was given through the New York City Chamber for the Commission of Grants, whatever the hell that is."

"It was an indie non-profit. They're out of business now, too," Tony said, impressing them. "Hey, only reading this here. Since she had the psych creds, she used it to work in the school. They pulled the grant from her within the first six months since she didn't set up seeing clients within the allotted time. As far as that grant commission knows, there is no clinic. That was in 2012. She just failed to tell her donors that. The clinic for the grant was on Ocean Avenue. It is closed. She opened this one on her own two years ago. And there's no one there for us to follow up with."

"Mrs. Bennett told me she started with her and went to Connecticut and then California and then came back. Why does she move so often? Did she go around the country doing this?"

"John, our job here is to find her, before she kills again, and figure out why she chose Reynolds. Let's focus on New York. I'm not bringing in the fucking FEDS for an interstate investigation." The desk phone rang. "Carlson."

"Lieutenant Carlson, this is Lieutenant Becker, Manhattan North. We have a bullet match from a shooting late last night off Central Park West and Ninety-Seventh, with ones your team put into the system. We know it's your active case."

Carlson put the phone on speaker. "Who?"

"A cabbie. His log showed he picked up at Sheepshead Medical Center and made three stops. The first two in Brooklyn. On Nostrand Avenue, then East Thirty-First, then Manhattan."

"Thanks. Send me all crime scene photos, exact location, and the cabbie's logs. We'll need it for a timeline."

"Will do, Lieutenant." The phone disconnected.

"Three fucking kills in one night. Not good. She's the most out of control psychopath I've seen in this borough."

"Central Park West? That's where Barbara's parents lived right?" John connected.

"Yeah. That's where the accident was. We'll bring up the case file and get their exact address," Sal said.

"See who owns the apartment now. Maybe that's Kellie's hideaway. I know she must have another Manhattan apartment."

Jennifer carried in a folder of new information from the clinic. "Thanks Jen." Carlson opened the file and scanned the first page. He read the report. "'Prints on the safe do not belong to Dr. Barbara Montgomery. They have her Department of Education prints here, and the ones on the safe." Carlson showed them to Sal, Tony, and John.

Tony grabbed the file. "It's obvious, even with the naked eye, they're different. Kellie has some scars on a few of her fingers. Either, she cut herself cooking, or got cut during some earlier kills. Barbara's fingerprints have nothing interfering with the lines and curvatures."

"Good. Is that the complete Department of Ed file?" John asked.

"Yeah. And something else worth noting. Her payroll checks get direct deposited to an account in Manhattan."

"What are you getting at, Loo?"

"There's only one Barbara Montgomery. The original one with the real social security. So the real Barbara can't be practicing in another state to leave Kellie to be a duplicate here. They would have been found out, if they were working together. Now what are you looking for, John?"

"The medical, for blood type. Kellie is A positive."

"Hold on, we got everything you wanted." Tony went through the medical. "Here it is, the real Barbara Montgomery is A positive."

"Okay we did it. We got the proof." John blew out a deep breath. "Kellie offed her twin Barbara and assumed her identity twelve years ago."

CHAPTER 38

John turned his laptop on and, while it booted up, he made a visit to the bathroom. He was an early riser and the heartbreak of learning that Barbara had killed Mrs. Bennett just an hour after her escape left him too depressed for words. A sleepless night didn't help even though that's not like him at all. After his long days with his complete devotion to the job and his wife, he was usually asleep before his head hit the pillow.

He heard the Skype bleep of an incoming call, thinking it was Sal or Tony, and he really wasn't in the mood to talk but he had to. The job. Could never refuse. His contract defined it. Could never refuse. Those words haunted him sometimes, and his parents, always. He dillydallied going into his office but he pressed the Skype call to answer, without looking at the number.

"John! It's me, Ricky!"

"Ricky!"

"I'm eight now. We've been tryin' to call you all night, well almost all night. Vicki made me go to bed at eleven. You'd probably think that's too late, knowin' you."

John sat there stunned, but immediately his state of mind changed and a big smile crossed his face. "Ricky, how did you—"

"It's a long story."

"Your stories were always long, champ. Tell me."

"It didn't work out with my aunt an' uncle that took me to

Miami. Well, for a year it did. They didn't have money to pay the bills for my asthma, so they took me back to social services. But that old lady that was there wasn't or somethin' like that. I told 'em I wanted to live with you an' Vicki, but when they tried to call her the phone was shut off, an' they couldn't find her. I still have the picture of you an' me. I carry it in my pocket every day."

"So do I, champ. So do I." Tears welled up inside him. "What happened?"

"I was in different foster homes, I think three, but no one wanted to keep me till I grow up, so they took me back. Everybody said 'he's difficult,' whatever that means. Maybe cause I didn't wanna to go to school an' I kept gettin' thrown out. Every time I asked them to call Vicki, they got no answer 'til a couple days ago. Vicki spoke to some lady an' said I can come live with you. I got here yesterday. I can, can't I?"

It immediately came to him and, though thrown off guard, he knew Vicki was coming back to him. And his deepest wish for the past three years had come true. "Yes of course, absolutely you can. Where's Vicki?"

"She's packin'. We're leavin' for your house this afternoon."

"Put her on, champ."

"Vicki, oh my God, Vicki, I've missed you so much and it's been the longest eighteen days of my life. I can't live without you, babe."

"Eighteen days, fifteen hours, and thirty three minutes to be exact. I can't live without you either. John, I can't believe you were right. You said he's coming back to us. It's a miracle."

"I believe in miracles, Vicki."

"John, it was meant for me to come back here. Just to get the call from social services. It was a miracle I got my old phone number back."

"The universe does things in wondrous ways, Vicki." He gazed at her very much-missed breasts. "You look at little puffy. Are you gaining weight?"

"I'll tell you when I see you tonight."

"No, Vicki, no. You can't come back today."

"What? John, are you seeing—"

"Vicki, no, babe, there'll never be anyone else for me, never in a million years."

Tears flowed. "Then why?"

"I'm working on a very serious murder case."

"So? You always are," she said, clearly trying to contain herself.

"This one's more dangerous. The killer escaped from custody, and there's a partner, and I don't want you or Ricky here. I'll be too pre-occupied with this case to spend time with you."

"But—That's BS!"

"No buts, Vicki. We'll have them in custody by the end of the week and then I'll come down. I'll need a vacation after this one. You stay there, tell Mark and Brian we spoke and tell him why you can't come back now. They'll understand. Okay? You'll tell them?"

"Yes, I will, of course. I want to be with you, John."

"Babe, I want to be with you, too. And we will. Just a few more days."

"Okay."

"All right, I have to get to the office. I'll call you when I can. I love you."

"I love you, too."

From the distance, John heard Ricky's voice.

"Don't hang up!" Ricky raced into view. "John, I forgot to tell you!"

"What, champ?"

"We're getting a dog!"

"A dog?"

"Yes."

"And that happened how?"

"Mark told Vicki his friend had puppies. An' you know how much she misses Duchess."

"How big of a dog?"

"Well, the dad is a hundred-ten an' the mom is ninety-seven."

"What kind of a dog is that?" John freaked out. A dog? Not on his white carpet.

"A German Shepherd. We saw the litter today an' they are

so cute. Nine puppies from a K-9 deputy. We drove an' drove an' drove up a dirt road an' Vicki's jeep got stuck in the sand an' they hadda come rescue us an' pull us outta the dirt cause the wheels spinned an' it took a long time an' I need a dog, John."

"You still talk without taking a breath. Why do you need a dog?"

"It'll teach me responsibility an' I swear I'll walk 'im an' feed 'im an' train it. They were all over me, John. Here look." He held up a pic with him sitting on the dirt road with his legs crossed and a four-week-old, tan and black male pup sat on his lap, licking him to death as his paws rested on Ricky's shoulders. "The deputy says from the size of his paws he'll be hundred-ten pounds. An' we named him Duke."

"Duke. Solid name. Uh, why don't we adjust to us being a family first?"

"Vicki wants a dog too an' she misses Duchess an' Mark says every kid should have a dog."

"Remind me to thank him."

"John, they were precious. You know how much I miss not having a dog. And the night I left, you said we could."

"I'd love to get a house first with a back yard. We'll talk about it when I see you two. Okay. Don't bring the puppy home yet or did you already? Vicki, you are so quick—"

"No. We can't take 'im home for five more weeks cause the deputy won't let 'im be adopted till they are nine weeks old an' he'll have some of his shots an' I dunno if I can wait five weeks."

"We'll talk about it when I see you. In a few days. Babe, I have to go."

The Skype disconnected.

Yeah right. A dog. Just what I need. In five weeks they'll be back in New York and he'll forget about it. All right. No stress.

∾∾∾

It was a cold February Sunday morning but that didn't prevent Morgan from working. Owning the company the past three months had made him grow up. He acknowledged the potential in his self-worth and, after seeking coaching from world-renowned leaders, the possibilities were endless. He grabbed onto them with fervor.

He worked diligently at the computer in his office, deep in concentration on an impending contract, making sure every element was in his favor, but providing his client a lot in terms of monetary incentives that encouraged return patronage. His repeat client roster was more extensive than most publishers', so through his narcissist quirks, he executed many things right. He had more people wanting to work with him than there was time for, and the books he published reached the right lists for more than the right sum. His authors consistently landed on the *New York Times* bestseller list, but he demanded that their work earn it. He would not budge on his benchmark criteria. No fluff, nor one-time or first-time authors for him unless their professionalism or pitch impressed him. He was a pro at recognizing talent.

Carol entered, unacknowledged, dressed to the hilt. He generously compensated her double for coming in on the weekends, even if it was just to admire her curves. "Mr. Reynolds, may I go to lunch now?"

He waved her off, without looking up. She departed meekly.

A few minutes later, the phone rang. "Damn, why didn't I tell her to put the machine on?" He reluctantly answered it. "Yes?"

"Have you recovered yet, mate?"

Pretending not to recognize the voice, he pushed the record button. "Who is this?"

"You know who."

"What do you want?"

"Ooh. You sound too strong after your ordeal. I think next time I'll have to do something a little more flamboyant."

"How much do you want?"

"More than you'd be willing to pay, mate, and I'm going to get it." Clancy hung up, leaving Morgan shivering, holding the phone close to his ear and feeling as if he'd lost another ten years of his life.

He shut off the computer, put the flash drive into his pocket, and nervously raced out of the room, forgetting to grab his
coat.

☙❧

*Max, you gave me one hell of a nightmare last night. I hope
you're wrong for once. I know I keep asking you to tell me the
connection between Carlson and Reynolds and you gave it to
me last night, boy. I'm not sure what I'm looking for, Max. All
I kept seeing is paper flying in the air, papers flying out of a
brown coat. Every pocket was spitting out paper. It was Carlson's coat. I saw him take it off and put it on the rack in his
office and then he disappeared into a thin mist. Actually, it was
more like a bomber jacket.*

*I'm in his office now, Max, sitting at his desk. It's after
hours and on Sunday. It's dinner time. Paul needs to eat, or we
hear his stomach rumbling from the next room. Not hearing
anything. No chance of Carlson appearing. So, Max, now
would work.*

A sudden epiphany hit!

*Oh, man, Max, am I looking for a jacket? A police file? Tell
me, please. I can deal with it. Am I looking for a file that will
make the connection between Carlson and Reynolds blow up
like a bomb?*

He remained calm for a minute and then received the usual
affirmative jolt through his right side. John jumped up and
opened the top drawer of the file cabinet. He was not exactly
sure what he was looking for. He thumbed through many files
and then the second drawer, and then the bottom one.

*He wouldn't be careless enough to leave it in here, in an
open cabinet.*

John sat back down at the desk, opened the center drawer,
and stared at Carlson's service revolver in its case. He opened
the large drawer on the bottom right. Under a stack of irrele-
vant papers was a wooden box. John saw a tiny padlock and
took a pair scissor out of the top middle drawer, stuck the tips
in, and spread the blades breaking the lock. He removed an
untitled legal size folder and the negative energy flowed

through him as he flipped open the cover. It was a feeling of churning in his stomach that made him nauseous.

It's a good thing I didn't eat. State income tax evasion. Conspiracy in vehicle transportation licensing, stock manipulations, insider trading. This guy is into some good stuff. No prosecutions. No active FBI investigations. Interesting, no publishing illegalities.

That's why Carlson didn't want to call in the FEDS and why he didn't show up at his apartment. And that's why he impeded the investigation. That's right! At Barbara's apartment, he recognized Reynolds voice on the answering machine. Damn it, Paul! How deep are you involved with this guy?

Carlson casually walked down the hall carrying a cup of joe and caught John looking at the file. He backed up with urgency, knocking into a metal trashcan, throwing him off balance and making his coffee fall out of his jittery hands. John, alerted to the noise ran to catch up with him but Carlson vanished around the corner, leaving John to stare in dismay at the splatter on the floor.

જીજી

Barbara relaxed, surrounded by luxury, on her oversized royal blue velvet couch in her living room with her legs up, bent at the knees, and her body leaning against a sky-blue lace-embellished pillow on the arm of the couch. Across the pillow, in hot pink embroidery, was the word "Princess." She grinned mischievously as she dialed the phone. She readied to begin her act. It would be the major starring role of her life.

"Hello."

As seductively as she could, she purred, "Morgan, hi, it's Barbara."

"Where the hell have you been?"

"At a conference in Connecticut. I got your messages but I was so busy with seminars and everything, I couldn't call you. I'm really sorry. You sounded so worried."

"To say the least. Can we talk over dinner?"

She had him exactly where she wanted him.

ᴄᴐᴇᴐ

Around eight p.m., Carlson sat at his desk in the precinct, panic-stricken that he'd been exposed. He removed his service revolver from the top middle drawer and loaded it with six rounds. He handled it contemplatively. "I couldn't hack it in the crib for ten years, or however long, not with the throat cancer." He raised the gun to his head, but before he could discharge a bullet, his phone rang. Startled, he put the gun back in his desk drawer and raced out of the office.

ᴄᴐᴇᴐ

In a crowded restaurant in Chelsea, where the average cost for a dinner was a hundred bucks for the entrée, and everything else was a' la carte, the maître d' escorted a dressed up Morgan and Barbara to an elegant table for two in a secluded corner. Morgan wore a Ralph Lauren blue pin stripped suit with a dark blue tie over a matching shirt and she stunned everyone in a low cut Vera Wang red dress, making the most of her smooth cleavage with a wide gold belt accentuating her narrow waist. Morgan couldn't take his eyes off her. The maître d' smiled warmly at them, holding the chair out for Barbara.

"Thank you." The maître d' nodded and left. "I never thought you'd want to see me again after our little fiasco," she told Morgan.

"Nah, that's water under the bridge. How's the car running?"

"Wonderfully. Is something wrong? You look preoccupied."

"No, nothing really."

They examined the menus but only his had the prices.

"Morgan, your eyes tell it all. Come on. What's wrong?"

"Ah, she's playing shrink."

"Aren't you lucky? You can get me for free."

"Funny lady. I'm just being bothered by a prankster with an irritating sense of humor. Don't worry about it."

"Blackmail?"

The waiter approached to take their order.

"We need some more time, please."

The waiter retreated.

"Morgan…"

"No, he hasn't mentioned money yet and it's been two times with a threat for a third."

"Have you called the police?"

"Yeah, had to. Steve forced the issue. My cousin is a lieutenant in Brooklyn, so he's handling it. I don't want to talk about it."

"You have to talk about it."

"Why?"

"That creep won't just go away. Whatever you do, don't give him any money. That'll never make him stop."

He hesitated. "I don't know about that. Maybe it will. Once and for all."

"Morgan, I know about people like this. It doesn't."

"Okay then, my free shrink. What would you do?" Barbara seized the opportunity to dive in. But before she could respond, he added, "I can't afford any police investigations now."

"Why not? What have you got to hide? Morgan, you're a very highly respected and generous philanthropist." He furrowed his brows and pursed his lips. "Oh, no!" she said. "Don't tell me you're laundering money for some Columbian drug cartel."

He laughed. "Nothing that adventurous."

She lowered her voice when she noticed stares. "Nothing that adventurous?"

"Look every large company finds practical loopholes. Forget it. Now what have you been up to?"

"Well, now that you asked. I'm thinking of expanding my clinic."

"To where?"

"A larger complex. My clientele is increasing, so I have to hire some more counselors. But I definitely want to stay in Brooklyn."

"Did you find a place yet?"

He was ready for the kill.

"Have any connections in real estate?"

⌘

Tony, Sal, and John convened with Jen a little after eleven p.m. in Loo's office.

"What do you mean he took a vacation?" Sal demanded of Jen.

"Sal, he called me a little while ago to get the team together to tell them he wasn't coming in for two weeks."

"Did he say why?"

"All he said, Tony, was that it was personal."

"Damn it! Thanks, Jen." She exited the room without looking back. "All right, John, what happened? Spill it," Sal demanded.

"Sit down. I've had the feeling he was involved with Reynolds, from the time he recognized the voice on Barbara's machine."

"Yeah, we got that. And he's been actin' real strange lately. Like he wants us out of the office more than in."

"That's what I meant, Tony, when I asked you if you noticed a change in him a couple of weeks ago. That's significant. He's been impeding the investigations, more lax than usual, and I knew something was up. I started to dig and found a file on Reynolds. Right in this drawer. Not good stuff. He caught me looking at it and took off."

Sal didn't look happy. "You broke the lock?"

"Yeah. With the scissors from here." John opened up the middle drawer.

"Wait a minute." Sal retrieved the engaged gun. "This isn't good. He was ready to use this, but something spooked him. Damn it, Paul. You better not be thinking of what we're thinking you're going to do."

"That was in its case when I saw it," John said. "We have to stop him before he does use it."

Sal took a flash drive out of his pocket. "Here, Reynolds's mouthpiece brought this over. Got another call."

Tony slammed his fist on the desk. "Man! What the fuck is he doing?"

"We'll set up a stakeout on Reynolds and see if Paul makes contact. Maybe we can save him from himself before we involve Internal Affairs," John said it, but he knew damn well that wouldn't be possible.

ℭ℘℘

Morgan and Barbara held onto each other under the sheets after making love. They were relaxed now, and he apparently enjoyed her while she faked enjoying him as she had faked it with every man. They lay face to face, sharing a pillow.

Lie, Barbara. Lie. "I knew you'd be good the moment you touched me in the elevator, and I wasn't disappointed, Morgan." She knew how to flatter a man's talents and, with Morgan, it was all below the belt. He was so self-absorbed, she'd bet he couldn't tell when a woman faked it.

He lapped up the compliments. "I told you so, blue eyes. You're not so bad yourself."

She uttered a childish giggle. "Listen, while I have you in a good mood." She gently pecked his cheek.

"Ah. Here it comes. What is it, honey?"

"Do you have any openings in your company?" Morgan hiked his brows. "Real entry level stuff?" she continued.

"Changing careers?"

"No. It's for the father of one of my patients. He spent most of his life in institutions. Now he's out. He really needs a chance, Morgan."

"A real gem, huh?"

"Look. I'm only asking you as a favor because he can't officially apply anywhere. He has no work history. But it was nothing criminal. I assure you. He only needs one, just one, person to give him a chance."

"He's got you."

She sounded so professional, it reeked. "Morgan, be realistic. I can't support him. That's not what the therapeutic process is about. Do you have anything? Stock boy? Mail room?

Housekeeping? For minimum wage. Just so he can build up a tiny piece of self-esteem."

"Can he read?"

"Yes."

"Yeah. Okay. Tell him to see Walter Banner first thing tomorrow morning. Eight a.m."

"Thanks. His name is Clancy Davis, and you won't be sorry."

"Famous last—" The doorbell rang. "What the—Stay here." He snatched a robe and angrily exited the bedroom.

"Believe me. I'm not going anywhere."

Morgan reached the front door. "Who's there?"

"It's me."

Morgan opened the door, annoyed, and didn't hesitate to show it. "I told you never to come here."

"Had no choice. Trenton read the file."

Barbara eavesdropped by the door.

"That file was supposed to be destroyed," Morgan snarled.

She grinned with satisfaction and looked upward. *Thank you, God.*

Morgan threw his hands up. "So now what?"

"He'll never keep quiet," Carlson said, insinuating what he wanted to do.

"No way, cous. I have over two mil invested in our relationship, but that doesn't include murder."

Barbara listened with a gleam in her eye.

"And I'll give you another million," Morgan said. "So pack up and get ready to leave the States. We'll meet at our usual drop off point tomorrow night."

Morgan slammed the door in Carlson's face without saying another word. Barbara watched him as he stood there livid, with his face turning red.

She performed a victory dance and raced back under the covers.

CHAPTER 39

Sal and Tony were grateful they were able to get hold of the superintendent of Barbara's Central Park West apartment building, Denver, early in the morning before he began his shift. Sal leaned against the beige-and-black marble tiled wall and relaxed as Tony, more on edge, fidgeted with his memo book in hand. Sal let him worry for both of them. He noticed not one light bulb was out in this place and the halls were immaculate.

"We need you at the precinct, Denver. Thanks for meeting us this early." Sal said.

"No problem, Detectives. We have the grandkids for their week off, so we're up early. Shame what happened to those folks. Such nice people. Lived here back when Barbara was a little one. What an adorable little thing." Denver smiled at the recollection. "She was their princess an' she was always dolled up like one."

Sal grinned. He conducted the interview while Tony recorded the notes. "Did they always live in the same apartment?"

"Yes, sir, 6-J."

"Do you know who they sold it to?"

"Barbara sold it. To her twin, Kellie."

The mental lightbulb flashed. Sal wished John was here.

"Right after her folks were killed, in fact. Told me they were separated at birth an' however it happened, they got together. Dunno how. Wasn't my place to ask. They bonded real fast, though. Guess it's being an only child an' she told me she

felt like an orphan so she now had a family. The apartment
was paid for an' this here paperwork, says it was done by fax.
Co-op board at the time approved it. Looked up what you
wanted. Kellie paid for it in cash, too. June 2003. Exactly one
and a half mil. Folks that were on the board then are gone now.
Either passed on or retired to Florida. That's our dream. Retire
to Florida, too. Needed though. To watch the grandkids. Barbara is in California now, a school psychologist, an' Kellie,
well she spends weekends an' holidays here, a real party girl.
Out most of the night."

Sal moved from the wall, putting things together. He let
Denver finish without interrupting him. "Kellie paid in cash?"

"Yeah."

"What did she list as her career?"

A hooker doesn't make that much."

"Dunno. Just printed out what you asked me. Didn't read it.
Couldn't understand it if I tried."

Sal examined the seemingly legit contract. "We have guys
to go through this. Thanks, Denver."

"Ever see any other family members coming and going?"

"No. Not even when the Montgomery's were alive. Real
strange, I know. Both the parents were only children, too."

"When did you see Kellie last, Denver?"

"Was here yesterday an' since Friday night. I was manning
the door after midnight on Friday."

"Know about what time?"

"Friday, came in about one a.m. Went out all dolled up
Saturday night, carrying an overnight bag. Wouldn't expect to
see her until later today, at the earliest."

"Know what she's driving?"

"Oh, yeah. Saw her driving outta the garage. Brand new
shiny red Camaro."

"Thanks Denver. You've been a great help."

"One more thing, Denver," Tony said. "Just a sec, Sal."

"Sure."

"When Kellie goes out at night, ever notice what she
wears?"

"Oh, yeah. Can't ignore that hot broad. The wife would kill
me if she heard me say that."

"Don't worry about it. Mine would, too," Sal said.

"And mine divorced me over it," Tony added.

"What was she wearing?" Sal asked.

"Tight designer jeans. Black and red high heeled boots. There's a name for them damn things."

"Stiletto." Tony had to explain that one. "We're learning some things. And when she went out Saturday night?"

"Only saw her top. Low cut. Red. She must love that red. Look like it coulda been a dress. Had to be goin' to meet up with a man, with all that cleavage showin'."

"Thanks again, Denver."

He entered his apartment.

"Tony, call for an unmarked to stakeout the apartment."

✄✃✄✃

Clancy stood in the clock-in line to punch in at eight a.m. in the corner of the main lobby of Reynolds Publishing Company. He waited his turn patiently, not saying a word to anyone. Most of the people were in executive attire and there he was the blue-collar laborer. Clancy, in the mailroom uniform—blue scratchy polyester button down shirt, matching slacks— loathed the assignment. So much for building his self-esteem. There were two racks on either side of the time clock. He punched his card, placed it in the appropriate slot, and then headed into a stairwell to get to the mailroom in the basement.

Some assignment. Take a wagon and empty the mail coming out of chute number six, sort it by department and then bring it up to the various department secretaries. That pompous Banner made it seem like a job for a Mensa scholar but little did he realize Clancy was. He just utilized his intelligence more creatively. He put the wagon in front of the chute, depressed the lever, and out poured the mail.

This is way too much snail mail. Haven't they heard of e-files? Damn! This will take forever.

Some of the mail plummeted to the floor and Clancy was about to leave it when he noticed the top envelope looked like a check. He seized up the pile. Mostly checks.

No direct deposit? That's a shock. Maybe royalty checks don't go in that way? Let's see what I have here. But she couldn't find me anything better. *Just because she hates her job.*

He approached a long stainless steel table and sorted the mail into the three departments he was assigned.

He noticed a lot were payroll checks.

This may not turn out so bad.

He placed all of the payroll checks into a different pile, satisfied that he was onto something. But he didn't know what he'd do with them yet, as the checks were not being delivered to anyone in the computer room, his first stop. Guess these geeks were smart enough to have direct deposit. He readied a camera pen and exited the room.

കൃകൃ

Ten men, late thirties to fifties, in dress shirts and slacks with not a jean among them, were positioned at their own computer stations, inputting data relevant to Reynolds Publishing. Each one had his own cubicle and Clancy made note of the type of mail each person received. One guy took care of advertising. One took care of the Reynolds Publishing's web site. Other stations were for publicity, humanitarian organizations, writer's contracts, writer's reviews. Separation seemed to be the key in Morgan keeping control. Smart man.

Clancy put stacks of mail next to various stations, signed the clipboard on the desk that he'd delivered the mail, and snapped pictures of the computer screens and room layout, merely by clicking the top of the pen in their direction. So what if they thought he had a nervous habit? He had made sure he kept an ample distance from them.

Wow. Barbara sure has the right tech contacts. A long distance camera in a pen? Hell, yeah.

There were printers in each cubicle and Clancy made notes as to the exact center that dealt with corporate finances, stocks, money transfers. He was interested in the money. Where it came from and went. He found the person controlling it. This must be one trusted employee. These men didn't take their eyes off their screens for a second. It was a good time for Clancy.

He departed before he out lived his welcome. No one bothered to get a glimpse of him.

☙❧

An irate Morgan argued with Steve in Morgan's office with the door shut tight.

"What the hell am I paying you for?" Morgan demanded.

"You've done pretty well so far, but you got yourself in too deep with Carlson. You never asked my advice and, when I gave it, you never took it. You just jumped right in and paid the bastard off."

"How did I know he wouldn't get rid of the file when you told him to?"

"How can you trust a crooked cop?"

"I know the questions. I don't have the answers. What will undo some of the miscalculation—"

"Miscalculations you've done over the years? Behind your father's back? Something really significant. So that the majority of people could see your good side."

"Hey. This is me you're talking about. How about if I donate a monumental sum of money to a cause and, if push comes to shove, I'll turn over the tax return?"

"What in hell are you talking about?"

"Let's go." Morgan snatched his jacket and raced out of his office. "I got an idea, a great idea."

☙❧

John sat in his office at Sheepshead Medical and looked over Barbara's files, trying to make sense of what had happened. Sergeant McDonald had gotten him the files he had wanted.

Yes, indeed, Kellie was here at the same time as Lois. Discharged at eighteen. John knew what had happened next.

The phone rang and, knowing his secretary was out to lunch, he answered it himself. "Dr. Trenton."

"Something is wrong with your Lieutenant Carlson, mate."

He recognized the voice from the tape Steven Katz had brought over, but pretended not to. "Who is this?"

"Let's just say I'm a citizen who wants him to get his due. There's a meet tonight, with him and Reynolds. As soon as the sun goes down. Something about a payoff and Carlson skipping the country. And, Doc, your life is in danger. Carlson wants you out of the equation."

The last comment surprised him, but John stayed on track. "Where's the meet?"

The phone clicked off. "Damn!"

෴

Sal and Tony staked out Barbara's Central Park West apartment at a busy time in the afternoon, right before rush hour. They felt cold and uncomfortable. They slouched in their unmarked car after just having relieved a shift of two very bored officers who had already discovered that Barbara wasn't home. They'd spent their day watching nannies wheeling baby carriages and dog walkers being pulled, sliding over ice. Nothing much happened in this neighborhood, much less anything criminal.

Sal lifted the cover off a container of cold coffee and flipped the lid onto the dash. "This is crazy."

A call came through and Tony pressed the Bluetooth. "Yeah?"

"You sound real entertained."

Sal sipped the coffee, grimacing at the stale taste. "They're just dancing in the streets here, John."

"Well, this should make you more depressed. Get over to the publishing company. There's a meet going down with Carlson, early evening tonight. A fix."

Sal spit out the coffee at the news. "Damn it, Paul. We were expecting something like this."

"Our perp gave me an informative call."

"Who does he want to nail?" Tony asked.

"Possibly both. Just get on it. See if he's with Reynolds or at his apartment. Let the guys know. Tail him from anywhere. No I don't know the T/P/O."

"Got any more good news?" Sal pitched his cup out the window. "Call the publishing company. See if Reynolds is there before we make the trip."

"On it. Is Mr. Reynolds there?"

Carol answered. "Sorry, sir. He's not in the office. Who is this?"

"This is Detective Mandella. I need to reach him."

"He's looking at real estate properties."

"Where?"

"Somewhere in Brooklyn. He didn't tell me where. Wasn't exactly sure where the agent was taking him."

"Who's the agent?"

"Lennox Real Estate on Avenue T off Ocean Avenue."

"Thanks. Is he coming back in tonight?"

"No. He has another meeting in Brooklyn."

"Thanks." Tony hung up. "Great. Somewhere in Brooklyn. But let's start with the agent."

∽∾

Morgan and Barbara descended the steps of a two family semi-attached house in a tree line residential, but commercially friendly area.

She surveyed the block cautiously and nervously at the same time. This area was too close for comfort. Less than a mile from the clinic. The business owners, at the least, would recognize her. Her heart palpitated and she sweated profusely. No matter how hard she tried to focus, her entire body trembled. The male agent followed behind them. He didn't look at Barbara once.

"What's the matter, honey? You look like you're panicked. What's going on?"

"Morgan, it's the excitement. I can't believe my dream is finally coming true. It's perfect. But I can't ask you to buy this for me."

"It's more than perfect, honey. It's still Sheepshead Bay. Easy for your patients to get to with the bus right on Avenue U. Several doctors have their offices on both sides of you. With seven rooms, you can have a couple of counselors see patients at the same time."

"Morgan, I can't make a decision like this so fast."

"And you can rent the second floor to another practitioner. It's move-in ready. You don't even have to paint. Barbara, it's a no brainer."

"Morgan, I can afford this on my own."

"You can?"

"Yes."

"This house is over $700,000 and the owners aren't budging because they know it's Doctor's Row."

"Well, I have donations sitting in the bank because I was looking for a bigger property. I have to use them sometime."

"Okay then. I'll buy the house. You won't have a mortgage. It'll be in my name for tax purposes, and you can furnish the offices, and pay the salaries. You have to pay top dollar salaries if you want quality staff. And I really believe that. Carol makes more money than any other person in her position in the industry. And her competence is worth every penny."

"Sounds like we have a plan."

"Okay, Henry, draw up a contract and I'll get Steve on it."

The agent grinned from ear to ear.

❦❦❦

Sal pulled up in front of Lennox Real Estate and they identified Morgan's limo, with the plate MRPUB, parked around the corner. He proceeded a block away toward Avenue S and parked behind a truck.

A brand new Infinity pulled up to the front door of the agency. Out stepped Morgan, the agent who was driving, and Barbara.

Tony peered through binoculars. "Who's the broad?"

"Probably one of the agents." Sal grabbed the eyes. "Wait a minute! That's Montgomery. No wonder our guys couldn't finger her. They were looking for a blonde, and so is everyone else. Gotta change that bolo. Bring her in or tail the limo?"

"Trenton wants her brought in."

"No, Tony, no. We protect our own first. Damn it, Paul! Why'dya have to make it personal?"

Barbara hurried to a Mercedes without kissing Morgan goodbye. Ignoring her as well, he had already entered the limo talking on the phone.

She drove off toward Ocean Parkway, melding in between cars in the heavy traffic before Sal or Tony could ID her plate.

Sal pulled out and drove down the block to tail the limo going east. Tony turned around to watch Barbara going west, straight on the avenue, but they needed to turn right on Bedford Avenue to follow Morgan. The limo made the lights. Barbara disappeared.

Tony rammed a broadcast. "Be on the lookout for Barbara Montgomery, now dark brown short hair with bangs, wearing a beige two piece business suit, straight skirt, driving a late model silver Mercedes-Benz CL-Class coupe, definitely not the base model, probably driving to upper West side in Manhattan. Last seen less than two minutes ago driving west on Avenue T. Probably going to Ocean Parkway to drive north to the Prospect Expressway. Get road block on Ocean Parkway going north and south and the Belt, just in case. Consider her armed and extremely dangerous."

Less than three blocks down Barbara turned right onto East Seventeenth and parked the Mercedes midway down the residential block toward Avenue S. She removed her suit jacket and skirt while in the driver's seat, and retrieved a black T-shirt and leggings out of a tote bag on the passenger seat. She dressed hurriedly and put on a long, dark red wig. Carrying a gray trench coat and a cheap canvas bag, she exited the Mercedes and trotted down the block to a white 2009 Honda Accord, base model, with the darkest tinted windows allowed in New York.

She continued to Ocean Avenue and Avenue R, double

parked a few cars from the corner, and performed her magic.

Universe, get me a parking spot.

She visualized a car leaving a spot and tapped on the dash three times. A minute later, a car pulled out. Parking, she exited the car, carrying her bag and trench, just in time for her to jump onto the four-thirty-five Express Bus, which would take her to Park Avenue South, a few blocks away from her destination.

CHAPTER 40

Barbara skipped down the Express Bus steps at five-twenty-five and looked around in the winter darkness, overjoyed her plan of sweet revenge was in motion. She enjoyed the cold breeze against her skin as it blew her hair away from her face. Exuding an air of self-confidence, humming "My Way," she jogged down Park Avenue to the outdoor parking lot.

Clancy had done his job. A Black Jeep Grand Cherokee Limited occupied spot three-sixteen. She waved to the attendant approaching her. "Pre-paid. Got it."

He turned around, eager to get back into the warmth of his cubicle. She found the hidden key on the driver's side rear wheel axel, got in, and drove a few blocks into the Reynolds Publishing indoor parking garage.

Barbara parked away from the few scattered cars in the lot. Amongst them was Clancy's van. Though surprised Clancy wasn't alert enough to know to park closest to the exit ramp, she dismissed the thought and his negligence, but she had carefully planned where to park, under the dimmest overhead lighting.

She stalked to the door, knocked twice. Clancy opened it.

They traversed down a long, gray concrete narrow corridor leading to the computer room. "I spent all afternoon deciphering codes and accessing the account."

"Did you expect it to be easy?" she asked. "Everything is ready overseas to accept the transfer."

They entered the room and Clancy led her to the computer, in the fifth cubicle from the right, that had the financial records. Barbara positioned herself at the computer with Clancy leaning in over her shoulder.

"All right. Let's do this." She keyed in the data from the sheets he handed her. "The password is MRPUB? How original? Doesn't he know you're not supposed to use words or phrases that you use publically?"

"Guess not. But Reynolds's lack of creativity will cost him now."

A list of financial institutions appeared on the screen with a drop down menu next to each. As she prepared to choose an account from the drop down menu, the screen turned blank and the words 'Access Denied, Incorrect Password' infiltrated the screen. Then audibly, 'Whoever you are, do you think you're going to access my account that easily?'

Barbara and Clancy sat stunned. "That bastard! You're sure MRPUB worked an hour ago?"

"Damn straight, I'm sure."

"Guess he's smarter than we give him credit for."

"No he's not. Something he said to me last night."

"You met him the last night?"

"Yes. To get you the job."

"And?"

Trying to be evasive, she said "We had dinner."

"You slept with him, didn't you?"

"None of your business."

"It certainly is my business."

"We'll talk about it later, okay? We have more important things to do now." It was a lot more complicated than she thought and, with her long nails, she made a lot of typos. "Good thing my hacker taught me everything he knows."

"Want me to do that? It'll take forever this way."

"No! This is something I need to do personally."

"Okay, just watch the typos. You don't want to send all that dough to someone else. That's just what we need."

"What a nauseating thought! Calm down. We have plenty of time. They're all involved at the meet in Brooklyn now, so the timing is perfect. All right, here it comes. Available cash flow forty-three mil. I'll transfer thirty-six."

"How did you know?"

She paused before she answered. "Something he mumbles when he comes."

"Excuse me?"

"Never mind. That'll keep us happy for a while." She depressed a few more keys, then a blue line appeared across the screen, *Transfer in Progress*, as Barbara leaned in with her fingers crossed under her chin. The words, *Transfer Complete*, appeared, and they stared eye to eye, smiling. "Now just one more thing to aggravate them." She closed the program, clicked on *Control Panel* on the Start menu, then Add or Remove Programs and then removed any files and programs related to banking. "Now, I'm happy."

"And you don't think they have backups?"

"Of course they do. Now let's get out of here. But first…" She carefully removed explosives from her gym bag. "Here, put this inside the computer main frame. Our very own bolt of lightning. And open all of the drawers and cabinets. Let's destroy all their paperwork, too. Make them spend extra money and time. And Morgan hates to waste either."

Clancy headed straight for the box on the wall, whose lock he'd picked earlier, and placed a miniature explosive device intertwined between a few red, blue, and yellow wires inside, while Barbara opened the drawers and cabinets. While his back was turned and he was preoccupied connecting the triggering element, Barbara left the room so hurriedly she ignored the gym bag. Clancy noticed it and snatched it.

❧❧

It was dark in Sheepshead Bay, Brooklyn, on Emmons Avenue and Bedford. Foghorns blew so loudly that Morgan cringed at the noise, even from across the street. Smells of freshly skinned fish penetrated his senses as he exited his limo, carrying a black briefcase. He headed over to the bay, wanting this to be over.

He bundled the collar of his long black wool trench coat around his neck. Morgan dodged cars as he crossed the wide four-lane avenue with the island in the middle. Anglers in wet blue jumpsuits, carrying poles over their shoulders and filled buckets, passed him, staring briefly. He was then, just as quickly, ignored.

Reaching the entry, he stared down at the marker on the ground at Pier Three, a blue circle with a sea bass encased within it with its tail extending beyond the circumference. This was the right dock. It was the dock where the boats fished for sea bass.

Fishing boats, named for women in the anglers' lives, docked one next to each other in the rough snow-capped water as swans, geese, and ducks bobbed up and down to the rhythm of the erratic waves. Some boats went out for porkies and sea bass. Others for blackfish and striped bass. Some looked well kept. Others needed a paint job, but no matter what, all of these boats, conveyed a story. It was a story of hard work, long hours, and sacrifice.

Tonight another sacrifice was about to happen. It was the dock where he'd be done with Carlson and his life could go on without interruption.

Morgan heard a small five-seater boat with an awning over the top approach. Aside from the American flag decal, no decoration indicated it was anything special. It was nothing that he would even consider going in.

As he walked down the dock to their meeting point, he looked down toward the ground so he wouldn't trip. The heel of his shoe entangled in a long fibrous white rope used as an anchor for the smaller boats. He nearly slipped on the icy, pitted from years of wear, gray concrete ground. Barrels and large containers for the caught fish and ice crowded the area and narrowed the path. Light generators, attached to the side railings with huge poles, provided just a glimmer to foster the anchoring of incoming boats. It was the last place Morgan wanted to be, slipping on the ice in the cold winter Brooklyn air, and smelling fish. He'd definitely need to take his coat to the dry cleaners tomorrow. He grabbed onto the white pigeon-excrement-filled railing to keep his balance.

He waited on the dock farther down toward the gate. There was room enough for one more motor boat to enter and one was approaching slowly. The rough waters forced it to bob up and down, and it was evident that the young man steering had lost control. He strayed from his path and was headed for a crash into the dock. He spun the wheel in opposite directions to guide it.

Morgan looked around, impatiently. The strong winds made him very uncomfortable. "Paul?"

⁓ೞ⁓ೞ

Carlson snuck out nervously from behind a barrier of gray cylinder crates which were piled high. He had taken many bribes over the years, but this one was of the magnitude that could not only cost him his career, which would be a minor consequence, but could put him away for over a decade and chuck his pension. He'd never finish the sentence, anyway. The doctor had given him less than six months to live. Carlson had thought long and hard about this moment for the last six years. When would it end? Would tonight be the night? When would be the last time he had to protect Morgan? What could he do for his own self-preservation? What could he do to protect Maria, the woman he'd loved for the past twelve years? Yes. He found the answer tonight.

"Here's the money and plane tickets." Morgan handed Carlson the briefcase, not being able to get rid of it fast enough.

"Not so fast."

"What's the matter with you, cous? You're jumping out of your skin. Don't trust me after all these years?"

John, Tony, Sal, and the Brooklyn South ESU team slipped in behind an angler's truck at the north side of the docks on Emmons Avenue. It provided the perfect barrier. They waited and tried to make out what the men said, but it was impossible with the wind. Morgan's back faced them. Carlson was jittery, and a jittery cop was never a good omen.

"It's not that, Morgan. But I can't let you leave. There's

bound to be an investigation. I can't put Maria through it." He pulled a Glock .40-caliber on Morgan.

"Don't do it, Paul!" Sal appeared from hiding with his weapon drawn.

ભળભ

Barbara jogged down the corridor without waiting for Clancy. She exited into the garage and jumped into the jeep, with Clancy yelling after her.

"Your bag!" He waved it.

"Bring it with you. I don't want to waste time. I'll meet you at the airport!" Clancy tossed it into the passenger seat of his van as Barbara sped up the exit ramp.

Clancy looked around and into a car close by and saw a flashy stereo unit. He wanted it. He sauntered over to the car, peered into the window to get a closer look, nodded in approval, and removed a tool kit from his pocket. After disengaging the alarm wires from underneath the car, he slipped into the passenger side seat.

ભળભ

Barbara stopped at a red light a block away, slipped on gloves, took the transmitter switch out of her canvas bag, and then depressed the red flashing button. Her glee at the situation overcame her and she burst into laughter as she tossed the transmitter out the window, under the wheels of a passing delivery truck. The evidence was crushed to smithereens.

ભળભ

Inside the computer room, each computer burst into flames one right after another. Ten quick explosions, ten seconds.

Nothing more.

The fire was contained because of the heavy steel doors but the room, its ceiling, and floors were scorched, and its contents, gone.

The flames subsided quickly and smoldering metal, paper ash, and smoke were all that remained.

In the garage, Clancy's van exploded. He came away from the driver's side of the car with the radio in hand. "That bitch! I should have killed her in the beginning, before I let her con me into her scam. And now I will!"

☙❦❧

John intervened. "Paul, take it easy."

Carlson pointed his weapon at John. "Don't fucking come near me, John. I'll fucking use it. I fucking swear, I'll use it. I've been itching to get rid of you for years, you fucking pompous son-of-a-bitch. The only one who'll miss you is my wife."

John extended his arms out. "Paul, you know I'm not armed."

"That means nothing to me. They all are. Go ahead, guys. End it. It's me or your sex addict shrink."

Sal hitched his breath. "We don't want to have to, Loo. Talk to us, Loo. Tell us what Morgan did to you. Come on, Loo, put your weapon down."

Carlson heard the out of control boat coming into the dock. He'd gone through how he'd do it a hundred times in his head. He had numbed himself. Valium had numbed him before. But he didn't take it tonight. He needed to remain alert to shoot. He stood here, practicing before every meet over the last six years with Morgan. What if this night was the night?

He'd felt the water with his bare feet, gotten used to the frigid temperature, studied its depth. He'd taken pictures and memorized them. There were six metal steps, comprised of seven small metal horizontal planks, with a one-inch space in between. It was six steps down to a tiny platform that wouldn't hold a baby's foot and then a ten-foot drop into the frigid water.

He'd studied the waves and their powerful undercurrent in the bay. He'd studied it all, while leaning over the railings on the avenue side. He knew the speed of the boats pulling in and which had the sharp propellers on their undersides that would tear him to shreds like the pulsating blades of a mix master. That was why he had chosen this pier. The propellers could tear him to shreds. Quickly.

He knew it was time. He backed up to the gate. It was open. No lock. No chain on the gate. It was always that way. He'd studied the pictures of the open gates. He'd studied how to position himself. He'd studied the exact time the boat, his weapon of choice, pulled in. He backed down three steps. He felt the splashing water drench his shoes and socks. His temperature rose from anxiety. "Sorry, Sal. If you don't have the guts to do it, I'll do it myself."

He jumped backward down the steps, just hitting the first one, into the path of the oncoming boat, which could not swerve in time to avoid hitting him. The boat's propellers sucked him in with more power than a fierce vacuum cleaner. The men rushed to the gate but all they saw was Carlson's blood spreading to the top of the water and out into the bay.

No body.

CHAPTER 41

In the Brooklyn precinct interrogation room with John and Sal, Morgan fidgeted as his right leg vibrated involuntarily at the conference table. At one point, he pushed down hard on his thigh to stop the movements. He perspired and loosened his shirt collar as he zoned out for a moment, staring blankly at the wall. John noticed his daydream and tapped on the metal table, startling him. Morgan shuddered, pulled a matching hankie out of his jacket pocket, and dabbed his forehead and hairline.

John snickered, seeing his reaction, but was not at all sympathetic. "Calm down, Mr. Reynolds. You're not going to be charged with murder at least. Did anyone hear you make the plans with Carlson?"

Steve shot Morgan an it's-the-time-to-come-clean look.

"Yes, Dr. Trenton, a date, possibly."

"Barbara Montgomery?"

Morgan whitened.

John continued. "All right. Listen up. Carlson locked her up. He didn't believe there was anyone after her until the same person went after you."

"But I still don't understand why Barbara would set me up. We were with her today. I financed a new clinic for her."

"We know. She could have wanted to set up Carlson for revenge. For incarcerating her. Or to divert us."

"Incarcerating—"

Tony stormed in. "Fire Marshall just called. Reynolds publishing was hit."

Morgan jumped out of his seat frantically. "What?"

"In the computer room, totally blown."

Morgan attempted to escape the room. Tony grabbed him by his arm. "You're not going anywhere, pal."

"I've got to get over there."

"What's the point of that?" Steve asked. "We have a full back up system on site and another one off. It's nuisance damage at the most."

Tony pointed to the chair, frowning. "Sit down, Reynolds. There's nothing you can do now. They know you're here. There's time to go to the scene. There was a van in the garage also blown to bits. Registered to a guy, yeah, here it is. Clancy Davis."

"Clancy Davis? We just hired him this morning. He's the father of one of Barbara's patients. She pleaded with me to give him a job. Dr. Trenton, what's going on?"

"You certainly did. And he's not. She had him snitch because she knew you'd be tied up with the meet. It gave her time to—what would she want in the computer room?"

"Money. She knows how I transfer money. My company gave her $400,000. She specifically asked for it that way."

John paced to get a handle on his thoughts. "Okay, hear me out. I'm just putting the dots together here. And, Mr. Reynolds and Mr. Katz, you don't even know the third of it. I'm not sure I should even go on with you two here, but again, I may need the validation."

"John, go ahead," Sal urged him. "Even your Max can join the party. Loo is dead. We need all the help we can get."

"All right, Sal. You two just listen until I ask you a question."

Morgan and Steve nodded.

"That means she's been planning this from the day she met you or before. Your father had been giving to her clinic for two years?" Morgan nodded. "I believe Clancy did start to go after her like he did you," John continued. "But she decided she could use him. She gets him to torment her, not planning on Carlson committing her five days ago."

Morgan's eyes widened. "That's must have been when I tried to reach her. She told me she was at a conference in Connecticut."

"She was in Sheepshead Psychiatric. She gets him to hit her apartment."

"You're kidding?"

"I said to be quiet, Mr. Reynolds. It takes the onus off her. Clancy is definitely her partner and we discussed this before. Mr. Reynolds, you're the real target."

"She already got what she wanted, money."

"Nah, that's a bonus. She wants you dead. And she plans to do it."

"What?"

"She's a murderer. She's been doing it for years and was never found out until a few days ago." John observed Morgan's fearful expression. "I'm going out on a limb here, but I could guess you slept with her. Why didn't she kill you then?"

Morgan reddened.

"For one, she wanted more money," John continued. "She probably got that today. We need you to access your accounts."

"Definitely. Who did she murder?"

"Mr. Reynolds, let me just say, we're privy to a lot of information and facts about her background, and all I can tell you is that you and your father were conned by a pro, and your life is really in danger. You have to trust me on this."

"Why my father? He adored her and couldn't wait for their meetings."

"Good question. Let's go there. How did their relationship start?"

"My father was a philanthropist and was in organizations to promote education, and he always read the grants teachers wrote for the funding of one program or another. And what I found odd, but my father was too impressed to think rationally, was that she included a roster of other publishing companies in other states that had donated to her clinics in their state. So she had established her credibility for her program being successful. My father met with her and was sucked in immediately. He didn't even bother checking out the claims."

"Did your father know that after six months, the grant was pulled from her for non-compliance of the regs?"

"No. Obviously not. Jesus! Wouldn't this mean tough jail time for her?"

"She's not going to let us catch her. We need to back up. Why publishing companies? I know she wants revenge for all the horrendous things that happened to her. We know she was adopted at birth. We know both adoptive parents died. Her father was a suicide. What triggered his suicide? Her real name isn't Montgomery. Does Wilson ring a bell? She was Kellie Wilson back then."

Morgan connected. "No. Can't be. Ralph Wilson?"

John smiled.

Sal looked at John. "Care to share, John?"

"Yes. His name was in Kellie Wilson's record as a child. Sergeant McDonald got it for me."

"Okay, wow, it was so long ago, but I re-read it," Reynolds said.

"When?"

"I took over the company when my father passed on three months ago. My hotshot lawyer here made sure I had the full company history, and I had to go through three decades of crap. I was only four at the time. Barbara and I are the same age. It was two years before my mother died. My father had to let go several employees. Times were bad and he didn't want to be forced to close the company. Ralph's wife had been killed in a hit and run and my father felt bad for him, but he had no choice but to let him go. He committed suicide six months later. Seems like my father was a colder bastard than I am. Even I wouldn't have done that. Because it was a suicide, they didn't put anything into a trust for the daughter. There was no life insurance policy and his salary just stopped. You think she's doing all this because my father fired hers?"

"Yes. It's a very simple motive. They usually are. She was thrown into the foster care system and a life of abuse began. It destroyed her. And we don't know if she killed other publishing company owners or just scammed them until she found the right one. And that is you, Mr. Reynolds."

"What I want to know is why did she wait till now?" Steve asked. "She had to know who Jacob was."

"Good question. Don't know if we'll ever get the answer to that one," John replied matter-of-factly.

"Oh, God. This can't be happening. I thought we had the beginning of something good."

"Morgan, wake up. You've been had."

"Thanks for your support, Steve."

"You can recognize great talent, I'll give you that. But you can't see when you've been conned. First, your cousin and then this whore."

"Remind me to fire you when all this is done."

John deepened the blow. "He may not be prosecuted for murder, but he should be prosecuted for stupidity. Could that backup system function now to see if any money was transferred?"

"I'll call the company," Katz said. "But hold on. My client wants some bargaining power here. If he cooperates and helps find these two, what's in it for him? He's not prosecuted—no charges will ever be brought against him. Carlson got all this together by himself, and he's a dead key witness."

"Save it for court. Mr. Reynolds, where can you stay until we have her in custody? But you can't leave the state. There is going to be an investigation. How much money did you give Carlson?"

"Over two mil."

"Where can you stay?"

"I have a lake house on Lake George," Reynolds said.

"Go there now," John insisted.

"Now?"

"Now. Out, both of you. And Mr. Katz. Make that call and let me know immediately."

Morgan and Steve couldn't get out of there fast enough.

"Listen to me, guys," John said. "She tried to eliminate Clancy. Now he'll be after her with a vengeance. Get a unit to Central Park West. Let's go."

ↄ∙ↄ∙ↄ

In the bedroom of her Central Park West Apartment, Barbara packed furiously, but lightly. Just some shorts, tees, no makeup or toiletries. Only a minimum amount of light seeped into the bedroom from a crack in the closed closet door. She assumed no one knew her whereabouts. The most she was aware of was that they were either, at the meet, or publishing company by now. It was only a matter of time.

I will not be caught. I can't be caught. I've got too many more to kill. I've got too many more for revenge. Death to all those who come near me!

She shimmied forward a modern décor fireplace, revealing a locked drawer on the back, and recovered three fake IDs, three more of her alias's over the years. She didn't have time now to use the tarot cards to help her make the selection, so she just stared at all three, with her eyes drawn to one, Emily Connors.

She pulled out a long straight hair brown wig from her dresser and makeup for the fair-skinned woman. Underneath the accessories was the matching forged passport for the personality of the day. She tossed it in her bag before she forgot. She perfected, practiced, and rehearsed everything down to Emily's cockney accent. Nothing would compromise her escape.

She looked around the bedroom, toward her California King bed with the princess-looking canopy and little girl bedding. She inhaled deeply, knowing right at this moment that now was the last time she would have the serenity of these surroundings. She was now on the run for however long she could manage to fight death. A moment of sadness overpowered her. It was short lived as she shook her body violently to bring her back to reality. She smiled. Everything was expendable—expensive, but replaceable.

She darted out the door, grabbing a small suitcase and a box that held a knitted sweater, from on top of the bed.

ↄ∙ↄ∙ↄ

Clancy stumbled into his disheveled apartment, more disoriented than ever. He would scream at the top of his lungs if he wouldn't alert anyone, and he didn't need that now. "I've got to find her! I'll get her!" Getting a serrated butcher knife with rats' blood on it, he concealed it in his jacket lining. "My van! My van! I'll get her and chop her into pieces like those measly rats!" He wobbled to the door. "She's going to the airport. I'll get her at the airport." He realized he carried a knife and wouldn't get through. Reluctantly, he pulled the knife out of his jacket and tossed it onto the floor.

❧❧

The Manhattan North, ESU team, Sergeants Shipman, Maxwell, Kramer, and Browne, in full protective gear that they had worn in the hostage situation almost three weeks earlier, checked out the door to Barbara's apartment for booby traps. Sal watched their every move. The bomb squad used heat-monitoring devices around the perimeter of the door to detect any sensors that might be around the lock. When they deemed it to be safe, the officer moved out of the way to let the sergeant unlock the door. He did so very slowly, with a device monitoring any strange, minute sound that indicated a danger. To their relief there was none.

A bomb-squad officer carefully opened the door, checking for any wiring across the room that could trigger an explosion or electricity. None. The bomb squad entered first then the ESU, checking each room. It was all business for them, not even absorbing the surroundings. All was clear. Everything was in its place. They leaned against the walls, not protruding into the doorways. Doorways would not be safe.

Then Sal, Tony, and John entered the magical fantasy land of Barbara's life.

Sal heard fairy music in his imagination. He stared in awe at the vibrant mix of pastel colors, alternating with bolder pinks and blues throughout the furnishings, walls, and art, creating a magical kingdom fit for royalty. Sal's senses overwhelmed him in this childlike fantasy world.

He spun around as if something tugged at him. His movements seemed involuntary as he absorbed each color, each picture on the walls. Having a daughter fostered his understanding when he observed Gina at home playing in fantasy, making her dolls come alive. This room was all lifelike. It was a castle built for his precious Gina. He smiled when he envisioned his thirteen-year-old daughter, with long flowing dark brown hair and eyes, basking on Barbara's throne—the huge Queen Victoria armchair in the hallway. It was bedecked with diamonds, rubies, and emeralds, running as studs along its arms and perimeter. A long pink-lace gown, her favorite color, enveloped Gina. He imagined her beckoning to him, her daddy, and he saw himself kneeling at her feet, presenting her with whatever she asked for, as he always did.

♥♥♥

Tony and John let Sal daydream. John was too preoccupied to care. He noticed there was not one masculine touch anywhere. This woman never had a man step into this place. She probably never had a real relationship in her entire life. It was the exact opposite of what would indicate that a violent, sick, perverted, murderous woman lived here. It was her fantasy world. Her calm world. The world of her missing childhood.

The ruby-and-emerald treasure box on the table drew John toward it. After putting on gloves, he lifted the separate lid to reveal the .38s. "Expensive bullet case."

"Is it real?" Tony asked.

John picked it up and examined it with a jeweler's eye. "Yeah, Tony, it's definitely real. I'd love this for Vicki. Oh, man, Vicki, haven't thought about her in two hours. I gotta call her. I'm getting her back. Just a few more days."

His phone rang. Sal re-entered reality at the ring but John remained with a blank gaze. "John. John."

"Oh." He snapped back as his cell continued to ring. Preoccupied, he placed the jewelry box down on the table but not from where he got it. He answered the phone after its last ring. "Dr. Trenton."

"Steve Katz. Thirty-six million was transferred into a Swiss bank account from us."

"Can you stop it?"

"It already went through. But get this. Her balance is 187 million."

"How do you know that?"

"Off-shore accounts aren't as private anymore."

"Thanks. Sounds like she's planning to leave the country," John said, hanging up. "Money is in a Swiss account."

"Let's go," Sal said. "Alert airport security to be on the lookout for her and Clancy,"

"What description should I give them?" Tony was clueless.

"Make one up. Guys, leave everything intact. She has to think we don't know of this place." John darted out.

CHAPTER 42

John F Kennedy airport bustled with its nightly overwhelming crowds, just like any major city airport, but times ten. Barbara followed the signs to her international gate. Cautious, cognizant of the stimuli, she fixated on the security guards. More armed guards than usual put her on the defensive. Her anxiety increased. She realized she treaded on thin ice. Death or prison? She'd definitely take death. And this was the worst feeling she could have. She might not win this one. The smells from the vendors made her nauseous, especially the differently flavored coffees she loved and craved. The chocolate caramel. That one forced the acid to scorch her throat.

The crowds lessened slightly as she headed to security for her midnight flight to freedom. The female attendant reviewed her passport and photo. It was uncanny how closely Barbara resembled the photo. Same hair, same makeup. She should, shouldn't she? Or was it a dead give-away to have an identical likeness? Barbara noticed the attendant giving her and the photo second, third, and fourth looks.

"Something wrong, ma'am?"

"Did you plan on dressing today, the same as in the photo?"

Barbara knew she had to notice her plaid mini skirt, black embroidered tights, ankle boots, and black ruffled blouse, the same blouse as in the photo. And to make it more unusual, it was the same hairstyle, with every strand in place.

"No, I didn't actually, but the photo is new, relatively. My passport expired and this is my first trip abroad with the new one. I'm sure you saw that."

Smile, smile, smile, Barbara, smile.

"No problem, Miss Connors." She handed her back the passport.

Barbara deposited her bag and the box on the conveyer belt, proceeded through the metal detectors without a hitch, retrieved her belongings, and whisked off to the gate for her flight.

⌘

Clancy meandered through the first floor of the airport, looking for Barbara. He'd created some of her disguises, but was unsure which she'd use. At least he had a hundred grand stashed. But she owed him big time.

He mumbled out loud. "Where is that bitch? She owes me. That bitch owes me. Wait till I have my hands around her neck." He wobbled, getting dizzy, startling those around him.

John, Sal, Tony, and the FBI agents, they had now called in, infiltrated the main lobby. They split up. Clancy passed by a Starbucks coffee vendor and was recognized easily by John who signaled to security guards that he was their man.

"Clancy!"

Clancy halted in his tracks, stunned, worried, and in a frenzy. His brain pushed him into a fight or flight response. But he couldn't move. He felt the tremors going down his left arm. He grabbed it with his right to stop the erratic movement. It wouldn't stop. His head pounded. His eyes reddened with fear. His pupils dilated.

"I'm Dr. Trenton, Clancy. We need to talk to you. Stay put."

Clancy couldn't breathe. He doubled over, trying to grasp onto a chair. John's arms wound around his torso, and eased Clancy onto the floor. Clancy's hand clutched his heart and he massaged his chest vigorously. Too late. He closed his eyes lapsing into a semi-conscious state.

The heart attack would win. In a last ditch effort to find

Barbara, John asked Clancy, "What flight is she taking?"

"Fourteen-forty-six to…" The last four words he mumbled.

They heard, 'Flight 1446 to Zurich Switzerland, now boarding at gate thirty-two.'

ᴇᴐᴇᴐ

Barbara stood in line at the gate, showing her boarding pass to one of the three uniformed women stationed there. She checked in and took back her half of the ticket. "Ooh. Oh, my God." She keeled over.

"Something wrong, miss?"

Barbara had spotted the FBI agents. "Ooh. My stomach, uh, I must go to the ladies' room. My stomach. Please, I'll be right back."

She darted off the line, zigzagging through the crowd into the ladies' room across the waiting area.

From the bathroom entry, she observed John with Tony and Sal. They showed a picture of Barbara, unrecognizable today, to the women checking everyone in.

They requested the manifest and photos of everyone on board. That would take hours to obtain and they wouldn't hold the plane. They hadn't obtained a warrant, either, so scrutinizing all the people on line and in the plane wouldn't be allowed. This would be the longest eight hours that John would ever have, waiting for the plane to land in Switzerland. He slouched in a chair, frustrated, observing the plane, easing away from the gate. A woman approached him holding a box.

"Dr. Trenton?" He looked up. "A woman who boarded that flight asked me to give this to you."

He was startled. "Who?"

"Didn't say her name, Doctor. Had a British accent."

"Thanks." He ripped off the giftwrap and opened the box. He lifted the tissue paper as he heard the plane taking off. He pulled out a jacquard sweater. The note read, *Dear John, I knew you would make it to see me off. Hope this fits. You earned it. Think of me, as I'll be on the slopes tomorrow. Love, Barbara.*

John didn't know whether to be relieved that she was gone

or aggravated they didn't catch her. He slipped the card into his shirt pocket and tossed the sweater over his shoulder, carrying the box for evidence.

∽∾∽

At the Brooklyn precinct after two a.m., John, Tony, and Sal, examined a folder with further crime scene evidence from the blast in Reynolds Publishing computer room.

"Damn! The one solid lead we had is dead." The ringing phone disturbed their thoughts. John answered it. "Dr. Trenton." He listened with eyes wide open. "What do you mean she wasn't on the plane?"

Tony and Sal put their pens down and paid attention to the call.

"Thanks." John hung up. "Oh, man. They checked all the passengers. Everyone accounted for except Emily Collins, a Brit. She checked in, but never got on the plane. They don't land for another six hours or so. They'll confiscate her luggage then. So where the hell is she?"

∽∾∽

Barbara exited the garage in her building and entered the elevator, not realizing the camera caught her. Denver was watching. It was his turn to be on duty tonight. He immediately called the precinct.

"Detective Valantino.

"Detective. Wow, three a.m. I thought I was the only one who worked these hours."

"No, sir. We do, more often than not. What can I do for you, Denver?"

"You wanted me to let you know when I saw Kellie again."

"Yes."

"She just pulled into the garage. I saw it on the monitor."

"Denver, thank you. Do nothing else and don't contact her."

"I won't."

"Let's go. She went back to her apartment. The one she doesn't think we know about."

"You stay here, John," Tony said.

"Like hell I will, Tony. I want her alive."

"She'll remain alive only if she gives us a choice. And by the time we get there she may leave."

"No way. I'm going. For Mrs. Bennett, I'm going."

CHAPTER 43

Barbara entered her apartment and her eyes nearly bulged out of their sockets, as she saw that some things were out of place. The gem treasure box that contained her bullets was at the opposite end of the table. Her favorite lace pillow on the royal blue couch had been put back upside down. Gemini statues were out of order on a shelf, re-shelved in descending order rather than ascending.

She was a stickler for detail, with a photographic memory that had served her well until she met that Doc. She fumed. She knew they'd been here. The nerve of them to violate her private space! She felt raped all over again. The feeling of restriction as she had felt when she had been held down on the bed by that seventeen-year-old boy and penetrated when she was only four, erupted through her. The panic and fear of not being in control shook her as energy drained through her, sapping her strength.

She examined the closets in the hall. They better not have touched her imported six hundred thread count Egyptian cotton sheets. Good. No linens or towels out of place.

She inspected the kitchen cabinets. All looked good.

What were they doing here? They obviously investigated the Montgomerys. Gotta be. How else would they have found out about my castle? Only a matter of time before they find out I had someone rig that van to explode. Right onto their car. Good thing I got rid of that driver, too. One shot to the head when he showed up for his payoff. Buried that driver in the foundation of a new midtown condo. Still buried there. The condo is still up with no ground reno in sight.

They were such creatures of habit. Right on the same street every day, picking up their precious daughter at the train station from graduate school. Jesus, twenty-eight and still picking her up. She had just achieved her doctorate for Christ's sake. This time they just went there to calm their souls. I took their precious daughter bitch from them just a couple of days before. And they didn't know it yet. She was nowhere to be found. No trace at her apartment, but everything was left for me to take over. Twenty-eight and still checked on her every day. Lucky for me, there was enough information for me just to slip into her shoes, quietly and unnoticed. And with no one to recognize I wasn't the brilliant Barbara, it was a gift from the heavens. They just had to go. I couldn't let them find out about me. Look at it this way. I saved them the grief. The agony. And now they're together with their precious little princess in heaven. Wonder if they met yet? Twelve years? Ah, who cares? It's not my problem. They just waited and waited and waited, hoping she'd show up. I knew she wouldn't. She's buried in a garbage dump on Long Island Sound. No remnants of her now. It was so perfect. Looking for my twin since I found out I had one. That PI was right on. He knew what I was up to. He knew I was up to no good. As soon as he told me about our birth mother, that she was a schizophrenic, who had given birth to us in a mental hospital, he saw the twinkle in my eye, and knew that I wouldn't be far behind. He gave me the Montgomery's info. He saw it coming. Took enough money from me, a hundred fifty grand, and then backed away.

Wouldn't turn his back on me. Think I'd pull a gun on a PI? Give me a break. He thought he got away. And then, surprise. His car went boom, along with all those small denomination bills as soon as he turned on the ignition. Yeah, he knew I was onto something. And I knew he knew.

I was twenty-eight and ready to leave the streets. She was so eager to meet me, the stupid bitch. Right at an all-night diner in the Bronx. Like I lived in the Bronx. Yeah, right. It was so easy to get that bitch outside. So gullible. More like our schizo mother than a shrink. Tried to be so sweet. So therapeutic.

What bullshit. Cried like a baby when I pulled my gun on her. It was only a twenty-two cal. Come on. It didn't hurt that much. And I only shot her twice. Of course with a silencer. I'm not dumb. Oh boy, that was one of my easier kills. She held her hands up to her face, crying as my gun went pop. Wow, I can't believe the memory is coming up now. Like I'm doing a confessional to myself. I'd better snap out of this, fast.

She immediately dashed into her bedroom and checked her closet. Filled with designer suits and corporate clothes for work and business meetings with potential donors, everything looked status quo. She lifted about a hundred filled hangers in a few tries, dumped them onto the bed in huge piles, and then opened the trap door on the back wall of the closet, that led into the vacant apartment next door. She crept through to her neighbor's closet and lugged out a huge, heavy chest.

Thank God, I ended that old geezer's life, just in time. But she sure is beginning to stink.

Once in her own bedroom, she popped open the latch, flipped up the top, and revealed her arsenal. Everything she needed was there.

All loaded and ready to kill.

Now it was time. She psychically heard them in the lobby as she set a trap right on top of the ledge over the front door. She then inserted a DVD Clancy had made for her into a hidden camera in the living room wall. Barbara then raced to take her place in the bedroom.

☙❧

John tensed up outside Barbara's apartment. Sal and Tony repeatedly adjusted the straps on their vests, even though they fit correctly. It was not what they usually wore. Not to this extent. Their already worn bodies wouldn't take much more. Tony fidgeted. His fingers trembled holding his weapon. Not sleeping in over seventy-two hours had taken its toll on him. He needed to use his left hand to position his trigger finger properly onto the right side of the Glock. He was too ready to shoot, and he needed to control his impulses. They were vulnerable. A vulnerable cop was automatically in trouble.

Sal showed more control. A firm hand on Tony's shoulder, momentarily, kept him back.

The three-man ESU team of Sergeant Shipman, Maxwell, and Kramer—suited up in their body armor with shields in front of them—didn't think too highly of Carlson's men.

"How hard can it be to take down a woman? What the hell is wrong with you guys?" Shipman meant every word.

Their annoyance perpetuated a non-cooperative operation. They had always had disputes, but not over incompetence. John felt empty-handed without a weapon as an ESU pushed him to the side to be suited in a Kevlar vest and helmet. They waited and listened. No sounds leaked from the apartment. They doubted that Barbara was in there. Good or bad omen they didn't know.

Then John noticed it. The front door stood slightly ajar. It was barely noticeable, but John pointed to it with his right index finger, while his left hand covered his mouth. Now it turned into a bad omen. Barbara was in there. And she had a plan.

"Don't do anything stupid, guys," Kramer implored. "I gotta get home to the baby,"

Tony just wanted her so badly, he ignored Kramer, barged in front of the ESU, and pushed the door in without hesitation, so fast they couldn't stop him. What was he thinking not to follow protocol? It'd been the same protocol he'd followed for fifteen years. ESU entered and secured the premises first. He knew that.

A sterling silver bucket filled with thirty pounds of ice cubes, toppled from the top ledge of the door, hitting Tony in his neck and shoulders, with the handle of the bucket hooking onto the bottom of the helmet. He collapsed to the ground, knocked out with his helmet torn off, and his gun disappeared under a couch.

John gasped as the ESU team stumbled in, slipping on the rolling ice, as the hologram that Clancy had created played on the walls. All four walls in the living room received vivid overlapping geometric graphics. Triangles, rectangles, parallelograms, octagons, and hexagons in kaleidoscopic intensity of the primary colors, red, green, blue, and yellow were so bright their eyes hurt. And the loud Reggae music compounded the sensory bombardment. Reflective lights bounced through the space onto all of the mirrors Barbara had in the room, on the ceilings, walls and tabletops, making the sense of time, space, and boundaries incomprehensible. They were entangled in a maze of mirrors and lights and couldn't figure out how to navigate their way through it. It stymied them. It resembled a huge life-like sensory bombardment chamber modeled after the ones in an experimental psychology college lab in the late 1960s.

John and Sal held their ears in agony so they couldn't focus on helping Tony who struggled to get on all fours. Sergeant Shipman helped Tony up—trembling, in pain, and wobbling—but he was alive. Shipman ushered Tony to a corner of the living room where he then put in a call for backup.

One wall cleared up and whitened. A hologram montage of John poured onto it. As he was repeatedly stabbed in his torso with silver, size-two knitting needles, gushing blood squirted out into the room, flooding Barbara's blue couch and turning it purple. The authentic representation stunned John. He had the same expression in his eyes as his team. Frantic, terrified were the words to describe it. The men looked around, panicked. They recovered John, trying to catch his breath in the corner with Tony.

"She has the best in store for me."

His comedic relief wasn't appreciated. Tony and Sal looked around, frantically, for the source, as Sergeant Shipman, Kramer, and Maxwell moved cautiously. The three of them had the stance of stiff soldiers equidistant in the living room. They froze. Never had they experienced something like this. In New York, they were prepared for everything, and had been, until now.

John was privy to the training they endured. Flexibility and adjustment to situations were key, but they entered situations for which they had been prepared. They were not prepared to go beyond reality into a fantasy world. A world they couldn't escape. A world that could kill them.

The job demanded that they risk their lives, unfalteringly.

Now the montage propelled from the wall and flashed onto John. His arms and legs were cut off by spinning serrated butcher blades controlled by a ghostly looking puppet. The puppet hung in front of him. In his aura. The men didn't know where to look first. Their bodies, the walls, carpets were all splashed with crimson blood. John's blood.

High-pitched screams, intermingled with low growls, wailed from the speakers in the ceiling in the four corners of the room, as if coming from a deranged woman. Visual stimuli pulsated off the mirrors. The ESU struggled to adjust their earphones. They couldn't control the noise level.

John fought to get the hologram off him. He swiped his arms and legs as the holographic knives repeatedly pierced him. Sal and Tony pulled him away from the spotlight but the images lingered right on top of him. Barbara was in control.

"All right, Kellie. You must have paid Clancy a hefty sum for this. Knock it off!"

She couldn't be seen, but she was heard loud and clear. "Death to all those who come near me!" It was more sick and more perverted than John had ever heard her yell it.

"Wait till you sees this, you arrogant bastard!"

The hologram continued with movie-like images on the wall. Barbara lunged at John with her knitting needles. He wore his long white lab coat over his suit and she wore the hospital gown. He caught one and seductively pulled her close to him, wanting what she wanted. She slowly pushed off his lab coat and jacket by slipping the other knitting needle underneath them. Then he slid his arms out and tossed the coats to the floor. With a long kiss, she dragged him down onto a bed. They kissed, slowly at first. His lips adorned her face, ears, neck.

"I want it the hottest you can give it, John." The voice on the montage was, indeed, Barbara's.

He recognized shots of him that had been on the internet in uncompromising situations. That one, he recalled, was a paparazzi plant.

What a time to regret his strong online presence. The hologram zipped to them both naked, him on top of her, his body molding into hers, his eyes ravenous, kissing, sucking her nipples, caressing her breasts.

While the montage held their focus, Barbara depressed a remote transmitter, triggering unrecognizable explosions throughout the apartment. The men whirled around, looking at everything. Glass splintered in the room. The glass tables caved in. Tony and Sal were splattered with flying glass before they could take cover. Though their faces and heads were protected, their arms and legs were slashed. Bloodied, Tony and Sal jumped behind a couch. Bookshelves collapsed, along with their contents. Heavy alabaster sculptures and books landed on top of Sergeant Shipman and Mike Kramer, crushing their torsos and legs. Their protective gear had failed them. They were gone.

Kramer's newborn had lost his father.

Maxwell pushed John down in the corner by the debris of the Queen Victoria chair and lay on top of him.

John and Barbara consumed each other. John was aggressive. Animalistic. The montage was snippets but devoid of emotion. John explored every inch of her with his tongue and his hands. She seized him, controlled him, forced him do whatever she demanded. She pushed his head down past her stomach. She ran her fingers through his hair, keeping his head down. He kissed her inner thigh. She spread her legs farther and farther apart. Her hands slithered up her stomach and over her breasts. She flailed them over her head as John came down on her, making her entrance wet with his saliva.

Sal and Tony crept, barely recovered, to John and Maxwell. Their breathing was labored and the sleeves of their shirts and pants legs were torn to shreds. Their wounds would require hours of stitching.

A condom wrapper floated to the floor. John rose on top of Barbara, penetrated.

"You slept with her! You did, didn't you?"

"No, Tony, I didn't. So help me God, I didn't."

"You piece of shit! Then where in hell did Clancy get these images?"

Barbara picked up the knitting needles lying by her side on

the bed and repeatedly plunged them up into John's stomach and chest just as he climaxed. The shiny silver needles spiked up and down. She didn't stop plunging. Blood flowed everywhere onto John, her, the carpet. John's eyes rolled back in his head as he collapsed, dead.

John's mind went to Vicki. No woman could satisfy him like his beautiful Vicki. For the love of God, he had to make it out of this.

Tony's gaze darted to the wall. He was breathing heavily. "I gotta—gotta stop this."

Tony pointed to the light coming from a closet door in the hall leading to the living room. John watched him as he crawled on his belly to the door, followed by the ESU officer. Tony opened it. A bomb positioned low to the ground on the other side of the door immediately exploded, decapitating him, and slicing Jackson Maxwell in his legs, propelling them to the other side of the room. Body parts and gray matter landed near Sal and John. Tony's head was sliced into minuscule sections. Shrapnel splintered all over the room with such a burst of power, it was worse than being in a war zone.

"Tony! Nooooo!" Fear escalated and shook Sal and John out of balance. Where the hell was backup? Sal screamed, frenzied. He just lost his partner of fifteen years—and John, his best friend.

Sal tossed a gun to John who expertly caught it. Trembling, Sal slipped to a doorway, just barely peering into it when the human Kellie unloaded an automatic machine gun into him from his head to groin and then disappeared from view into a bedroom. At first, John didn't know if it was a hologram or not. Frantic, he knelt by his dead friend. Feeling the real blood and seeing it drip from his hands made him explode with terror. Then he heard it ripple through the room.

"Death to all those who come near me!"

John grabbed Sal's Glock. Standing, weak and broken, he screamed, "All right you bitch! You want me, come get me!"

A flash of Barbara appeared on the wall. It spun around and around until it was a total blur.

"Talk to me, bitch! I don't even know what to call you. Who are you now?"

Flashes of Barbara's identities through the years material-ized on the wall, Kellie Wilson, Pauline Jones, Emily Connors, and Barbara Montgomery. They allied side by side. John fired into all of them, hitting them right in the chest, trying to find the human behind them. His gun emptied.

He dropped that gun, ripped Sal's service weapon from his ankle holster, and sprang over what was left of the couch. He pitched pillows out of his way. The rubies, emeralds, and dia-monds from the bullet jewelry box sparkled on the carpet with-in the shards of glass.

He stumbled into the bedroom, sweating, fear ridden, and near collapse. Blood dripped through his tattered shirt, and his slacks had gaping bloodied holes. The inflexible Kevlar vest was the only thing giving him the support to stand. Barbara was in bed naked and waiting for him. Piles of her clothing lay on the floor. He was not sure what he saw with blood dripping into his eyes from the gashes on his forehead.

"I've been waiting for you, John. I want it the hottest you can give it."

He lunged at the image of Barbara in bed and dove through it. The image disappeared and he lay face down on the bed, on the edge of consciousness. He was saturated with a combina-tion of sweat, his own blood and the body parts and plasma of his best friends. He must survive, for Vicki, their unborn child, and Ricky.

The real Barbara appeared from out of the closet, naked. She tiptoed up behind him and jumped on his back. The shock of her being real made the gun slip out of his sweaty grip onto the floor. He used his last bit of strength to turn over in an at-tempt to grab her.

"Come on, John. You know you want me."

Red and bright purple lights from the corner of the room flashed into his eyes, blinding him. He continued to try to grab her but he missed each time. He thought he was really becom-ing blind. He rolled off the bed onto the floor, landing on his back. After a few moments to recoup from the lights, which she surprisingly gave him, he saw her stand erect right over him. He grabbed her leg to get her off balance, but this was

one strong and in-shape woman, and he was almost unconscious.

She toyed with him with a paring knife, pretending to slit
his throat. He defended with his arm and the knife flew backward. He attempted to get up but she kicked him in his chin,
making him fall back, banging his head on the night table.

She backed off quickly, grabbing a coat off a chair. "Sorry
to cut this playtime short, John. Got some more kills to do before you."

She climbed out the open window and down the fire escape. He lay on the floor completely worn out going into un-
consciousness.

℮ℭ℮ℭ

Another ESU team dashed in looking at the devastation.
They saw the demise of Tony, Sal, and their team members,
and knew they needed to control themselves. They split up, in
shock. The now-eerie silence was deafening. They found everyone but John.

"Doc? Dr. Trenton where are you?"

"Here." His voice was barely audible.

After cleansing some clumps of skin and bone from one or
more of the victims from John's face, a paramedic put an oxygen mask tightly on his face. He strained to talk. John had all
the signs of trauma, a weak pulse, shallow breathing, a very
pale complexion, perspiration dripping from his pores, and his
eyes held a dazed panicked expression. He was totally limp

"Dr. Trenton, I know you can hear me. Be still. Don't talk
yet. You have shards of glass all over and you're bleeding,
heavily." He was disoriented and couldn't even tell where the
voice was coming from, even though the tech kneeled right in
front of his face. "We get what happened. You're lucky to still
be alive."

John blankly stared at them, moaning unintelligible words
as he struggled to sit up, but they restrained him. He comprehended what he heard, but he couldn't get the words out with
any meaning. He looked around in bewilderment as the room
spun before his eyes, and he felt like he was on a cloud drifting

off into heaven. He was in a whirlwind of despair and the techs didn't have a clue as to what raced through his mind, which was twelve hundred miles south.

He wasn't focused on who worked on him and he lost awareness of where he was. He smelled medicinal odors, but he couldn't place it. He felt someone rolling up his sleeve, but he couldn't fathom why. He felt like a Ken doll being poked, prodded, contorted out of shape, rolled, and folded up, which for a Ken doll would be broken in half.

Only he knew what he was saying. Only he knew what he envisioned. Only he knew what messages he was receiving from his unconscious at this moment. He saw Vicki and Barbara in the same scene. A scene that lasted two seconds. That meant one thing.

Vicki was in trouble.

He had to get to Florida to save his Vicki and his soon to be children, Ricky and the baby Vicki carried. He couldn't die. He couldn't let her die. He couldn't let their unborn child be taken from him. Didn't Vicki know he'd noticed? He needed to snap back. He must.

The last twenty minutes had become a vague nightmare. He wasn't aware if it was real or if he was dreaming. How could that be? He was always the guy on top of everything. He was the rock. How could this be happening to him? He must be the rock for his family.

"Breathe, Dr. Trenton, breathe. You've got to relax. You can't fight us. We've got to stop the bleeding. We're going to give you something to calm you down."

He shook his head, but he couldn't talk. His breathing was too tight. His diaphragmatic breathing wasn't working. Max wasn't coming to hit them over the head to make them listen to him. Not that they would understand him. He struggled with the tech's hold on him and he lost. His eyes must have looked scared to them, not forewarning of what he desired to say. They must have assumed it was fright from the devastation around them. He felt a needle go into his arm. And a moment later he was asleep.

CHAPTER 44

John's breathing deepened. He moaned in his sleep, but couldn't move a muscle. They had restrained his wrists and ankles so he couldn't disrupt, or pull out, the IV tubes if he awakened. Bandages covered both arms, which were stitched in sixteen places from his wrists to his shoulders. He had cardiac and respiratory monitors counting every beat and every breath in the ICU.

The sedative relaxed him enough to enable him to slip into a deep meditative state. He could usually go there himself, but the sedative took him deeper. First, he saw in black and white, kaleidoscopic round swirls in front of his eyes as if they originated in his eyes. They rotated slowly from directly on top of him, and then moved slowly farther and farther away in front of his third eye, until his mind was a blank slate, and he could participate in the vision. It seemed like it took a long time. The sounds of the ICU lessened and then were replaced by others. He couldn't discern them at first. As he traveled farther, he knew. He was able to make contact with Barbara and see her in real time, where she was, and what she was doing. He felt himself travel to Barbara.

He astral traveled.

He heard the sounds in the club, the voices, house and techno music, as he perched on top of the bar invisible to everyone.

Barbara's moves were slower and more strained than usual tonight. She wore a Marilyn Monroe blonde wig, bright red lipstick, and she revealed her own baby blues. She was disengaged, unfocused; just not sexy enough for the men who gazed at her, willing to pay for what they wanted. She danced on stage like a matronly woman who was having trouble keeping her balance after consuming three or four unusually strong cocktails a few weeks after having a hip replacement. She soaked up the effects of the sensory bombardment as well as the men she'd just murdered.

"Unappetizing" as they told the manager of the club Raunchy. It lived up to its name. The women were more scantily dressed than at Zodiac. Whiskey, her stage name, wasn't cutting it. Even though wearing the same outfit as in Zodiac, minus the boots, her lethargy wasn't doing her any favors.

"Whiskey, off the stage now!" The middle-aged balding, rotund, brusque manager wasn't at all pleased with the talent for the evening, and she'd be the one he'd make an example of for the other dancers. He was pissed they had all chosen tonight to make an appearance for his stage. Usually there was one good one among the bunch, but tonight he'd lose money.

She jumped off. "Yeah, Yeah, I know all about it, Brett. Don't even have to pay me for tonight. See ya!" She grabbed her purse that laid at the back corner of the stage.

He stared at her, not catching her agenda. "And don't come back till ya get your act together."

Her willingness to be dismissed so easily didn't penetrate this numbskull at all. He didn't even see where she went.

But John did, from the his room in the ICU.

"Sure thing," she said, knowing Brett didn't hear her.

She looked around for her mark for the night and spotted them in a corner. There were three of them, positioned strategically, where they could view the meat in the club from the best vantage point. They were young, twentyish, cute, in a boyish way, certainly not manly. They sipped watered-down drinks, dressed alike, all in black from their unbuttoned rayon shirts showing minimal chest hair like they'd barely reached puberty, and skin-tight black leatherette jeans, with their hair greased up in spikes. The cool look. All but one, having a Coke, who looked more innocent than the rest, but more worn out. He was not the one she intended to approach. Young meant computer savvy and that's what she needed. She realized it was too hot out there to contact her hacker, so she had resigned herself to finding new talent. "Hi, guys."

"Hi there, honey."

One of them was very intrigued and tried to be seductive beyond his years. Barbara decided to play with him even though she was just shy of twice his age.

"I may need your help. Are you game?"

"What kind of help, doll?" He got closer, peering down at her breasts. Salivating, he almost drooled right on her.

"Oh, sweetie, you are so cute." She patted his cheek adoringly. "Here's what I need." She plucked a photo out of her tiny purse. "How are you on the computer, sweetie? I need to find their address."

The intrigued one took it. He read the headline. "Dr. John Trenton and his gorgeous wife Vicki."

The kid with the Coke gulped.

"She's a looker. Why do you need to find him?"

"Well, sweetie pie." She wasn't thrilled with the question. She hated questions by anyone, but he deserved a nibble. "There's ten grand in it if you can find his address with no questions asked from you or your friends. Deal?"

"I think I can do that. You definitely came to the right place, doll." He laughed with confidence and an immature bravado. "Didn't she, guys?"

They sounded so dumb. "Yeah, she sure did, AJ."

"I can find anything, even personal stuff. My fingers on the keyboard sing, doll, and I don't mean on a piano. Got the drift, doll?"

"Oh, sweetie."

"How do I know you'll pay up?"

"I'm a woman of my word." She handed him a card with just a phone number. "Call me when you have what I need and don't contact me if you don't have it. I need it by ten a.m. A second later and the deal's off. Got it?"

"Oh, yeah. I got it, doll." She cringed at him even thinking he could have her and paraded away with an extra sexy wiggle. "This will be the easiest ten grand I'll ever make."

John moaned, still deeply under sedation. He stayed with the vision.

The kid with the Coke snatched the card. "Just wanna see the number." He handed it back to his friend after he read it and committed it to memory. "I gotta go, guys. I have a curfew at this place."

John wasn't waking up. He followed Bobby outside.

☙❧

As soon as Bobby was outside, he raced down the block, making sure he wasn't followed. He breathed with a lot of effort and couldn't get his mind to focus. But he must try, just like he'd been taught the last couple of weeks.

He leaned against the graffiti-filled wall, with his mind reeling, and rubbed his hands over his face. What had he just become involved in? Oh, man! This was going to thrust him backward. A decision like this, he didn't want to have to make. It was his future. He had sacrificed his entire life. He'd lost his childhood, teens, and part of his young adult life. Now he could throw away the rest of it.

Oh, man. What should he do? He was never good at making decisions, least of all the right ones. That's why he had been in trouble for all those years. Now, at twenty-two, he had a chance. Finally a chance. Why risk it now? He knew they would put him away in lock-up, possibly costing him his freedom for a long time. It had only been two weeks. They wouldn't believe him. No one could change in two weeks. No one, before two weeks ago, had ever given him a chance.

He had to do it. He had to do it for the man who saved his life. He took out his cell and dialed.

The phone rang five times as he paced nervously, and the call transferred to voicemail. "Dr. Trenton. It's Bobby. I know you're gonna kill me and lock me up. I know. I know it for sure. Judge Marks hates me. I violated my probation. But this is urgent. Life and death urgent. You gotta call me as soon as you get this. I know it's five a.m. and I should be at the house, but I'm not. Damn! Please call me." He hung up with his body sliding down the side of the building and landed, sitting on the pavement, pulling his knees into his chest, and wrapping his arms around them. He concealed his head in his knees and sobbed, heart-wrenching sobs.

CHAPTER 45

Barbara exited the plane with a huge smile on her face. The two-hour-twenty-minute flight gave her the chance to rest and recoup. She'd donned a long brown hair wig tied back in a ponytail, perfect for Florida weather, with her natural bangs.

Her eyes were emerald and she was casually dressed in light blue denim crop jeans and a solid blue T-shirt. No cops picked her up. They didn't know about her yet? The entire team on her case was dead. Who else knew about her? The thought of "no one" invigorated her. She held a light carry on and she couldn't wait to get into the Florida sun.

As she waited in the long taxi line, she took out her iPad and looked up lodging in Serento. She located a Best Western not too far from Vicki's address and dialed on her cell.

"Hi. I just landed in Tampa and I need a room. Single occupancy. Yes. Non-smoking please. I can be there in a couple of hours. Yes, of course, Susan Miller. Can I please give you my card number when I get there? I'm sort of around a lot of people and—Oh, thank you. Yes, I have ID. See you soon."

Huh? It wouldn't be that easy in New York.

Before long, she rode in a Lincoln Town Car, traveling ninety miles north, after paying the driver one-hundred-twenty bucks in advance. She checked her watch. Taking out her cell, she dialed.

∽∾∽

Ricky scampered to answer the phone. "Dad?"

"Is this Vicki Trenton's house?"

"Yes. Who's this?"

"Sweetheart, I'm a friend of your dad's. Is your mom there?"

"Yes. Hold on." Vicki took the phone. "She says she's a friend of John's."

"Hello."

"Vicki?"

"Yes."

"Hi, I'm so glad I reached you. I'm Susan Miller, a colleague of John's at Sheepshead Medical."

"Oh. Hi. Are you a psychiatrist?"

"No. I'm a school psychologist there and I work with teens in short term admissions."

"Did he tell you to call me?" Right away Vicki thought John had referred Susan to work with Ricky, but why would he do that so quickly without even seeing him yet?

"No, but he gave me your number."

"That doesn't make sense."

"Why?"

"Why would he give you my number if he didn't tell you to call?"

"Let me explain, because we might be on the wrong track here."

"Please do."

"I just landed in Tampa. I'm looking around the area for a nice serene adult community for my parents. John told me how peaceful it is by you and wooded. My parents love the Adirondacks, but it's way too cold for them year round, and south Florida is way too crowded. So he thought this area would be great for them, and my father loves golf."

"Yes, we were on the wrong track, Susan, sorry."

"Trust me, I'm not sleeping with your husband. Mine is possessive enough."

"I wasn't thinking of that either." *Why would she go there? Something isn't right here.*

"Oh. Can we do lunch or something? I'm staying at the Best Western in Serento."

"Sure. That's not far from me. How long will you be in town?"

"Just a couple of days."

"Perfect. How about coming over for dinner tonight, around seven? I'm making a country barbeque."

"That would be wonderful. Thank you! What's the exact address?"

☙☙

In John's hospital room, a couple of detectives he didn't know surrounded him, but they knew of him—John the player, John the moronic risk taker—and boy was he one last night. What was a civilian doing in a situation like that? What did he have to prove?

To them, this was one shrink who had more than his own share of issues.

They were able to access the forensics and all of the police files in hard copy, that had loaded up three boxes, which alone were more than overwhelming. Lex Withers, with twelve years on the force, was a top-notch investigator with his newbie partner Bella Richards, who just made the rank, and neither was thrilled with taking on this case in its escalated proportion. They were told they could wait in John's room until he woke up, and he still wasn't stirring. A nurse entered to check the IV.

"Can't you give this dude somethin' to wake him up? We gotta get on this case."

"Sorry, Detective, he has to wake up on his own. He probably needed this sleep badly." The nurse removed the wrist and ankle restraints.

"Well, so do I, and my little partner here ain't used to the long hours yet."

The nurse smiled and walked out without responding.

Withers looked at the door before going over to the side of the bed and putting his hand on John's shoulder. "Come on Trenton, wake up. You've had more sleep than us."

John began to stir and moan, and he opened his eyes.

"Whoa." He moved his eyes around but couldn't focus. "How long was I out?"

"Close to seven hours. I'm Withers. She's Richards. We got the case now. Real sorry to hear about your team. They were good people."

"Oh, man. I need my cell. I've got to make some calls. I got a message. I need my cell." His hands were uncoordinated and it took him a few minutes to control them. When he did, he pulled the oxygen tube out of his nose.

"Hold on, brother. You're in an ICU unit. Can't use the cell in here. What do you mean a message? A voicemail?"

"Where's my cell?"

"Hey! Tell me what's going on!"

"Barbara Montgomery or whatever alias she's using is probably down in Florida by now and she's going to attempt to kill my wife and son."

"No, she's not. She's dead."

John scowled at him.

"They found a body of a woman burned to a crisp in the living room."

"Wasn't her. She grabbed a coat and ran down the fire escape outside the bedroom window."

"You're kiddin', right?" After the signature look from John, Wither's stomach sank. "Didn't get forensics back yet. Fuck! We gave her a seven-hour head start."

"Now get me a phone. And a plane ready at the airport. Where are my clothes?"

"Doc. You're not going anywhere. You're hooked up. Not to mention stitched up."

"Get me a phone now!" John screamed as loudly as he could, which was minimal, not having any strength. "Get me my phone! I have to validate something!" He breathed heavily and his head sank back into the pillow.

"Damn it, Trenton. We don't have time for your bullshit."

John grasped Wither's forearm. "Where's my phone?"

"Hold on, lunatic. I have it. The EMS tech gave it to me." Withers took it out of his pocket.

"Check for messages. Put them on speaker phone."

Withers followed the order, though doubting John's mental state.

"Dr. Trenton, it's Bobby again. Some woman had a picture of you and your wife. And she wanted to find your address. My friend said he would do it and she promised him ten grand. He found out and met with the guy she sent to get the address to pay him. He shot my friend in cold blood, Dr. Trenton. He's dead. I was around the corner. He gave the guy your address and told him your wife is visiting her parents in Serento, Florida. Dr. Trenton, that woman is going to Florida to kill your wife."

"How the hell did you know that with the phone shut off and in my damn pocket?"

"I told you I got a message. The sedation let me go into deep meditation and see things."

"Oh, yeah. You're that psychic shrink."

"My wife's life is in danger and you're not going to stop me," John growled. He ripped the IV tape off and pulled out the needle with some of his blood from the tubing splashing onto Withers. He couldn't have cared less. He reattached the gauze and tape to cover the incision. "I'm taking care of this myself."

"All right, hold on. You said she left by the fire escape?"

"Yes." John struggled to sit up, but Withers held him down only to get himself kneed in the stomach with as much force as John could muster.

Withers didn't back off. He remained leaning over John. "When?"

"A few minutes before EMS came into the bedroom. Get off me. Every minute we spend doing this, is more time she can get to my wife and kids."

"Thought you didn't have any kids."

"We're adopting an eight year old and Vicki is pregnant. So now's not the time to prove you're almost as strong as me."

"I'm stronger. It's called youth. I've ten less years of deterioration on me."

Withers received a sneer of disapproval for that remark. "I've got to call my brother-in-law," John said.

"Why him?"

"He's the commander of SWAT in the county. He'll know what to do."

"Jesus, wait a second." Withers yelled out into the hall, "Get me a phone hook-up in here!"

❧❧

Barbara meandered down the trail in the woods, leading to Vicki's house. She double-checked the Pink Lady she'd concealed in her bag. *Boy, was it easy to get a gun down here. Cash and carry right from a couple of rednecks off a truck. Just the way I like it. And with the serial number already buffed off, it will be untraceable. This part of the county is great. With all these woods, it's so easy to bury a body here, or two. When I'm done, Vicki and their kid won't be found for decades. This is one isolated house. Hell, I could never live here. I'd die of boredom. Jesus, this chick is going to be an easy mark. What could a cracker know?*

A jeep in the driveway signaled that Vicki was home. Barbara confidently rang the bell.

"Who's there?"

"It's Susan, sweetheart."

The door opened and sweet and adorable Ricky, with his long curly blond hair almost to his shoulders, greeted her. "I thought you were coming for dinner. It's only two o'clock."

Barbara gave him the once over. "Are you in the military?"

He looked down at his outfit, shorts and a tank top in army camouflage. "No, I'm too young."

Barbara walked in, laughing. "I know, baby, and I know I'm early, but I didn't know where to go today. I'm just not used to seeing all these cows and horses so close up. I thought your mom could give me some ideas." She looked up when Vicki entered from the bedroom.

"Hi, Susan, I'm Vicki and this is Ricky." Vicki extended her hand to shake. Barbara reciprocated. "Can I get you something to drink? Lemonade? Unsweet tea?"

"Tea would be great, thanks."

Vicki smiled. "I'll be right back, darlin'."

Ricky made himself comfortable next to Barbara on the couch. "You work with John?"

"Yes. And you call your dad by his first name?"

"Well, he's not my dad yet, but he's going to be."

"How so?"

"John an' Vicki are going to adopt me. Then they'll be my mom an' dad for real. I can't wait. I'll have a real family that loves me for the first time in my life."

"That's wonderful." Her stomach sank. If only she could have had a family of her own. She did once, but it was all taken from her. Now she begrudged everyone a family. "How did you meet them?"

"I was five an' I met John the same night he met Vicki in the hospital. I had an asthma attack an' John helped me when I was waiting there for the kid doctor. An' John talked to my mom an' got her to leave my dad because he was doing really bad things to me. Really bad. Then my dad took my mom, grandma an' grandpa hostage, He had a lot of guns, rifles too, an' John got me out of there an' put them in jail. He wanted me to live with them then, but the judge wouldn't let him take me to New York, an' I've been in different foster homes, an' finally they reached Vicki an' she said I could come live with them."

"Mommy is in jail, too?"

"Yes. She was doing bad things to me, too. The lady at social services told Vicki they gave up their parental rights, whatever that is, so they can adopt me now." He took out the photo from his pocket of John and him sleeping together when he was five. "See? This is John an' me, the first night after he saved me. I was a little kid, then."

"Oh, my God, Ricky, that's so beautiful, sweetheart."

He had a huge smile on his face while Barbara sank into in her own sick little world into a daydream....

Oh no. How am I going to get myself to kill this little angel? And Vicki? At least he was rescued. I was never rescued. I never had a John or Vicki in my life. But he could have helped me. I didn't let him. I would have been put away for life. No, I was never rescued. I can't let that stop me. He gave me so much grief and anguish in that God-forsaken hospital, I have to get even with him. He made me tell him things I never would have said. I never should have said. I took away his two best friends. He has no reason to live now except for them. No one stayed alive for me. Both my parents left me, left me for garbage. Why should I care about them?

Vicki returned with the tea. Barbara was in her distant world. "Susan? You Okay?"

She almost didn't snap out of it. "Oh, yes. I'm just mesmerized, looking out at the lanai and seeing all that greenery." She took the glass from Vicki with jittery hands.

☙❧❧

"Mark, its John. Get Vicki and Ricky out of the house."

"What's going on?"

"Didn't Vicki tell you why I didn't want her to come back?"

"Yeah. So?"

"You didn't get it."

"The only thing I get is that you're pushing her away."

"Damn it, Mark! A female killer escaped from custody and is probably down there now to attempt to kill your sister. Wake up! I didn't want her back here to be an easy target. I didn't think she'd find Vicki in Florida, but she did."

"Jesus Christ John. If my sister gets—I'll get the teams in place. I don't even know if the surveillance system is activated."

"For once, I hope it is. I'm coming down. Have a copter ready for me at the Tampa heliport."

"Where are you now?"

"Hooked up to an IV in ICU."

"What the hell happened?"

"This woman, Barbara Montgomery, but even that's not her real name. She uses many aliases. She pretends to be a school psychologist. She killed Tony and Sal and three ESU guys last night and that's not all of her kills. She's a weapons expert and master of disguises. Be careful. She kills with a vengeance and without hesitation."

"On it." The phone died.

"I'm okay, really. I've got to get down there. Call 555-637-0122 to get me the commissioner's plane to leave at the Manhattan center."

"You talkin' police commissioner? You have access to the police commissioner's private plane?"

"Just do it."

CHAPTER 46

Vicki's cell jingled as she sat next to Barbara on the couch. She answered it, getting to her feet. The southern gal came flying out of her. "Be right back, darlin'. Need more ice in my tea. Want more ice, Susan?"

"No, I'm fine, thanks."

"Hi," Vicki said into the phone.

"Vicki, it's Mark."

"I know. Oh my goodness, Mark. Want to hear something great? Really great?"

"Sure."

"John's friend came down from New York to look for a place for her parents. She's a school psychologist in the same hospital as John, Sheepshead."

"She's there now?"

"Yes. We're having tea and Ricky really likes her. Ooh, he really does."

"Remember what he told you about why he didn't want you in New York?"

"Uh, yes, really? Oh my, a blizzard today? Yes, good thing I didn't. Listen, it's really rude of me to be on the phone with company, so can we talk later?"

"Get it on."

"Oh, what a sweet brother you are. Is that what you're calling to remind me? Yes it's done, and the roast is plugged into the skewers on the pit, too. Susan is joining us for the barbeque tonight. So come well-armed to shovel a lot of food into your bellies. And tell our daddy sheriff he can bring extra friends. They'll be so much food. In fact, I have more cooking to do now. Susan, do you cook?"

She got a negative head shake and an I-can't-stand-to-be-in-the-kitchen, grimace. Now, Vicki knew how to irk the hell out of her. And how to keep her there.

"We'll be there soon. Sit tight."

"Don't worry, I won't frazzle myself in the kitchen." She hung up. "My twin brother, he checks on me every day. We're very close. But he tries to run my life when I'm here, like he runs his department."

"And how's that?"

"Well, he's the Commander of SWAT down here so he's really tough and so overprotective. Has a huge team. Helicopters and everything. And you should see their Hummer. Oh my God. Little kids just stop them every time to take pictures with them. And they love it. The cops down here are so friendly and they really care about everyone."

Barbara became more wide eyed.

"Wanna come into the kitchen? My potatoes should be done by now. I roast them in the oven with garlic and rosemary before I make them into potato salad. So tell me about you, Susan. I totally envy women who can make it in New York. I have a hard time. And John, the darlin' that he is, tries to give me everything I want to make it up to me. He spoils me so much. More than I ever was as a child. Come in the nook while I check on the potatoes. We can do our chatting up close and personal."

ಌಌ

Mark mobilized his team and the Crisis Negotiation Team at the Emergency Operations Center and all of their equipment had been put into the truck.

On his laptop, he observed Vicki and Barbara in the kitchen while Vicki cooked. Good place to get Barbara into. Vicki had some of her weapons in there. "Smart move, sis. We're on our way. Be there in forty."

coco

Vicki let out a big sigh. How nauseatingly sweet did she have to be to Barbara? How much time did she have left to go along? "How about some lunch? I'll whip up some cheese omelets and grill some turkey bacon. We have herb biscuits I'll reheat and the potatoes are absolutely delish. Ricky and I had breakfast hours ago."

"Oh, my God. That sounds irresistible. Yes. Thank you. You always cook for John?"

Vicki popped the biscuits and bacon onto sheets and into the oven. "John can eat. Believe me. But mostly healthful stuff. That's how he keeps his hot body."

Barbara laughed.

"Sorry if I embarrassed you," Vicki said. "Yes. He has dinner on the table when he comes home every night. I'm only back down here for three weeks, visiting my folks, but I always bake for the doctors' lounge and the precinct. So I'm sure you've had my pastries at Sheepshead. I stocked his fridge and freezer before I left. He has the most amazing kitchen in that condo—a kitchen a chef would die for. Oh, look at me. I shouldn't be rambling. Tell me about you, Susan, please."

Barbara was comfortable at the table as Vicki cooked. "Well, I've been a school psychologist for twelve years. The last three I've been in Brooklyn. My husband, Clancy, got relocated from LA to New York three years ago for a couple of film projects. He's a cinematographer. So we moved there."

"Oh, how exciting! From Hollywood. Look Ricky, it's so great! Susan's from California."

"I've never been to California!"

"Me neither, honey. Brooklyn. Wow! That's a big city! So do you know Tony, Sal, and Paul?"

"Actually, Brooklyn is a borough." Barbara's tone was quite condescending. "Yes. I've worked with them on some teen weapons suspensions from school."

Vicki caught the attitude and taunted her more. "They're great guys. When we get to New York, Ricky, we'll get you together with their kids. They're John's bestest friends in the whole world." She turned back to her guest. "Do you have any kids?"

"Unfortunately, no."

"Well, we have one in the oven. We tried for a couple of years. But please, don't tell John. I want to surprise him when we go back to New York."

"You do look a little puffy in the girls there."

"I know, and we Skyped yesterday. I hope he didn't notice."

"You mean to tell me your husband doesn't know you're pregnant?"

"No, I want it to be a surprise."

Barbara laughed. "John has a residency in Gyno, and you don't think he noticed? You're something else, girlfriend."

They both giggled like they'd been BFFs a long time. Barbara relaxed and enjoyed herself. Vicki served and they all dug in.

"Oh my God. This is so good, Vicki. Thank you!"

"Eat to your heart's content, darlin'." *I need you as sluggish as I can get you on all these carbs.*

Barbara devoured her second biscuit.

☙❧☙

Mark saw a clear view in real time on the laptop. He couldn't believe his sister was doing so well, and she'd gotten this murderer to relax and actually laugh. But he was aware a psychopath could play any role. Any time. He had to move fast. He put on the metal scanner and scanned Barbara from head to toe.

She wasn't carrying on her person. Her bag rested on the couch in the great room. Bingo. "Thirty-eight in her bag, Vicki. Keep her away from it. We're right outside."

He signaled to two of his team to go around to either side of the lanai. The kid sniper vanished to the left side, closest to the kitchen. The men remained out of view, awaiting instructions. It took time to set up. As long as it was calm, they had a few minutes.

ℰᏜℰᏜ

Vicki fingered her hair to acknowledge she heard him through her earwig. "Now, I'm stuffed."

"Me too, Vicki. Thank you, again!"

"Want some coffee and dessert? I made an outrageous pumpkin cheesecake. Or would you prefer chocolate layer?" Vicki took two cake trays from the ledge behind her and put them on the table, hoping this would give the team time to bust in and grab Barbara.

Without a moment's notice, Barbara's blood sugar spiked and her aggression mounted. "Don't you do anything else but cook and bake?"

Vicki feigned little girl whining. "Oh, oh, that's insulting. I happen to have a bachelor's degree and I'm a kindergarten teacher. You're just like the rest of John's friends who look down on me because I'm not a doctor."

Barbara fidgeted and struggled to find the words. "I'm sorry. I'm sorry, Vicki. I didn't mean to insult you. That was so rude of me."

Ricky unexpectedly stepped up to be the man of the house and threw them and the teams ready to bust in off guard. He stood right up in front of Barbara, blocking the kid sniper's shot. "You're being mean to my mom. Leave our house now!"

"I guess I better." She backed off to the couch in the great room, grabbed her bag, pulled out her Pink Lady and pointed it aggressively at Vicki, whose arm was around Ricky. "On second thought, no. I'm not leaving till your wonderful husband is down here on his knees begging for your life. Get in here and sit down on the couch. And you, you little blond mop, get into that chair."

That's all she's got! That little girly girl gun? This is going to be fun. Thank you, brothers for teaching me what you know. I have some time to think. I'll break you down, but good.

"Don't hurt us. Please. What do you want? Jewelry? I've got some diamond pieces John bought me. You can have them."

"I don't want jewelry. Get in here and sit down. I'm not killing you yet."

She heard Mark through the earwig. "Vicki, listen to her."

Vicki shoved Ricky into the chair and sat on the couch opposite it. She signaled to him to be quiet.

"Just sit there and be quiet," Barbara said. "Call your husband and tell him to get his sexy ass down here."

Vicki picked up her cell. Barbara paused about five feet away in between Vicki and Ricky so she could see them both.

"How do you know he has a sexy ass?" Vicki pretended to be in tears. "It's more than sexy. And it belongs to me."

Through a megaphone, they heard Mark's bellowing voice. "Barbara Montgomery! We know you're in there!"

"Oh, my God! What signals were you giving to your brother, you cracker piece of shit?" Barbara didn't know where to look. She paced to the lanai, backward, with her gun still on Vicki, took a glance, and saw no one.

"Barbara, front door. This is Commander Mark Marin. Sun County SWAT. John is on his way here. He just landed in Tampa."

"Barbara, I'm Lieutenant Randy Leigh. I want you to talk to me."

"An hour and a half. I'll wait. When John comes, I'll talk."

"He's coming by copter. It'll be sooner than that. Tell me what's going on?"

"What did he tell you, Lieutenant?"

"Not as much as we need to know."

"The less you know the better."

"Not true, Barbara. You're in our jurisdiction, now. We need to know what you're willing to tell us."

"All you have to know is that I have a gun on the commander's sister and the kid."

"Don't hurt them, Barbara. There's no need for that. Why are you doing this?"

"I want that bastard shrink to suffer."

"Why?"

"He locked me in a hospital. He did things to me to make me talk with that therapy of his. It hurt, damn it. It hurt. And he didn't care. He kept pressing and pressing and pressing until he found out what he wanted. That bastard shrink. I was just about to get what I wanted and he stopped me," she screamed at the top of her lungs.

"All I needed was two more days. Two more fucking days! Twenty-two years, twenty-two years of work, down to two fucking days! I was just about to get the revenge for my life. But he stopped me. Couldn't mind his own fucking business. I almost had what I wanted. That bastard shrink. I was so close. I almost got that guy, but he stopped me. He made me kill more. It's his fault I killed more. But I got even. I killed his best friends." Vicki stared at her. "That's right, cracker bitch! I killed Sal and Tony, but Paul did it to himself. So you won't see them in New York. Hey, you might meet them all when you get to heaven. Even though that bastard shrink belongs in hell."

She hyperventilated but Vicki remained still and calm. Ricky was too scared to move. Vicki calmed Ricky with her hands, moving slowly to signal to him that it'd be okay.

"Barbara, when John comes, what do you want me to tell him?"

"I want him in here. I want him on his knees. I want him to watch while I shoot his pregnant wife right in the belly, and then put a bullet in that brat's head."

"Do you think we can allow that to happen?"

"Well, if you bust in here, I'll kill them now."

"We won't bust in. If you take some deep breaths and calm down, we'll all wait for John to come. How's that?"

"Deep breaths? You and John with the deep breaths. You can both fuck off!"

"You're getting more aggravated, pacing. Why don't you sit down?"

"How can you see what I'm doing?"

"It's our job. I can see you didn't hurt Vicki and Ricky. That's good. You want me to see that, don't you?"

She peered out the window and saw the SWAT Hummer, but not the other command vehicles. She couldn't see the commander or the lieutenant.

"Good news, Barbara, John is coming up the path. He can talk to you. Hold on a few minutes while I read him in. Okay?"

"Finally, yes. Do what you have to do." She looked out the

side window and caught a glimpse of a haggard John with Mark and Randy.

⌘

Mark looked at John's bandaged forehead. He wore a long sleeved shirt so Mark couldn't see the rest of his stitchery. "You look like shit."

"Yeah, suit me up."

"You're not going in there. That's what she wants and she wants to kill Vicki and Ricky right in front of you. Them first, then you."

"Suit me up." He staggered to the trucks and selected his own gear. His arms stung from the several places he had needed stitching and his movements were rigid. Some spots of blood had trickled though his shirt from him stretching the wounds. Vest, helmets, boots, fingerless gloves—he grabbed everything. He was wild and on the attack. It was a John that Mark had never encountered before. John had neared his breaking point. Mark and his team attempted to hold him back. "I have to end this," John insisted. "I have to end this, now. Give me your weapon."

"You're out of your mind! You're not licensed to carry down here."

"Why didn't you bust in there? Where is that kid sniper?"

"He's in the back. Doesn't have a clear shot. Can't risk that Ricky won't get up in the way. Vicki will know what to do."

"You're not putting my wife in harm's way."

"We've trained her more than you. Knock it off!"

"Then I'll go in like I always do."

⌘

"Come here, little blondie." Barbara whisked Ricky off the chair and clutched him in front of her. "He dares to raise a gun to me and he's dead. Got it, cracker bitch?"

Vicki pretended to nod in fear. She planned her strategy.

She knew the teams required more time. She heard John and Mark arguing. Right now, she did what Mark had told her to do in a case like this—sit still and let his team do the intervention. Don't cause the perp to have more anxiety. Don't get them rattled. Just "yes" them. But she couldn't help herself.

"Who's dead? Ricky or John? You didn't say."

"Your husband goes last. No matter what. So I guess it's the kid. You are so stupid. How in the hell did John fall in love with you?"

The opening. The strategy to weaken her. "Sex. The sex is beyond great. Wanna know how many times we do it? Two to three times a day and he makes me come a couple of times each. And, now that I'm pregnant, it'll be—oh my goodness, I won't be able to describe it. How often does your husband wrap his arms around you and make passionate love to you? Like you're the only woman in the world?"

ᔕᓇᔕ

"Vicki's trying to distract her," Mark said.

"Talking sex? That should do it," John said. "That woman feels nothing."

Mark sneered at him.

"It came out in the therapy. Your men are in position. I'm going in."

ᔕᓇᔕ

"How often, Barbara? You look like one cold potato to me."

"Shut up!" Barbara's hands trembled. The gun rattled in her grip.

"Don't like to talk about sex, huh?"

"Shut up!"

"John and I love to talk sex. We've been doing it over the phone and Skype the past three weeks."

Barbara turned toward Vicki. Her face had reddened. She held firmly onto Ricky, who obeyed Vicki's hand signals to remain still. That was what Vicki wanted. To get Barbara not to focus on the door, so John could get her from behind. Or the team.

Barbara was so bent on her revenge to shoot Vicki and Ricky in front of John that she didn't waiver. Vicki counted on that.

"When he comes down on me, it's so amazing. His tongue brings out the nectars of the gods. I quiver and moan and my entire body floats. And John, he just loves the feel of my body riveting underneath him. Ooh." She shook her body as if she was going through it now.

Barbara bent down to hit Vicki in the head with the gun. Vicki pulled off her wig with her left hand, to divert her, and then defended with her right arm, pushing Barbara's arm away. Then she kicked Barbara in the shoulder so hard the she fell to the left side of the door. The sniper still had no shot. Ricky toppled right on top of Barbara, with his head blocking Barbara's face.

At that moment, John swung open the door, too fast. He miscalculated. He bellowed, not looking in Barbara's direction. "Kellie, drop the gun!"

With Ricky in her arms on top of her, he was a body shield. Barbara moved her head and shot John without hesitation in his right shoulder, as he turned toward her. He collapsed backward onto the floor. Vicki, even though she was scared stiff about John, retrieved her weapon from a side table.

The men heard the shot, and the kid sniper bust into the lanai. Mark's team dashed up the path to the house.

Barbara, still on the floor, struggled to hold onto Ricky. The front door was pushed closed in their struggle and Barbara was confined against it. Vicki mouthed "Now" to Ricky and he began to fight Barbara. Her gun, still held in her firm grip, was hot against his face. He kicked Barbara hard in her legs, as he tried to move his face out of the way. Ricky was too erratic in his movements for the sniper to take the shot, even though it was at a closer than normal range. The team outside couldn't open the door.

"Ricky, move to the left!"

He used all of his strength to fight Barbara and rolled off her to the left.

Vicki fired once, hitting Barbara between the eyes. She wasn't even proud of herself. It was at very close range.

Vicki and Ricky ran to John, as the sniper stormed in and pushed Barbara's limp body to the side to open the door for Mark's team. Vicki handed her gun to Mark. She collapsed on John's chest with tears streaming down her face. She wrapped her arms around him and ran her fingers though his hair. He struggled to raise his right arm to touch her but he couldn't.

John's voice was barely audible as he whispered in Vicki's ear, "Don't you ever leave me again, babe."

THE END

About the Author

Ronnie Allen is a New York City native, born and bred in Brooklyn, New York, where she was a teacher in the New York City Department of Education for 33 years including the obtaining of a New York State license as School Psychologist. Her various roles included classroom teacher, staff developer, crisis intervention specialist, and mentor for teachers who were struggling. Always an advocate for the child, Allen carries this through as a theme in her novel *Gemini*, with the reader seeing the horrors of child abuse through the eyes of three characters.

In the early 1990s she began a journey into holistic healing and alternative therapies and completed her PhD in Parapsychic Sciences in 2001.

Along the way, Allen has picked up many certifications. She is a Board Certified Holistic Health Practitioner as well as a crystal therapist, Reiki practitioner, metaphysician, dream analyst, and Tarot Master Instructor. She has taught workshops in New York City and in Central Florida where she now lives.

Combining a love of the crime genre and her psychology background, with her alternative therapies experiences, writing psychological thrillers is the perfect venue for her.